Joanne Harris is the author of four previous novels, *Sleep, Pale Sister*, *The Evil Seed*, the Whitbread-shortlisted *Chocolat* (a major film starring Juliette Binoche) and *Blackberry Wine*. Her latest novel, *Coastliners*, is published by Doubleday. She lives in Barnsley, Yorkshire, with her husband and small daughter.

Acclaim for *Five Quarters of the Orange*:

'As lyrically succulent as *Chocolat* and *Blackberry Wine*, this book probes darker corners of loss, enmity and betrayal'
PS Magazine

'Beautifully told, it's a haunting and tantalizing tale that stays with you long after turning the last page'
The Mirror

'Vastly enjoyable and utterly gripping, *Five Quarters of the Orange* is a dark antithesis to *Chocolat*'
The Times

'Harris's vividly sensual account of a nine-year-old's loves, loyalties and misunderstandings is a powerful and haunting story of childhood betrayal'
Good Housekeeping

'The author of the Whitbread-shortlisted *Chocolat* must win more plaudits for this elegant and epicurean novel permeated with the tantalizing flavours of rustic France'
Publishing News

'Gripping . . . Harris is on assured form'
Sunday Times

'Harris indulges her love of rich and mouthwatering descriptive passages, appealing to the senses . . . Thoroughly enjoyable'
Observer

'If Joanne Harris didn't exist, someone would have to invent her'
Sunday Express

'Harris has a gift for injecting magic into the everyday . . . She is an old-fashioned writer in the finest sense, believing in a strong narrative, fully rounded characters, a complex plot, even a moral'
Daily Telegraph

'Rich in detail, engaging all the senses and drawing one compulsively on to the unexpected climax'
Time Out

'Hugely enjoyable'
Sunday Mirror

'Harris evocatively balances the young Framboise's perspectives on life against grown-up truths with compelling, zestful flair'
Elle

'Evocative descriptions of food and rural France are what we have come to expect from the best-selling author of *Chocolat*. With recipes and luscious descriptions of food, this is the perfect book for a gastronome'
Eve

'*Five Quarters of the Orange* completes a hat-trick of food-titled tales with a riveting story about a young girl brought up in occupied France who's now an old woman harbouring a terrible secret. Harris is light-years ahead of her contemporaries. She teases you with snippets of a bigger story, gently pulling you in with her vivid descriptions of rural France until you can actually smell the oranges. Read it'
Now

'Joanne Harris's latest novel indulges in familiarities from her earlier books; a sensuality rising from the smells, tastes and colours of lusciously described dishes, so that old men become "sweetened with dementia" and Reinette's eyes are "almost gold, the colour of boiling syrup"; a strong, powerful but damaged woman at the centre, in this case Framboise's mother; the inescapability of the past. This mix is served up in the kind of delicate, precise yet rich prose that has reviewers reaching irresistibly for those foodie metaphors which are spread generously over the jacket covers of every Harris book'
Independent on Sunday

'Just as she did in *Chocolat*, Harris indulges her love of rich and mouth-watering descriptive passages, appealing to the senses with seductively foreign names, and evoking the textures and smells of food. These descriptions are suffused with a child's wide-eyed wonder that lends the story a magical quality, almost like a folk tale or a children's story. Even having the Occupation as a backdrop, Harris sets out to tell a story that proves, like her previous books, to be thoroughly enjoyable . . .'
Guardian Weekly

'Joanne Harris's rather brilliant *Five Quarters of the Orange* is a fascinating page-turner with a compelling climax . . . This is an absolutely remarkable book that deserves to be read over and over again'
Punch

'Harris presents a complicated but beautiful tale involving misfortune, mystery and intense family relations . . . This intense work brims with sensuality and sensitivity'
Publishers Weekly

'If you enjoyed *Chocolat* and *Blackberry Wine*, you are certainly ready to embark on this journey back to war-torn France, an unresolved past and a fraught future'
The Oxford Times

'This shape-shifting drama switches easily between Occupied France and the present day. Recipes for luscious meals and homebrewed liqueurs interlace a storyline that spoons suspense and black humour into the blender in equal measures'
Irish Independent

'Joanne Harris is masterly in her conjuring of the sense of time and place in the wartime segments of the book, and with almost poetic style she brings to life the smell of country cooking, and the movement of fish in the Loire and the stifling smell of orange oil'
Yorkshire Evening Post

'The double-plot, past and present, is well paced, and keeps the reader guessing until the very last minute. The luscious prose, abounding in culinary metaphors and similes, which made *Chocolat* so readable, is once more in evidence . . . a satisfying page-turner'
Irish Examiner

Acclaim for *Chocolat*:

'Is this the best book ever written? This is a truly excellent book, one of the best it has been my pleasure to read in the line of duty for years. Joanne Harris achieves everything a novelist should aim for, with no sense of effort or striving . . . Harris' achievement is not only in her story, in her insight and humour and the wonderful picture of small-town life in rural France, but also in her writing. Like good cooking, it is in turn rich without being fussy and plain without being dull. In short, this is what we call a rave review'
Literary Review

'Moody and atmospheric . . . Harris writes confident and stylish prose . . . a richly textured tale, evoking the claustrophobia of village life, and its amusements, with an impressively light touch'
Independent

'This novel is mouthwatering. Its title and its rich blue, pink and gold dustjacket entice you to try it and, once you do, you find yourself unable to stop until you've finished feasting on this delightful, quirky, sensuous story. This is also a feelgood book of the first order. One to curl up with. To luxuriate in . . . so full of colour, tastes and scents, that as you are lured by the plot and the wonderful descriptions, your senses are left reeling. This novel is a celebration of pleasure, of love, of tolerance. Read it'
The Observer

'This delicious, bewitching novel provides the antidote to all those late 20th century body shape obsessions; to all those tired and tiring Bridget Jones stereotypes. Here's a story, written by a woman, that celebrates chocolate *without guilt!* . . . Harris unfolds a huge tale of life, love, death and bereavement, of fear and violence, of murder and bravery and – most imporant – happiness. The author's joy in her creation is obvious and infectious'
Scotland on Sunday

'An enjoyable, not to say addictive, read . . . short enough to be read at a sitting, and light enough for its unashamedly hedonistic message to be swallowed without indigestion. A chocolate soufflé of a novel – with a pleasantly bitter aftertaste'
Christina Koning, *The Times*

Also by Joanne Harris

THE EVIL SEED
SLEEP, PALE SISTER
CHOCOLAT
BLACKBERRY WINE
COASTLINERS

Dear Nelly,
   Enjoy this book for
your trip home. I hope
that you like it & may

FIVE QUARTERS
OF THE ORANGE

It inspire us (by the
title alone) to create

Joanne Harris more
   culinary masterpieces
with orange!
   Haha!
      Love Laura x

BLACK SWAN

FIVE QUARTERS OF THE ORANGE
A BLACK SWAN BOOK : 0 552 99883 4

Originally published in Great Britain by Doubleday,
a division of Transworld Publishers

PRINTING HISTORY
Doubleday edition published 2001
Black Swan edition published 2002

7 9 10 8 6

Set in 11/12pt Melior by
Kestrel Data, Exeter, Devon.

Black Swan Books are published by Transworld Publishers,
61–63 Uxbridge Road, London W5 5SA,
a division of The Random House Group Ltd,
in Australia by Random House Australia (Pty) Ltd,
20 Alfred Street, Milsons Point, Sydney, NSW 2061, Australia,
in New Zealand by Random House New Zealand Ltd,
18 Poland Road, Glenfield, Auckland 10, New Zealand
and in South Africa by Random House (Pty) Ltd,
Endulini, 5a Jubilee Road, Parktown 2193, South Africa.

Printed and bound in Great Britain by
Clays Ltd, St Ives plc.

To my grandfather, Georges Payen (aka P'tit Père),
who was there

Acknowledgements

Heartfelt thanks to those who have taken part in the series of armed encounters which became this book. To Kevin and Anouchka for manning the cannons; to my parents and my brother for support and supplies; to Serafina, Warrior Princess, for defending my corner; to Jennifer Luithlen for foreign policy; to Howard Morhaim for defeating the Norsemen; to my loyal editor Francesca Liversidge; to Jo Goldsworthy and the heavy artillery at Transworld; to my standard-bearer Louise Page; and to Christopher for being on my side.

PART ONE

The Inheritance

1

When my mother died she left the farm to my brother, Cassis, the fortune in the wine cellar to my sister, Reine-Claude, and to me, the youngest, her album and a two-litre jar containing a single black Périgord truffle, large as a tennis ball and suspended in sunflower oil, which, when uncorked, still releases the rich dank perfume of the forest floor. A fairly unequal distribution of riches, but then Mother was a force of nature, bestowing her favours as she pleased, leaving no insight as to the workings of her peculiar logic.

And as Cassis always said, I was the favourite.

Not that she ever showed it when she was alive. For my mother there was never much time for indulgence, even if she'd been the type. Not with her husband killed in the war, and the farm to run alone. Far from being a comfort to her widowhood, we were a hindrance to her, with our noisy games, our fights, our quarrels. If we fell ill, she would care for us with reluctant tenderness, as if calculating the cost of our survival, and what love she showed took the most elementary forms: cooking pots to lick, jam pans to scrape, a handful of wild strawberries collected from the straggling border behind the vegetable patch, and delivered without a smile in a twist of handkerchief. Cassis would be the man of the family. She showed even less softness towards him than to the rest of us. Reinette was already turning heads before she reached her teens, and my mother was vain enough to feel pride at the attention she received. But I was the extra mouth, no second son to expand the farm and certainly no beauty.

I was always the troublesome one, the discordant one, and after my father died I became sullen and defiant. Skinny and dark, like my mother, with her long, graceless hands, flat feet and wide mouth, I must have reminded her too much of herself, for there was often a tightness at her mouth when she looked at me, a kind of stoic appraisal, of fatalism. As if she foresaw that it was I, not Cassis or Reine-Claude, who would carry her memory forward. As if she would have preferred a more fitting vessel.

Perhaps that was why she gave me the album, valueless, then, except for the thoughts and insights jotted in the margins alongside recipes and newspaper cuttings and herbal cures. Not a diary, precisely; there are no dates in the album, no precise order. Pages were inserted into it at random, loose leaves later bound together with small, obsessive stitches, some pages thin as onion skin, others cut from pieces of card trimmed to fit inside the battered leather cover. My mother marked the events of her life with recipes, dishes of her own invention or interpretations of old favourites. Food was her nostalgia, her celebration, its nurture and preparation the sole outlet for her creativity. The first page is given to my father's death – the ribbon of his Légion d'Honneur pasted thickly to the paper beneath a blurry photograph and a neat recipe for black-wheat pancakes – and carries a kind of gruesome humour. Under the picture my mother has pencilled, 'Remember – dig up Jerusalem artichokes. Ha! Ha! Ha!' in red.

In other places she is more garrulous, but with many abbreviations and cryptic references. I recognize some of the incidents to which she refers. Others are twisted to suit the moment's needs. Others seem to be complete inventions, lies, impossibilities. In many places there are blocks of tiny script in a language I cannot

14

understand – '*Ini tnawini inoti plainexini. Ini canini inton inraebi inti ynani eromni.*' Sometimes a single word, scrawled across the top or side of the page, seemingly at random. On one page, 'seesaw' in blue ink, on another, 'wintergreen, rapscallion, ornament' in orange crayon. On another, what might be a poem, though I never saw her open any book other than one of recipes. It reads:

> this sweetness
> scooped
> like some bright fruit
> plum peach apricot
> watermelon perhaps
> from myself
> this sweetness

It is a whimsical touch which surprises and troubles me. That this stony and prosaic woman should in her secret moments harbour such thoughts. For she was sealed off from us – from everyone – with such fierceness that I had thought her incapable of yielding.

I never saw her cry. She rarely smiled, and then only in the kitchen with her palette of flavours at her fingertips, talking to herself – so I thought – in the same toneless mutter, enunciating the names of herbs and spices – 'cinnamon, thyme, peppermint, coriander, saffron, basil, lovage' – running a monotonous commentary. 'See the tile. Has to be the right heat. Too low, the pancake is soggy. Too high, the butter fries black, smokes, the pancake crisps.' I understood later that she was trying to educate me. I listened because I saw in our kitchen seminars the one way in which I might win a little of her approval, and because every good war needs the occasional amnesty. Country recipes from her native Brittany were her favourites; the buckwheat pancakes we ate with everything, the *far breton* and *kouign amann* and *galette bretonne*, which we sold in down-river Angers, with our goat's cheeses, sausage and fruit.

She always meant Cassis to have the farm. But Cassis was the first to leave, casually defiant, for Paris, breaking all contact, except for his signature on a card every Christmas, and when she died, thirty-six years on, there was nothing to interest him in a half-derelict farmhouse on the Loire. I bought it from him with my savings, my widow money, and at a good price, too, but it was a fair deal, and he was happy enough to make it then. He understood the need to keep the place in the family.

Now, of course, all that's changed. Cassis has a son of his own. The boy married Laure Dessanges, the food writer, and they own a restaurant in Angers – Aux Délices Dessanges. I met him a few times before Cassis died. I didn't like him. Dark and flashy, already running to fat, as his father did, though still handsome and knowing it. He seemed to be everywhere at once in his eagerness to please; called me *Mamie*, found a chair, insisted I take the most comfortable seat, made coffee, sugared, creamed, asked after my health, flattered me on this and that till I was almost dizzy with it. Cassis, sixty-odd then, and swollen with the seeds of the coronary that would later kill him, looked on with barely restrained pride. *My son. See what a fine man he is. What a fine, attentive nephew you have.*

Cassis called him Yannick, after our father, but I liked my nephew no more for that. That's my mother in me, the dislike of conventions, of false intimacies. I don't like to be touched and simpered over. I don't see why the blood we share should tie us in affection. Or the secret of spilled blood we hid for so long between us.

Oh yes. Don't think I forgot that business. Not for a minute, I didn't, though the others tried hard enough. Cassis scrubbing *pissoirs* outside his Paris bar. Reinette working as an usherette in a porno cinema in Pigalle, and sniffing from man to man like a lost dog. So much for her lipstick and silk stockings. At home she'd been the harvest queen, the darling, the undisputed village beauty. In Montmartre all women look the same. Poor Reinette.

I know what you're thinking. You wish I'd get on with the story. It's the only story about the old days which interests you now; the only thread in this tattered flag of mine which still catches the light. You want to hear about Tomas Leibniz. To have it clear, categorized, ended. Well, it isn't as easy as that. Like my mother's album, there are no page numbers. No beginning, and the end is as raw as the seamless edge of an unhemmed skirt. But I'm an old woman – seems here everything gets old so quickly; must be the air – and I have my own way of going about things. Besides, there are so many things for you to understand. Why my mother did what she did. Why we hid the truth for so long. And why I'm choosing to tell my story now, to strangers, to people who believe a life can be condensed to a two-page spread in a Sunday supplement, a couple of photographs, a paragraph, a quote from Dostoevsky. Turn the page and it's over. No. Not this time. They're going to take down every word. Can't make them print it, of course, but by God they'll listen. I'll *make* them do it.

2

My name is Framboise Dartigen. I was born right here, in the village of Les Laveuses, not fifteen kilometres from Angers, on the Loire. I'll be sixty-five in July, baked and yellowed by the sun like a dried apricot. I have two daughters, Pistache, married to a banker in Rennes, and Noisette, who moved to Canada in '89 and writes to me every six months, and two grandchildren, who come to stay at the farm every summer. I wear black for a husband who died twenty years ago, under whose name I returned in secret to the village of my birth to buy back my mother's farm, long-abandoned and half-gutted by fire and the elements. Here I am Françoise Simon, *la veuve Simon*, and no-one would think to connect me with the Dartigen family, who left in the wake of that dreadful business. I don't know why it had to be this farm, this village. Perhaps I'm just stubborn. That was how it was. This is where I belong. The years with Hervé seem almost a blank now, like the strange, calm patches you sometimes get in a stormy sea; a moment of waiting, of forgetfulness. But I never really forgot Les Laveuses. Not for a moment. Something in me was always here.

It took almost a year to make the farmhouse habitable, during which time I lived in the south-facing wing, where at least the roof had held. While the workmen replaced the roofing, tile by tile, I worked in the orchard – what was left of it – pruning and shaping and dragging down great wreaths of devouring mistletoe from the trees. My mother had a passion for all fruit except oranges, which she refused to allow in the house. She named each one of us, on a seeming whim, after a fruit and a recipe – Cassis, for her thick blackcurrant cake, Framboise, her raspberry liqueur, and Reinette for her greengage tart, after the *reine-claude* – greengages – which grew against the south wall of the house, thick as grapes and syrupy with wasps in midsummer. At one time we had over a hundred trees – apples, pears, plums, gages, cherries, quinces, not to mention the raspberry canes and the fields of strawberries, gooseberries and currants, the fruits of which were dried, stored, made into jams and liqueurs and wonderful cartwheel tarts on *pâte brisée* and *crème pâtissière* and almond paste. My memories are flavoured with their scents, their colours, their names. My mother tended them as if they were her favourite children. Smudge pots against the frost, which we fed with our own winter fuel. Barrows full of manure dug around the base every spring. And in summer, to keep the birds away, we would tie shapes cut out of silver paper onto the ends of the branches, which would shiver and flick-flack in the wind, mooseblowers made out of string drawn tightly across empty tin cans to make eerie, bird-frightening sounds, windmills of coloured paper which would spin wildly, so the orchard was a carnival of baubles, shining ribbons and shrieking wires, like a Christmas party in midsummer.

The trees all had names. 'Belle Yvonne,' my mother would say as she passed a gnarled pear tree. 'Rose d'Aquitaine. Beurre du roi Henry.' Her voice at these times was soft, almost monotone. I could not tell whether she was speaking to me or to herself. 'Conference. Williams. Ghislaine de Penthièvre.'

This sweetness.

Today there are fewer than twenty trees left in the orchard, though I have quite enough for my needs. My sour-cherry liqueur is especially popular, though I feel a little guilty that I cannot remember the cherry's name. The secret is to leave the stones in. Layer cherries and sugar one on the other in a wide-mouthed glass jar, covering each layer gradually with clear spirit – kirsch is best, but you can use vodka or even armagnac – up to half the jar's capacity. Top up with spirit and wait. Every month, turn the jar carefully to release any accumulated sugar. In three years' time the spirit has bled the cherries white, staining itself deep red, penetrating even to the stone and the tiny almond inside it, becoming pungent, evocative, a scent of autumn past. Serve in tiny liqueur glasses, with a spoon to scoop out the cherry, and leave it in the mouth until the macerated fruit dissolves under the tongue. Pierce the stone with the point of a tooth to release the liqueur trapped inside and leave it for a long time in the mouth, playing it with the tip of the tongue, rolling it under, over, like a single prayer bead. Try to remember the time of its ripening, that summer, that hot autumn, the time the well ran dry, the time we had the wasps' nests, time past, lost, found again in the hard place at the heart of the fruit.

I know, I know. You want me to get to the point. But this is at least as important as the rest, the *method* of telling, and the *time* taken to tell. It has taken me fifty-five years to begin, at least let me do it in my own way.

When I came back to Les Laveuses I was almost sure no-one would recognize me. All the same, I showed myself clearly, almost brazenly, about the village. If someone did know me, if they managed to distinguish in my features those of my mother, then I wanted to know it immediately. I wanted to know where I stood.

I walked to the Loire every day and sat on the flat stones where Cassis and I had fished for tench. I stood on the stump of the Lookout Post. Some of the Standing Stones are missing now, but you can still see the pickets where we hung our trophies, the garlands and ribbons and Old Mother's head when we finally caught her.

I went to Brassaud's tobacconist's – his son runs it now, but the old man is still alive, his eyes black and baleful and aware – to Raphaël's café, the post office where Ginette Hourias is postmistress. I even went to the war memorial. On one side, the eighteen names of our soldiers killed in the war, beneath the carved motto, '*Morts pour la patrie*'. I noticed that my father's name had been chiselled off, leaving a rough patch between Darius G. and Fenouil J-P. On the other side, a brass plaque with ten names in larger letters. I did not need to read them; I knew them by heart. But I feigned interest, knowing that inevitably someone would tell me the story, perhaps show me the place against the west wall of Saint-Benedict's, tell me that every year there was a special service to remember them, that their names were read out from the steps of the memorial and flowers laid out. I wondered whether I could bear it. I wondered whether they would know from my face.

Martin Dupré, Jean-Marie Dupré, Colette Gaudin, Philippe Hourias, Henri Lemaître, Julien Lanicen, Arthur Lecoz, Agnès Petit, François Ramondin, Auguste Truriand. So many people still remember. So many people with the same names, the same faces. The families have stayed here, the Hourias, the Lanicens, the Ramondins, the Duprés. Sixty years later they still remember, the young coached in casual hatred by the old.

There was some interest in me for a time. Some curiosity. That same house, abandoned since she left it, that Dartigen woman – 'I can't quite remember the details, madame, but my father . . . my uncle' – Why had I bought the place, anyway? they asked. It was an eyesore, a black spot. The trees still standing were half rotten with mistletoe and disease. The well had been concreted over, filled in with rubble and stones. But I remembered a farm that was neat and thriving and

21

busy; horses, goats, chickens, rabbits. I liked to think that perhaps the wild ones that ran across the north field might be their descendants, and occasionally I glimpsed patches of white amongst the brown. To satisfy the curious, I invented a childhood on a Breton farm. The land was cheap, I explained. I made myself humble, apologetic. Some of the old ones viewed me askance, thinking, perhaps, that the farm should have stayed a memorial for ever. I wore black and hid my hair beneath a succession of scarves. You see, I was old from the beginning.

Even so, it took some time for me to be accepted. People were polite but unwelcoming, and because I am not of a naturally social disposition – surly, my mother used to call it – they remained so. I did not go to church. I know how it must have looked, but I could not bring myself to go. Arrogance, perhaps, or the kind of defiance that led my mother to name us after fruit rather than the Church's saints. It took the shop to make me part of the community.

It began as a shop, though I had always intended to expand later. Two years after my arrival, Hervé's money was almost gone. The house was habitable now, though the land was still virtually useless – a dozen trees, a vegetable patch, two pygmy goats and some chickens and ducks. Clearly it would be some time before I could make a living from the land. I began to make and sell cakes – the brioche and *pain d'épices* of the region, as well as some of my mother's Breton specialities, packets of *crêpes dentelle*, fruit tarts and packs of *sablés*, biscuits, nutbread, cinnamon snaps. At first I sold them from the local bakery, then from the farm itself, adding other items little by little: eggs, goat's cheeses, fruit liqueurs and wines. With the profits I bought pigs, rabbits, more goats. I used my mother's old recipes, working most often from memory, but consulting the album from time to time.

Memory plays such strange games. No-one in Les Laveuses seemed to remember my mother's cooking.

Some of the older people even said what a difference my presence had made, that the woman who had lived here before had been a hard-faced sloven. Her house had reeked, her children had run barefoot. Good riddance to her, to them. I winced inwardly but said nothing. What could I have said? That she waxed the floorboards every day, made us wear felt overslippers in the house so that our shoes would not scuff the floor? That her window boxes were always brimming with flowers? That she scrubbed us with the same fierce impartiality with which she scrubbed the steps, Chinese-burning our faces with the flannel so that we were sometimes afraid we might bleed?

She is an evil legend here. There was even a book once. Not more than a pamphlet really; fifty pages and a few photographs – one of the memorial, one of Saint-Benedict's, a close-up of the fateful west wall. Only a passing reference to the three of us, not even our names. I was grateful for that. A blurry blow-up photograph of my mother, hair scraped back so fiercely from her face that her eyes looked Chinesed, mouth crimped into a tight little line of disapproval. The official photograph of my father, the one from the album, in uniform, looking absurdly young, rifle slung casually over one arm, grinning. Then, almost at the end of the book, the photograph that made me catch my breath like a fish with a hook in its throat. Four young men in German uniforms, arms linked except for the fourth, who stood a little to the side, self-consciously, a saxophone in one hand. The others are also carrying musical instruments – a trumpet, a side drum, a clarinet – and though their names are not given, I know them all. Les Laveuses military ensemble, circa 1942. Far right, Tomas Leibniz.

It took me some time to understand how they could have found out so many details. Where had they discovered the picture of my mother? As far as I knew there *were* no pictures of her. Even I had only ever seen one, an old wedding photo in the bottom of a bedroom drawer, two people in winter coats on the steps of Saint-Benedict's church, he wearing a broad-brimmed hat and she loose-haired, with a flower behind one ear. A different woman, then, smiling stiffly, shyly at the camera; the man beside her standing with one arm protectively around her shoulders. I understood that if my mother knew I had seen the photograph she would be angry, and replaced it, trembling a little, troubled almost without knowing why.

The photograph in the book is more like her, more like the woman I thought I knew but never knew at all, hard-faced and eternally on the brink of rage. Then, looking at the author's picture on the flyleaf of the book, I finally understood from where the information had come. Laure Dessanges, journalist and food writer, short red hair and practised smile. Yannick's wife; Cassis's daughter-in-law. Poor, stupid Cassis. Poor, blind Cassis, blinded by his pride in his successful son. Risking our undoing for the sake of . . . what? Or had he really come to believe his fiction?

3

You have to understand that for us the occupation was a very different matter than for those in the towns and the cities. Les Laveuses has barely changed since the war. Look at it now: a handful of streets, some still no more than broad dirt roads, reaching out from a main crossroads. There's the church at the back, the monument in the Place des Martyrs, with its bit of garden and the old fountain behind it, then, on the Rue Martin et Jean-Marie Dupré, the post office, Petit's butcher's, the Café de la Mauvaise Réputation, the bar-tabac, with its rack of postcards of the war memorial and old Brassaud sitting in his rocker by the step, the florist-funeral director opposite – food and death, always good trade in Les Laveuses – the general store – still run by the Truriand family, though fortunately a young grandson who only moved back recently – the old yellow-painted postbox.

Beyond the main street runs the Loire, smooth and brown as a sunning snake and broad as a wheatfield, its surface broken in irregular patches by islands and sandbanks, which to the tourists driving by on the way to Angers might look as solid as the road beneath them. Of course, we know otherwise. The islands are moving all the time, rootless. Insidiously propelled by the movements of the brown water beneath, they sink and surface like slow yellow whales, leaving small eddies in their wake, harmless enough when seen from a boat, but deadly for a swimmer, the undertow pulling mercilessly beneath the smooth surface, dragging the unwary down to choke undramatically, invisibly. There are still fish in the old Loire, tench and pike and eels grown to monstrous proportions on sewage and the rotting stuff of upriver. Most days you'll see boats out there, though half the time the fishermen throw back what they catch.

By the old jetty, Paul Hourias has a shack from which he sells bait and fishing tackle, not spitting distance from where we used to fish, he and Cassis and I, and where Jeannette Gaudin was bitten by the water-snake. Paul's old dog lies at his feet, eerily like the brown mongrel which was his constant companion in the old days, and he watches the river, dangling a piece of string into the water as if he hopes to catch something.

I wonder if he remembers. Sometimes I see him looking at me – he's one of my regulars – and I could almost think he does. He's aged, of course. So have we all. His moony round face has darkened, grown pouchy and mournful. A limp moustache the colour of chewed tobacco. A cigarette end between his teeth. He seldom speaks – he never was talkative – but he watches with that sad-dog expression, a navy beret crammed over his skull. He likes my pancakes and my cider. Perhaps that's why he never said anything. He was never one to cause a scene.

4

I had been back for almost four years when I opened the crêperie. By then I had money set aside, custom, acceptance. I had a boy working for me on the farm – a boy from Courlé, not from one of the Families – and I took on a girl, Lise, to help with the service. I started with only five tables – the trick has always been to think small at first, to avoid alarming people – but eventually I had double that, plus what I could fit on the *terrasse* in front on fine days. I kept it simple. My menu was limited to buckwheat pancakes with a choice of fillings, plus one main dish every day and a selection of desserts. That way I could handle the cooking myself, leaving Lise to take the orders. I called the place Crêpe Framboise, after the house speciality, a sweet pancake with raspberry coulis and my home-made liqueur, and I smiled a little to myself, thinking of their reaction if they could have known. Several of my regulars even came to calling the place Chez Framboise, which made me smile all the more.

It was at this point that men began to pay attention to me again. You understand, I had become quite a wealthy woman by Les Laveuses standards. I was barely fifty, after all. Plus I could cook and keep house. A number of men paid a kind of court to me, honest, good men like Gilbert Dupré and Jean-Louis Lelassiant, lazy men like Rambert Lecoz, who wanted a life-time meal ticket. Even Paul, sweet Paul Hourias with his drooping nicotine-streaked moustache and his silences. Of course anything like that was out of the question. That was one foolishness I could never succumb to. Not that it caused me more than the occasional pang of regret. I had the business, I had my mother's farm; I had my memories. A husband would lose me all that. There would be no way I could conceal forever my assumed identity, and though the villagers might have forgiven me my origins at first, they would not forget five years of deceit. So I refused every offer, the tentative and the bold, until I was generally held to be first inconsolable, then impregnable, and then, finally, years later, too old.

I had been in Les Laveuses for almost ten years. For the last five I had begun to invite Pistache and her family to stay during the summer holidays. I watched the children grow from curious big-eyed bundles to small brightly coloured birds, flying over my meadow and through my orchard on invisible wings. I have a good daughter in Pistache. Noisette, my secret favourite, is more like me: sly and rebellious, black eyes like mine and a heart full of wildness and resentment. I could have stopped her leaving – a word, a smile might have done it – but I did not, fearing, perhaps, that she would turn me into my mother. Her letters are flat and dutiful. Her marriage has ended badly. She works as a waitress in an all-night café in Montreal. She refuses my offers of money. Pistache is the woman Reinette might have been, plump and trusting, gentle with her children and fierce in their defence, with soft brown hair and eyes as green as the nut from which she takes her name. Through her, and through her children, I have learned to relive the good parts of my childhood.

For them I learned to be a mother again, cooking pancakes and thick herb-and-apple sausages. I made jam for them from figs and green tomatoes and sour cherries and quinces. I let them play with the little brown mischievous goats and feed them with crusts and pieces of carrot. We fed the hens, stroked the soft noses of the ponies, collected sorrel for the rabbits. I showed them the river and how to reach the sunny sandbanks. I warned them, with a catch in my heart, of the dangers – the snakes, roots, eddies, quicksand – made them promise never, *never* to swim there. I showed them the woods beyond, the best places to find mushrooms, the ways of telling the fake chanterelle from the true, the sour bilberries growing wild under the thicket. This was the childhood my daughters should have had. Instead there was the wild coast of Côte d'Armor, where Hervé and I lived for a time, the windy beaches, pine forests and slate-roofed stone houses. I tried to be a good mother to them, really I did, but I felt there was always something missing. I realize now it was this house, this farm, these fields, the sleepy, reeking Loire of Les Laveuses. This is what I wanted for them, and I began again with my grandchildren. Indulging them, I indulged myself.

I like to think my mother might have done the same, given the chance. I imagine her as a placid grandmother, accepting my rebukes – '*Really, Mother, you're going to spoil those children rotten*' – with an impenitent twinkle, and it does not seem as impossible as once it did. Or maybe I'm reinventing her. Maybe she really *was* as I remember her: a stony woman who never smiled, who watched me with that look of flat, incomprehensible hunger.

She never saw her granddaughters, never even knew they existed. I told Hervé my parents were dead, and he never questioned the lie. His father was a fisherman, his mother a little round partridge of a woman who sold the fish on the markets. I pulled them around me like a borrowed blanket, knowing that one day I would have to go back into the cold without them. A good man, Hervé, a calm man with no sharp edges in him upon which I could be cut. I loved him, not in the searing, desperate way I had loved Tomas, but enough.

When he died in 1975 – struck by lightning on an eel-fishing trip with his father – my grief was tinged with a feeling of inevitability, almost of relief. It had been good for a time, yes. But business – *life* – has to move on. I went back to Les Laveuses eighteen months later with the feeling of waking up after a long, dark sleep.

It may seem strange to you that I waited for so long before reading my mother's album. It was my only legacy – except for the Périgord truffle – and in five years I had barely glanced at it. Of course, I knew so many of the recipes by heart that I hardly needed to read them, but even so. I had not even been present for the reading of the Will. I can't tell you on what day she died, though I can tell you where – in an old folks' home in Vitré called La Gautraye – of stomach cancer. She's buried there, too, in the local cemetery, though I only went there once. Her grave is close to the far wall, by the refuse bins. 'Mirabelle DARTIGEN', it says, then some dates. I notice, with little surprise, that my mother lied to us about her age.

I don't really know what prompted my initial studies of her album. It was my first summer in Les Laveuses after Hervé's death. There had been a drought, and the Loire was maybe a couple of metres lower than usual, showing ugly, shrunken verges like the stumps of sick teeth. Roots straggled down into the water, bleached yellow-white by the sun, and children played among them on the sandbanks, paddling barefoot in the filthy brown puddles, poking with sticks at the rubbish floating from upstream. Until then I had avoided looking at the album, feeling absurdly at fault, a voyeuse, as if my mother might come in at any time and see me reading her strange secrets. Truth is, I didn't *want* to know her secrets. Like walking into a room at night and hearing your parents making love, an inner voice told me it was wrong, and it took more than ten years for me to understand that the voice I heard was not my mother's, but my own.

As I said, much of what she wrote was incomprehensible. The language – Italian-sounding and unpronounceable – in which much of the album was written was alien to me, and after a few abortive attempts to decipher it, I abandoned the idea. The recipes were clear enough, printed in blue or violet ink, but the mad scrawlings, poems, drawings and accounts between them were written with no apparent logic, no order that I could discover.

Saw Guilherm Ramondin today. With his new wooden leg. He laughed at R-C staring. When she asked, Didn't it hurt? he said he was lucky. His father makes clogs. Half the work of a pair, ha ha, and half the chance of standing on your toes during the waltz, my pretty. I keep thinking about what it looks like inside the pinned-up trouser-leg. Like an uncooked white pudding, tied up with a piece of string. Had to bite my mouth to stop myself from laughing.

The words are written, very small, above a recipe for white puddings. I found these short anecdotes disturbing, with their joyless humour.

In other places my mother speaks of her trees as if they are living people: 'Stayed up all night with Belle Yvonne; she was so sick with cold.' And though she only ever seems to refer to her children by abbreviation – R-C, Cass and Fra – my father is never mentioned. Never. For many years I wondered why. Of course, I had no way of knowing what was written in the other sections, the secret sections. My father – what little I knew of him – might never have existed.

5

Then came the business with the article. I didn't read it myself, you understand; it came in the kind of magazine which seems to view food simply as a style accessory – 'This year we're all eating couscous, darling, it's absolutely *de rigueur*' – while, for me, food is simply food, a pleasure for the senses, a carefully constructed piece of ephemera, like fireworks, hard work sometimes, but not to be taken seriously. Not *art*, for heaven's sake; in one end and out the other. Anyway, there it was one day, in one of these fashion magazines. 'Travels down the Loire', or some such thing, a famous chef sampling restaurants on his way to the coast. I remember him, too; a thin little man with his own salt and pepper pots wrapped in a napkin, and a notebook on his lap. He had my *paëlla antillaise* and the warm artichoke salad, then a piece of my mother's butter-sugar pastries, with my own *cidre bouché* and a glass of *liqueur framboise* to finish. He asked me a lot of questions about my recipes, wanted to see my kitchen and garden, was amazed when I showed him my cellar with its shelves of *terrines*, preserves and aromatic oils – walnut, rosemary, truffle – and vinegars – raspberry, lavender, sour apple – asked where I trained and seemed almost upset when the question made me laugh.

Perhaps I said too much. I was flattered, you see. I invited him to taste this and that. A slice of *rillettes*, another of my *saucisson sec*. A sip of my pear liqueur, the *poiré* my mother used to make in October with the windfall pears, fermenting already as they lay on the hot ground, gloved with brown wasps so that we had to use the wooden tongs to pick them up. I showed him the truffle my mother had left me, carefully preserved in the oil like a fly in amber, and smiled as his eyes widened in amazement.

'Have you any idea what a thing like that is worth?' he said.

Yes, I was flattered in my vanity. A little lonely, too, perhaps; glad to talk to this man who knew my language, who could name the herbs in a terrine as he tasted it, and who told me I was too good for this place, that it was a crime. Perhaps I dreamed a little. I should have known better.

The article came a few months later. Someone brought it to me, torn out of the magazine. A photograph of the crêperie, a couple of paragraphs.

'Visitors to Angers in search of authentic gourmet cuisine may head for the prestigious Aux Délices Dessanges. In so doing they would certainly miss one of the most exciting discoveries of my travels down the Loire . . .' Frantically I tried to remember whether I had told him about Yannick. 'Behind the unpretentious façade of a country farmhouse, a culinary miracle is at work . . .' A great deal of nonsense followed about 'country traditions given a new lease of life by this lady's creative genius'. Impatiently, with a rising sense of panic, I scanned the page for signs of the inevitable. A single mention of the name Dartigen and all my careful building work might begin to crumble.

It may seem I'm exaggerating. I'm not. The war is vividly remembered in Les Laveuses. There are people here who still don't speak to each other. Denise Mouriac and Lucile Dupré, Jean-Marie Bonet and Colin Brassaud. Wasn't there that business in Angers a few years ago, when an old woman was found locked in a room above a top-floor flat? Her parents had shut her there in 1945, when they found out she'd collaborated with the Germans. She was sixteen. Fifty years later they brought her out, old and mad, when her father finally died.

And what about those old men – eighty, ninety, some of them – locked away for war crimes? Blind old men, sick old men, sweetened by dementia, their faces slack and uncomprehending. Impossible to believe they might once have been young. Impossible to imagine bloody dreams inside those fragile, forgetful skulls. Smash the vessel, the essence evades you. The crime takes on a life, a justification, of its own.

'By a strange coincidence, the owner of Crêpe Framboise, Mme Françoise Simon, just happens to be related to the owner of Aux Délices Dessanges . . .' My breath stopped. I felt as if a flake of fire had blocked my windpipe and suddenly I was underwater, brown river clutching me under, fingers of flame reaching into my throat, my lungs. '. . . our very own Laure Dessanges! Strange that she hasn't managed to find out many of her great-aunt's secrets. I, for one, much preferred the unpretentious charm of Crêpe Framboise to any of Laure's elegant – but all-too meagre! – offerings.

I breathed again. Not the nephew, but the niece. I had escaped discovery.

I promised myself then that there would be no more foolishness, no more talking to kind food writers. A photographer from another Paris magazine came to interview me a week later, but I refused to see him. Requests for interviews came by post, but I left them unanswered. A publisher wrote to me with an offer to write a book of recipes. For the first time Crêpe Framboise was deluged by people from Angers, by tourists, by elegant people with flashy new cars. I turned them away by the dozen. I had my regulars and my ten to fifteen tables; I could not accommodate so many people.

I tried to behave as normally as I could. I refused to take advance bookings. People queued on the pavement. I had to engage another waitress, but otherwise I ignored the unwelcome attention. Even when the little food writer returned to argue – to reason with me – I would not listen to him. No, I would not allow him to use my recipes in his column. No, there was to be no book. No pictures. Crêpe Framboise would stay as it was, a provincial crêperie.

I knew that if I stonewalled for long enough they would leave me alone. But by that time the damage was done. Now Laure and Yannick knew where to find me.

Cassis must have told them. He had settled in a flat near the city centre, and though he had never been a good correspondent, he wrote to me occasionally. His letters were filled with reports of his famous daughter-in-law and his fine son. Well, after the article and the stir it caused, they made it their business to find me. They brought Cassis with them, like a present. They seemed to think we would be moved, somehow, at seeing one another again after so many years, but though his eyes watered in a rheumy, sentimental sort of way, mine stayed resolutely dry. There was hardly a trace of the older brother with whom I had shared so much; he was fat now, his features lost in a shapeless dough, his nose reddened, his cheeks crack-glazed with broken veins, his smile vacillating. What I once felt for him, the hero-worship of the big brother who, in my mind, could do anything – climb the highest tree, brave wild bees to steal their honey, swim *right across* the Loire at its broadest point – was reduced to a faint nostalgia, coloured with contempt. All that was such a long time ago, after all. The fat man at the door was a stranger.

At first they were clever. They asked for nothing. They were concerned for me living alone, gave me presents – a food processor, shocked that I didn't already have one; a winter coat, a radio – offered to take me out. They even invited me to their restaurant once, a big barn of a place, with gingham-print faux-marble tables and neon signs and dried starfish and brightly coloured plastic crabs wreathed in fisherman's netting on the walls. I commented, rather diffidently, on the décor.

'Well, Mamie, it's what you'd call kitsch,' explained Laure kindly, patting my hand. 'I don't suppose *you're* interested in things like that, but believe me, in Paris this is very fashionable.' She levelled her teeth at me. She has very white, very large teeth, and her hair is the colour of fresh paprika. She and Yannick often touched and kissed each other in public. I have to say it all rather embarrassed me. The meal was . . . modern, I suppose. I'm no judge of such things. Some kind of salad in a bland dressing, lots of little vegetables cut to look like flowers. Might have been some endive in there, but mostly just plain old lettuce leaves and radishes and carrots in fancy shapes. Then a piece of hake – a nice piece, I have to say, but very small – with a white wine shallot sauce and a piece of mint on top – don't ask me why. Then a sliver of pear tartlet, fussed over with chocolate sauce, dusted sugar and chocolate curls. Looking furtively at the menu I noticed a great deal of self-congratulatory stuff along the lines of 'a nougatine of assorted candies on a mouth-watering bed of wafer-thin pastry, bound with thick dark chocolate and served with a tangy apricot coulis'. Sounded like a plain old florentine to me, and when I saw it, it looked no bigger than a five-franc piece. You'd have thought Moses had brought it down from the mountain to read how they'd described it. And the price! Five times the price of my most expensive menu, and that was without the wine. Course, I didn't pay for any of it. But I was beginning to think there might be a hidden price in all this sudden attention.

There was.

Two months later came the first proposal. A

thousand francs to me if I would give them my recipe for *paëlla antillaise* and allow them to put it on their menu. Mamie Framboise's *paëlla antillaise*, as mentioned in *Hôte & Cuisine*, July 1991, by Jules Lemarchand. At first I thought it was a joke. 'A delicate blend of freshly caught seafood, subtly melded with green bananas, pineapple, muscatels and saffron rice.' I laughed. Didn't they have enough recipes of their own?

'Don't laugh, Mamie.' Yannick was almost curt, his bright black eyes very close to mine. 'I mean, Laure and I would be *so* grateful.' He gave a wide, open smile.

'Now don't be coy, Mamie.' I wished they wouldn't call me that. Laure put her cool bare arm around me. 'I'd make sure everyone knew it was *your* recipe.'

I relented. I don't actually mind giving out my recipes; after all, I've given enough out already to people in Les Laveuses. I'd give them the *paëlla antillaise* for nothing, plus anything else they took a shine to, but on condition that they left Mamie Framboise off the menu. I'd had one narrow escape. I wasn't going to court more attention.

They agreed so quickly to my demands and with so little argument, and three weeks later the recipe for Mamie Framboise's *paëlla antillaise* appeared in *Hôte & Cuisine*, flanked by a gushing article by Laure Dessanges. 'I hope to be able to bring you more of Mamie Framboise's country recipes soon,' she promised. 'Till then, you can taste them for yourself at *Aux Délices Dessanges*, Rue des Romarins, Angers.'

I suppose they never imagined I would actually read the article. Perhaps they thought I hadn't meant what I'd told them. When I spoke to them about it they were apologetic, like children caught out in some endearing prank. The dish was already proving extremely successful, and there were plans for an entire Mamie Framboise section of the menu, including my *couscous à la provençale*, my *cassoulet trois haricots* and *Mamie's Famous Pancakes*.

'You see, Mamie,' explained Yannick winningly. 'The beauty of it is that we're not even expecting you to do anything. Just to be yourself. To be *natural*.'

'I could run a column in the magazine,' added Laure. '"Mamie Framboise Advises", something like that. Of course, *you* wouldn't need to write it. *I'd* do all that.' She beamed at me, as if I were some child who needed reassurance.

They'd brought Cassis with them again, and he too was beaming, though he looked a little confused, as if this was all a little too much for him.

'But I told you.' I kept my voice level, hard, to keep it from trembling. 'I told you before. I don't want any of this. I don't want to be a part of it.'

Cassis looked at me, bewildered. 'But it's such a good chance for my son,' he pleaded. 'Think what the publicity might do for him.'

Yannick coughed. 'What my father means', he amended hastily, 'is that we could *all* benefit from the situation. The possibilities are endless, if the thing catches on. We could market Mamie Framboise jams, Mamie Framboise biscuits. Of course, Mamie, you'd have a substantial percentage.'

I shook my head. 'You're not listening,' I said in a louder voice. 'I don't *want* publicity. I don't *want* a percentage. I'm not interested.'

Yannick and Laure exchanged glances.

'And if you're thinking what I think you're thinking,' I said sharply, 'that you might just as easily do it *without* my consent – after all, a name and a photograph's all you *really* need – then listen to this. If I hear of one more so-called Mamie Framboise recipe appearing in that magazine – in *any* magazine – then I'll be on the phone to the editor that very same day. I'll sell him the rights to every recipe I've got. Hell, I'll *give* them to him for free.'

I was out of breath, my heart hammering with rage and fear. But no-one railroads Mirabelle Dartigen's daughter. They knew I meant what I said, too. I could see it in their faces.

Helplessly, they protested: 'Mamie—'

'And stop calling me Mamie!'

'Let me talk to her.' That was Cassis, rising with difficulty from his chair. I noticed that age had shrunk him, had softly sunk him into himself, like a failed soufflé. Even that small effort caused him to wheeze painfully. 'In the garden.'

Sitting on a fallen tree trunk, beside the disused well, I felt an odd sense of doubling, as if the old Cassis might pull aside the fat man's mask from his face and reappear as before, intense, reckless and wild.

'Why are you doing this, 'Boise?' he demanded. 'Is it because of me?'

I shook my head slowly. 'This has nothing to do with you,' I told him, 'or Yannick.' I jerked my head at the farmhouse. 'You notice I managed to get the old farm fixed up.'

He shrugged. 'Never saw why you'd want to, myself,' he said. 'I wouldn't touch the place. Gives me the shivers just to think of you living here.' Then he gave me a strange look, knowing, almost sharp.

'But it's very like you to do it.' He smiled. 'You always were her favourite, 'Boise. You even look like her nowadays.'

I shrugged. 'You won't talk me round,' I said flatly.

'Now you're beginning to sound like her, too.' His voice, complex with love, guilt, hate. ''Boise—'

I looked at him. '*Someone* had to remember her,' I told him. 'And I knew it wasn't going to be you.'

He made a helpless gesture. 'But *here*, in Les Laveuses—'

'No-one knows who I am,' I said. 'No-one makes the connection.' I grinned suddenly. 'You know, Cassis, to most people, all old ladies look pretty much the same.'

He nodded. 'And you think Mamie Framboise would change that.'

'I know it would.'

A silence.

'You always were a good liar,' he observed casually. 'That's another thing you got from her. The capacity to hide. Me, I'm wide open.' He flung his arms wide to illustrate.

'Good for you,' I said indifferently. He even believed it himself.

'You're a good cook, I'll give you that.' He stared over my shoulder at the orchard, the trees heavy with ripening fruit. 'She'd have liked that. To know you'd kept things going. You're so *like* her,' he repeated slowly, not a compliment, but a statement of fact, with some distaste, some awe.

'She left me her book,' I told him. 'The one with the recipes in it. The album.'

His eyes widened. 'She did? Well, you were her favourite.'

'I don't know why you keep saying that,' I said impatiently. 'If ever Mother had a favourite it was Reinette, not me. You remember—'

'She told me herself,' he explained. 'Said that of the three of us you were the only one with any sense or any guts. "There's more of me in that sly little bitch than the pair of you ten times over." That's what she said.'

It sounded like her. Her voice in his, clear and sharp as glass. She must have been angry with him, in one of her rages. It was rare that she struck any of us, but God, her tongue!

Cassis grimaced. 'It was the way she said it, too,' he told me softly. 'So cold and dry, with that curious look in her eyes, as if it was a kind of test. As if she was waiting to see what I'd do next.'

'And what did you do?'

He shrugged. 'I cried, of course. I was only nine.'

Of course he would, I told myself. That was always

his way. Too sensitive beneath his wildness. He used to run away from home regularly, sleeping out in the woods or in the treehouse, knowing that Mother would not whip him. Secretly she encouraged his misbehaviour, because it looked like defiance, like strength. Me, I'd have spat in her face.

'Tell me, Cassis' – the idea came to me in a rush and I was suddenly almost out of breath with excitement – 'did Mother . . . Do you ever remember if she spoke Italian? Or Portuguese? Some foreign language?'

Cassis looked puzzled and shook his head.

'Are you sure? In her album . . .' I explained about the pages of foreign writing, the secret pages I had never learned to decipher.

'Let me see.'

We looked over it together, Cassis fingering the stiff yellow leaves with reluctant fascination. I noticed he avoided touching the writing, though he often fingered the other things, the photographs, the pressed flowers, butterflies' wings, pieces of cloth stuck to the pages.

'My God,' he said in a low voice. 'I never had any idea she'd made something like this.' He looked up at me. 'And you say you weren't her favourite.'

At first he seemed more interested in the recipes than anything else. Flicking through the album, his fingers seemed to have retained some of their old deftness.

'*Tarte mirabelle aux amandes,*' he whispered. '*Tourteau fromage. Clafoutis aux cerises rouges.* I remember these!' His enthusiasm was suddenly very young, very like the old Cassis. 'Everything's here,' he said softly. 'Everything.'

I pointed at one of the foreign passages.

Cassis studied it for a moment or two, and then began to laugh. 'That's not Italian,' he told me. 'Don't you remember what this is?' He seemed to find the whole thing very funny, rocking and wheezing. Even his ears shook, big old-man's ears, like bluecap mushrooms. 'This is the language Dad invented. Bilini-enverlini, he used to call it. Don't you remember? He used to speak it all the time.'

I tried to recall. I was seven when he died. There must be something left, I told myself. But there was so little. Everything swallowed up into a great hungry throat of darkness. I can remember my father, but only in snatches. A smell of moths and tobacco from his big old coat. The Jerusalem artichokes he alone liked, and which we all had to eat once a week. How I'd once accidentally sunk a fish-hook through the webby part of my hand, between finger and thumb, and his arms around me, his voice telling me to be brave. I remember his face through photographs, all in sepia. And at the back of my mind, something, a remote something, disgorged by the darkness. Father jabbering to us in nonsense-talk, grinning, Cassis laughing, myself laughing, without really understanding the joke, and Mother, for once, far away, safely out of earshot, one of her headaches, perhaps, an unexpected holiday.

'I remember *something*,' I said at last.

He explained then, patiently. A language of inverted syllables, reversed words, nonsense prefixes and suffixes. *Ini tnawini inoti plainexini* – I want to explain. *Minini toni nierus niohwni inoti* – I'm not sure who to.

Strangely enough Cassis seemed uninterested by my mother's secret writings. His gaze lingered over the recipes. The rest was dead. The recipes were something he could understand, touch, taste. I could feel his discomfort at standing so close to me, as if my similarity to her might infect him, too.

'If my son could only see all these recipes,' he said in a low voice.

'Don't tell him,' I said sharply. I was beginning to know Yannick. The less he learned about us, the better.

Cassis shrugged. 'Of course not. I promise.'

And I believed him. It goes to show that I'm not as like my mother as he thought. I trusted him, God help me, and for a while it seemed as if he'd kept his promise. Yannick and Laure kept their distance, Mamie Framboise vanished from view and summer rolled into autumn, dragging a soft train of dead leaves.

6

'Yannick says he saw Old Mother today,' she writes.

He came running back from the river half wild with
excitement and babbling. He'd forgotten his fish on the
verge in his haste, and I snapped at him for wasting time.
He looked at me with that sad helplessness in his eyes,
and I thought he was going to say something, but he
didn't. I suppose he feels ashamed. I feel hard inside,
frozen. I want to say something, but I'm not sure what it
is. Bad luck to see Old Mother, everyone says, but we've
had enough of that already. Perhaps that's why I am what
I am.

I took my time over Mother's album. Part of it was
fear – of what I might find out, perhaps; of what I
might be forced to remember. Part of it was that the
narrative was confused, the order of events deliberately and expertly shuffled, like a clever card trick. I
barely remembered the day of which she had spoken,
though I dreamed of it later. The handwriting, though
neat, was obsessively small, giving me terrible headaches if I studied it for too long. In this, too, I am like
her. I remember her headaches quite clearly, often
preceded by what Cassis used to refer to as her 'turns'.
They had worsened when I was born, he told me. He
was the only one of us old enough to remember her
before.
Below a recipe for mulled cider, she writes:

44

I can remember what it was like to be in the light. To be whole. It was like that for a time, before C. was born. I try to remember how it was to be so young. If only we'd stayed away, I tell myself. Never come back to Les Laveuses. Y. tries to help. But there's no love in it any more. He's afraid of me now, afraid of what I might do. To him. To the children. There's no sweetness in suffering, whatever people might think. It eats away everything in the end. Y. stays for the sake of the children. I should be grateful. He could leave and no-one would think the worse of him for it. After all, he was born here.

Never one to give in to her complaints, she bore the pain for as long as she could before retiring to her darkened room, while we padded silently, like wary cats, outside. Every six months or so she would suffer a really serious attack, which would leave her prostrate for days. Once, when I was very young, she collapsed on the way back from the well, crumpling forwards over her bucket, a wash of liquid staining the dry path in front of her, her straw hat slipping sideways to show her open mouth, her staring eyes. I was in the kitchen garden gathering herbs, alone. My first thought was that she was dead. Her silence, the black hole of her mouth against the taut yellow skin of her face, her eyes like ball-bearings. I put down my basket very slowly and walked towards her.

The path seemed oddly warped beneath my feet, as if I were wearing someone else's glasses, and I stumbled a little. My mother was lying on her side. One leg was splayed out, her dark skirt hiked up a little to show boot and stocking. Her mouth gaped hungrily. I felt very calm.

She's dead, I told myself. The rush of feeling which came in the wake of the thought was so intense that for a moment I was unable to identify it. A bright comet's tail of sensation, prickling at my armpits and flipping my stomach like a pancake. Terror, grief, confusion – I looked for them inside myself and found no trace of them. Instead, a burst of poison fireworks filled my head with light. I looked flatly at my mother's corpse and felt relief, hope and an ugly, primitive joy.

This sweetness . . .

I feel hard inside, frozen.

I know, I know. I can't expect you to understand how I felt. It sounds grotesque to me, too, remembering how it was, wondering whether this is not another false memory. Of course, it might have been shock. People experience strange things under the effects of shock. Even children. *Especially* children, the prim, secret savages we were. Locked in our mad world between the Lookout Post and the river, with the Standing Stones keeping watch over our covert rituals. But it was joy I felt all the same.

I stood beside her. The dead eyes stared at me, unblinking. I wondered whether I ought to close them. There was something disturbing about their round, fishy gaze, which reminded me of Old Mother, the day I finally nailed her up. A thread of drool glistened at her lips. I moved a little closer.

Her hand shot out and grabbed me by the ankle. Not dead, no; but waiting, her eyes bright with mean intelligence. Her mouth worked painfully, enunciating every word with glassy precision. I closed my eyes to stop myself from screaming.

'Listen. Get my stick.' Her voice was grating, metallic. 'Get it. Kitchen. Quickly.'

I stared at her, her hand still clutching my bare ankle.

'Felt it coming this morning,' she said tonelessly. 'Knew it was going to be a big one. Only saw half the clock. Smelt oranges. Get the stick. Help me.'

'I thought you were going to die.' My voice sounded eerily like hers, clear and hard. 'I thought you were dead.'

One side of her mouth hitched, and she made a low yarking sound, which eventually I recognized as laughter. I ran to the kitchen with that sound in my ears, found the stick – a heavy piece of twisted hawthorn she used to reach the higher branches of the fruit trees – and brought it to her. She was already on her knees, pushing against the ground with her hands. From time to time she shook her head with a sharp, impatient gesture, as if plagued by wasps.

'Good.' Her voice was thick, like a mouthful of mud. 'Now leave me. Tell your father. I'm going . . . to . . . my room.' Then, jerking herself savagely to her feet with the stick, swaying and keeping upright with a simple effort of will: 'I said *go away*!'

And she struck at me clumsily with one clawing hand, almost losing balance, stubbing at the path with her stick. I ran then, turning back only when I was well out of her range, ducking down behind a stand of redcurrants to watch her stagger towards the house, dragging her feet in great loops in the dirt behind her.

It was the first time I became truly aware of my mother's affliction. My father explained it to us later, the business with the clock and the oranges, while she lay in darkness. We understood little of what he told us. Our mother had bad spells, he said patiently, headaches that were so terrible that sometimes she didn't even know what she was doing. Had we ever had sunstroke? Felt that woozy, unreal feeling, imagined that objects were closer than they were, sounds louder? We looked at him, uncomprehending. Only Cassis, nine then to my four, seemed to understand.

'She does things,' said my father. 'Things she doesn't really remember afterwards. Because of the bad spells.'

We stared at him solemnly. *Bad spells*.

My youthful mind associated the phrase with stories of witches. The gingerbread house. The Seven Swans. I imagined my mother lying on her bed in the dark, eyes open, strange words sliding between her lips like eels. I imagined her looking through the walls and seeing me, seeing right inside me and rocking with that dreadful, yarking laughter. Sometimes Father slept on the kitchen chair when Mother had her bad spells. And one morning we had got up to find him bathing his forehead in the kitchen sink, and the water full of blood. An accident, he told us. A stupid accident. But I remember seeing blood, glossy on the clean terracotta tiles. A length of stove wood had been left on the table. There was blood on that, too.

'She wouldn't hurt us, would she, Papa?'

He looked at me for a moment. A second's hesitation, maybe two. And in his eyes a look of calculation, as if deciding how much to tell.

Then he smiled. 'Of course not, sweetheart.' What a question, his smile said. 'She wouldn't ever hurt *you*.' And he folded me into his arms and I smelled tobacco and moths and the biscuity smell of old sweat. But I never forgot that hesitation, that measuring look. For a second he had considered it. Turned it over in his mind, wondering how much to tell us. Perhaps he'd thought he had time, plenty of time to explain to us when we were older.

Later that night I heard sounds from my parents' room: shouting and breaking glass. I got up early to find that my father had slept all night in the kitchen. My mother got up late but cheery – as cheery as she ever was – singing to herself in a low, tuneless voice as she stirred green tomatoes into her round copper jamming-pan, slipping me a handful of yellow gages from her apron pocket. Shyly, I asked her if she felt any better. She looked at me without comprehension, her face white and blank as a clean plate. I sneaked into her room later and found my father taping waxed paper over a broken window pane. There was glass on the floor from the window and the face of the mantel clock, now lying face down on the boards. A reddish smear had dried against the wallpaper, just above the bedstead, and my eyes sought it with a kind of fascination. I could see the five commas of her finger-tips where they had stabbed at the paper, and the blot which was her palm. When I looked a few hours later, the wall had been scrubbed clean and the room was tidy again. Neither of my parents mentioned the incident, both behaving as if nothing untoward had happened. But after that, my father kept our bedroom doors locked and our windows bolted at night, almost as if he were afraid of something breaking in.

7

When my father died I felt little true grief. When I looked for sorrow I found only a hard place inside myself, like a stone in a fruit. I tried to tell myself that I would never see his face again, but by that time I had almost forgotten it anyway. Instead he had become a kind of icon, with rolling eyes like a plaster saint's, his uniform buttons gleaming mellowly. I tried to imagine him lying dead on the battlefield, lying broken in some mass grave, exploded by the mine that blew up in his face. I imagined horrors, but they were as unreal to me as nightmares. Cassis took it worst. He ran away for two days after we got the news, finally returning exhausted, hungry and covered in mosquito bites. He'd been sleeping out on the other side of the Loire, where the woods tail off into marshland. I think he'd had some mad idea of joining the army, but had got lost instead, going round in circles for hours until he'd found the Loire again. He tried to bluff it out, to pretend he'd had adventures, but for once I didn't believe him.

After that he took to fighting other boys, and often came home with torn clothes and blood under his fingernails. He spent hours in the woods alone. He never cried for Father, and took pride in that, even swearing at Philippe Hourias when he once tried to offer comfort. Reinette, on the other hand, seemed to enjoy the attention Father's death brought her. People called round with presents, or patted her head if they met her in the village. In the café the matter of our future – and our mother's – was discussed in low, earnest voices. My sister learned to make her eyes brim at will, and cultivated a brave, orphaned smile that earned her gifts of sweets and the reputation of being the sensitive one in the family.

My mother never spoke of him after his death. It was as if Father had never lived with us at all. The farm went on without him, if anything with even greater efficiency than before. We dug up the rows of Jerusalem artichokes, which only he had liked, and replaced them with asparagus and purple broccoli, which swayed and whispered in the wind. I began to have bad dreams in which I was lying underground, rotting, overwhelmed by the stench of my own decay. I drowned in the Loire, feeling the ooze of the river bed crawl over my dead flesh, and when I reached out for help I felt hundreds of other bodies there with me, rocking gently with the under-river current, crammed shoulder to shoulder against each other, some whole, some in pieces, faceless, grinning brokenly from dislocated jaws, and rolling dead eyes in garish welcome. I awoke from these dreams sweating and screaming, but Mother never came. Instead, Cassis and Reinette came to me, impatient and kind by turns. Sometimes they pinched and threatened me in low, exasperated voices. Sometimes they took me in their arms and rocked me back to sleep. Sometimes Cassis would tell stories and Reine-Claude and I would both listen, eyes wide in the moonlight. Stories of giants and witches and man-eating roses and mountains and dragons masquerading as men. Oh, Cassis was a fine storyteller in those days, and though he was sometimes unkind, and often made fun of my night terrors, it is the stories I remember most now, and his eyes shining.

8

With father gone, we grew to know mother's bad spells almost as well as he had. As it began, she would speak with a certain vagueness, and she would suffer tension around the temples which would betray itself through the impatient little pecking movements of her head. Sometimes she would reach for something – a spoon or a knife – and miss, slapping her hand repeatedly against the table or the sink top, as if feeling for the object. Sometimes she would ask, 'What's the time?' even though the big round kitchen clock was just in front of her. And always at these times, the same sharp, suspicious question, 'Have any of you brought oranges into the house?'

We shook our heads silently. Oranges were scarce; we'd only tasted them occasionally. At the market in Angers we might see them sometimes – fat Spanish oranges with their thick, dimpled rind; finer-grained blood oranges from the south, cut open to reveal their grazed purple flesh. Our mother always kept away from these stalls, as if the sight of them sickened her. Once, when a friendly woman on the market gave us an orange to share, our mother refused to let us into the house until we had washed, scrubbed under our nails and rubbed our hands with lemon balm and lavender. Even then she claimed she could smell the orange oil on us, and left the windows open for two days until it finally vanished. Of course, the oranges of her bad spells were purely imaginary. The scent heralded her migraines, and within hours she was lying in darkness with a lavender-soaked handkerchief across her face and her pills to hand beside her. The pills, I later learned, were morphine.

She never explained. What information we gleaned was gathered from long observation. When she felt a migraine approaching, she simply withdrew to her room, without giving any reason, leaving us to our own devices. So it was that we viewed these spells of hers as a kind of holiday – lasting from a couple of hours to a whole day, or even two – during which we ran wild. They were wonderful days for us, days I wished would last for ever; swimming in the Loire or catching crayfish in the shallows, exploring the woods, making ourselves sick with cherries or plums or green gooseberries, fighting, sniping at each other with potato rifles and decorating the Standing Stones with the spoils of our adventuring.

The Standing Stones were the remains of an old jetty, long since swept away by the currents. Five stone pillars, one shorter than the rest, protruding from the water. A metal staple stuck out from the side of each, bleeding tears of rust into the rotten stone where boards had once been fixed. It was onto these metal protrusions that we hung our trophies; barbaric garlands of fish-heads and flowers, signs lettered in secret codes, magical stones and driftwood sculptures. The last pillar stood well into the deep water, at a point where the current was especially strong, and it was here we hid our treasure chest. This was a tin box wrapped in oilcloth and weighted with a piece of chain. The chain was secured to a rope, which in its turn was tied to the pillar we all referred to as the Treasure Stone. To retrieve the treasure it was necessary first to swim to the last pillar – no mean feat – then, holding on to the pillar with one arm, to haul up the sunken chest, detach it and swim back to the shore with it. It was accepted that only Cassis could do this. The 'treasure' consisted mainly of things no adult

53

would recognize as being of value. The potato guns, chewing gum wrapped in greased paper to make it last, a stick of barley sugar, three cigarettes, some coins in a battered purse, actresses' photographs – these, like the cigarettes, belonged to Cassis – and a few copies of an illustrated magazine specializing in lurid stories.

Sometimes Paul Hourias came with us on what Cassis called our 'hunting trips', though he was never fully initiated into our secrets. I liked Paul. His father sold bait on the Angers road and his mother took in mending to make ends meet. He was an only child of parents old enough to be his grandparents, and much of his time was spent keeping out of their way. He lived as I longed to live. In summer he spent whole nights out in the woods without arousing any concern from his family. He knew where to find mushrooms on the forest floor and how to make whistles out of willow twigs. His hands were deft and clever, but he was often awkward and slow in speech, and when adults were near he stuttered. Though he was close to Cassis in age, he did not go to school, but instead helped on his uncle's farm, milking the cows and bringing them to and from the pasture. He was patient with me, too, more so than Cassis, never making fun of my ignorance or scorning me because I was small. Of course, he's old now. But I sometimes think that, of the four of us, he is the one who has aged the least.

PART TWO

Forbidden Fruit

1

It was already, in early June, promising to be a hot summer, and the Loire was low and surly with quicksand and landslides. There were snakes, too, more than usual, flat-headed brown adders which lurked in the cool mud in the shallows. Jeannette Gaudin was bitten by one of these as she paddled one dry afternoon, and they buried her a week later in Saint-Benedict's churchyard, beneath a little cross and an angel. 'Beloved Daughter . . . 1934–1942'. I was three months older than she was.

Suddenly I felt as if a gulf had opened beneath me, a hot, deep hole, like a giant mouth. If Jeannette could die, then so could I. So could anyone. Cassis looked down from the height of his thirteen years in some scorn. 'You expect people to die in wartime, stupid. Children, too. People die all the time.'

I tried to explain and found I could not. Soldiers dying – even my own father – was one thing. Even civilians killed in the bombing, though there had been little enough of that in Les Laveuses. But this was different. My nightmares worsened. I spent hours watching the river with my fishing net, catching the evil brown snakes in the shallows, smashing their flat, clever heads with a stone and nailing their bodies to the exposed roots at the river bank. A week of this and there were twenty or more drooping lankly from the roots, and the stink – fishy and oddly sweet, like something bad fermented – was overwhelming. Cassis and Reinette were still at school – they both went to the *collège* in Angers – and it was Paul who found me with a clothes-peg on my nose to keep out the stench, doggedly stirring the muddy soup of the verge with my net.

He was wearing shorts and sandals, and held his dog, Malabar, on a leash made of string.

I gave him a look of indifference and turned back to the water. Paul sat down next to me and Malabar flopped onto the path, panting. I ignored them both. At last Paul spoke. 'Wh-what's wrong?'

I shrugged. 'Nothing. I'm just fishing, that's all.'

Another silence. 'For s-snakes.' His voice was carefully uninflected.

I nodded, rather defiantly. 'So?'

'So nothing.' He patted Malabar's head. 'You can do what you like.' A pause which crawled between us like a racing snail.

'I wonder if it hurts,' I said at last.

He considered it for a moment, as if he knew what I meant, then shook his head. 'Dunno.'

'They say the poison gets into your blood and makes you go numb. Just like going to sleep.'

He watched me non-committally, neither agreeing nor disagreeing. 'C-Cassis sez that Jeannette Gaudin musta seen Old Mother,' he said at last. 'You know. That's why the snake b-bit her. Old Mother's curse.'

I shook my head. Cassis, the avid storyteller and reader of lurid adventure magazines, with titles like *The Mummy's Curse*, or *Barbarian Swarm*, was always saying things like that.

'I don't think Old Mother even exists,' I said defiantly. 'I've never seen her, anyway. Besides, there's no such thing as a curse. Everyone knows that.'

Paul looked at me with sad, indignant eyes. 'Course there is,' he said. 'And she's down there all right. M-my dad saw her once, way back before I was born. B-biggest pike you ever saw. Week later, he

58

broke his leg falling off of his b-bike. Even *your* dad got—' He broke off, dropping his eyes in sudden confusion.

'Not my dad,' I said sharply. 'My dad was killed in battle.' I had a sudden, vivid picture of him marching, a single link in an endless line which moved relentlessly towards a gaping horizon.

Paul shook his head. 'She's there,' he said stubbornly. 'Right at the deepest point of the Loire. Might be forty years old, maybe fifty. Pikes live a long time, the old uns. She's black as the mud she lives in. And she's clever, crazy-clever. She'd take a bird sitting on the water as easy as she'd gulp a piece of bread. My dad sez she's not a pike at all, but a ghost, a murderess, damned to watch the living for ever. That's why she hates us.'

This was a long speech for Paul, and in spite of myself I listened with interest. The river abounded with stories and old wives' tales, but the story of Old Mother was the most enduring. The giant pike, her lip pierced and bristling with the hooks of anglers who had tried to catch her. In her eye, an evil intelligence. In her belly, a treasure of unknown origin and inestimable worth.

'My dad sez that if anyone was to catch her, she'd hafta give you a wish,' said Paul. 'Sez *he'd* settle for a million francs and a look at that Greta Garbo's underwear.' He grinned sheepishly. That's grown-ups for you, his smile seemed to say.

I considered this. I told myself I didn't believe in curses or wishes for free, but the image of the old pike wouldn't let go.

'If she's there, we could catch her,' I told him abruptly. 'It's our river. We could.'

It was suddenly clear to me; it was not only possible, but an obligation. I thought of the dreams which had plagued me ever since father died; dreams of drowning, of rolling blind in the black surf of the swollen Loire with the clammy feel of dead flesh all around me, of screaming and feeling my scream forced back into my throat, of drowning in myself. Somehow the pike personified all that, and though my thinking was certainly not as analytical as that, something in me was suddenly certain; certain that if I were to catch Old Mother, *something* might happen. What it might be I would not articulate, even to myself. But something, I thought in mounting, incomprehensible excitement. *Something*.

Paul looked at me in bewilderment. 'Catch her?' he repeated. 'What for?'

'It's our river,' I said stubbornly. 'It shouldn't be in our river.' What I wanted to say was that the pike *offended* me in some secret, visceral way, much more so than the snakes; its slyness, its age, its evil complacency. But I could think of no way to say it. It was a monster.

''Sides, you'd never do it,' Paul went on. 'I mean, people have tried. Grown-up people. With lines and nets anall. It bites through the nets. And the lines . . . it breaks them right snap down the middle. It's strong, see. Stronger than either of us.'

'Doesn't have to be,' I insisted. 'We could trap it.'

'You'd hafta be bloody clever to trap Old Mother,' said Paul stolidly.

'So?' I was beginning to get angry now, and I faced him with fists and face clenched in frustration. 'So we'll *be* clever. Cassis and me and Reinette and you. All four of us. Unless you're scared.'

'I'm not s-scared, but it's im-im-impossible.' He was beginning to stutter again, as he always did when he felt under pressure.

I looked at him. 'Well, I'll do it on my own if you won't help. And I'll catch the old pike, too. You just wait.' For some reason my eyes were stinging. I wiped them furtively with the heel of my hand. I could see Paul watching me with a curious expression, but he said nothing. Viciously, I poked at the hot shallows with my net. ''S'only an old *fish*,' I said. Poke. 'I'll catch it and hang it on the Standing Stones.' Poke. 'Right *there*.' I pointed at the Treasure Stone with my dripping net. 'Right there,' I said again in a low voice, spitting on the ground to prove that what I said was true.

2

My mother smelt oranges all through that hot month. As often as once a week, though it was not every time that a bad spell ensued. While Cassis and Reinette were at school I ran to the river, mostly on my own but sometimes accompanied by Paul, when he could get away from his chores on the farm.

I had reached an awkward age, and separated from my siblings for most of those long days I grew bold and defiant, running away when my mother gave me work to do, missing meals and coming home late and dirty, my clothes streaked yellow with river-bank dust, hair untied and plastered back with sweat. I must have been born confrontational, but in the summer of my ninth year I grew more so than ever before. My mother and I stalked each other, like cats staking out their territory. Every touch was a spark which hissed with static. Every word was a potential insult, every conversation a minefield. At mealtimes we sat face to face, glowering over our soup and pancakes. Cassis and Reine flanked us like frightened courtiers, big-eyed and silent.

I don't know why we pitted ourselves against each other; maybe it was the simple fact that I was growing up. The woman who had terrified me during my infancy took on a different light as I approached adolescence. I could see the grey in her hair, the lines bracketing her mouth. I could see now, with a flash of contempt, that she was only an ageing woman whose bad spells sent her helpless to her room.

And she baited me. Deliberately, or so I thought. Now I think that maybe she couldn't help it, that it was as much in her unhappy nature to bait me as it was in mine to defy her. It seemed, during that summer, that every time she opened her mouth it was to criticize. My manners, my dress, my appearance, my opinions. Everything, according to her, was reprehensible. I was slovenly; I left my clothes unfolded at the foot of my bed when I went to sleep. I slouched when I walked; I would become a hunchback if I wasn't careful. I was greedy, stuffing myself with fruit from the orchard. Otherwise I had little appetite; I was growing thin and scrawny. Why couldn't I be more like Reine-Claude? At twelve, my sister had already ripened. Soft and sweet as dark honey, with amber eyes and autumn hair, she was every storybook heroine, every screen goddess I had ever imagined and admired. When we were younger she would let me plait her hair, and I would twist flowers and berries into the thick strands and circle her head with convulvulus so she looked like a woodland sprite. Now there was something almost adult about her composure, her passive sweetness. Next to her I looked like a frog, my mother told me, an ugly, skinny little frog, with my wide sullen mouth and my big hands and feet.

I remember one of those dinner-time conflicts in particular. We had *paupiettes*, those little parcels of veal and minced pork, tied up with string and cooked in a thick stew of carrots, shallots and tomatoes in white wine. I looked at my plate with sullen disinterest. Reinette and Cassis looked at nothing, carefully detached.

My mother clenched her fists, infuriated by my silence. After my father's death there was no-one to temper her rage, and it was always close by, boiling under the surface. She seldom struck us – very unusual in those days, almost a freak – though it was not, I suspect, from any great sense of affection.

63

Rather, she was afraid that, having begun, she might not be able to stop.

'Don't *slouch*, for God's sake.' Her voice was tart as an unripe gooseberry. 'You know that if you slouch you'll end up staying that way.'

I gave her a quick, insolent look and put my elbows on the table.

'Elbows off the table,' she almost moaned. 'Look at your sister. Look at her. Does she slouch? Does she behave like a sulky farmhand?'

It did not occur to me to resent Reinette. It was my mother I resented, and I showed it with every movement of my sly young body. I gave her every excuse to hound me. She wanted the clothes on the washing-line hung by the hems: I hung them by the collars. The jars in the pantry had to have the labels facing the front: I turned them backwards. I forgot to wash my hands before meals. I changed the order of the pans hanging on the kitchen wall from largest to smallest. I left the kitchen window open so that when she opened the door the draught would make it bang. I infringed a thousand of her personal rules, and she reacted to each trespass with the same bewildered rage. To her, those petty rules mattered because those were the things she used to control our world. Take them away and she was like the rest of us, orphaned and lost.

Of course, I didn't know that then.

'You're a hard little bitch, aren't you?' she said at last, pushing away her plate. 'Hard as nails.' There was neither hostility nor affection in her voice, merely a kind of cool disinterest. 'I used to be like that,' she said. It was the first time I had ever heard her speak of her own childhood. 'At your age.' Her smile was stretched and mirthless. Impossible to imagine her ever being young. I stabbed at my *paupiette* in its congealing sauce.

'I always wanted to fight everybody, too,' said my mother. 'I would have sacrificed everything, hurt anyone, to prove myself right. To win.' She looked at me intently, curiously, her black eyes like pinpricks in tar. 'Contrary, that's what you are. I knew from the moment you were born that's what you were going to be. You started it all again, worse than ever. The way you screamed in the night and wouldn't feed, and me lying awake with the doors closed and my head pounding.'

I did not answer. After a moment my mother laughed rather jeeringly and began to clear the dishes. It was the last time she spoke of the war between us, though that war was far from over.

3

The Lookout Post was a large elm on the near bank of the Loire, half overhanging the water, a clutch of thick roots dangling down deep from the dry soil of the bank. It was easy to climb, even for me, and from the higher branches I could see all of Les Laveuses. Cassis and Paul had built a primitive treehouse there – a platform and some branches bent over to make a roof – but I was the one who spent most time in the completed shelter. Reinette was reluctant to climb to the top, though the way had been made easier by means of a knotted rope, and Cassis rarely went there any more, so I often had the place to myself. I went there to think and to watch the road, where sometimes I could see the Germans in their jeeps – or more often motorcycles – passing by.

Of course, there was little to interest the Germans in Les Laveuses. There was no barracks, no school, no public buildings for them to occupy. They settled in Angers instead, with only a few patrols around the neighbouring villages, and all I saw of them, except for the vehicles on the road, were the groups of soldiers sent every week to requisition produce from Hourias' farm. Our own was less frequented, as we had no cows, only a few pigs and goats. Our main source of income was fruit, and the season had barely begun. A couple of soldiers came, half-heartedly, once a month, but the best of our supplies were well hidden, and Mother always sent me out into the orchard when the soldiers came. Even so, I was curious about their grey uniforms, sometimes sitting in the Lookout Post and shooting imaginary rockets at the jeeps as they sped by. I was not truly hostile, none of the children were; we were merely curious, repeating the insults our parents taught us – filthy Boche, Nazi swine – out of an instinct for mimicry. I had no idea of what was happening in Occupied France, and little notion even of where Berlin was.

Once they came to requisition a violin from Denis Gaudin, Jeannette's grandfather. Jeannette had told me about it the next day. It was getting dark and the blackout shutters were already in place when she'd heard a knocking at the door. She'd opened it and seen a German officer. In polite though laborious French he addressed her grandfather.

'Monsieur, I . . . understand . . . you have . . . a violin. I . . . need it.'

A few of the officers, it seemed, had decided to form a military band. I suppose even Germans needed some way of passing the time.

Old Denis Gaudin looked at him. 'A violin, *mein Herr*, is like a woman,' he replied pleasantly. 'Not to be lent out.' And very gently he closed the door. There was a silence as the officer digested this. Jeannette looked up at her grandfather with wide eyes. Then, from outside, came the sound of the German officer laughing and repeating: '*Wie eine Frau! Wie eine Frau!*'

The officer never came back, and Denis kept his violin until much later, almost until the end of the war.

4

For the first time that summer, however, my main interest was not the Germans. I spent most of my waking and many of my sleeping hours devising ways of trapping Old Mother. I studied the various techniques of fishing. Lines for eels, pots for crays, dragnets, straight nets, live bait and skim lures. I went to Hourias and plagued him until he told me all he knew about bait. I dug bloodworms from the sides of the banks and learned to keep them in my mouth for warmth. I trapped bluebottles and threaded them on lines bristling with fish-hooks, like strange tinsel. I made traps from cages of willow and thread, and baited them with scraps. A single touch on one of the threads in the cage and it would spring shut, jerking the whole contraption out of the water as the bent branch underneath it was released. I stretched pieces of net across the narrower channels between the sandbanks. I left static lines baited with boluses of rotting meat hanging from the far bank. In this way I caught any number of perch, small bleaks, gudgeons, minnows and eels. Some I took home to eat and watched my mother prepare them. The kitchen was now the only neutral place in the house, a place of brief respite from our private war. I used to stand beside her, listening to her low monotone, and together we would make her *bouillabaisse angevine* – a fish stew with red onions and thyme – and perch roasted in tinfoil with tarragon and wild mushrooms. Some of my catches I left at the Standing Stones in gaudy, stinking garlands: a warning and a challenge.

But Old Mother did not come. On Sundays, when Reine and Cassis were away from school, I would try to infuse them with my passion for the hunt. But since Reine-Claude's admission to the *collège* earlier that year, the two of them had become a race apart. Five years separated me from Cassis; three from Reine. And yet they seemed closer than that in age, gilded with adulthood, so alike, with their golden faces and high cheekbones, that they might almost have been twins. They often talked together in secret whispers, secret laughter, naming friends I had never heard of, laughing at private jokes. Alien names punctuated their conversations. Monsieur Toupet, Madame Froussine, Mademoiselle Culourd. Cassis had nicknames for all his teachers, and could mimic their habits and voices to make Reine laugh. Other names, whispered under cover of darkness when I was asleep, seemed to be those of their friends. Heinemann. Leibniz. Schwartz. Laughter when these names were whispered, strange, spiteful laughter with a bright note of guilt and hysteria. They were names I did not recognize, foreign names, and when I asked about them, Cassis and Reine-Claude simply giggled and ran away, arm in arm, towards the orchards.

This elusiveness troubled me more than I could have imagined. They had become conspirators where before they were my equals. Suddenly all our shared activities had become childish to them. The Lookout Post and the Standing Stones were mine alone. Reine-Claude claimed to be afraid to go fishing for fear of snakes. Instead she stayed in her room, brushing her hair into complicated styles and sighing over photographs of film actresses. Cassis listened with polite inattention to my excited plans, then made excuses to leave me on my own: a lesson to copy, Latin verbs to learn for Monsieur Toubon. I'd understand later, when I was older. They made every effort to keep me away from them. They made appointments with me which they did not keep, sending me across Les Laveuses on an imaginary errand, promising to meet me at the river, then making for the forest alone, while I waited, angry tears burning my eyes. They pretended innocence when I challenged them, clapping sly hands to their mouths – 'Did we really say the big elm? I was so sure we agreed the second oak' – and giggling when I stalked away.

They only went occasionally to the river to swim, Reine-Claude entering the water gingerly, and only in the deeper, clearer parts, where snakes were unlikely to venture. I sought their attention, making extravagant dives from the bank and swimming underwater for such long stretches that Reine-Claude would scream that I was drowned. Even so I felt them slipping from me little by little, and loneliness overwhelmed me.

Only Paul stayed loyal during this time. Though he was older than Reine-Claude and almost the same age as Cassis, he seemed younger, less sophisticated. He was inarticulate when they were there, smiling in agonized embarrassment when they talked about school. Paul could barely read, and his writing was the stilted, painful printing of a much younger child. He liked stories, though, and I would read to him from Cassis' magazines when he came to the Lookout Post. We used to sit on the platform, he whittling at a piece of wood with his small knife, while I read *The Mummy's Tomb* or *The Martian Invasion*, half a loaf of bread on the board between us, from which we would occasionally cut a slice. Sometimes he brought a piece of *rillettes* wrapped in a sheet of greaseproof paper, or half a camembert. To our little feast, I would add a pocketful of strawberries or one of the goat's cheeses rolled in ash, which my mother called *petits cendrés*. From the post I could see all my nets and traps, which I checked every hour, resetting them as necessary and removing the small fry.

'What'll you wish for when you catch her?' By now

he believed implicitly that I would catch the old pike, and he spoke with a kind of reluctant awe.

I considered. 'Dunno.' I took a bite of bread and *rillettes*. 'There's no point making plans till I've caught it. That might take time.'

It was time I was willing to take. Three weeks into June and my enthusiasm had not faltered. Quite the opposite. Even the indifference of Cassis and Reine-Claude only served to increase my stubbornness. Old Mother was a talisman in my mind, a slinking black talisman which, if I could only reach it, might put right everything which was skewed.

I'd show them. The day I caught Old Mother they'd all look at me in amazement. Cassis, Reine, and to see that look in my mother's face, to make her *see* me, perhaps to clench her fists in rage . . . or to smile with peculiar sweetness and open her arms.

But here my fantasy stopped; I dared not imagine further.

''Sides,' I said with studied languor. 'I don't believe in wishes. I told you that already.'

Paul looked cynical. 'If you don't believe in wishes,' he pointed out, 'then what're you doing it for?'

I shook my head. 'Dunno,' I said at last. 'Just for something to do, I expect.'

He laughed. 'That's you, 'Boise,' he said between gusts of laughter. 'That's you all over, that is. Catch Old Mother for *something to do*!' And he was off again, rolling alarmingly close to the edge of the platform in his incomprehensible hilarity until Malabar, tied by string to the foot of the tree, began to bark sharply and we fell silent before our cover was blown.

5

Soon after that I found the lipstick under Reine-Claude's mattress. A stupid place to hide it, really – anyone could have found it, even Mother – but Reinette was never imaginative. It was my turn to make the beds, and the thing must have worked its way under the bottom sheet, because that was where I found it, tucked between the lip of the mattress and the bedboard. At first I didn't recognize it. Mother had never used make-up. A small golden cylinder, like a stubby pen. I turned the cap, encountered resistance and opened it. I was experimenting rather gingerly on my arm when I heard a gasp behind me and Reinette jerked me round. Her face was pale and contorted.

'Give me that!' she hissed. 'That's mine!' She snatched the lipstick from my fingers and it fell to the floor, rolling under the bed. Quickly she scrabbled to retrieve it, her face flaring.

'Where did you get that?' I asked curiously. 'Does Mother know you've got it?'

'None of your business,' gasped Reinette, emerging from under the bed. 'You've no right to go snooping in my private things. And if you dare tell *anyone*—'

I grinned. 'I might tell,' I told her. 'And I might not. It just depends.' She took a step forwards, but I was almost as tall as she was, and though rage had made her reckless, she knew better than to try and fight me.

'Don't tell,' she said in a wheedling voice. 'I'll go

fishing with you this afternoon, if you like. We could go to the Lookout Post and read magazines.'

I shrugged. 'Maybe. Where did you get it?'

Reinette looked at me. 'Promise you won't tell.'

'I promise.' I spat in my hand. After a moment's hesitation she followed suit. We sealed the bargain with a spit-clammy handshake.

'All right.' She sat down on the edge of the bed, legs curled underneath her. 'It was at school, in spring. We had a Latin teacher there, Monsieur Toubon. Cassis calls him Monsieur Toupet because he looks as if he wears a wig. He was always getting at us. He was the one who made the whole class stay in that time. Everybody hated him.'

'A *teacher* gave it to you?' I was incredulous.

'No, stupid. Listen. You know the Boches requisitioned the lower and middle corridors and the rooms around the courtyard. You know, for their quarters. And their drilling.'

I'd heard this before. The old school, with its location near the centre of Angers, its large classrooms and enclosed playgrounds, was ideal for their purposes. Cassis had told us about the Germans on manoeuvres with their grey cow's head masks, how no-one was allowed to watch and the shutters had to be closed around the courtyard at those times.

'Some of us used to creep in and watch them through a slit under one of the shutters,' said Reinette. 'It was boring, really. Just a lot of marching up and down and shouting in German. Can't see why it all has to be so secret.' Her mouth drooped in a moue of dissatisfaction.

'Anyway, old Toupet caught us at it one day,' she continued. 'Gave us all a big lecture – Cassis and me and, oh, people you wouldn't know. Made us miss our free Thursday afternoon. Gave us a whole lot of extra Latin to do.' Her mouth twisted viciously. 'I don't know what makes *him* so holy anyhow. He was only coming to watch the Boches himself.' Reinette shrugged. '*Anyway,*' she continued in a lighter voice. 'We managed to get him back eventually. Old Toupet lives in the *collège* – he has rooms next to the boys' dorm – and Cassis looked in one day when Toupet was out, and what do you think?'

I shrugged.

'He had a big radio in there, pushed under his bed. One of those long-wave contraptions.' Reinette paused, looking suddenly uneasy.

'So?' I looked at the little gold stick between her fingers, trying to see the connection.

She smiled an unpleasantly adult smile. 'I know we're not supposed to have anything to do with the Boches, but you can't avoid people all the time,' she said in a superior tone. 'I mean, you see them at the gate, or going into Angers to the pictures.' This was a privilege I greatly envied Reine-Claude and Cassis, that on Thursdays they were allowed to cycle into the town centre, to the cinema or the café – and I pulled a face.

'Get on with it,' I said.

'I *am,*' complained Reinette. 'God, 'Boise, you're so *impatient.*' She touched her hair. 'As I was saying, you're bound to see Germans *some* of the time. And they're not all bad.' That smile again. 'Some of them can be quite nice. Nicer than old Toupet, anyway.'

I shrugged indifferently. 'So one of *them* gave you the lipstick,' I said with scorn. Such a fuss over so little, I thought to myself. It was just like Reinette to get so excited about nothing at all.

'We told them – well, we just *mentioned* to one of them – about Toupet and his radio,' she said. For some reason she was flushed, her cheeks bright as peonies. 'He gave us the lipstick, and some cigarettes for Cassis, and, well, all kinds of things.' She was speaking rapidly now, unstoppably, her eyes bright.

'And later Yvonne Cressonnet said that she saw them come to old Toupet's room, and they took the radio away, and he went with them, and now instead of Latin we have an extra geography lesson

74

with Madame Lambert, and no-one knows what's happened to him.'

She levelled her gaze at me. I remember her eyes were almost gold, the colour of boiling sugar syrup as it begins to turn.

I shrugged. 'I don't suppose anything happened,' I said reasonably. 'I mean, they wouldn't send an old man like that to the Front just for having a radio.'

'No, course they wouldn't.' Her reply was too hasty. 'Besides, he shouldn't have had it in the first place, should he?'

I agreed he shouldn't. It was against the rules. A teacher should have known that. Reine looked at the lipstick, turning it gently, lovingly in her hand.

'You won't tell, then?' She stroked my arm gently. 'You won't, will you, 'Boise?'

I pulled away, automatically rubbing my arm where she had touched me. I never did like being petted. 'Do you and Cassis see these Germans often?' I questioned.

She shrugged. 'Sometimes.'

'D'you tell them anything else?'

'No.' She spoke too quickly. 'We just talk. Look, 'Boise, you won't tell anyone, will you?'

I smiled. 'Well, I *might* not. Not if you do something for me.'

She looked at me narrowly. 'What do you mean?'

'I'd like to go into Angers sometimes, with you and Cassis,' I said slyly. 'To the pictures and the café and stuff.' I paused for effect, and she glared at me from eyes as bright and narrow as knives. 'Or,' I continued in a falsely holy tone, 'I might tell Mother that you've been talking to the people who killed our father. Talking to them and spying for them. Enemies of France. See what she says to *that*.'

Reinette looked agitated. ''Boise, you *promised*!'

I shook my head solemnly. 'That doesn't count, it's my patriotic duty.'

I must have sounded convincing. Reinette turned pale. And yet the words themselves meant nothing to me. I felt no real hostility to the Germans. Even when I told myself that they had killed my father, that the man who did it might even be *there*, actually *there* in Angers, an hour's cycle ride down the road, drinking *Gros-Plant* in some *bar-tabac* and smoking a Gauloise. The image was clear in my mind, and yet it had little potency. Perhaps because my father's face was already blurring in my memory. Perhaps in the same way that children rarely get involved in the quarrels of adults, and adults rarely understand the sudden hostilities which erupt for no comprehensible reason between children. My voice was prim and disapproving, but what I really wanted had nothing to do with our father, France or the war. I wanted to be involved again, to be treated as an adult, a bearer of secrets. And I wanted to go to the cinema, to see Laurel and Hardy or Bela Lugosi or Humphrey Bogart, to sit in the flickering dark, with Cassis on one side and Reine-Claude on the other, maybe with a cornet of chips in one hand or a strip of liquorice.

Reinette shook her head. 'You're crazy,' she said at last. 'You know Mother would never let you go into town on your own. You're too young. Besides—'

'I wouldn't be on my own. You or Cassis could take me on the back of your bike,' I continued stubbornly. She rode my mother's bike, and Cassis took Father's bike to school with him, an awkward, black gantry-like thing. It was too far to walk, and without bikes they would have had to board at the *collège*, as many country children did. 'Term's nearly over. We could all go into Angers together, see a film, have a look round.'

My sister looked mulish. 'She'll want us to stay home and work on the farm,' she said. 'You'll see. She never wants anyone to have any fun.'

'The number of times she's been smelling oranges recently,' I told her practically, 'I don't suppose it will matter. We could sneak off. The way she is, she'll never even know.'

It was easy. Reine was always easy to move. Her

passivity was an adult thing, her sly, sweet nature hiding a kind of laziness, almost indifference. She faced me now, throwing her last weak excuse at me like a handful of sand.

'You're crazy!' In those days everything I did was crazy to Reine. Crazy for swimming underwater, for teetering at the top of the Lookout Post on one leg, for answering back, for eating green figs or sour apples.

I shook my head. 'It'll be easy,' I told her firmly. 'You can count on me.'

You see from what innocent beginnings it grew. We none of us meant for anyone to be hurt, and yet there is a hard place in the centre of me which remembers implacably and with perfect precision. My mother knew the dangers before any of us did. I was sweaty and unstable as dynamite. She knew it, and in her strange way she tried to protect me by keeping me close, even when she would have preferred otherwise. She understood more than I imagined.

Not that I cared. I had a plan of my own, a plan as intricate and carefully laid as my pike traps on the river. I once thought Paul might have guessed, but if he did, he never spoke a word. Small beginnings, leading to lies, deceit and worse.

It began with a fruit stall, one Saturday market day. July fifth, it was, two days after my ninth birthday.

It began with an orange.

6

Until then I had always been judged too young to go into town on market days. My mother would arrive in Angers for nine and set up her little stall by the church. Quite often Cassis or Reinette would accompany her. I stayed behind at the farm, supposedly to do chores, though I usually spent the time by the river, fishing, or in the woods with Paul.

But that year was different. I was old enough now to make myself useful, she told me in her brusque way. Couldn't stay a little girl for ever. She looked at me once, searchingly. Her eyes were the colour of old nettles. Besides – casually, without giving the impression of a favour conferred – I might want to go into Angers later that summer, maybe to the cinema, with my brother and sister . . .

I guessed then that Reinette must have been at work. No-one else could have persuaded her. But Reinette knew how to cajole her. Hard she might be, but I thought there was a softer look in her eyes when she spoke to Reinette, as if, beneath her gruff exterior, something was moved. I mumbled something graceless in reply.

'Besides,' continued my mother. 'Maybe you need a little responsibility. Keep you from running wild. Teach you something about what matters in life.'

I nodded, trying for some of Reinette's docility.

I don't think my mother was fooled. She raised a satirical eyebrow. 'You can help me on the stall,' she said.

And so, for the first time, I accompanied her into town. We rode in the trap together, with our goods packed into boxes beside us and covered with tarpaulin. We had cakes and biscuits in one box, cheeses and eggs in another, fruit in the rest. It was early in the season, and though the strawberries had been good, there was little else ready. We supplemented our income by selling jam, sugared with last year's autumn beets, before the season really began.

Angers was busy on market day. Carts crammed axle to axle in the main street, bicycles pulling wicker baskets, a small open-topped wagon laden with churns of milk, a woman carrying a tray of loaves on her head, stalls piled high with greenhouse tomatoes, aubergines, courgettes, onions, potatoes. Here a stall sold wool or pottery; there wine, milk, preserves, cutlery, fruit, second-hand books, bread, fish, flowers. We settled early. There was a fountain beside the church where the horses could drink, and it was shady. My job was to wrap the food and hand it to the customers while my mother took the money. Her memory and speed of calculation were phenomenal. She could add a list of prices in her head without ever having to write them down, and she never hesitated over change. Notes in one side, coins in the other, she kept the money in the pockets of her overall, then the surplus went into an old biscuit tin she kept under the tarpaulin. I remember it still: pink, with a pattern of roses around the rim. I remember the coins and notes as they slid against the metal; my mother didn't believe in banks. She kept our savings in a box under the cellar floor, along with the more valuable of her bottles.

That first market day we sold all the eggs and all the cheeses within an hour of arrival. People were aware of the soldiers standing at the intersection, guns crooked casually into the elbow, faces bored and indifferent. My mother caught me staring at the grey uniforms and snapped me sharply to attention.

'Stop that gawping, girl.'

Even when they came through the crowd we had to ignore them, though I could feel my mother's restraining hand on my arm. A tremor went through her as he stopped in front of our stall, but her face remained impassive. A stocky man with a round, red face, a man who might have been a butcher or a wine merchant in another life. His blue eyes shone gleefully.

'*Ach, was für schöne Erdbeeren.*' His voice was jovial, slightly beery, the voice of a lazy man on holiday. He took a strawberry between plump fingers and popped it into his mouth. '*Schmeckt gut, ja?*' He laughed, not unkindly. His cheeks bulged. '*Wu-n-der-schön!*' He pantomimed rapture, rolling his eyes comically at me. In spite of myself I smiled.

My mother gave my arm a warning squeeze. I could feel nervous heat burning from her fingers. I looked at the German once more, trying to understand the source of her tension. He looked no more intimidating than the men who came to the village sometimes; less so, in fact, with his peaked cap and his single pistol in its holster at his side. I smiled again, more in defiance of my mother than for any other reason.

'*Gut, ja,*' I repeated and nodded. The German laughed again, took another strawberry and made his way back through the crowd, his black uniform oddly funereal amongst the bright patchwork of the market.

Later my mother tried to explain. All uniforms were dangerous, she told me, but the black ones above all. The black ones weren't just the army; they were the army's police. Even the other Germans were afraid of them. They could do anything. It didn't matter that I was only nine years old. Put a foot wrong and I could be shot. *Shot*, did I understand? Her face was stony, but her voice trembled and she kept putting one hand to her temple in a strange, helpless gesture, as if one of her headaches were on the way. I barely listened to her warning. It was my first face-to-face encounter with the enemy. Thinking it over later from the top of the Lookout Post, the man I had seen seemed oddly innocuous, rather disappointing. I had expected something more impressive.

The market finished at twelve. We had sold out before that, but we stayed to do a little shopping of our own and to collect the spoiled goods we were sometimes given by the other stallholders: overripe fruit, scraps of meat, damaged vegetables which would not last another day. My mother sent me to the grocer's stall while she bought a piece of discarded parachute silk from under the counter of Madame Petit's sewing shop, tucking it carefully into her apron pocket. Fabrics of any kind were hard to come by, and we all wore hand-me-downs. My own dress was made from the pieces of two others, with a grey bodice and a blue linen skirt. The parachute, Mother told me, had been found in a field just outside Courlé, and would make Reinette a new blouse.

'Cost me the earth,' grumbled Mother, half-sullen, half-excited. 'Trust her kind to get along, even through the war. Always land on their feet.'

I asked what she meant.

'Jews,' said my mother. 'They've got a knack for making money. Charges the earth for that piece of silk, and never paid a penny for it herself.' Her tone was unresentful, almost admiring. When I asked her what Jews did, she shrugged dismissively. I guessed she didn't really know.

'Same as we do, I imagine,' she said. 'They get by.' She stroked the parcel of silk in her apron pocket. 'All the same,' she said softly, 'it's not right. It's taking advantage.'

I shrugged inwardly. So much excitement for a piece of old silk. But what Reinette wanted, she had to have. Scraps of velvet ribbon, queued and bartered for; the best of Mother's old clothes; white ankle-socks to wear to school every day and, long after the rest of us had been reduced to wooden-soled clogs, Reinette was wearing patent black shoes with buckles.

I didn't mind. I was used to Mother's odd inconsistencies.

Meanwhile, I went around the other stalls with my empty basket. People saw me, and knowing our family's history, gave me what they could not sell; a couple of melons, some aubergines, endives, spinach, a head of broccoli, a handful of bruised apricots. I bought bread from the baker's stall, and he threw in a couple of croissants, ruffling my hair with his big floury hand. I swapped fishing stories with the fishmonger, and he gave me some good scraps, wrapped in newspaper. I lingered beside a fruit-and-vegetable stall as the owner bent to move a box of red onions, trying not to betray myself with my eyes.

That was when I saw it, on the ground just beside the stall, next to a box of chicory. Oranges were scarce then, wrapped singly in purple tissue paper and laid on a tray out of the sun. I'd hardly hoped to see any on my first visit to Angers, but there they were, smooth and secret in their paper shells, five oranges lined up carefully for repacking. Suddenly I wanted one, *needed* one with such urgency that I barely even paused to think. There would be no better opportunity; Mother was out of the way.

The closest orange had rolled to the edge of the tray, almost touching my foot. The grocer still had his back to me. His assistant, a boy of Cassis' age or thereabouts, was busy packing boxes into the back of his van. Vehicles other than buses were rare. The grocer was a wealthy man, then, I thought. That made what I was planning easier to justify.

Pretending to look at some sacks of potatoes, I shuffled off my wooden clog. Then I reached out my bare foot stealthily, and with toes grown clever from years of climbing, flicked the orange from out of the tray. It rolled, as I knew it would, a little distance away, half-hidden by the green cloth which covered a nearby trestle.

Immediately I put the shopping basket on top of it,

then bent as if to remove a stone from my clog. Between my legs I observed the grocer as he picked up the remaining cases of produce and hoisted them into the van. He did not notice me as I manoeuvred the stolen orange into my basket.

So easy. It had been so easy. My heart was beating hard, my face flaring so wildly that I was sure someone would notice. The orange in my basket felt like a live grenade. I stood up, very casually, and turned towards my mother's pitch.

Then I froze. From across the square, one of the Germans was watching me. He was standing by the fountain, slouching a little, a cigarette cupped into his palm. The market-goers avoided going too close to him, and he stood in his little circle of stillness, his eyes fixed upon me. He must have seen my theft. He could hardly have missed it.

For a moment I stared at him, unable to move. My face was rigid. Too late I remembered Cassis' stories about the cruelty of the Germans. He was watching me still; I wondered what the Germans did with thieves. Then he winked at me.

I stared at him for a second, then turned abruptly away, my face burning, the orange almost forgotten at the bottom of my basket. I didn't dare look at him again, even though my mother's pitch was quite close to where he was standing. I was shaking so badly that I was sure my mother would notice, but she was too preoccupied with other things. Behind us I sensed the German's eyes on me, felt the pressure of that sly, humorous wink, like a nail in my forehead. For what seemed like for ever, I waited for a blow that never came.

We left then, after dismantling the stall and putting the canvas and the trestle back onto the trap. I took the bag from the mare's nose and guided her gently between the shafts, feeling the German's eyes on the nape of my neck all the time. I had hidden the orange in my apron pocket, wrapping it in a piece of the damp newspaper from the fishmonger's so my mother would not smell it on me. I kept my hands in my pockets so that no unexpected bulge would alert her to its presence, and I rode silently during the journey home.

7

I told no-one but Paul about the orange, and that was because he came unexpectedly to the Lookout Post and found me gloating. He had never seen an orange before. At first he thought it was a ball. He held the fruit between his cupped hands, almost reverently, as if it might spread magical wings and fly away.

We sliced the fruit in two, holding the halves over a couple of broad leaves so that none of the juice would be lost. It was a good one, thin-skinned and tart beneath its sweetness. I remember how we sucked every drop of the juice, how we rasped the flesh clear of the skin with our teeth, then sucked at what remained until our mouths were bitter and cottony. Paul made as if to throw the discarded skin from the top of the Lookout Post, but I stopped him in time.

'Give that to me,' I told him.

'Why?'

'I need it for something.'

When he had gone, I carried out the last part of my plan. With my pocket knife I chopped the two halves of orange skin into tiny pieces. The scent of the oil, bitter and evocative, filled my nostrils as I worked. I chopped up the two leaves we had used for plates, too; their scent was faint, but they would help to keep the whole moist for a while. Then I tied the mixture into a piece of muslin – stolen from my mother's jamming room – and secured it firmly. After that, I placed the muslin bag with its fragrant contents in a tobacco tin, which I replaced in my pocket.

Everything was ready.

I would have made a good murderer. Everything was meticulously planned, the few small traces of the crime kicked over in minutes. I washed in the Loire to eliminate all traces of the scent from my mouth, face and hands, rubbing the coarse grit of the banks into my palms so they glowed pink and raw, scouring under my fingernails with a piece of sharpened stick. On the way home, through the fields, I picked bunches of wild mint and rubbed them into my armpits, hands, knees and neck, so that any lingering perfume would be overwhelmed by the hot green of the fresh foliage. In any case, Mother noticed nothing when I came into the house. She was making fish stew with the scraps from the market, and I could smell the rich aroma of rosemary and garlic and tomatoes and frying oil coming from the kitchen.

Good. I touched the tobacco tin in my pocket. Very good.

I should have preferred it to be a Thursday, of course. That was when Cassis and Reinette usually went into Angers – the day they received their pocket money. I was judged too young to have pocket money – what would I spend it on? – but I was sure I could contrive something. Besides, I told myself, there was no guarantee that my plan would work at all. I had to try it first.

I hid the tin – opened, now – beneath the living-room stove. It was cold, of course, but the pipes which connected it to the hot kitchen were warm enough for my purpose. In a few minutes the contents of the muslin bag had begun to release a sharp scent.

We sat down to dinner.

The stew was good; red onions and tomatoes cooked in garlic and herbs and a cupful of white wine, the fish scraps simmering tenderly amongst fried potatoes and whole shallots. Fresh meat was scarce in those days, but the vegetables we grew ourselves, and my mother had three dozen bottles of olive oil hidden beneath the cellar floor, along with the best of the wine. I ate hungrily.

''Boise, take your elbows off the table!'

Her voice was sharp, but I saw her fingers creeping unwillingly to her temple in the familiar gesture, and I smiled a little. It was working.

My mother's place was closest to the pipe. We ate in silence, but twice more her fingers crept, stealthily, to her head, cheek and eyes, as if checking the density of the flesh. Cassis and Reine said nothing, heads lowered almost to their plates. The air was heavy as the day's heat turned leaden, and I almost found my own head aching in sympathy.

Suddenly she snapped, 'I can smell oranges. Have any of you brought oranges into the house?' Her voice was shrill, accusing. 'Well? *Well?*'

We shook our heads dumbly.

Again, that gesture. More gently now, the fingers massaging, probing.

'I know I can smell oranges. You're *sure* you haven't brought oranges into the house?'

Cassis and Reine were furthest away from the tobacco tin, and the pot of stew was between them and it, releasing its good smell of wine, fish and oil. Besides, we were used to Mother's bad spells; it would never have occurred to them that the orange scent of which our mother spoke was anything but a figment of her imagination. I smiled again, and hid the smile beneath my hand.

''Boise, the bread, please.'

I passed it to her in its round basket, but the piece she took stayed untasted throughout the meal. Instead, she turned it reflectively around and around on the waxed red tablecloth, pressing her fingers into the soft centre, spreading crumbs about her plate. If I had done that, she would have had something sharp to say.

''Boise, go get the dessert, please.'

I left the table with barely suppressed relief. I felt almost sick with excitement and fear, pulling gleeful faces at myself in the shining copper saucepans. Dessert was a dish of fruit and a few of my mother's biscuits – broken, of course; she sold the good ones, keeping only the misshapen ones for home. I noticed that my mother examined the apricots we had brought from the market with suspicion, turning them over in her hand one after the other, even smelling them, as if one of them might somehow be an orange in disguise. Her hand stayed at her temple now, as if to protect her eyes from blinding sunlight. She took half a biscuit, crumbled it into pieces, discarded it on her plate.

'Reine, do the dishes. I think I'll go to my room and lie down. I can feel one of my headaches coming.' My mother's voice was uninflected, only that tic of hers – the small, repetitive movement of her fingers across her face and temple – betraying her discomfort. 'Reine, don't forget to close the curtains. The shutters. 'Boise, make sure the plates are put away properly. Mind you don't forget.' Even now she was anxious to maintain her own strict order. The plates, stacked in order of size and colour, each one wiped with a cloth and dried with a clean, starched tea towel. Nothing left to drain sluttishly on the board; that would have been too easy. The tea towels hung out to dry in neat rows. 'Hot water for my good plates, do you hear?' She sounded edgy now, anxious for her good plates. 'And mind you wipe them, wipe both sides. No putting my plates away still damp, do you hear me?'

I nodded. She turned, grimacing. 'Reine, make sure she does it.' Her eyes were bright, almost feverish-looking. She looked at the clock with a peculiar ticking movement of the head. 'And lock the doors. The shutters, too.' At last she seemed almost ready to go. Turning, pausing, still reluctant to leave us to our own devices, our secret freedoms. Speaking to me in that sharp, stilted way that hid anxiety.

'You just mind those plates, 'Boise, that's all.'

Then she was gone. I heard her pouring water in the bathroom sink. I closed the blackout curtains in the living room, bending to retrieve the tobacco tin as I did so, then, stepping out into the corridor, I said loudly enough for her to hear me, 'I'll do the bedrooms.'

My mother's room first. I secured the shutter, drew the curtain and fastened it in place, then looked around quickly. Water was still splashing in the bathroom, and I could hear the sound of my mother brushing her teeth. Moving quickly and silently, I removed her pillow from its striped cover, then, with the tip of my pocket knife, made a tiny slit in the seam and poked the muslin bag inside. I pushed it in as far as I could with the hilt of my knife, so that no bulge could betray its presence. Then I replaced the cover, my heart hammering wildly, smoothing the quilt carefully to prevent creases. Mother always noticed things like that.

I was only just in time. I met her in the passageway, but although she gave me a suspicious look she said nothing. She looked vague and distracted, her eyes creased small, her grey-brown hair unbound. I could smell soap on her, and in the gloom of the passageway she looked like Lady Macbeth – a tale I had culled recently from another of Cassis' books – her hands rubbing against each other, lifting to her face, caressing, cradling it, rubbing again, as if blood, and not the juice of oranges, were the stain she could not wash away.

For a moment I hesitated. She looked so old, so tired. My own head had begun to throb sharply and I wondered what she would do if I went up to her and pressed it against her shoulder. My eyes stung briefly. Why was I doing this, anyway? Then I thought of Old Mother waiting in the murk, of her mad and baleful gaze, of the prize in her belly.

'Well?' My mother's voice was harsh and stony. 'What are you gawping at, idiot?'

'Nothing.' My eyes were dry again. Even my headache was fading as suddenly as it had appeared. 'Nothing at all.'

I heard the door snick shut behind her and returned to the living room, where my brother and sister were waiting for me. Inside, I was grinning.

8

'You're crazy.' That was Reinette again, her usual help-less cry when all other arguments had been exhausted. Not that it took long to exhaust her; lipsticks and filmstars apart, her capacity for argument was always limited.

'It's as good a time as any,' I told her straightly. 'She'll sleep late in the morning. As long as we get the chores done, we'll be able to go wherever we like afterwards.' I looked at her, hard. There was still that business of the lipstick between us, my eyes reminded her. Two weeks earlier. I hadn't forgotten. Cassis looked at us with curiosity; I was sure she hadn't told him.

'She'll be furious if she finds out,' he said slowly.

I shrugged. 'Why should she find out? We'll say we went into the woods looking for mushrooms. Chances are she might not even be out of bed by the time we get back.'

Cassis paused to consider the idea. Reinette shot him a look which was pleading and anxious at the same time.

'Go on, Cassis,' she said. Then, in a lower voice, 'She knows. She found out about . . .' Her voice trailed off. 'I had to tell her some of it,' she finished miserably.

'Oh.' He looked at me for a moment, and I felt something pass between us, something *change*; his look was almost admiration. He shrugged – *who cares anyway?* – but his eyes remained watchful, cautious.

'It wasn't my fault,' said Reinette.

'No. She's smart, aren't you?' said Cassis lightly. 'She would have found out sooner or later.' This was high praise, and a few months earlier it might have made me weak with pride, but now I just stared at him levelly. 'Besides,' said Cassis in the same light tone. 'If she's in on it, she won't be able to run blabbing to Mother.' I was still only nine, old for my age, but still childish enough to be stung by the casual contempt of his words.

'I don't *blab*!'

He shrugged. 'Fine with me if you come, as long as you pay your own way,' he continued levelly. 'Don't see why either of us should pay for you. I'll take you on my bike. That's all. You work the rest out for yourself. All right?'

It was a test. I could see the challenge in his eyes. His smile was mocking, the not-quite-kind smile of the older brother who sometimes shared his last square of chocolate with me, and sometimes Chinese-burned my arm so hard that the blood gathered in dark flecks under my skin.

'But she doesn't get any pocket money,' said Reinette plaintively. 'What's the point of taking—'

Cassis shrugged. It was a typically final gesture, a man's gesture – *I have spoken*. He waited for my reaction, arms crossed, that little smile on his lips.

'That's fine,' I said, trying to sound calm. 'That's fine by me.'

'All right, then,' he decided. 'We'll go tomorrow.'

9

This was where the day's chores began. Buckets of water were brought from the well into the kitchen for cooking and washing. We had no hot water – no running water, in fact, except for the handpump by the well, a few yards from the kitchen door. Electricity was slow to come to Les Laveuses, and when bottled gas became too scarce we cooked on a wood-burning stove in the kitchen. The oven was outside, a large, old-fashioned charcoal oven the shape of a sugar loaf, and beside it was the well. When we needed water, that was where we got it from, one of us pumping while the other held the bucket. There was a wooden lid on the well, closed and padlocked since long before my birth to prevent accidents. When Mother was not watching we washed under the pump, dousing ourselves with cold water. When she was around we had to use basins of water, warmed in copper pans on the stove, and the gritty coal-tar soap that abraded our skin like pumice, leaving a scum of grey froth on the surface of the water.

That Sunday we knew Mother would not make an appearance until later. We had all heard her during the night, moaning to herself, turning and rolling on the old bed she had shared with my father, sometimes standing up and walking to and fro in the room, opening the windows for air, the shutters slamming back against the sides of the house and making the floor shake. I lay awake listening for a long time as she moved, paced, sighed and argued with herself in her percussive whisper. At about midnight I fell asleep, but awoke, an hour or so later, to hear her still awake.

It sounds callous now, but all I felt was triumph. There was no guilt at what I had done, no pity for her suffering. I didn't understand it then, I had no idea of what a torment insomnia can be. That the little bag of orange peel inside her pillow could have provoked such a reaction seemed almost impossible. The more she tossed and sighed on her pillow, the stronger the scent must have become, warmed by the feverish nape of her neck. The stronger the scent, the greater her anxiety. The headache *must* come soon, she thought to herself. Somehow the anticipation of pain can be even more troubling, more of a misery than the pain itself. The anxiety, which was a permanent crease in her forehead, nibbled at her mind like a rat in a box, killing sleep. Her nose told her there were oranges, but her mind said it was impossible – *how could there be oranges, for God's sake?* – and yet the scent of orange, bitter and yellow as old age, sweated from every dark mote of that room.

She rose at three and lit a lamp to write in her album. I can't know for sure that it was then – she never wrote dates – and yet I know.

'Worse now than it's ever been,' she writes. The script is tiny, a column of ants scrawled across the page in violet ink. 'I lie in bed and wonder whether I'll ever sleep again. Whatever happens can't be worse than this. Even going insane might be a relief.' And a little later, under a recipe for vanilla-potato pie, she writes, 'Like the clock, I am divided. At three in the morning, anything is possible.'

After that she got up to take her morphine pills. She kept them in the bathroom cabinet, next to my dead father's shaving things. I heard the door open and the tired squeak of her sweating feet against the polished boards. The bottle rattled, and I heard the clink of a cup as she poured water from the jug. I suppose that six hours' insomnia might well have finally provoked one of her headaches. In any case, she was out like a light when, some time later, I got up.

Reinette and Cassis were still asleep, and the light which bled from beneath the thick blackout curtain was greenish and pale. It might have been five o'clock; there was no timepiece in our bedroom. I sat up in bed, felt for my clothes in the dark and dressed quickly. I knew every corner of the little room. I could hear Cassis and Reine breathing – he with shallower, almost wheezing breaths – and very quietly I stepped past their beds. There was a great deal to do before I woke them.

First I listened at the door of my mother's room. Silence. I knew she had taken her pills, and the chance was that she would be sleeping heavily, but I could not run the risk of being caught. Very gently I turned the doorknob. A board beneath my bare foot popped with a sound like a firecracker. I stopped mid-gesture, listening for her breathing, for any change in its rhythms. There was none. I pushed the door. One shutter had been left slightly open and the room was light. My mother was lying across the bed. She had kicked off the covers during the night, and one pillow had fallen to the floor. The other was half covered by her outflung arm, and her head was hanging uncomfortably at an angle, her hair brushing the floor-boards. I noticed, with no surprise, that the pillow in which I had concealed the muslin bag was the one upon which she was resting. I knelt beside her. Her breathing was thick and slow. Beneath her bruise-coloured eyelids the pupils moved erratically. Slowly I worked my fingers into the pillowcase beneath her.

It was easy. My fingers worked at the knot in the centre of the pillow, coaxing it back towards the slit in the lining. I touched the bag, drew it closer with my fingernails, finally pulling it from its hiding place and safe into the palm of my hand. My mother never stirred. Only her eyes ticked and skittered under the

95

darkened flesh, as if constantly following something bright and elusive. Her mouth was half open, and a thread of drool had crawled down her cheek to the mattress. On an impulse, I put the sachet beneath her nostrils, crushing it to release the scent, and she whimpered in her sleep, turning her head away from the scent and frowning. I put the orange sachet into my pocket again.

Then I began in earnest, with a final glance behind me at my mother, as if she might be a dangerous animal feigning sleep. Then I moved to the mantelpiece. There was a clock there, a heavy piece with a round dial under a gilt-and-glass dome. It looked strange above the bare little black grate, too ornate for my mother's room, but she had inherited it from her mother and it was one of her most prized possessions. I lifted the glass dome and carefully turned the clock's hands back. Five hours. Six. Then I replaced the dome.

I rearranged the ornaments on the mantelpiece – a framed photograph of my father, another of a woman I knew to be my grandmother, a pottery vase of dried flowers, a dish containing three hairpins and a single sugared almond from Cassis' christening. I turned the photographs against the wall, placed the vase on the floor, took the hairpins from the dish and put them in the pocket of my mother's discarded apron. Then I picked up her clothes and draped them artistically around the room. One clog balancing on the lampshade, the other on the window ledge. Her dress hanging neatly on a hanger behind the door, but her apron spread out on the boards like a picnic tablecloth. Finally, I opened her wardrobe and positioned the door so the mirror inside it would reflect the bed from where she was lying. The first thing she would see as she awoke was herself.

I did none of this from any real sense of mischief. My intention was not to hurt but to disorientate, to fool her into thinking that her imagined attack had been real and that she herself had, unknowingly, moved the objects, arranged the clothes, changed the clock. I knew from my father that she sometimes did things and lost track of doing them, that in the extremity of her pain and confusion her vision was troubled and her thoughts more so. The clock on the kitchen wall might suddenly appear bisected, one half clearly visible and the other suddenly not there, nothing but the bare wall behind it; or a wineglass might seem to change place on its own, to shift slyly from one side of the plate to the other. Or a face, a human face – mine, my father's, Raphaël's at the café – would suddenly have half its features sheared away, as if by some terrible surgery, or half of the page of a cookery book removed as she read, the remaining letters dancing incomprehensibly before her.

Of course, I didn't know all that then. I learned most of this from the album, from her scribbled notes, some frantic, almost despairing – 'At three in the morning, anything seems possible' – others almost clinical in their detachment, noting symptoms with cool scientific curiosity.

'Like the clock, I am divided.'

10

Reine and Cassis were still asleep when I left, and I guessed I had about half an hour to take care of my business before they awoke. I checked the sky, which was clear and greenish, with a faint yellow stripe on the horizon. Dawn was maybe ten minutes away. I would have to hurry.

I took a bucket from the kitchen, pulled on my clogs, which were waiting on the doormat, and ran as fast as I could towards the river. I took the shortcut through the Hourias' back field, where summer sunflowers raised hairy, still-green heads at the pale sky. I kept low, invisible beneath the spread of leaves, my bucket clanging against my leg at every step. It took me less than five minutes to arrive at the Standing Stones.

At five in the morning the Loire is still and sumptuous with mist. The water is beautiful at that time of the day, cool and magically pale, the sandbanks rising like lost continents. The water smells of night, and here and there a spray of new sunlight makes mica shadows on the surface. I took off my shoes and my dress and surveyed the water critically. It looked deceptively still.

The last of the Standing Stones, the Treasure Stone, was maybe thirty feet from the bank, and the water at its base looked oddly silky at the surface, a sign that a strong current was at work. I could drown here, I told myself suddenly, and no-one would even know where to look for me.

But I had no choice. Cassis had issued a challenge. I had to pay my own way. How could I do that, with no pocket money of my own, without using the purse hidden in the Treasure Chest? Of course, there was a chance he might have removed it. If he had, I would risk stealing from my mother's purse. But that I was reluctant to do. Not because stealing was especially wrong, but because of my mother's unusual memory for figures. She knew what she had to the last *centime*, and she would know at once what I had done.

No. It had to be the Treasure Chest.

Since Cassis and Reinette had finished school there had been few expeditions to the river. They had treasure of their own – *adult* treasure – to gloat over. The few coins in the purse amounted to a couple of francs, no more. I was counting on Cassis' laziness, his conviction that no-one but he would be able to reach the box tied to the pillar. I was sure the money was still there.

Carefully, I scrambled down the bank and into the water. It was cold and river mud oozed between my toes. I waded out until the water was waist deep. I could feel the current now, like an impatient dog at the leash. God, it was already so strong! I put out a hand against the first pillar, pushing away from it into the current, and took another step. I knew there was a drop just ahead, a point at which the still-shallow verge of the Loire sheared away into nothingness. Cassis, when he was making the trip, always pretended to drown at this point, turning belly-up into the opaque water, struggling and screaming, with a mouthful of brown Loire spurting from between his lips. He always fooled Reine, however many times he did this, making her squeal in horror as he sank beneath the surface.

I had no time for such an exhibition. I felt for the drop with my toes. There. Pushing against the riverbed, I propelled myself as far as I could with my first kick, keeping the Standing Stones downriver to my right. The water was warmer on the surface, and the drag of current not as strong. I swam steadily, in a smooth arc, from the first Standing Stone to the second. The stones were maybe twelve feet apart at their widest stretch, spread unevenly from the bank. I could make five feet with a good strong kick against each pillar, aiming slightly upstream so the current would bring me back to the next pillar in time to begin again. Like a small boat tacking against a strong wind, I limped towards the Treasure Stone, feeling the current grow stronger each time. I was gasping with cold. Then I was at the fourth pillar, making my final lunge towards my goal. As the current dragged me towards the Treasure Stone I overshot the pillar, and there was a moment of sudden, sparkling terror as I began to move downstream into the main drag of the river, my arms and legs pinwheeling against the water. Panting, almost crying with panic, I managed to kick myself within range of the stone, and grabbed the chain that secured the Treasure Chest to the pillar. It felt weedy and unpleasant in my hand, slimed with the brown ooze of the river, but I used it to manoeuvre myself around the pillar.

I clung there for a moment, letting my pounding heart quiet. Then, with my back wedged safely against the pillar, I hauled the Treasure Chest up and out of its muddy cradle. It was a difficult job. The box itself was not especially heavy, but weighted with chain and tarpaulin as it was, it seemed a dead weight. Trembling with cold now, my teeth clattering, I struggled with the chain and finally felt something give. Kicking my legs frantically to keep my position against the pillar, I hauled at the box. I knew another moment of near panic as the mud-slimed tarpaulin caught at my feet, then my fingers were working at the rope which held the box. For an instant I was sure my numbed fingers would not be able to open the tin, then the catch gave way and water rushed into the Treasure Chest. I swore. Still, there was the purse, an old brown leather thing

Mother had discarded because of a faulty catch. I grabbed it and jammed it between my teeth for safety, then, with a final effort, I slammed the box closed and let it sink, weighted by its chain, to the bottom again. The tarpaulin was lost, of course, the remaining treasure waterlogged, but that couldn't be helped. Cassis would have to find somewhere drier to hide his cigarettes. I had the money, and that was all that mattered.

I swam back to the bank, missing the last two pillars and drifting 200 yards down towards the Angers road before I managed to steer myself out of the current, which was now more like a dog than ever, a mad, brown dog with its leash twined crazily around my frozen legs. The whole episode, I guessed, had taken maybe ten minutes.

I forced myself to rest awhile, feeling the slight warmth of the sun's first rays on my face, drying the mud of the Loire on my skin. I was trembling with cold and exhilaration. I counted the money in the purse; there was certainly enough for a cinema ticket and a glass of squash. Good. Then I walked upstream to where I had left my clothes. I dressed in my old skirt and a red sleeveless man's shirt, cut down to make an overall, and clogs. I did a perfunctory check on my fishing traps, tipping out the small fry or leaving it in place as bait. In a cray-pot by the Lookout Post there was the unexpected bonus of a small pike – not Old Mother, of course – and this I slid out into the bucket I had brought from the house. Other catches – a mess of eels from the muddy flats beside the big sandbank, a sizeable bleak from one of my catch-all nets – I piled into the bucket. They would be my alibi if Cassis and Reine were awake when I returned. Then I made my way home through the fields as unobtrusively as I had come.

I did well to bring the fish. Cassis was washing under the pump when I got back, and Reinette had warmed a basin of water and was dabbling delicately at her face with a soapy washrag. They looked at me curiously for a moment, then Cassis' face relaxed into an expression of cheery contempt.

'You never give up, do you?' he said, jerking his dripping head at the fish bucket. 'What you got in there, anyway?'

I shrugged. 'Couple of things,' I said carelessly. The purse was in the pocket of my overall, and I smiled inwardly at its comforting weight. 'Pike. Just a small one,' I said.

Cassis laughed. 'You might catch the small ones, but you'll never catch Old Mother,' he said. 'Even if you did, what'd you do with it? A pike that old wouldn't be any good to eat. Bitter as wormwood and full of bones.'

'I'll catch her,' I said stubbornly.

'Oh?' His tone was careless, disbelieving. 'And what then? You'll make a wish, will you? Wish for a million francs and an apartment on the Left Bank?'

I shook my head mutely.

'I'd wish to be a movie star,' said Reine, towelling her face. 'To see Hollywood, and the lights, and Sunset Boulevard, and to drive in a limousine and have dozens and dozens of dresses.'

Cassis gave her a brief look of scorn, which cheered me immensely. Then he turned to me. 'Well, what about it, 'Boise?' His grin was brash and irresistible. 'What's it going to be? Furs? Cars? A villa in Juan-les-Pins?'

I shook my head again. 'I'll know when I've caught it,' I said flatly. 'And I'll get it, too. See if I don't.'

Cassis studied me for a moment, the grin sliding from his face. Then he made a little noise of disgust and turned back to his ablutions. 'You're something, 'Boise,' he said. 'Really something, you know?'

Then we raced out to finish the day's chores before Mother woke up.

11

There is always plenty to do on a farm. Water to bring in from the pump, leaving it in metal buckets on the cellar tiles so the sun doesn't warm it; goats to milk, the pail to be covered in a muslin cloth and left in the dairy; the goats then to be taken to the pasture so they don't eat all the vegetables in the garden; hens and ducks to feed; the day's crop of ripe strawberries to pick; the baking oven to stoke, even though I doubted Mother would be doing much baking that day; the horse, Bécassine, to be let out into the pasture and fresh water brought to the troughs. Working at maximum speed it took us the best part of two hours to finish, and by the time we did the sun's heat was gaining, the night damp already steaming off the baked-earth paths and the dew drying on the grass. It was time to go.

Neither Reinette nor Cassis had mentioned the money question. There was no need. I paid my way, Cassis had told me, assuming that this would be impossible. Reine looked at me oddly as we picked the last of the strawberries, wondering perhaps at my self-assurance, and when she caught Cassis' eye she giggled. I noticed that she had dressed with special care that morning, in her pleated school skirt, red short-sleeved jumper, ankle socks and shoes, and her hair was rolled into a fat sausage at the back of her head, secured with hairpins. She smelt unfamiliar, too, a kind of sweetish powdery smell, like marshmallow and violets, and she was wearing the red lipstick. I wondered if she was meeting someone. A boy, perhaps. Someone she knew from school. She certainly seemed more nervous than usual, picking the fruit with the delicate haste of a rabbit feeding amongst weasels. As I moved between the rows of strawberry plants I heard her whisper something to Cassis, then I heard her high, nervous giggle.

I shrugged inwardly. I supposed they were planning to go off somewhere without me. I had persuaded Reine to take me, and they would not go back on that promise. But as far as they knew, I had no money. That meant they could go to the pictures without me, perhaps leaving me by the fountain in the market square to wait for them, or sending me on an imaginary errand while they went to meet their friends. Sourly, I bit down on the thought. That was *supposed* to be how it went. They were so sure of themselves that they'd overlooked the one obvious solution to my problem. Reine would never have swum the Loire to the Treasure Stone. Cassis still saw me as the little sister, too much in awe of the adored older brother to hazard the slightest thing without his permission. Occasionally he looked at me and grinned his satisfaction, his eyes gleaming with mockery.

We left for Angers at eight o'clock, I riding on the back wheel of Cassis' huge, ungainly bike, my feet wedged perilously beneath the handlebars. Reine's bicycle was smaller and more elegant, with high handlebars and a leather saddle. There was a bicycle basket across the handlebars, in which she carried a flask of chicory coffee and three identical packets of sandwiches. She had tied a white scarf around her head to protect her coiffure, and the tails whipped at her nape as she rode. We stopped three or four times on our way, to drink from the flask in Reine's bicycle basket, to check a soft tyre, to eat a piece of bread and cheese in lieu of breakfast. At last we came to the suburbs of Angers, passing the *collège* – closed now for the holidays and guarded by a pair of German soldiers at the gate – and down streets of stucco houses towards the town centre.

The cinema, the Palais-Doré, was in the main square, close to where the market was held. Several rows of small shops lined the square, most of which were opening for the morning, and a man was washing down the pavement with a bucket of water and a broom. We pushed the bikes then, steering them into an alley between a barber's and a blindly shuttered butcher's shop. The alley was barely wide enough to walk through, and the ground was piled with rubble and debris; it seemed safe to assume our bikes would be left alone. A woman at the *terrasse* of a café smiled at us and called a greeting; a few Sunday customers were already there, drinking bowls of chicory and eating croissants or hard-boiled eggs. A delivery boy went by on a bicycle, ringing his bell importantly. By the church, a newspaper kiosk sold single-sheet bulletins. Cassis looked around, then made his way to the kiosk. I saw him hand something to the newspaper man, then the man handed Cassis a bundle, which quickly vanished into Cassis' trouser waistband.

'What was that?' I asked curiously.

Cassis shrugged. I could see that he was pleased with himself, too pleased to withhold the information just to annoy me. He lowered his voice conspiratorially and allowed me a glimpse of rolled-up papers which he immediately covered up again.

'Comic books. Serial story.' He winked at Reine self-importantly. 'American film magazine.'

Reine uttered a squeak of excitement and made as if to grab his arm. 'Let me. Let me see!'

Cassis shook his head irritably. 'Shh! For God's sake, Reine!' He lowered his tone again. 'He owed me a favour. Black market,' he mouthed. 'Kept them under the counter for me.'

Reinette looked at him in awe. I was less impressed. Perhaps because I was less aware of the scarcity of such items; perhaps because the seeds of rebellion already growing in me pushed me to scorn anything of which my brother seemed overly proud. I gave a shrug to show my indifference. Still, I wondered what kind of favour the newspaper man might have owed Cassis, and finally concluded that he must have been bragging. I said as much.

'If I had contacts with the black market,' I said with a passable show of scepticism, 'I'd make sure I got better stuff than a few old papers.'

Cassis looked stung. 'I can get anything I want,' he said quickly. 'Comics, smokes, books, real coffee, *chocolate*—' He broke off with a scornful laugh. 'You can't even get the money for a rotten cinema ticket,' he said.

'No?' Smiling, I took the purse from my apron pocket. I jingled it a little, so that he could hear the coins inside. His eyes widened as he recognized the purse.

'You little thief!' he breathed at last. 'You rotten, bitching little thief!'

I looked at him, but said nothing.

'How did you get that?'

'Swum out and got it,' I answered defiantly. 'Anyway, it wasn't stealing. The treasure belonged to all of us.'

But Cassis was hardly listening. 'You bitching, thieving,' he said again. Clearly he was disturbed that anyone other than he should obtain anything by guile.

'I don't see that it's any different from you and your black market,' I said calmly. 'It's all the same game, isn't it?' I let this sink in before I continued. 'And you're just upset because I'm better at it than you.'

Cassis glared at me. 'It isn't anything like the same thing,' he said at last.

I kept my expression disbelieving. It was always so easy to make Cassis give himself away. Just like his son, all those years later. Neither of them understood anything about guile. Cassis was red-faced, almost shouting now, his conspiratorial tone forgotten. 'I could get you anything you liked. Proper fishing tackle for your stupid pike,' he hissed savagely. 'Chewing gum, shoes, silk stockings, silk *underwear*, if you wanted.' I laughed aloud at that. Brought up as we had been, the idea of silk underwear was ludicrous. Enraged, Cassis grabbed me by the shoulders and shook me.

'*You stop that!*' His voice cracked with fury. 'I got *friends!* I know people! I could get–you–anything–you–*wanted*!'

You see how easy it was to take him off-balance. Cassis was spoilt in his way, too used to being the great older brother, the man of the house, the first to go to school, the tallest, the strongest, the wisest. His occasional bouts of wildness – his escapades into the woods, his daredevilry on the Loire, his small thefts from market stalls and shops in Angers – were uncontrolled, almost hysterical. He took no enjoyment from them. It was as if he needed to prove something to both of us, or to himself.

I could tell I perplexed him. His thumbs were digging so deeply into my arms that they would make great ripe-blackberry marks on my skin the next day, but I did not show any sign of it. Instead, I just looked at him steadily and tried to stare him out.

'We've got friends, Reine and me,' he said in a lower voice, almost reasonable now, his thumbs still gouging into my arms. 'Powerful friends. Where do you think she got that stupid lipstick? Or the perfume? Or that stuff she puts on her face at night? Where d'you think we got all that from? And how d'you think we *earned* it?'

He let go of my arms then, with an expression of mingled pride and consternation, and I realized that he was sick with fear.

12

I don't remember very much about the film. *Circonstances Atténuantes*, with Arletty and Michel Simon, an old film which Cassis and Reine had already seen. Reine at least was untroubled by the fact; she stared at the screen the whole time, rapt. I found the story unlikely, too removed from my realities. Besides, my mind was on other things. Twice the film in the projector broke; the second time the house lights went on and the audience roared disapproval. A harassed-looking man in a dinner jacket shouted for silence. A group of Germans in a corner, feet resting on the seats in front of them, began slow-clapping. Suddenly Reine, who had come out of her trance to complain irritably about the interruption, gave a squeak of excitement.

'Cassis!' She leaned over me and I could smell a sweetish chemical scent in her hair. 'Cassis, *he's here*!'

'*Shh!*' hissed Cassis furiously. 'Don't look back.' Reine and Cassis sat facing the front of the auditorium for a moment, expressionless as dummies. Then he spoke, from the corner of his mouth, like someone whispering in church.

'Who?'

Reinette flicked a glance at the Germans from the corner of her eye.

'Back there,' she replied in the same fashion. 'With some others I don't know.' Around us the crowd stamped and yelled. Cassis ventured a quick look.

'I'll wait till the lights go down,' he said.

Ten minutes later the lights dimmed and the film continued. Cassis wriggled from his seat towards the back of the auditorium. I followed him. On the screen Arletty pranced and eye-fluttered in a tight, low-cut dress. The mercury reflection lit our low-bent, running figures, making Cassis' face a livid mask.

'Go back, you little idiot,' he hissed at me. 'I don't want you with me, getting in the way.'

I shook my head. 'I won't get in the way,' I told him. 'Not unless you try to stop me coming with you.'

Cassis made an impatient gesture. He knew I meant what I said. In the dark I could feel him trembling with excitement or nerves. 'Keep down,' he told me at last. 'And let me do the talking.'

We finally squatted down at the back of the auditorium, close to where the group of German soldiers made an island amongst the regular crowd. Several of the men were smoking; we could see dimps of red fire on their flickering faces.

'See him there, at the end?' whispered Cassis. 'That's Hauer. I want to talk to him. You just stay with me and don't say a word, all right?'

I did not reply. I wasn't going to promise anything.

Cassis slid into the aisle next to the soldier called Hauer. Looking around curiously I could see that no-one was paying us the slightest attention except the German standing behind us, a slight, sharp-faced young man, with his uniform cap tilted back at a rakish angle and a cigarette in one hand. Beside me I heard Cassis whispering urgently to Hauer, then the crackle of papers. The sharp-faced German grinned at me and gestured with the cigarette.

Suddenly, with a jolt, I recognized him. It was the soldier from the market, the one who had seen me take the orange. For a minute I could do nothing but stare at him, transfixed.

The German gestured again. The glow from the cinema screen lit his face, throwing dramatic shadows from his eyes and cheekbones.

I cast a nervous glance at Cassis, but my brother was too deep in conversation with Hauer to notice me. The German was still watching expectantly, a little smile on his lips, standing some distance away from where the others were seated. He held his cigarette with the tip cupped into his palm, and I could see the dark smudge of his bones beneath the glowing flesh. He was in uniform, but his jacket was undone. For some obscure reason, that reassured me.

'Come here,' said the German softly.

I could not speak. My mouth felt as if it were full of straw. I would have run, but I was not sure my legs would carry me. Instead, I put up my chin and moved towards him.

The German grinned and dragged another breath from his cigarette.

'You're the little orange girl, aren't you?' he said as I came closer.

I did not reply.

The German seemed unconcerned by my silence. 'You're quick. As quick as I was when I was a boy.' He reached into his pocket and brought out something wrapped in silver paper. 'Here. You'll like it. It's chocolate.'

I eyed him with suspicion. 'I don't want it,' I said.

The German grinned again. 'You like oranges better, do you?' he asked.

I said nothing.

'I remember an orchard by a river,' the German said softly. 'Near the village where I grew up. It had the biggest, blackest plums you ever saw. High wall all around. Farm dogs prowling. All through summer I tried to get at those plums. I tried everything. I could hardly think of anything else.'

His voice was pleasant and lightly accented, his eyes bright behind a scrawl of cigarette smoke. I observed him warily, not daring to move, unsure whether or not he was making fun of me.

110

'Besides, what's stolen tastes so much better than what you get for free, don't you think?'

Now I was sure he was mocking me, and my eyes widened indignantly.

The German seemed to see my expression and laughed, still holding out the chocolate. 'Go on, *Backfisch*, take it. Imagine you're stealing it from the Boches.'

The square was half melted and I ate it straightaway. It was real chocolate, too, not the whitish, gritty stuff we occasionally bought in Angers. The German watched me eat, amused, as I eyed him with undiminished suspicion, but with growing curiosity.

'Did you get them in the end?' I asked at last, in a voice thick with chocolate. 'The plums, I mean?'

The German nodded. 'I did, *Backfisch*. I still remember the taste.'

'And you weren't caught?'

'That, too.' The grin became rueful. 'I ate so many that I made myself sick, and so I was found out. I got such a hiding. But I got what I wanted in the end. That's what matters, isn't it?'

'That's good,' I agreed. 'I like to win.' I paused. 'Is that why you didn't tell anyone about the orange?'

The German shrugged. 'Why should I tell anyone? It was none of my business. Besides, the grocer had plenty more. He could spare one.'

I nodded. 'He's got a van,' I said, licking the square of silver paper so that none of the chocolate would be lost.

The German seemed to agree. 'Some people want to keep everything they've got to themselves,' he said. 'That isn't fair, is it?'

I shook my head. 'Like Madame Petit at the sewing shop,' I said. 'Charges the earth for a bit of parachute silk she got for free.'

'Precisely.'

It struck me then that perhaps I shouldn't have mentioned Madame Petit, and I shot him a quick glance, but the German seemed hardly to be listening. Instead he was looking at Cassis, still whispering to Hauer at the end of the row of seats. I felt a stab of annoyance that Cassis should interest him more than I did.

'That's my brother,' I said.

'Is it?' The German looked back at me again, smiling. 'You're quite a family. Are there any more of you, I wonder?'

I shook my head. 'I'm the youngest. Framboise.'

'I'm very pleased to meet you, Françoise.'

I grinned. 'Fram*boise*,' I corrected.

'Leibniz. Tomas.' He held out his hand. After a moment's hesitation I shook it.

13

So that was how I met Tomas Leibniz. For some reason Reinette was furious with me for talking to him, and sulked all the way through the rest of the film. Hauer had slipped Cassis a packet of Gauloises, and we both crept back to our seats, Cassis smoking one of his cigarettes and myself lost in speculation. Only when the film was finished was I ready to ask questions.

'Those cigarettes,' I said, 'is that what you meant when you said you could get things?'

'Of course.' Cassis was looking pleased with himself, but I still sensed anxiety beneath the surface. He held his cigarette in the palm of his hand, as if in imitation of the Germans, but on him the gesture looked awkward and self-conscious.

'Do you tell them things? Do you?'

'We sometimes . . . tell them things,' admitted Cassis, smirking.

'What kind of things?'

Cassis shrugged. 'It started with that old idiot and his radio,' he said in a low voice. 'That was only fair. He shouldn't have had it anyway, and he shouldn't have pretended to be so shocked when all we were doing was watching the Germans. Sometimes we leave notes with a delivery man, or at the café. Sometimes the newspaper man gives us stuff they've left. Sometimes *they* bring it.' He tried for nonchalance, but I could sense he was anxious, edgy.

'It's nothing important,' he continued. 'Most of the

Boches use the black market themselves anyway, to send stuff home to Germany. You know, stuff they've requisitioned. So it doesn't really matter.'

I considered this. 'But the Gestapo—'

'Oh grow up, 'Boise.' Suddenly he was angry, as he always was when I put him under pressure. 'What do you know about the Gestapo?' He looked around nervously, then lowered his voice again. 'Of *course* we don't deal with *them*. This is different. I told you, it's just business. And anyway, it's nothing to do with you.'

I faced him, feeling resentful. 'Why not? I know things too.' I wished now that I had made more of Madame Petit with the German, that I had told him she was a Jew.

Cassis shook his head scornfully. 'You wouldn't understand.'

We rode home in slightly apprehensive silence, perhaps expecting Mother to have guessed about our unsanctioned trip, but when we got home we found her in unusual spirits. She did not mention the smell of oranges, her sleepless night or the changes I had made in her room, and the meal she prepared was almost a celebration dinner, with carrot-and-chicory soup, *boudin noir* with apple and potatoes, black buckwheat pancakes and *clafoutis* for dessert, heavy and moist with last year's apples and crusted with brown sugar and cinnamon. We ate in silence, as always, but Mother seemed abstracted, quite forgetting to tell me to take my elbows off the table and failing to see my tangled hair and smudged face.

Perhaps the orange had tamed her, I thought.

She made up for it the next day, however, reverting to her usual self again with a vengeance. We avoided her as best we could, doing our chores in haste, then retreating to the Lookout Post and the river, where we played half-heartedly. Sometimes Paul came with us, but he sensed that he was no longer a part of us, that he was excluded from the circle we made. I felt sorry for him, even a little guilty, knowing what it was like to be excluded, but I could do nothing to prevent it. Paul would have to fight his own battles, as I had fought mine.

Besides, Mother disliked Paul, as she disliked the entire Hourias family. In her eyes Paul was an idler, too lazy to go to school, too stupid even to learn to read in the village with the other children. His parents were just as bad – a man who sold bloodworms by the side of the road and a woman who mended other people's clothes. But my mother was especially vicious about Paul's uncle. At first I thought this was simply village rivalry. Philippe Hourias owned the biggest farm in Les Laveuses, acres of sunflower fields, potatoes, cabbages and beets, twenty cows, pigs, goats, a tractor at a time when most local people still used hand ploughs and horses, and a proper milking machine. It was jealousy, I told myself, the resentment of the struggling widow against the wealthy widower. Still, it was odd, given that Philippe Hourias had been my father's oldest friend. They had been boys together, fishing, swimming, sharing secrets. Philippe had carved my father's name on the war memorial himself, and always laid flowers at its base on Sundays. But Mother never acknowledged him with more than a nod. Never a gregarious soul, after the orange incident she seemed more hostile than ever towards him.

In fact, it was only much later that I began to guess at the truth. When I read the album, in fact, more than forty years afterwards. That tiny, migraine-inducing script staggering across the bound pages.

'Hourias knows already,' she wrote. 'I see him looking at me sometimes. Pity and curiosity, like I was something he ran over in the road. Last night he saw me coming out of La Rép with the things I need to buy there. He didn't say anything, but I knew he'd guessed. He thinks we should marry, of course. It makes sense to him, widow and widower, marrying their land together. Yannick had no brother to take

115

over when he died, and a woman isn't expected to run a farm alone.'

If she had been a naturally sweet woman, perhaps I might have suspected something sooner. But Mirabelle Dartigen was not a sweet woman; she was rock salt and river mud, her rages as quick and furious and inevitable as summer lightning. I never sought the cause, merely avoiding the effect as best I could.

14

There were no more trips to Angers that week, and neither Cassis nor Reinette seemed inclined to speak of our meeting with the Germans. As for myself, I was reluctant to mention my conversation with Leibniz, though I was unable to forget it. It made me feel by turns apprehensive and oddly powerful.

Cassis was restless, Reinette sullen and discontented, and to add to that it drizzled for a week, so that the Loire swelled ominously and the sunflower fields were blue with rain. Seven days had passed since our last visit to Angers. Market day came and went; this time Reinette accompanied Mother to town, leaving Cassis and myself to prowl discontentedly through the dripping orchard. The green plums on the trees made me think of Leibniz, with an odd mixture of curiosity and disquiet. I wondered whether I would ever see him again.

Then, unexpectedly, I did.

It was market day, in the early morning, and it was Cassis' turn to help with the provisions. Reine was fetching the new cheeses, wrapped in vine leaves, from the coolroom and Mother was collecting eggs from the hen house. I was just back from the river with the morning catch: a couple of small perches and bleaks, which I had chopped for bait and left in a bucket by the window. It was not the Germans' usual day to call, and as a result it was I who happened to open the front door when they knocked.

There were three of them; two I did not recognize, and Leibniz, very correct now in uniform, standing with a rifle slung into the crook of his arm. His eyes widened a little in surprise when he saw me, then he smiled.

If it had been any other German standing there I might have shut the door in their faces, as Denis Gaudin did when they came to requisition his violin. I would certainly have called Mother. But on this occasion I was unsure; I fidgeted uneasily on the doorstep, wondering what to do.

Leibniz turned to the other two and spoke to them in German. I thought I understood from the gestures which accompanied his words that he intended to search our farm himself while the others moved down the lane towards Ramondin's and Hourias' places. One of the other Germans looked at me and said something. The three of them laughed, then Leibniz nodded and, still smiling, stepped past me into our kitchen.

I knew I should call Mother. When the soldiers called she was always more sullen than ever, stonily resentful of their presence and their casual appropriation of anything they required. And today of all days. Her temper was bad enough as it was; this would be the final blow.

Supplies were getting scarce, Cassis had explained when I had asked him about it. Even Germans had to eat. 'And they eat like pigs,' he had continued with indignation. 'You should see their canteen – whole loaves of bread, with jam and pâté and *rillettes* and cheese and salted anchovies and ham and sour cabbage and apple – you wouldn't believe it!'

Leibniz closed the door behind him and looked around. Away from the other soldiers his posture was relaxed, more like a civilian's. He reached in his pocket and lit a cigarette.

'What are you doing here?' I demanded at last. 'We don't have anything.'

'Orders, *Backfisch*,' said Leibniz. 'Is your father about?'

'I don't have a father,' I replied with a touch of defiance. 'Germans killed him.'

'Ah, I'm sorry.' He seemed embarrassed, and I felt a little swell of pleasure inside. 'Your mother, then?'

'Out back.' I glared at him. 'It's market day today. If you take our market stuff we won't have anything left. We just manage as it is.'

Leibniz glanced around, a little shamefacedly, I thought. I saw him take in the clean tiled floor, the patched curtains, the scarred stripped-pine table. He hesitated.

'I have to do it, *Backfisch*,' he said softly. 'I'll be punished if I don't obey orders.'

'You could say you didn't find anything. You could say there was nothing left when you came.'

'Perhaps.' His eyes lit on the bucket of scraps by the window. 'Fisherman in the family, is there? Who is it? Your brother?'

I shook my head. 'Me.'

Leibniz was surprised. 'Fishing?' he echoed. 'You don't look old enough.'

'I'm nine,' I said, stung.

'Nine?' Lights danced in his eyes, but his mouth stayed serious. 'I'm a fisherman myself, you know,' he whispered. 'What is it you fish for around here? Trout? Carp? Perch?'

I shook my head.

'What then?'

'Pike.'

Pikes are the cleverest of freshwater fish. Sly and cautious in spite of their vicious teeth, they need carefully selected bait to lure them to the surface. Even the smallest thing can make them suspicious: a fraction of a change in temperature, the hint of a sudden movement. There's no quick or easy way to do it; blind luck apart, catching pike takes time and patience.

'Well, that's different,' said Leibniz thoughtfully. 'I

don't think I could let down a fellow fisherman in trouble.' He grinned at me. 'Pike, eh?'

I nodded.

'What d'you use, bloodworms or boluses?'

'Both.'

'I see.' This time he did not smile; it was a serious business. I watched him in silence. It was a ploy which never failed to make Cassis uneasy.

'Don't take our market stuff,' I repeated.

There was another silence.

Then Leibniz nodded. 'I suppose I could manage to think of some story to tell them,' he said slowly. 'You'd have to keep quiet, though. Or you could get me into real trouble. Do you understand?'

I nodded. It was fair. After all, he'd kept quiet about the orange. I spat on my palm to seal the bargain. He did not smile, but shook hands with perfect seriousness, as if this were an adult arrangement between us. I half expected him to ask me for a favour in return, but he did not, and the thought pleased me. Leibniz wasn't like the others, I told myself.

I watched him go. He did not look back. I watched him as he sauntered down the lane towards the Hourias farm and flicked his cigarette end into the outhouse wall, its glowing tip striking red sparks against the dull Loire stone.

15

I said nothing to Cassis or Reinette about what had occurred between Leibniz and myself. To have spoken of it to them would have robbed it of its potency. Instead, I hugged my secret close, turning it over in my mind like a stolen treasure. It gave me a peculiarly adult feeling of power.

I now thought of Cassis' film magazines and Reinette's lipstick with a certain contempt. They thought they'd been so clever. But what had they really done? They'd behaved like children telling tales in school. The Germans treated them like children, bribing them with trinkets. Leibniz had not tried to bribe me. He had spoken to me as an equal, with respect.

The Hourias farm had been badly hit. A week's supply of eggs requisitioned, half the milk, two whole sides of salted pork, seven pounds of butter, a barrel of oil, twenty-four bottles of wine, ill-concealed behind a partition in the cellar, plus any number of terrines and preserves. Paul told me about it. I felt a small pang for him – his uncle provided most of the family's supplies – but promised myself I would share my own food with him whenever I could. Besides, the season was just beginning. Philippe Hourias would make up his losses soon enough. And I had other things on my mind.

The orange bag was still hidden where I had left it. Not under my mattress, though Reinette still insisted upon keeping her original cache for the beauty aids she imagined to be secret. My secret place was a great deal more imaginative. I placed the bag in a small screw-topped glass jar and sunk it elbow-deep in a barrel of salted anchovies which my mother kept in the cellar. A piece of string tied around the lip of the jar would enable me to locate it when needed. Discovery was unlikely, as my mother disliked the pungent scent of the anchovies, and usually sent me to fetch any which might be required.

I knew it would work again.

I waited until Wednesday evening. This time I hid the bag in the spill-tray under the stove, where the heat would release the vapour the quickest. Sure enough, Mother was soon rubbing her temple as she worked at the stove, snapping sharply at me if I was late in bringing her flour or wood, scolding, 'Mind you don't chip my good plates, girl!' and sniffing the air with that animal look of confusion and distress. I closed the kitchen door for maximum effect, and the scent of orange invaded the room once again. I hid the bag in her pillow as before – the pieces of orange peel were crisp by then, blackened by the heat of the stove, and I felt sure this would be the last time I could use the orange bag – sewing it in, beneath the striped slip.

Dinner was burnt.

No-one dared mention it, though, and my mother fingered the black brittle lace of her charred pancakes and touched her temple over and over until I was sure I would scream. This time she did not ask whether we had brought oranges into the house, though I could tell she wanted to. She just touched and crumbled and fingered and fidgeted, sometimes breaking the silence with a fierce exclamation of rage at some trivial in-fringement of the house rules.

'Reine-Claude! Bread on the breadboard! I don't want you getting crumbs on my clean floor!'

Her voice was waspish, exasperated. I cut a slice of bread, deliberately turning the bread over onto the breadboard so that the flat underside was uppermost. For some reason this always enraged Mother, as did my habit of cutting off the crusty piece from either end of the loaf and discarding the middle section.

'Framboise, turn that bread over!' She touched her head again, fleetingly, as if checking it was still there. 'How many times have I told you about—' Then she froze mid-sentence, head on one side, mouth open.

She stayed that way for thirty seconds or so, staring at nothing with the face of a slow pupil trying to remember Pythagoras' Theorem or the rule of the ablative absolute. Her eyes were glassy-green and blank as winter ice. We looked at each other in silence, watching her as the seconds passed. Then she moved again, a brusque and typical gesture of irritation, and began to clear the dishes, even though we were only halfway through the meal. No-one mentioned that, either.

The next day, as I had predicted, she kept to her bed, and we went to Angers as before. Not to the pictures this time; instead we loitered in the streets, Cassis ostentatiously smoking one of his cigarettes, and settled on the *terrasse* of a town-centre café, Le Chat Rouget. Reinette and I ordered *diabolo-menthe*, and Cassis began to order pastis, changing meekly to *panaché* beneath the supercilious gaze of the waiter.

Reine drank carefully, trying not to smear her lipstick. She seemed nervous, her head ticking from side to side, as if watching out for something.

'Who are we waiting for?' I enquired curiously. 'Your Germans?'

Cassis glared at me. 'Tell everyone, won't you, you idiot!' he snapped. He lowered his voice. 'We sometimes meet here,' he explained. 'You can pass messages. No-one notices. We trade information.'

'What kind of information?'

Cassis made a sound of derision. 'Anything,' he said impatiently. 'People with radios. Black market.

123

Traffickers. *Resistance*.' He gave this last word a heavy emphasis, lowering his voice still further.

'Resistance,' I repeated.

Try to see what that meant to us. We were children. We had our own rules. The adult world was a distant planet inhabited by aliens. We understood so little of it. Least of all the Resistance, that fabulous quasi-organization. Books and the television made it sound so focused in later years, but I remember none of that. Instead I remember a mad scramble, in which rumour chased counter-rumour and drunkards in cafés spoke loudly against the new *régime*, and people fled to relatives in the country, out of reach of an invading army already stretched beyond tolerance in the towns. The one Resistance – the secret army of popular understanding – was a myth. There were many groups, communists and humanists and socialists, and people seeking martyrdom and swaggarts and drunkards and opportunists and saints, *all* sanctified by time, but in those days nothing like an army, and hardly a secret. Mother spoke of them with scorn. According to her, we'd all be better off if people just kept their heads down.

Even so, Cassis' whisper awed me. *Resistance*. It was a word which appealed to my sense of adventure, of drama. It brought images of rival gangs struggling for power, of night-time escapades, shootings, secret meetings, treasures and dangers braved. In a sense this was similar to the games we had played in previous years, Reine, Cassis, Paul and I – the potato-guns, passwords, the rituals. The game had broadened a little, that was all. The stakes were higher.

'You don't know any Resistance,' I said cynically, trying not to sound impressed.

'Not yet, maybe,' said Cassis. 'But we could find out. We've found out all kinds of things already.'

'It's all right,' continued Reinette, 'we don't talk about anyone in Les Laveuses. We wouldn't tell on our neighbours.'

I nodded. That wouldn't be fair.

'Anyway, in Angers it's different. Everyone's doing it here.'

I considered this. 'I could find things out, too.'

'What do you know?' said Cassis scornfully.

I almost told him what I'd said to Leibniz about Madame Petit and the parachute silk, but decided against it. Instead I asked the question which had been troubling me since Cassis had first mentioned their arrangement with the Germans.

'What do they do when you tell them things? Do they shoot people? Do they send them to the Front?'

'Of course not. Don't be silly.'

'Then what?'

But Cassis was no longer listening to me. Instead his eyes were on the newspaper stand by the church opposite, where a black-haired boy of about his age was watching us insistently. The boy made an impatient gesture in our direction.

Cassis paid for our drinks and stood up. 'Come on,' he said.

Reinette and I followed him. Cassis seemed on friendly terms with the other boy – I supposed he knew him from school. I caught a few words about holiday work, and a snort of low, nervous laughter. Then I saw him slip a folded piece of paper into Cassis' hand.

'See you later,' said Cassis, moving casually away.

The note was from Hauer.

Only Hauer and Leibniz spoke good French, Cassis explained as we took turns reading the note. The others – Heinemann and Schwartz – knew only basic French, but Leibniz especially might have been a Frenchman himself, someone from Alsace-Lorraine perhaps, with the guttural dialect of the region. For some reason I sensed that this pleased Cassis, as if passing information to an almost-Frenchman were somehow less reprehensible.

'Meet me at twelve by the school gate,' said the note briefly. 'I have something for you.'

Reinette touched the paper with her fingertips. Her face was flushed with excitement. 'What time is it now?' she said. 'Will we be late?'

Cassis shook his head. 'Not with the bikes,' he replied, trying for a laconic tone. 'Let's see what they've got for us.'

As we retrieved the bikes from their usual place in the alley, I noticed that Reinette took a compact from her pocket and quickly checked her reflection. She frowned; snaking the gold lipstick from the pocket of her dress she retouched her lips in scarlet, smiled, retouched and smiled again. The compact closed. I was not entirely surprised. It was clear to me from the first trip that she had something on her mind besides moving-picture shows. The care with which she dressed, the attention she paid to her hair, the lipstick and the perfume, all this must be for the benefit of someone. To tell the truth, I was not especially interested. I was used to Reine and her ways. At twelve she already looked sixteen. With her hair curled in that sophisticated style and her lips reddened, she might have been older. I had already seen the looks she got from people in the village. Paul Hourias grew tongue-tied and bashful when she was around – even Jean-Benet Darius, who was an old man of nearly forty, and Guguste Ramondin or Raphaël at the café. Boys looked at her; I knew that. And she noticed them. From her first day at school she'd been full of tales about the boys she met there. One week it might be Justin, who had such wonderful eyes, or Raymond, who made the whole class laugh, or Pierre-André, who could play chess, or Guillaume, whose parents moved from Paris last year. Thinking back, I could even remember when those tales stopped. It must have been at about the same time the German garrison moved in. I gave an inward shrug of indifference. There was certainly a mystery of some kind, I told

126

myself, but Reinette's secrets rarely intrigued me.

Hauer was standing guard at the gate. I could see him better in the daylight – a broad-faced German with an almost expressionless face. In a low voice he told us, 'Upriver; about ten minutes,' speaking from the corner of his mouth, then waved at us in mock impatience, as if to send us packing. We got on our bikes again without giving him a second glance, even Reinette, which led me to think that Hauer could not be the object of her infatuation.

Less than ten minutes later we caught sight of Leibniz. At first I thought he was out of uniform, but then I saw that he had simply removed his jacket and boots and was dangling his feet over the parapet, beneath which the sly brown Loire was rushing. He greeted us with a cheery wave and beckoned for us to join him. We dragged the bikes down the banking so they would not be visible from the road, then came to sit beside him. He looked younger than I remembered, almost as young as Cassis, though he moved with a careless assurance that my brother would never have, however much he tried to achieve it.

Cassis and Reinette looked at him in silence, like children at the zoo watching some dangerous animal. Reinette was scarlet. Leibniz seemed unimpressed by our scrutiny and lit a cigarette, grinning.

'The widow Petit,' he said at last through a mouthful of smoke. 'Very good.' He chuckled. 'Parachute silk and a thousand other things; she was a real black-market free-for-all.' He gave me a wink. 'Good work, *Backfisch*.'

The others looked at me in surprise, but said nothing. I remained silent, torn between pleasure and anxiety at his approving words.

'I've had some luck this week,' continued Leibniz in the same tone. 'Chewing gum, chocolate and' – he reached into his pocket and brought out a package – 'this.'

This turned out to be a handkerchief, lace-edged,

which he handed to Reinette. My sister blushed scarlet with confusion.

Then he turned to me. 'And what about you, *Back-fisch*, what is it *you* want?' He grinned. 'Lipstick? Face cream? Silk stockings? No, that's more your sister's line. Doll? Teddy bear?' He was mocking me gently, his eyes bright and filled with silvery reflections.

Now was the time to admit that my mention of Madame Petit had been nothing but a careless slip of the tongue. But Cassis was still looking at me with that expression of astonishment, Leibniz was smiling, and suddenly a gleam of an idea came into my head.

I did not hesitate. 'Fishing tackle,' I said at once. 'Proper, good fishing tackle.' I paused and fixed him with an insolent look, staring him straight in the eyes. 'And an orange.'

16

We met him again, in the same place, a week later. Cassis gave him a rumour about late-night gambling at Le Chat Rouget, and a few words he'd overheard from *Curé* Traquet outside the cemetery about a secret cache of church silver.

But Leibniz seemed preoccupied.

'I had to keep this from the others,' he told me. 'They might not have liked me giving it to you.' From under the army jacket lying carelessly on the river bank he drew out a narrow, green canvas bag, about four feet long, which made a small rattling sound as he pushed it towards me. 'It's for you,' he said as I hesitated. 'Go on.'

In the bag was a fishing rod. Not a new one, but even I could see that it was a fine piece, dark bamboo, worn almost black with age, and a gleaming metal reel, which span beneath my fingers just as neatly as if it were on ball-bearings. I gave a long, slow sigh of amazement.

'Is it . . . mine?' I asked, not quite daring to believe it.

Leibniz laughed, a bright, uncomplicated sound. 'Of course,' he said. 'We fishermen have to stick together, don't we?'

I touched the rod with tentative, eager fingers. The reel felt cool and slightly oily to touch, as if it had been packed in grease.

'But you'll have to keep it safe, eh, *Backfisch*?' he

told me. 'No going telling your parents and friends. You do know how to keep a secret, don't you?'

I nodded. 'Of course.'

He smiled. His eyes were a clear, dark grey. 'Get that pike you were telling me about, eh?'

I nodded again and he laughed. 'Believe me, with *that* rod you could catch a *U-Boot*.'

I looked at him critically for a moment, just to see how much he was teasing me. Clearly he was amused, but it was a kind mockery, I decided, and he had kept his side of the bargain. Only one thing troubled me.

'Madame Petit,' I began hesitantly. 'Nothing very bad will happen to her, will it?'

Leibniz dragged on his cigarette, then flicked the stub into the water.

'I shouldn't think so,' he said carelessly. 'Not if she minds her mouth.' He gave me a sudden sharp look, which included Cassis and Reinette. 'And you, all three of you, you keep this to yourselves, all right?'

We nodded.

'Oh, one more thing for you.' He put his hand into his pocket. 'You'll have to share, I'm afraid. I could only find one.' And he held out an orange.

He was charming, you see. We were all charmed; Cassis less so than Reine and I, perhaps, because he was the eldest and understood more about the dangers we were courting. Reinette rosy-cheeked and shy, and I . . . well, perhaps it was I most of all. It began with the fishing rod, but there were a dozen other things, his accent, the lazy ways he had, the careless look of him and his laughter. Oh, he was a real charmer, all right, not like Cassis' son Yannick tried to be, with his brash ways and his weaselly eyes. No, Tomas Leibniz had a natural way with him, even for a lonely child with a headful of nonsense.

It was nothing I could put my finger on. Reine might have said that it was the way he looked at you without saying anything, or the way his eyes changed colour – sometimes grey-green, sometimes brown-grey, like the river – or how he walked with his cap tilted back on his head and his hands in his pockets, like a boy playing truant from school. Cassis might have said that it was his *reckless* quality; the way he could swim the Loire at its widest point, or hang upside down from the Lookout Post, just as if he were a boy of fourteen, with a boy's contempt for danger. He knew all about Les Laveuses before he even set foot there. He was a country lad from the Black Forest, and he was full of anecdotes about his family, his sisters, his brothers, his plans. He was always making plans. There were days when everything he said seemed to begin with the same words, 'When I'm rich and the war is over . . . 'Oh, there was no end to what he'd do. He was the first adult we had ever met who still *thought* like a boy, planned like a boy, and maybe in the end that was what attracted us to him. He was one of us, that was all. He played by our rules.

He had killed one Englishman and two Frenchmen so far in the course of the war. He made no secret of it, but the way he told the story you would have sworn he had no choice. It could have been our father, I thought afterwards. But even so, I would have forgiven him. I would have forgiven him anything.

Of course, I was guarded at first. We met him three more times, twice alone at the river, once in the cinema with the others – Hauer; Heinemann, squat and red-haired; and slow, fat Schwartz. Twice we sent notes via the boy at the newspaper stand, twice more we received cigarettes, magazines, books, chocolate and a packet of nylon stockings for Reinette. People are less wary of children, as a rule. They guard their tongues less. We gleaned more information that way than you could ever imagine, and we passed it all on to Hauer, Heinemann, Schwartz and Leibniz. The other soldiers hardly spoke to us. Schwartz, who spoke little French, would sometimes leer at Reinette and whisper at her in guttural, greasy-sounding German. Hauer was stiff and awkward, and Heinemann was full of nervous energy, scratching incessantly at the reddish stubble which seemed an indelible part of his face. The others made me uneasy.

But not Tomas. Tomas was one of us. He was able to reach us in a way no-one else did. It was nothing as obvious as our mother's indifference or the loss of our father, or even the lack of playmates or the privations of war. We were barely aware of those things ourselves, living as we did in our savage little world of the imagination. We were certainly taken by surprise at how desperately we needed Tomas. Not for what he brought us; the chocolate and chewing gum, make-up and magazines. We needed someone to tell about our exploits, someone to impress, a fellow conspirator with the energy of youth and the polish of experience, a teller of finer stories than even Cassis could dream of. It didn't happen overnight, of course. We were wild animals, just as Mother said, and we took some taming. He must have known that from the start, because of the clever way he set out to take us, one by one, making each of us feel special. Even now, God help me, I can almost believe it. Even now.

I hid the rod in the Treasure Chest for safekeeping. I had to be careful when I used it, because everybody in Les Laveuses was apt to mind your business for you if you didn't mind it yourself, and it wouldn't take more than a chance comment to alert Mother. Paul knew, of course, but I told him that the rod had belonged to my father, and with the stammer he had, he was never one to gossip. In any case, if he ever suspected anything, he kept it to himself, and I was grateful for that.

July turned hot and sour, with thunderstorms every other day and the sky roiling mad and purple-grey over the river. At the end of the month the Loire burst its banks, washing all my traps and nets away downstream, then spilling down into Hourias' maize fields, with the maize just yellow-green and three weeks from full ripeness. It rained almost every night that month, and lightning sheeted down like great crackling rolls of silver paper, so that Reinette screamed and hid under her bed, and Cassis and I stood at the open window with our mouths open to see if we could catch radio signals on our teeth. Mother had more headaches than ever, and I only used the orange bag – revitalized now with the skin of the orange Tomas had given us – twice that month and into the next. The rest was her own problem, and she often slept badly and woke with a mouth full of barbed wire and not a kind thought in her head. On those days, I thought of Tomas like a starving man thinks of food. I think the others did the same.

The rain was hard to our fruit, too. Apples, pears and plums swelled grotesquely, then split and rotted on the trees, and wasps squeezed into the sickly clefts so that the trees were brown with them and buzzing sluggishly. My mother did what she could. She covered some of her favourites with tarpaulins to keep the rain off, but even that was little use. The soil, baked hard and white by the June sun, turned to slush beneath the feet, and the trees stood in pools of water, rotting their exposed roots. Mother piled sawdust and earth around their bases to protect them from the rot, but it was no good. The fruit fell to the ground and made sweetish mud soup. What could be retrieved we saved and made into greenfruit jam, but we all knew the harvest was spoiled before it had even had a chance. Mother stopped talking to us altogether. In those weeks her mouth was perpetually set in a small white line, her eyes holes. The tic that heralded her headaches was almost permanent, and the level of pills in the jar in the bathroom diminished more rapidly than ever.

Market days were especially silent and cheerless. We sold what we could – harvests were bad all through the county, and there wasn't a farmer along the Loire who hadn't suffered – but beans, potatoes, carrots, squash and even tomatoes had sickened with the heat and rain, and there was precious little to sell. Instead we took to selling our winter stocks, the preserves and dried meats, terrines and confits, which Mother had made last time a pig was slaughtered, and because she was desperate, she treated every sale as if it were her last. Some days her look was so black and sour that customers turned tail and fled rather than buy from her, and I was left writhing in embarrassment for her – for us – while she stood stony-faced and unseeing, one finger at her temple, like the barrel of a gun.

One week we arrived at the market to find Madame Petit's shop boarded up. Monsieur Loup, the fishmonger, told me she just packed her things and went one day, giving no reason and leaving no forwarding address.

'Was it the Germans?' I demanded with a slight unease. 'I mean, her being a Jew and everything?'

Monsieur Loup gave me a strange look. 'Don't know anything about that,' he said. 'I just know she upped and left one day. I never heard anything about the other thing, and if you've any sense you won't go round telling anyone, either.' His expression was so cool and disapproving that I apologized, abashed, and backed away, almost forgetting my packet of scraps.

My relief that Madame Petit had not been arrested was tempered by an odd feeling of disappointment. For a while I brooded in silence, then I began to make discreet enquiries in Angers and in the village, concerning the people about whom we had passed on information. Madame Petit; Monsieur Toupet or Toubon, the Latin teacher; the barber opposite Le Chat Rouget, who received so many parcels; the two men we had heard talking outside the Palais-Doré one Thursday after the film. Strangely enough, the idea that we might have passed on worthless information – perhaps to the amusement or scorn of Tomas and the others – troubled me more than the possibility of causing harm to any of the people we denounced.

I think Cassis and Reinette already knew the truth. But nine is a different continent to twelve and thirteen.

Little by little I came to realize that not a single one of the people we had denounced had been arrested or even questioned, or a single one of the places we had named as suspect raided by the Germans. Even the mysterious disappearance of Monsieur Toubon was easily explained.

'Oh, he was called to go to his daughter's wedding in Rennes,' said Monsieur Doux airily. 'No mystery there, little puss. I delivered the invitation myself.'

I fretted about it for almost a month, until the uncertainty was like a barrel of wasps in my head, all buzzing at once. I thought about it when I was out fishing, or laying traps, or playing gunfights with Paul, or digging dens in the woods. I grew thinner. My mother looked at me critically and announced that I was growing so fast it was affecting my health. She took me to Docteur Lemaître, who prescribed a glass of red wine for me every day, but even this made no difference. I began to imagine people following me, talking about me. I lost my appetite. I imagined that somehow Tomas and the others might be secret members of the Resistance, even now taking steps to eliminate me. Finally I told Cassis about my worries.

We were alone at the Lookout Post. It had been raining again, and Reinette was at home with a cold. I didn't set out to tell him everything, but once I had started the words began to spill out of me like grain from a burst sack. There was no stopping them. I had the green bag with my fishing-rod in one hand, and in a rage I flung it right out of the tree and into the bushes, where it fell in a tangle of blackberries.

'We're not *babies*!' I yelled furiously. 'Don't they believe the things we tell them? Why did Tomas give me this' – a wild gesture at the distant fishing bag – 'if I didn't earn it?'

Cassis looked at me, bewildered. 'Anyone would think you *wanted* someone to get shot,' he said uncomfortably.

'Of course not.' My voice was sullen. 'I just thought—'

'You never *thought* at all.' The tone was that of the old, superior Cassis, impatient and rather scornful. 'You really think we'd help to get people locked up or shot? That's what you think we'd do?' He sounded shocked, but underneath I knew he was flattered.

That's just what I think, I thought to myself. If it suited you, Cassis, I'm sure that's exactly what you'd do. I shrugged.

'You're so naïve, Framboise,' said my brother loftily. 'You're really too young to be involved in something like this.'

It was then I knew that even he hadn't understood at the start. He was quicker than I was, but at the beginning he hadn't known. On that first day at the cinema he'd been really afraid, sour with sweat and excitement. And later, talking to Tomas, I had seen fear in his eyes. Later, only later, had he understood the truth.

Cassis made a gesture of impatience and turned his gaze away. '*Blackmail!*' he spat furiously into my face, starring me with spittle. 'Don't you get it? That's all it is! Do you think *they're* having an easy time of it, back in Germany? Do you think they're any better off than we are? That *their* children have shoes or chocolate or any of that stuff? Don't you think *they* might sometimes want those things, too?'

I gaped at him.

'You never thought at all.' I knew that he was furious, not with my ignorance, but with his own. 'It's just the same over there, stupid!' he shouted. 'They're putting things away to send home. Getting to know stuff about people, then making them pay to keep quiet. You heard what he said about Madame Petit: 'A real black-market free-for-all.' You think they'd have let her go if he'd told anyone about it?' He was panting now, close to laughter. 'Not on your life! Haven't you ever heard of what they do to Jews in Paris? Haven't you ever heard of the death camps?'

I shrugged, feeling stupid. Of course I had *heard* of these things. It was just that in Les Laveuses things were different. We'd all heard rumours, of course, but in my mind they had got somehow tangled with the Death Ray from *The War of the Worlds*. Hitler had been muddled with the pictures of Charlie Chaplin from Reinette's film magazines, fact fusing with folk-lore, rumour, fiction and newsreel broadcast melting into serial-story star-fighters from beyond the planet Mars and night flights across the Rhine, gunslingers and firing-squads, *U-Boots* and the *Nautilus* 20,000 leagues under.

'Blackmail?' I repeated blankly.

'Business,' corrected Cassis in a sharp voice. 'Do you think it's fair that some people have chocolate and coffee and proper shoes and magazines and books, while others have to do without? Don't you think they should pay for those privileges? Share a little of what they've got? And hypocrites, like Monsieur Toubon, and liars? Don't you think *they* should pay, too? It's not as if they can't afford it. It's not as if anyone gets hurt.'

It might have been Tomas speaking. That made his words very difficult to ignore, and slowly I nodded.

I thought Cassis looked relieved. 'It isn't even steal-ing,' he continued eagerly. 'That black-market stuff belongs to everyone. I'm just making sure we all get our fair share of it.'

'Like Robin Hood.'

'Exactly.'

I nodded again. Put that way, it seemed perfectly fair and reasonable.

Satisfied, I went to retrieve my fishing bag from where it lay in the blackberry tangle, happy in the knowledge that I had earned it, after all.

PART THREE

The Snack Wagon

1

It was maybe five months after Cassis died – three years after the Mamie Framboise business – that Yannick and Laure came back to Les Laveuses. It was summer, and my daughter Pistache was visiting with her two children, Prune and Ricot, and until then it had been a happy time. The children were growing so fast and so sweet, just like their mother – Prune chocolate-eyed and curly-haired, and Ricot tall and velvet-cheeked, and both of them so full of laughter and mischief that it almost breaks my heart to see them, it takes me back so. I swear I feel forty years younger every time they come, and that summer I taught them how to fish and bait traps and make caramel macaroons and green-fig jam, and Ricot and I read *Robinson Crusoe* and *Twenty Thousand Leagues Under the Sea* together, and I told Prune outrageous lies about the fish I'd caught, and we shivered at stories of Old Mother's terrible gift.

'They used to say that if you caught her and set her free, she'd give you your heart's desire, but if you saw her – even out of the corner of your eye – and *didn't* catch her, something dreadful would happen to you.'

Prune looked at me with wide pansy-coloured eyes, one thumb corked comfortingly in her mouth. 'What kind of a dreadful?' she whispered, awed.

I made my voice low and menacing. 'You'd *die*, sweetheart,' I told her softly. 'Or someone else would. Someone you loved. Or something worse even than that. And in any case, even if you survived, Old Mother's curse would follow you to the grave.'

Pistache gave me a quelling look. '*Maman*, I don't know why you want to go telling her that kind of thing,' she said reproachfully. 'D'you want her to have nightmares and wet the bed?'

'I *don't* wet the bed,' protested Prune. She looked at me expectantly, tugging at my hand. '*Mémée*, did *you* ever see Old Mother? Did you? *Did* you?'

Suddenly I felt cold, wishing I had told her another story. Pistache gave me a sharp look and made as if to lift Prune off my knee.

'Prunette, you just leave *Mémée* alone now. It's nearly bedtime, and you haven't even brushed your teeth or—'

'Please, *Mémée*, did you? Did you *see* her?'

I hugged my granddaughter, and the coldness receded a little. 'Sweetheart, I fished for her during one entire summer. All that time I tried to catch her, with nets and line and pots and traps. I fixed them every day, checked them twice a day and more if I could.'

Prune looked at me with solemn eyes. 'You must really have wanted that wish, hmm?'

I nodded. 'I suppose I must have.'

'And did you catch her?'

Her face glowed. She smelt of biscuit and cut grass, the wonderful warm, sweet scent of youth. Old people need to have youth about them, you know, to remember.

I smiled. 'I did catch her.'

Her eyes were wide with excitement. She dropped her voice to a whisper. 'And what did you wish?'

'I didn't make a wish, sweetheart,' I told her quietly.

'You mean she got away?'

I shook my head. 'No, I caught her all right.'

Pistache was watching me now, her face in shadow. Prune put her small plump hands on my face and asked impatiently, 'What then?'

I looked at her for a moment. 'I didn't throw her

back,' I told her. 'I caught her at last, but I didn't let her go.'

Except that wasn't quite right, I told myself then. Not quite true. And then I kissed my granddaughter and told her I'd tell her the rest later, that I didn't know why I was telling her a load of old fishing stories anyway; and in spite of her protests, between coaxing and nonsense, we finally got her to bed. I thought about it that night, long after the others were asleep. I've never had much trouble sleeping, but this time it seemed like hours before I could find any peace, and even then I dreamed of Old Mother down in the black water, and myself pulling, pulled, pulling, as if neither of us could bear to ever let go.

Anyway, it was soon after that that Yannick and Laure came. To the restaurant to begin with, almost humbly, like ordinary customers. They had the *brochet angevin* and the *tourteau fromage*. I watched them covertly from my post in the kitchen, but they behaved well and caused no trouble. They spoke to each other in low voices, made no unreasonable demands on the wine cellar, and for once refrained from calling me Mamie. Laure was charming, Yannick hearty; both were eager to please and to be pleased. I was somewhat relieved to see that they no longer touched and kissed each other so often in public, and I even unbent enough to talk to them for a while over coffee and petits fours.

Laure had aged in three years. She had lost weight – it may be the fashion, but it didn't suit her at all – and her hair was a sleek copper helmet. She seemed edgy, too, with a habit of rubbing her abdomen, as if she had a pain there. As far as I could see, Yannick hadn't changed at all.

The restaurant was doing well, he declared cheerfully. Plenty of money in the bank. They were planning a trip to the Bahamas in the spring; they hadn't had a holiday together in years. They spoke of Cassis with affection and, I thought, genuine regret.

143

I began to think I'd judged them too harshly.

I was wrong.

Later that week they called at the farm, when Pistache was about to put the children to bed. They brought presents for us all – sweets for Prune and Ricot, flowers for Pistache. My daughter looked at them with that expression of vacant sweetness which I know to be dislike, and which they no doubt took for stupidity. Laure watched the children with a curious insistence, which I found unsettling; her eyes flicked constantly towards Prune, playing with some pine cones on the floor. Yannick settled himself in an armchair by the fire. I was very conscious of Pistache sitting quietly near by, and hoped my uninvited guests would leave soon. However, neither of them showed any desire to do so.

'The meal was simply wonderful,' said Yannick lazily. 'That *brochet*; I don't know what you did with it, but it was absolutely marvellous.'

'Sewage,' I told him pleasantly. 'There's so much of it pours into the river nowadays that the fish practically feed on nothing but. Loire caviare, we call it. Very rich in minerals.'

Laure looked at me, startled. Then Yannick gave his little laugh, '*Hé, hé, hé,*' and she joined him.

'Mamie likes her joke. *Hé, hé.* Loire caviare. You really are a tease, darling.'

But I noticed they never ordered pike again.

After a while they began to talk about Cassis. Harmless stuff at first – how papa would have loved to see his niece and her children.

'He was always saying how much he wanted us to have children,' said Yannick. 'But at that stage in Laure's career—'

Laure interrupted him. 'There'll be plenty of time for that,' she said, almost harshly. 'I'm not so old, am I?'

I shook my head. 'Of course not.'

'And of course, at that time there was the added expense of looking after papa to think about. He had hardly anything left, Mamie,' said Yannick, biting into one of my *sablés*. 'All he had came from us. Even his house.'

I could believe it. Cassis was never one to hoard wealth. He slid it through his fingers in smoke, or more often into his belly. Cassis was always his own best customer in the Paris days.

'Of course, we wouldn't think of begrudging him that.' Laure's voice was soft. 'We were very fond of poor papa, weren't we, *chéri*?'

Yannick nodded with more enthusiasm than sincerity. 'Oh yes. *Very* fond. And, of course, such a *generous* man. Never felt any resentment at all about this house, or the inheritance, or anything. Extraordinary.' He glanced at me then, a sharp, ratty slice of a look.

'What's that supposed to mean?' I was up at once, almost spilling my coffee, still very conscious of Pistache sitting next to me, listening. I had never told my daughters about Reinette or Cassis. They never met; as far as they knew I was an only child. And I had never spoken a word about my mother.

Yannick looked sheepish. 'Well, Mamie, you know *he* was really supposed to inherit the house—'

'Not that we blame you—'

'But he *was* the eldest, and under your mother's Will . . .'

'Now wait a minute!' I tried to keep the shrillness from my voice, but for a moment I sounded just like my mother, and I saw Pistache wince. 'I paid Cassis good money for that house,' I said in a lower tone. 'It was only a shell after the fire, anyway, all burned out, with the rafters poking through the slates. He could never have lived in it, and wouldn't have wanted to either. I paid good money, more than I could afford, and—'

'Shh. It's all right.' Laure glared at her husband. 'No-one's suggesting your agreement was in any way improper.'

Improper.

That's a Laure word all right: plummy, self-satisfied and with just the right amount of scepticism. I could feel my hand tightening around the rim of my coffee cup, printing bright little points of burn on my fingertips.

'But you have to see it from our point of view.' That was Yannick, his broad face gleaming. 'Our grandmother's legacy . . .'

I didn't like the way the conversation was heading. I especially hated Pistache's presence, her round eyes taking everything in.

'You never even knew my mother, any of you,' I interrupted harshly.

'That's not the point, Mamie,' said Yannick quickly. 'The point is that there were *three* of you. And the legacy was divided into three. That's right, isn't it?'

I nodded cautiously.

'But now, since poor papa has passed away, we have to ask ourselves whether the informal arrangement you two made between you is entirely fair to the remaining members of the family.' His tone was casual, but I could see the gleam in his eyes, and I shouted out, suddenly furious.

'*What* informal arrangement? I told you, I paid good money. I signed papers—'

Laure put her hand on my arm. 'Yannick didn't mean to upset you, Mamie.'

'No-one's upset me,' I said stonily.

Yannick ignored that and continued: 'It's just that some people might think that an arrangement such as you made with poor papa – a sick man desperate for cash –' I could see Laure watching Pistache, and cursed under my breath. 'Besides the unclaimed third which should have belonged to Tante Reine –' The fortune under the cellar floor. Ten cases of Bordeaux, laid down the year she was born, tiled over and cemented into place against the Germans, and what came later, worth a thousand francs or more per bottle today, I daresay, all awaiting collection. Damn. Cassis could never keep his mouth shut when it was needed. I interrupted harshly.

'That's being kept for her. I haven't touched any of it.'

'Of course not, Mamie. All the same,' Yannick grinned unhappily, looking so like my brother that it almost hurt. I glanced briefly again at Pistache, sitting bolt upright in her chair, face expressionless. 'All the same, you have to admit that Tante Reine is hardly in a position to claim it now, and don't you think it would be fairer to all concerned—'

'All that belongs to Reine,' I said flatly. 'I won't touch it. And I wouldn't give it to you if I could. Does that answer your question?'

Laure turned to me then. In her black dress, with the yellow lamplight on her face, I thought she looked quite ill.

'I'm sorry,' she said, with a meaningful glance at Yannick. 'This was never meant to be about money. Obviously we wouldn't expect you to give up your home, or any part of Tante Reine's inheritance. If either of us gave the impression . . .'

I shook my head, bewildered. 'Then what on earth was all that—'

Laure interrupted, her eyes gleaming. 'There was a *book*.'

'A book?' I repeated.

Yannick nodded. 'Papa told us all about it,' he said. 'You showed it to him.'

'A *recipe* book,' said Laure with strange calmness. 'You must have all the recipes by heart already. If we could only see it – borrow it.'

'Of course, we'd pay for anything we used,' added Yannick hastily. 'Think of it as a way to keep the Dartigen name alive.'

It must have been that, that name, which did it. Confusion, fear and disbelief warred in me for a while, but at the mention of that name a great spike of

147

terror pierced me and I swept the coffee cups off the table, where they shattered against my mother's terracotta tiles. I could see Pistache looking at me strangely, but could do nothing but follow the seam of my rage.

'*No! Never!*' My voice rose like a red kite in the little room, and for a second I left my body and looked down upon myself emotionlessly, a drab, sharp-faced woman in a grey dress, her hair drawn fiercely back into a knot behind her head. I saw strange comprehension in my daughter's eyes and veiled hostility in the faces of my nephew and niece, then the rage slammed into place again and I lost myself for a while.

'I know what you want!' I snarled. 'If you can't have Mamie Framboise, then you'll settle for Mamie Mirabelle. Is that it?' My breath tore through me like barbed wire. 'Well, I don't know what Cassis told you, but he had no business, and nor have you. That old story's dead. *She's* dead, and you'll get none of it from me, not if you were to wait fifty years for it!' I was out of breath now, and my throat hurt from shouting. I picked up their most recent present – a box of linen handkerchiefs lying on the kitchen table in their silver wrapping – and pushed it fiercely at Laure.

'So you can take your bribes,' I yelled hoarsely, 'and you can stick them up your fancy arse, with your Paris menus and your tangy apricot *coulis* and your poor old papas.'

For a second our eyes met, and I saw hers unveil at last and fill with spite.

'I could talk to my solicitor,' she began.

I began to laugh. 'That's right,' I hooted. 'Your solicitor. It always comes to that in the end, doesn't it?' I yarked savage laughter. 'Your solicitor!'

Yannick tried to calm her down, his eyes bright with alarm. 'Now, *chérie*, you know how we—'

Laure turned on him savagely. 'Get your fucking hands off me!'

I howled laughter, cramping my stomach. Points of

darkness danced before my eyes. Laure's eyes shot me with hate-shrapnel, then she recovered.

'I'm sorry.' Her voice was chilly. 'You don't know how important this is to me. My career—'

Yannick was trying to steer her towards the door, keeping a wary eye on me. 'No-one meant to upset you, Mamie,' he said hastily. 'We'll come back when you're more reasonable. It's not as if we were asking to *keep* the book.'

Words like spilled cards sliding. I laughed harder. The terror in me grew, but I couldn't control my laughter, and even when they had gone, the screech of their Mercedes tyres oddly furtive in the night, I still felt the occasional spasm, souring into half sobs as the adrenalin fell from me, leaving me feeling shaken and old.

So old.

Pistache was looking at me, her face unreadable. Prune's face appeared around the bedroom door.

'*Mémée*? What's wrong?'

'Go to bed, sweetheart,' said Pistache quickly. 'It's all right. It's nothing.'

Prune looked doubtful. 'Why was *Mémée* shouting?'

'Nothing.' Her voice was sharp now, anxious. 'Go to bed!'

Prune turned reluctantly. Pistache closed the door.

We sat in silence.

I knew she'd talk when she was ready, and I knew better than to rush her. She looks sweet enough, but there's a stubborn streak in her all the same. I know it well; I have it too. Instead I washed the dishes and put them away. After that I took out a book and pretended to read.

After a while Pistache spoke. 'What did they mean about a legacy?'

I shrugged.

'Nothing. Cassis made out he was a rich man so that they'd look after him in his old age. They should have known better. That's all.' I hoped she might leave it at that, but there was a stubborn line between her eyes that promised trouble.

'I never even knew I had an uncle,' she said tonelessly.

'We weren't close.'

Silence. I could see her going over it in her mind, and I wished I could stop the circle of her thoughts, but knew I couldn't.

'Yannick's very like him,' I told her, trying for lightness. 'Handsome and feckless. And his wife leads him like a dancing bear.' I demonstrated mincingly, hoping for a smile, but if anything her thoughtful look deepened.

'They seemed to think you'd cheated him somehow,' she said. 'Bought him out when he was ill.'

I forced myself to pause. Anger at this stage would not help anyone.

'Pistache,' I said patiently. 'Don't believe everything those two tell you. Cassis wasn't ill. At least, not in the way you think. He drank himself into bankruptcy, left his wife and son, and sold off the farm to pay his debts.'

She watched me curiously, and I had to make an effort to keep my voice from rising. 'Look, that was all a long time ago. It's over. My brother's dead.'

'Laure said there was a sister.'

I nodded. 'Reine-Claude.'

'Why didn't you tell me?'

I shrugged. 'We weren't—'

'Close. I gathered.' Her voice was small and flat-sounding.

Fear pricked at me again, and I said more sharply than I had intended, 'You understand that, don't you? After all, you and Noisette were never—' I bit the words short, but too late. I saw her flinch and cursed myself inwardly.

'No. But at least I tried. For you.'

Damn. I'd forgotten how sensitive she was. All those years I took her for the quiet one, watching my other daughter grow wilder and more wilful day by day. Yes, Noisette was always my favourite, but until now I thought I'd hidden it better. If she had been Prune I would have put my arms around her, but to see her now, this calm, close-faced woman of thirty, with her small, hurt smile and sleepy cat's eyes . . . I thought of Noisette, and how, out of pride and stubbornness, I had made her a stranger to me. I tried to explain.

'We were separated a long time ago,' I told her. 'After . . . the war. My mother was . . . ill . . . and we went to live with different relatives. We didn't keep in touch.' It was almost true, at least as close as I could bear to tell her. 'Reine went to . . . work . . . in Paris. She . . . fell ill, too. She's in a private hospital near Paris. I visited her once, but . . .' How could I explain? The institution-stink of the place – boiled cabbage and laundry and sickness – televisions blaring in soft rooms full of lost people who wept when they didn't like the stewed apples and who sometimes shouted at each other with unexpected viciousness, flailing their fists helplessly and pushing each other against the pale green walls. There had been a man in a wheelchair – a relatively young man with a face like a scarred fist and rolling, hopeless eyes – who had screamed, 'I don't like it here! I don't like it here!' during the whole of my visit, until his voice faded into a drone and even I found myself ignoring his distress. One woman stood in a corner, with her face to the wall, and wept unheeded. And the woman on the bed, the huge bloated thing with the dyed hair, round white thighs and arms cool and soft as fresh dough, smiling serenely to herself, murmuring. Only the voice was the same, without which I would never have believed it – a little girl's voice, chiming nonsense syllables, the eyes as blank and round as an owl's. I made myself touch her.

'Reine. Reinette.'

Again that vapid smile, the little nod, as if in her dreams she were a queen and I her subject. She had forgotten her name, the nurse told me quietly, but she was happy enough; she had her 'good days' and she loved the television, especially the cartoons, and to have her hair brushed while the radio played.

'Of course we still have our bad spells,' said the nurse, and I froze at the words, feeling something shrivel in my stomach to a bright, hard knot of terror. 'We wake in the night' – strange, that pronoun, as if by taking on part of the woman's identity she might somehow be able to share in the experience of being old and mad – 'and sometimes we have our little tantrums, don't we?' She smiled brightly at me, a young blonde of twenty or so, and I hated her so much in that moment for her youth and cheery ignorance that I almost smiled back.

I felt the same smile on my face as I looked at my daughter, and hated myself for it. I tried again for a lighter note.

'You know what it's like,' I said apologetically. 'Can't bear old people and hospitals. I sent some money.'

It was the wrong thing to say. Sometimes everything you say is wrong. My mother knew that.

'*Money*,' said Pistache contemptuously. 'Is that all people care about?'

She went to bed soon after, and nothing was right again between us that summer. Two weeks later she left, a little earlier than usual, pleading fatigue and the approach of the school term, but I could see something was wrong. I tried to talk about it to her once or twice, but it was no good. She remained distant, her eyes wary. I noticed she was receiving a lot of mail, but I thought nothing of it until much later. My mind was on other things.

2

A few days after the business with Yannick and Laure, the snack wagon arrived. A large trailer van brought it and parked its load on the grass verge just opposite Crêpe Framboise. A young man in a red-and-yellow paper hat got out. I was busy with customers at the time and paid little attention, so that when I looked out again later that afternoon I was surprised to see that the van had gone, leaving on the verge a small trailer, upon which the words 'Super Snak' were painted in bright red capitals. I came out of the shop to take a closer look. The trailer seemed abandoned, though the shutters which closed it were heavily chained and padlocked. I knocked on the door, but there was no answer.

The next day the snack wagon opened. I noticed it at about eleven thirty, when my first customers usually begin to arrive. The shutters opened to reveal a counter, above which a red-and-yellow awning gaped, and a string of bunting, with each coloured flag bearing the name of a dish and a price – '*steak-frites*, 17F, *saucisse-frites*, 14F' – and finally a number of brightly coloured posters advertising 'Super Snaks' or 'Big Value Burgers' and a variety of soft drinks.

'Looks like you've got competition,' said Paul Hourias, exactly on time at twelve fifteen. I didn't ask him what he wanted to order; he always orders the special and a *demi* – you could set your watch by him. He never says much, just sits in his usual place by the window and eats and watches the road. I decided he was making one of his rare jokes.

'Competition!' I repeated derisively. 'Monsieur Hourias, the day Crêpe Framboise has to compete with a grease merchant in a caravan is the day I pack up my pots and pans for good.'

Paul chuckled. The day's special was grilled sardines, one of his favourites, with a basket of my walnut bread, and he ate reflectively, watching the road, as usual, as he did. The presence of the snack wagon did not seem to affect the number of clients in the crêperie, and for the next two hours I was busy overseeing the kitchen while my waitress, Lise, took the orders. When I looked out again there were a couple of people at the snack wagon, but they were youngsters, not regulars of mine, a girl and a boy, with cornets of chips in their hands. I shrugged. I could live with that.

The next day there were a dozen of them, all youngsters, and a radio playing raucous music at maximum volume. In spite of the day's heat I closed the crêperie door, but even so the tinny ghosts of guitars and drums marched through the glass, and Marie Fenouil and Charlotte Dupré, both regulars, complained about the heat and the noise.

The next day the crowd was larger, the music louder, and I complained. Marching up to the snack wagon at eleven forty, I was immediately enswarmed by adolescents, some of whom I recognized, but many out-of-towners, too – girls in halter-tops and summer skirts or jeans, young men with turned-up collars and motorcycle boots with jingling buckles. I could see several motorbikes already propped up against the sides of the snack wagon, and there was a smell of petrol mingled in amongst the frying and beer. A young girl with cropped hair and a pierced nose looked at me insolently as I marched up to the counter, then thrust her elbow in front of me, just missing my face.

'Waitcher turn, *'hé, mémère,*' she said smartly, through a mouthful of gum. 'Can'tcher see there's people waiting?'

'Oh, is *that* what you're doing, sweetheart?' I snapped. 'I thought you were just touting for custom.'

The girl gaped at me, and I elbowed past her without a second glance. Mirabelle Dartigen, whatever else she might have done, never raised any of her children to mince their words.

The counter was high, and I found myself looking up at a young man of about twenty-five. He was good-looking, in a dirty-blond sharpish kind of way, with hair past his collar and a single gold earring – a cross, I think – dangling. He had eyes which might have done something for me forty years ago, but nowadays I'm too old and too particular. I think that old clock stopped ticking just about the same time men stopped wearing hats. Come to think of it, he looked a little familiar, but I wasn't thinking about that then.

Of course, he already knew me.

'Good morning, Madame Simon,' he said in a polite, ironic voice. 'What can I do for you? I've got a lovely *burger américain* if you'd care to try it.'

I was angry, but I tried not to show it. His smile showed that he was expecting trouble, and that he felt confident of withstanding it. I gave him one of my sweetest.

'Not today, thank you,' I told him. 'But I would be grateful if you'd consider turning your radio down. My customers—'

'But of course.' His voice was smooth and cultured, his eyes gleaming porcelain blue. 'I had no idea I was disturbing anyone.'

Beside me, the girl with the pierced nose made an incredulous sound. I heard her say to a companion, another girl in a crop-top and shorts so small that fleshy half-moons showed beneath the hem, 'Did you hear what she said to me? Did you hear?'

The young blond man smiled, and reluctantly I saw charm there, and intelligence, and something oh-so familiar which needled and nibbled. Leaning over to turn the music down. Gold chain around the neck, sweat stains on a grey T-shirt, hands too smooth for a cook. Oh there was something wrong about him, about the whole thing, and for the first time I felt not anger but a kind of fear.

Solicitous: 'Is that all right for you, Madame Simon?'

I nodded.

'I'd hate to be thought an intrusive neighbour.'

The words were all right, but I still couldn't shake the thought that there was something wrong, some mockery in that cool, courteous tone which I'd missed somehow. And though I'd got what I wanted, I fled the place, almost turning my ankle on the gravel of the verge, with the press of young bodies against me – there must have been forty of them now, maybe more – and the sound of their voices drowning me. I got out quickly – I never liked to be touched – and as I went back into Crêpe Framboise I heard the sound of raucous laughter, as if he had waited for me to leave before making some comment. I looked back sharply, but he had his back to me by then and was flipping a row of burgers with practised ease.

But still that feeling of wrongness remained. I found myself watching out of the window more than usual, and when Marie Fenouil and Charlotte Dupré, the customers who had complained about noise the previous day, did not arrive at their usual time, I began to feel edgy. It might be nothing, I told myself. There was only a single empty table, after all. The majority of my customers were there as usual. And yet I found myself watching the snack wagon with a reluctant fascination, watching *him* as he worked, watching the crowd which remained by the roadside, young people eating from paper cornets and polystyrene boxes while he held court. He seemed on friendly terms with everyone. Half a dozen girls – the one with the pierced nose among them – propped up the counter, some with cans of soda in their hands. Others lolled in languid attitudes near by, and there was much studied perking-out of bosoms and flicking of hips. Those eyes, it seemed, had touched softer hearts than mine.

At twelve thirty I heard the sound of motorcycles from the kitchen. A terrible sound, like pneumatic drills in unison, and I dropped the skillet with which I was turning a row of *bolets farcis* to run out into the road. The sound was unbearable. I clapped my hands over my ears and even then felt sharp pain lancing my eardrums, made sensitive from years of diving in the old Loire. Five motorcycles which I had last seen propped against the sides of the snack wagon were now parked on the road just opposite, and their owners – three with girls perched delicately behind them – were revving up to leave, each trying to outdo the rest in volume and attitude. I shouted at them, but could hear nothing but the tortured screech of the machines. Some of the young customers at the snack wagon laughed and clapped. I waved my arms furiously, unable to make myself heard against the din, and the riders saluted me mockingly, one rising onto his back wheels, like a prancing horse in a redoubled gale of sound.

The whole performance lasted five minutes, by which time my *bolets* were burnt and my ears ringing painfully and my temper risen to melting point. There was no time to complain again to the manager of the snack wagon, though I promised myself that I would as soon as my customers left. By then, however, the wagon had closed, and though I thumped furiously against the shutters, no-one answered.

The next day the music was playing again. I ignored it for as long as I could, then stamped off to complain. There were even more people than before, and a number of them, recognizing me, made insolent comments as I pushed my way through the little crowd. Too angry to be polite today, I glared up at the snack wagon's owner and spat, 'I thought we had an agreement!'

He gave me a smile as wide as a barn door. Enquiringly: 'Madame?'

But I was in no mood to be cajoled. 'Don't go trying to pretend you don't know what I'm talking about. I want the music off, right now!'

Polite as always, and now looking slightly hurt at my ferocious attack, he switched the music off.

'But of course, madame. I didn't mean to offend you. If we're to be such close neighbours, we should try to accommodate each other.'

For a few seconds I was too angry even to hear the warning bell.

'What do you mean, close neighbours?' I managed at last. 'How long do you imagine you're going to be staying here?'

He shrugged. 'Who knows?' His voice was silky. 'You know the catering business, madame. Such an unpredictable thing. Crowds one day, the next half empty. Who knows what may happen?'

The warning bells had grown to a jangle now, and I was beginning to feel cold. 'Your trailer's on a public road,' I said drily. 'I imagine the police will move you on as soon as they spot you.'

He shook his head. 'I've got permission to be here, on the verge,' he told me gently. 'All my papers bear scrutiny.' Then he looked at me with that insolent politeness of his. 'Do yours, madame, I wonder?'

I kept my face stony, while my heart flipped over like a dying fish. He knew something. The thought spun dizzily in my head. Oh God, he knew something. I ignored his question.

'Another thing.' I was pleased with my voice, with its low, sharp quality. The voice of a woman who is not afraid. Beneath my ribs my heart beat faster. 'Yesterday there was a commotion with motorcycles. If you allow your friends to disturb my customers again, then I shall report you for creating a public nuisance. I'm sure the police—'

'I'm sure the police will tell you that the cyclists themselves are responsible, not I.' He sounded amused. 'Really, madame, I'm trying to be reasonable, but threats and accusations aren't going to solve the problem.'

I left feeling strangely culpable, as if I, not he, had made the threats. That night I slept fitfully, and in the morning I snapped at Prune for spilling her milk, and at Ricot for playing football too close to the kitchen garden. Pistache looked at me oddly – we had barely spoken since the night of Yannick's visit – and asked if I felt all right.

'It's nothing,' I said shortly, and returned to the kitchen in silence.

3

For the next few days the situation gradually worsened. There was no music for two days, then the music began again, louder than ever. Several times the gang of motorcyclists called, each time revving violently as they arrived and left, and doing laps around the block, where they raced each other and uttered long, ululating cries. The group of regulars at the snack wagon showed no sign of diminishing, and every day I spent longer and longer picking up discarded cans and papers from the sides of the road. Worse still the wagon began to open in the evenings, too, from seven until midnight – coincidentally, these were identical to my own opening hours – and I began to fear the sound of the wagon's generator as it powered up, knowing that my quiet crêperie would soon be facing an ever-growing street party. A pink neon strip above the wagon's counter announced, 'Chez Luc, Sandwiches-Snacks-Frites', and the fair-ground smells of frying and beer and sweet hot waffles filled the soft night air.

Some of my customers complained, some simply stayed away. By the end of the week seven of my regulars had seemingly stopped coming altogether and the place was half empty on weekdays. On Saturday a group of nine came from Angers, but the noise was especially bad that evening, and they looked nervously at the crowd at the roadside where their cars were parked, finally leaving without dessert or coffee and with a conspicuous absence of a tip.

This couldn't go on.

Les Laveuses has no police station, but there is one *gendarme*, Louis Ramondin – François' grandson – though I'd never had much to do with him, he being from one of the Families. A man in his late thirties, lately divorced following a too-early marriage to a local girl, he had the look of his great-uncle Guilherm, the one with the wooden leg. I didn't want to talk to him now, but I could feel everything slipping away from me, pulling me apart in every direction, and I needed help.

I explained the situation with the snack wagon. I told him about the noise, the litter, my customers, the motorcycles. He listened with the look of an indulgent young man talking to a fussy grandmother, nodding and smiling so that I longed to knock heads with him. Then he told me, in the cheery, patient tone the young reserve for the deaf and the elderly, that no law was as yet being infringed. Crêpe Framboise was on a main road, he explained. Things had changed since I'd first moved to the village. He might be able to talk to the wagon's owner, Luc, but I must try to understand.

Oh, I understood. I saw him later by the snack wagon, out of uniform, chatting with a pretty girl in a white T-shirt and jeans. He had a can of Stella in one hand and a sugared waffle in the other. Luc gave me one of his satirical smiles as I went by with my shopping basket, and I ignored them both. I understood.

In the days which followed, business at Crêpe Framboise slumped. The place was only half full now, even on Saturday nights, and weekday lunchtimes were even poorer. Paul stayed, though, loyal Paul with his special every day and his *demi*, and out of simple gratitude I began to give him a beer on the house, though he never asked for more than the single glass.

Lise, my little waitress, told me that Luc was staying over at La Mauvaise Réputation, where they still rent a few rooms.

'I don't know where he's from,' she told me. 'Angers, I think. He's paid his rent three months in advance, so it looks as if he's planning to stay.'

Three months. That would take us almost to December. I wondered whether his *clientèle* would be as keen when the first frost came. It was always a low season for me, with only a few regulars to keep things going, and I knew that, with things as they were, I might not even be able to count on those. Summer was my high time, and in those holiday months I usually managed to set aside enough money to make me comfortable until the spring. But this summer . . . As things were at present, I told myself coolly, I might make a loss. It was all right; I had money put away, but there was Lise's wage, plus the money I sent for Reine, feed for the animals, stores, fuel and machine hire. And with autumn coming soon there would be the labourers to pay, the apple-pickers and Michel Hourias with his combine, though I could sell my grain and cider in Angers to tide myself over.

Still, it might be hard. For some time I fretted uselessly over figures and estimates. I forgot to play with my grandchildren, and for the first time wished that Pistache had not come for the summer. She stayed another week, then left with Ricot and Prune, and I could see in her eyes that she felt I was unreasonable, but I could not find enough warmth in me to tell her what I felt. There was a cold, hard place where my love for her should have been, a hard, dry place, like the stone in a fruit. I held her briefly as we said goodbye, and turned away dry-eyed. Prune gave me a bunch of flowers she had picked in the fields, and for a moment a sudden terror overwhelmed me. I was behaving like my mother, I told myself. Stern and impassive, but secretly filled with fears and insecurities. I wanted to reach out to my daughter, to explain that it wasn't anything *she* had done, but somehow I couldn't. We were always raised to keep things to ourselves. It isn't a habit which can be easily broken.

4

And so the weeks passed. I spoke to Luc again on several occasions, but met with nothing but his ironic civility. I could not shake the thought that he was familiar somehow, but could not place where I might have seen him before. I tried to find out his surname, in the hope that it might give me a clue, but he paid cash at La Mauvaise Réputation, and when I went there the café seemed full of the out-of-towners who haunted the snack wagon. There were a few locals too – Murielle Dupré and the two Lelac boys with Julien Lecoz – but mostly they weren't locals, but pert-looking girls in their designer jeans and crop-tops, and young men in cycle leathers or Lycra shorts. I noticed that young Brassaud had added a jukebox and a pool table to his assortment of shabby slot machines; it seemed that not all trade had been bad in Les Laveuses.

Perhaps that was why support for my campaign was so half-hearted. Crêpe Framboise is at the far side of the village, on the Angers road. The farm was always isolated from the others, and there are no other houses for half a kilometre into the village. Only the church and the post office are within any kind of hearing distance, and Luc took care to keep his crowd silent when there was a service. Even Lise, who knew what it was doing to our business, made excuses for him. I complained to Louis Ramondin twice more, but I might as well have spoken to the cat for all the use he was to me.

The man really wasn't hurting anyone, he said firmly. If he broke the law, then perhaps something could be done. Otherwise I was to let the man get on with running his business. Did I understand?

It was then the other affair began. Little things at first. One night it was fireworks going off somewhere in the street, then motorcycles revving up outside my door at two in the morning. Litter tipped onto my doorstep during the night, a pane of my glass door broken. One night a motorcyclist rode about in my big field and made figures-of-eight and skid-marks and crazy loops all over my ripening wheat. Little things. Nuisances. Nothing you could tie down to *him*, or even to the out-of-towners he brought in his wake. Then someone opened the door of the hen house and a fox got in and killed every one of those nice brown Polands of mine. Ten pullets, good layers all of them, gone in a single night. I told Louis – he was supposed to deal with thieves and trespassers – but he practically accused me of forgetting to close the door myself.

'Don't you think perhaps it might have just swung open in the night?' He gave me his big friendly countryman's smile, as if maybe he could smile my poor hens back to life. I gave him a sharp look.

'Locked doors don't just *swing* open,' I told him tartly. 'And it takes a clever fox to cut open a padlock. Someone mean did that on purpose, Louis Ramondin, and you're paid to find out who.'

Louis looked shifty and muttered something under his breath.

'What did you say?' I asked sharply. 'There's nothing wrong with my ears, young Louis, and you'd better believe it. Why, I remember when—' I bit off the end of my sentence in a hurry. I'd been about to say that I remembered his old granddaddy snoring in church, drunk as a lord and with piss down his pants, hidden inside the confessional during the Easter service, but that was nothing *la veuve* Simon would ever have known about, and I felt cold to think that I might have given myself away with a piece of stupid gossip. You understand now why I didn't have more to do with the Families than I could help.

Anyway, Louis finally agreed to have a look round the farm, but he didn't find anything, and I just got on with things as best I could. The loss of the hens was a blow, though. I couldn't afford to replace them, besides, who was to say it might not happen again? So I had to buy eggs from the old Hourias farm, now owned by a couple called Pommeau, who grew sweetcorn and sunflowers, which they sold upriver to the processing plant.

I knew Luc was behind what was happening. I knew it but I couldn't prove anything, and it was driving me half crazy. Worse, I didn't know *why* he was doing it, and my rage grew until it was like a cider press squeezing my old head like an apple, ripe and ready to burst. The day after the fox got into the hen house I took to sitting up at my darkened window with my shotgun slung across my chest, and a strange sight it must have been to anyone who saw me in my nightdress and light autumn coat, keeping watch over my yard. I bought some new padlocks for the gates and the paddock, and I stood guard night after night, waiting for someone to come calling, but no-one came. The bastard must have known what I was doing, though how he could have guessed I don't know. I was beginning to think he could see right into my mind.

5

It didn't take long for sleeplessness to take its toll on me. I began to lose concentration during the day. I forgot recipes. I couldn't remember whether I'd already salted the omelette, and salted it twice or not at all. I cut myself seriously as I was chopping onions, only realizing I'd been asleep on my feet when I awoke with a handful of blood and one of my fingers gaping. I was abrupt with my remaining customers, and even though the loud music and the motorcycles seemed to have quietened down a little, word must have got around, because the regulars I had lost didn't come back. Oh, I wasn't entirely alone. I did have a few friends who took my part, but the deep reserve, the constant feeling of suspicion, which had made Mirabelle Dartigen such a stranger in the village, must be in my blood, too. I refused to be pitied. My anger alienated my friends and frightened my customers away. I existed on rage and adrenalin alone.

Oddly enough, it was Paul who finally put a stop to it. Some weekday lunchtimes he was my only customer, and he was regular as the church clock, staying for exactly an hour, his dog lying obediently under his chair, watching the road in silence as he ate. He might have been deaf, for all the notice he took of the snack wagon, and he rarely said anything to me except hello and goodbye.

One day he came in, but didn't sit down at his usual table, and I knew something was wrong. It was a

167

week after the fox had got into the hen house, and I was dog-tired. My left hand was bound up in thick bandage after I'd cut myself, and I'd had to ask Lise to prepare the vegetables for the soup. I still insisted on making the pastry myself – imagine having to make pastry with a plastic bag mittened over one hand – and it was hard work. Standing half asleep on my feet by the kitchen door, I barely returned Paul's greeting. He looked at me sideways, taking off his beret and stubbing out his small black cigarette on the doorstep.

'*Bonjour*, Madame Simon.'

I nodded and tried to smile. The fatigue was like a sparkling grey blanket over everything. His words were a yawning of vowels in a tunnel. His dog went to lie under their table at the window, but Paul stayed standing, his beret in one hand.

'You don't look well,' he observed in his slow way.

'I'm all right,' I said shortly. 'I didn't sleep too well last night, that's all.'

'Or any night this month, I'd say,' said Paul. 'What is it, insomnia?'

I gave him a sharpish look. 'Your dinner's on the table,' I said. 'Chicken fricassée and peas. I won't be heating it up for you if it gets cold.'

He gave a sleepy smile. 'You're beginning to sound like a wife, Madame Simon. People will talk.'

I decided this was one of his jokes and ignored it.

'Perhaps I can help,' insisted Paul. 'It isn't right for them to treat you this way. Somebody ought to do something about it.'

'Please don't trouble yourself, monsieur.' After so many broken nights I could feel tears coming closer to the surface by the day, and even this simple, kind talk brought a stinging to my eyes. I made my voice dry and sarcastic to compensate, and looked pointedly in the opposite direction. 'I can deal with it perfectly well by myself.'

Paul remained unquelled. 'You can trust me, you know,' he said quietly. 'You should know that by now.

All this time . . .' I looked at him then, and suddenly I knew.

'Please, 'Boise.'

I stiffened.

'It's all right. I haven't told anyone, have I?'

Silence. The truth stretched between us like a string of chewing gum.

'Have I?'

I shook my head. 'No, you haven't.'

'Well, then.' He took a step towards me. 'You never would take help when you needed it, not even in the old days.' Pause. 'You haven't changed that much, Framboise.'

Funny. I thought I had. 'When did you guess?' I asked at last.

He shrugged. 'Didn't take long,' he said laconically. 'Probly the first time I tasted that *kouign amann* of your mother's. Or maybe it was the pike. Never could forget a good recipe, could I?' And he smiled again beneath his drooping moustache, an expression which was both sweet and kind and unutterably sad at the same time.

'It must have been hard,' he commented.

The stinging at my eyes was almost unbearable now. 'I don't want to talk about it,' I said.

He nodded. 'I'm not a talker,' he said simply.

He sat down then to eat his fricassée, stopping occasionally to look at me and smile, and after a while I sat down next to him – after all, we were alone in the place – and poured myself a glass of *Gros-Plant*. We sat in silence for a time. After a few minutes I laid my head down on the table top and wept quietly. The only sounds were my weeping and those of Paul's cutlery as he ate reflectively, not looking at me, not reacting. But I knew his silence was kind.

When I had finished I wiped my face carefully on my apron. 'I think I'd like to talk now,' I said.

6

Paul is a good listener. I told him things I never meant to tell a living soul, and he listened in silence, nodding occasionally. I told him about Yannick and Laure, about Pistache and how I had let her go without a word, about the hens, the sleepless nights, and how the sound of the generator made me feel as if ants were crawling inside my skull. I told him of my fears for the business, for myself, my nice home and the niche I had made for myself among these people. I told him of my fear of growing old, of how the young today seemed so much stranger and harder than we had ever been, even with what we had seen during the war. I told him of my dreams, of Old Mother with a mouthful of orange and of Jeannette Gaudin and the snakes, and little by little I began to feel the poison inside me drain away.

When at last I finished, there was silence.

'You can't stand guard every night,' said Paul at last. 'You'll kill yourself.'

'I have no choice,' I told him. 'Those people, they could come back at any time.'

'We'll share watches,' said Paul simply, and that was that.

I let him have the guest room now that Pistache and the children were gone. He was no trouble, keeping to himself, making his own bed and keeping things tidy. A lot of the time you'd hardly have noticed him, and yet he was there, calm and unobtrusive. I felt guilty that I had ever thought him slow. In fact, he was quicker than I was in some ways; certainly it was he who finally made the connection between the snack wagon and Cassis' son.

We spent two nights watching for trespassers – Paul from two till six, and I from ten till two – and already I was beginning to feel more rested and more able to cope. Sharing the problem was enough for me then, just knowing there was someone else. Of course, the neighbours began to talk almost at once. You can't really keep a secret in a place like Les Laveuses, and too many people knew that old Paul Hourias had left his shack by the river to move in with the widow. People fell silent as I came into shops. The postman winked at me as he delivered letters. Some disapproving glances came my way, mostly from the *curé* and his Sunday-school cronies, but for the most part there was little but quiet, indulgent laughter. Louis Ramondin was heard to say that the widow had been behaving strangely in recent weeks, and now he knew why. Ironically, many of my customers came back for a while, if only to see for themselves whether the rumours were true.

I ignored them.

Of course, the snack wagon hadn't moved, and the noise and nuisance from the daily crowds did not abate. I'd given up trying to reason with Luc; the authorities, such as they were, seemed uninterested, which left us – Paul and me – with only one remaining alternative. We investigated.

Every day Paul took to drinking his lunchtime *demi* at La Mauvaise Réputation, where the motorcyclists and town girls hung out. He questioned the postman. Lise, my waitress, also helped us, even though I'd had to lay her off for the winter, and she set her little brother Viannet onto the case, too, which must have made Luc the most watched man in Les Laveuses. We found out a few things.

He was from Paris. He'd moved to Angers six months ago. He had money, and plenty of it, which he spent freely. No-one seemed to know his last name, though he wore a signet ring with the initials L.D. He had an eye or two for the girls. He drove a white Porsche, which he kept at the back of La Mauvaise Réputation. He was generally reckoned to be all right, which probably meant he bought a lot of rounds.

Not a great deal for our trouble.

Then Paul thought of inspecting the snack wagon. Of course I'd done that before, but Paul waited until it was closed and its owner was safely in the bar of La Mauvaise Réputation. It was sealed, locked and padlocked, but at the back of the trailer he found a small metal plate with a registration and a contact telephone number inscribed on it. We checked the telephone number and traced it . . . to the restaurant Aux Délices Dessanges, Rue des Romarins, Angers.

I should have known from the start.

Yannick and Laure would never have given up so easily on a potential source of income. And knowing what I did now, it was easy to see where I'd seen him before. He had that same slightly aquiline nose, clever, bright eyes and sharp cheekbones – Luc Dessanges, Laure's brother.

My first reaction was to go straight to the police – not to our Louis but the Angers police – to say I was being harassed. Paul talked me out of it.

There was no proof, he told me gently. Without proof there was nothing anyone could do. Luc hadn't done anything openly illegal. If we could have caught him, well, that would have been something else, but he was too careful, too clever for that. They were waiting for me to cave in, waiting for just the right moment to step in and make their demands – 'If only we could help you, Mamie. Just let us try. No hard feelings.'

I was all for taking the bus to Angers there and then – find them in their lair, embarrass them in front of their friends and customers, screech to all and sundry that I was being hounded, blackmailed – but Paul said we should wait. Impatience and aggression had already lost me more than half my customers. For the first time in my life, I waited.

They came calling a week later.

It was Sunday afternoon, and for the past three weeks I had closed the crêperie on Sundays. The snack wagon too was closed – he followed my opening hours almost to the minute – and Paul and I were sitting in the yard, with the last of the autumn sun warming our faces. I was reading, but Paul – never a reader in the old days – seemed content to sit doing nothing, occasionally looking at me in that mild, undemanding way of his, or maybe whittling at a piece of wood.

I heard the knock and went to answer the door. It was Laure, businesslike in a dark-blue dress, with Yannick in his charcoal suit behind her. Their smiles were like piano keyboards. Laure was carrying a large plant with red and green leaves. I kept them on the doorstep.

'Who's died?' I asked coolly. 'Not me, not yet, though it isn't for want of both of you bastards trying.'

Laure put on her pained look. 'Now, Mamie,' she began.

'Don't you "Now, Mamie" me,' I snapped. 'I know all about your dirty little intimidation games. It isn't going to work. I'd die rather than let you make a penny out of me, so you can tell your brother to pack up his grease cart and clear off, because I know what he's up to, and if it doesn't stop right now, then I swear I'll go to the police and tell them exactly what you've been doing.'

Yannick looked alarmed and began to make placating noises, but Laure was made of tougher stuff. The surprise in her face lasted for maybe ten seconds, then hardened into a tight, dry smile.

'I knew from the start that we'd be better off telling you everything,' she said, with a flick of a contemptuous glance at her husband. 'None of this is helping either of us, and I'm sure that once I explain everything you'll understand the value of a little cooperation.'

I folded my arms. 'You can explain what you like,' I said. 'But my mother's legacy belongs to me and Reine-Claude, whatever my brother told you, and there's nothing more to be said about it.'

Laure gave me a broad, hateful smile of dislike. 'Is that what you thought we wanted, Mamie? Your bit of money? Oh *really*! What a dreadful pair you must think us.' Suddenly I saw myself through their eyes, an old woman in a stained apron, sloe eyes and hair dragged back so tightly it stretched the skin. I growled at them then, like a bewildered dog, and grabbed hold of the doorpost to steady myself. My breath came in gasps, each one a journey through thorns.

'It isn't that we couldn't do with the money,' said Yannick earnestly. 'The restaurant business isn't doing well right now. That review in *Hôte & Cuisine* didn't help. And we've been having trouble—'

Laure quelled him with a glance. 'I don't want the money at all,' she repeated.

'I know what you want,' I said again, harshly, trying not to let my confusion show. 'My mother's recipes. But I won't give them to you.'

Laure looked at me, still smiling. I realized that it wasn't just recipes she wanted, and a cold fist tightened around my heart.

'No,' I whispered.

'Mirabelle Dartigen's album,' said Laure gently. 'Her very own album. Her thoughts, her recipes, her

175

secrets. Our grandmother's legacy to all of us. It's a crime to keep something like that hidden away for ever.'

'*No!*'

The word wrenched from me, and I felt as if it were taking half my heart with it. Laure started and Yannick took a step back. My breath was a throatful of fish-hooks.

'You can't keep it secret for ever, Framboise,' said Laure reasonably. 'It's incredible no-one found out before this. Mirabelle Dartigen' – she was flushed, almost pretty in her excitement – 'one of the most elusive and enigmatic criminals of the twentieth century. Out of the blue she murders a young soldier, and stands by coolly while half her village is shot in retribution, then she just walks off without a word of explanation.'

'It wasn't like that,' I said in spite of myself.

'Then tell me what it *was* like,' said Laure, taking a step forwards. 'I'd consult you on everything. We've got the chance of a wonderful exclusive insight here, and I know it will make a fabulous book.'

'What book?' I said stupidly.

Laure looked impatient. 'What do you mean, *what book*? I thought you'd guessed. You said . . .'

I felt my tongue cleave to the roof of my mouth. With difficulty I said, 'I thought you were after the recipe book. After what you told me—'

She shook her head impatiently. 'No, I need it to research *my* book. You read my pamphlet, didn't you? You must have known I was interested in the case. And when Cassis told us she was actually *related* to us. Yannick's grandmother.' She broke off again to grasp at my hand. Her fingers were long and cool, her nails painted shell-pink, like her lips. 'Mamie, you're the last of her children. Cassis dead, Reine-Claude useless.'

'You went to see her?' I said blankly.

Laure nodded. 'She doesn't remember anything. A

complete vegetable.' Her mouth was wry. 'Plus no-one in Les Laveuses remembers anything worth mentioning, or if they do, they won't talk.'

'How do you know?' Rage had given way to a cold feeling, a realization that this was much worse than anything I had previously suspected.

She shrugged. 'Luc, of course. I asked him to come over here, ask a few questions, buy some rounds at the old anglers' club, you know what I mean.' She gave me that impatient, quizzical look. 'You told me you knew all that.'

I nodded in silence, too benumbed to speak.

'I have to say you've managed to keep it quiet for longer than I would have thought possible,' continued Laure admiringly. 'No-one imagines that you're anything but a nice Breton lady, *la veuve Simon*. You're very much respected. You've done well for yourself here. No-one suspects a thing. You never even told your daughter.'

'Pistache?' I sounded stupid to myself, my mouth yawning like my mind. 'You've not been talking to her?'

'I wrote her a few letters. I thought she might know something about Mirabelle. But you never told her, did you?'

Oh, God. Oh, Pistache. I was in a landslide where every movement starts a new rockfall, bringing a new collapse of the world I thought steady.

'But what about your other daughter? When did you last hear from her? And what does she know?'

'You have no right, *no right*.' The words were harsh as salt in my mouth. 'You don't understand what it means to me, this place. If people get to know—'

'Now, now, Mamie.' I was too weak to push her away, and she put her arms around me. 'Obviously, we'd keep your name out of it. And even if it got out – and you have to face the fact that it might one day – then we'd find you another place. A better place. At your age you shouldn't be living in a dilapidated old farm like this anyway; it doesn't even have proper plumbing, for Christ's sake. We could settle you in a nice flat in Angers. We'd keep the press away from you. We care about you, Mamie, whatever you may think. We're not monsters. We want what's best for you.'

I pushed her away with more strength than I knew I had.

'*No!*'

Gradually I became aware of Paul, standing silently behind me, and my fear blossomed into a great flower of rage and elation. I was not alone. Paul, my loyal old friend, was with me now.

'Think what it might mean to the family, Mamie.'

'*No!*' I began to push the door closed, but Laure put her high heel into the crack.

'You can't hide away for ever.'

Then Paul stepped forward into the doorway. He spoke in a calm and slightly drawling voice, the voice of a man who is either deeply at peace or a little slow in the head.

'Maybe you didn't hear Framboise.' His smile was almost sleepy, but for the wink he gave me, and in that moment I loved him completely and with a suddenness that startled away my rage. 'If I've understood this right, then she doesn't want to do business. Isn't that so?'

'Who's this?' said Laure. 'What's *he* doing here?'

Paul gave her his sweet, sleepy smile. 'A friend,' he told her simply. 'From way back.'

'Framboise,' called Laure from behind Paul's shoulder. 'Think about what we said. Think about what it *means*. We wouldn't ask you if it wasn't important. Think about it.'

'I'm sure she will,' said Paul kindly, and closed the door. Laure began to knock persistently upon it, and Paul drew the latch and put on the safety chain. I could hear her voice, muffled by the thickness of the wood, now with a high buzzing note to it.

'Framboise! Be reasonable! I'll tell Luc to go away! Things can go back to the way they were! *Framboise!*'

'Coffee?' suggested Paul, going into the kitchen. 'Make you feel, you know, better.'

I glanced at the door. 'That woman,' I said in a shaking voice. 'That hateful woman.'

Paul shrugged. 'Take it outside,' he suggested simply. 'We won't hear her from there.'

It was as easy as that to him, and I followed, exhausted, as he brought me hot black coffee with cinnamon cream and sugar, and a slice of blueberry *far* from the kitchen cupboard. I ate and drank in silence for a while, until I felt my courage return.

'She won't give up,' I told him at last. 'Either way she'll keep at me until she forces me out. Then she knows there won't be any point in me keeping the secret any longer.' I put my hand to my aching head. 'She knows I can't hang on for ever. All she has to do is wait. I won't last long anyhow.'

'Are you going to give in to her?' Paul's voice was calm and curious.

'No,' I said harshly.

He shrugged. 'Then you shouldn't talk as if you are. You're smarter than she is.' For some reason he was blushing. 'And you know you can win if you try.'

'How?' I knew I sounded like my mother, but I couldn't help it. 'Against Luc Dessanges and his friends? Against Laure and Yannick? It hasn't been two months and already they've half ruined my business. All they need to do is go on the way they began, and by spring . . .' I made a furious gesture of frustration. 'And what about when they start talking? All they have to say—' I choked on the words. 'All they have to do is mention my mother's name.'

Paul shook his head. 'I don't think they'll do that,' he said calmly. 'Not at once, anyway. They want something to bargain with. They know you're afraid of that.'

'Cassis told them,' I said dully.

He shrugged. 'Doesn't matter,' he said. 'They'll leave you alone for a while; hope to make you come round, try to make you see sense. They'll want you to do it of your own accord.'

'So?' I could feel my anger reaching towards him now. 'How long does that leave me? A month? Two? What can I do with two months? I could rack my brains for a year and it still wouldn't do any—'

'That's not true.' He spoke flatly, without resentment, pulling a single crumpled Gauloise from his top pocket and popping a match against his thumb to light it. 'You can do anything you've a mind to. Always could.' He looked at me then over the red eye of the cigarette and gave his small, sad smile. 'Remember from the old days. You caught Old Mother, didn't you?'

I shook my head. 'That isn't the same thing,' I told him.

'It is, though, just about,' replied Paul, dragging on acrid smoke. 'You must know that. You can learn a lot about life from fishing.'

I looked at him, puzzled. He went on: 'Take Old Mother, now. How d'you catch her when all those others didn't?'

I considered that for a moment, thinking back to my nine-year-old self. 'I studied the river,' I said at last. 'I learned about the old pike's habits, where it fed, what it fed on. And I waited. I was lucky, that's all.'

'Hmm.' The cigarette flared again, and he breathed smoke through his nostrils. 'And if this Dessanges was a fish. What then?' He grinned suddenly. 'Find where he feeds, find the right bait, and he's yours. Isn't that right?'

I looked at him.

'Isn't that right?'

Maybe. Hope scratched a thin silver trail across my heart. Maybe.

'I'm too old to fight them,' I said. 'Too old and too tired.'

Paul put his rough brown hand over mine and smiled. 'Not to me,' he said.

8

He's right, of course. You can learn a lot about life
from fishing. Tomas had taught me that, among other
things. We'd talked a lot, the year we'd been friends.
Sometimes Cassis and Reine were there, and we'd talk
and exchange news for small items of contraband: a
stick of chewing gum or a bar of chocolate or a jar of
face cream for Reine or an orange. Tomas seemed to
have an unlimited supply of these items, which he
distributed with casual indifference. He almost always
came alone then.

Since my conversation with Cassis in the treehouse
I felt that things were settled between us, Tomas and
I. We followed the rules; not the mad rules of our
mother's devising but simple rules that even a child of
nine could understand: *keep your eyes open; look after
number one; share and share alike*. We three had been
self-sufficient for so long that it was a blissful, if
unspoken, relief to have someone in charge again; an
adult, someone to keep order.

I remember one day, we were together, the three of
us, and Tomas was late. Cassis still called him Leibniz,
though Reine and I had long since progressed to first-
name terms, and today Cassis was jumpy and sullen,
sitting apart from the rest of us on the river bank,
pinging stones into the water. He'd had a shouting
match with mother that morning over some matter of
no importance:

'If your father was alive you wouldn't dare talk to me like that!'

'If our father was alive he'd do as he was told, just as you do!'

Beneath the lash of her tongue, Cassis fled, as always. He kept Father's old hunting jacket on a straw mattress in the treehouse, and he was wearing it now, hunched in it like an old Indian in a rug. It was always a bad sign when he wore Father's jacket, and Reine and I left him alone.

He was still sitting there when Tomas came.

Tomas noticed at once, and sat a little further down the bank without saying anything.

'I've had enough,' said Cassis at last, without looking at Tomas. 'Kid's stuff. I'm nearly fourteen. I've had enough of all that.'

Tomas took off his army greatcoat and tossed it aside for Reinette to go through the pockets. I lay on my stomach on the bank and watched.

Cassis spoke up again. 'Comics, chocolate; it's all rubbish. That's not war. It's nothing.' He stood up, looking agitated. 'None of it's serious. It's just a game. My father got his head blown off and it's all a stinking game to you, isn't it?'

'Is that what you think?' said Tomas.

'I think you're a Boche,' spat Cassis.

'Come with me,' said Tomas, standing up. 'Girls, you stay here. OK?'

Reine was happy to do that, to flick through the magazines and treasures in the greatcoat's many pockets. I left her to it, and slunk after them through the undergrowth, keeping low to the mossy ground. Their voices filtered towards me distantly, like motes from the tree canopy.

I didn't hear all of it. I was crouching low behind a fallen stump, almost afraid to breathe. Tomas unholstered his gun and held it out to Cassis.

'Hold it if you like. Feel how it feels.'

It must have felt very heavy in his hand. Cassis levelled it and looked over the sights at the German. Tomas seemed not to notice.

'My brother was shot as a deserter,' said Tomas. 'He'd only just finished his training. He was nineteen and scared. He was a machine-gunner, and the noise must have sent him a little crazy. He died in a French village, right at the beginning of the war. I thought that if he'd been with me I could have helped him, kept him cool somehow, kept him out of trouble. I wasn't even there.'

Cassis looked at him with hostility. 'So?'

Tomas ignored the question. 'He was my parents' favourite. It was always Ernst who got to lick the pots when my mother was cooking, Ernst who got the least chores to do, Ernst who made them proud. Me? I was a plodder, just about good enough to take out the rubbish or feed the pigs. Not much else.'

Cassis was listening now. I could feel the tension between them, like something burning.

'When we got the news, I was home on leave. A letter came. It was supposed to be a secret, but within half an hour everyone in the village knew the Leibniz boy had deserted. My parents couldn't understand what was going on; they behaved like people who'd been struck by lightning.'

I began to crawl closer, using the fallen tree as cover. Tomas went on. 'The funny thing was that I'd always thought I was the coward in the family. I kept my head down. I didn't take risks. But from then on, to my parents, I was a hero. Suddenly I'd taken Ernst's place. It was as if he'd never existed. I was their only son. I was everything.'

'Wasn't that . . . scary?' Cassis' voice was almost inaudible.

Tomas nodded.

I heard Cassis sigh then, a sound like a heavy door closing.

'He wasn't *supposed* to die,' said my brother. I

guessed it was Father to whom he referred.

Tomas waited patiently, seemingly impassive.

'He was always supposed to be so clever. He had everything under control. *He* wasn't a coward—' Cassis broke off and glared at Tomas, as if his silence implied something. His voice and his hands were shaking. Then he began to scream in a high, tortured voice; words I could hardly make out, spilling over themselves in furious eagerness to be free.

'*He wasn't supposed to die!* He was supposed to sort everything out and make everything better, and instead he went and got his stupid self blown up. And now it's me in charge and I – don't – know – what to do any more, and I'm s–s–sc—'

Tomas waited until it was over. It took some time. Then he put out his hand and casually retrieved the gun.

'That's the trouble with heroes,' he remarked. 'They never quite live up to expectations, do they?'

'I could have shot you,' said Cassis sullenly.

'There's more than one way of fighting back,' said Tomas.

I sensed they were reaching a close, and began to retreat back through the bushes, not wanting to be there when they turned round. Reinette was still there, absorbed in a copy of *Ciné-Mag*. Five minutes later Cassis and Tomas were back, arm-in-arm like brothers, and Cassis was wearing the German's cap at a rakish angle.

'Keep it,' advised Tomas. 'I know where I can get another one.'

The bait was taken. Cassis was his slave from that moment.

9

After that our enthusiasm for Tomas' cause redoubled. Any piece of information, however trivial, was grist to his mill. Madame Henriot at the post office was opening mail in secret, Gilles Petit at the butcher was selling catmeat and calling it rabbit, Martin Dupré had been heard speaking against the Germans in La Mauvaise Réputation with Henri Drouot, everyone knew the Truriands had a radio hidden under a trap in their back garden and that Martin Francin was a communist. And day by day he would visit these people with the excuse of collecting supplies for the barracks and would leave with a little more than he came for – a pocketful of notes or some black-market cloth or a bottle of wine. Sometimes his victims paid with more information; a cousin from Paris hiding in a cellar in downtown Angers, or a stabbing behind the Chat Rouget café. By the end of summer Tomas Leibniz knew half the secrets in Angers and two-thirds of those in Les Laveuses, and he already had a small fortune tucked away in his mattress in the barracks. Fighting back, he called it. Against what, he never needed to say.

He was sending money home to Germany, though I never knew how. There were ways, of course. Diplomatic bags and couriers' cases, food trains and hospital trucks. Plenty of ways for an enterprising young man to exploit, given the right contacts. He exchanged duties with friends in order to visit local farms. He listened at the door of the officers' mess. People liked Tomas, trusted him, talked to him. And he never forgot anything.

It was risky. He told me as much, meeting me one day down by the river. If he made a mistake he might be shot. But his eyes were bright with laughter as he told me. Only a fool gets caught, he said, grinning. A fool gets slack and careless, greedy, too, perhaps. Heinemann and the others were fools. He'd needed them once, but now it was safer to play alone. Liabilities, all of them. Too many weaknesses – fat Schwartz had an eye for the girls, Hauer drank to excess and Heinemann, with his constant scratching and nervous tics, seemed a prime candidate for the sanatorium. No, he said lazily, lying on his back with a clover stem between his teeth, it was better to work alone, to watch and wait and let others take the big risks.

'Take your pike,' he said reflectively. 'It hasn't lived so long in the river by taking risks all the time. It's a bottom-feeder mostly, even though its teeth allow it to tackle just about any fish on the river.' He paused to discard the clover stem and pull himself into a seated position overlooking the water. 'It knows it's being hunted, *Backfisch*, so it waits on the bottom, eating bits of rotted stuff and sewage and mud. From the bottom it's safe. It watches the other fish, the smaller ones, closer to the surface, sees their bellies reflecting the sun, and when it sees one a little further from the rest, maybe one in trouble – *whap*!' He demonstrated with a rapid movement of the hands, closing imaginary jaws on the invisible victim.

I watched him with wide eyes.

'It keeps away from traps and nets; it knows them by sight. Other fish get greedy, but the old pike just bides its time. It knows to wait. And the bait; it knows that, too. Lures don't work for the old pike. Live bait's all it will take, and even then only sometimes. Takes a clever man to catch a pike.' He smiled. 'You and I could both learn a few lessons from an old pike like that, *Backfisch*.'

I took him at his word. I met him once a fortnight, or even once a week, once or twice alone, more often the three of us. It was usually a Thursday, and we met by the Lookout Post and went into the woods or down-river, away from the village, where no-one would see us. Often Tomas wore civilian clothing, leaving his uniform hidden in the treehouse so that no-one would ask questions. On Mother's bad days I used the orange bag to keep her to her room while we met Tomas. On all other days I rose at four thirty every morning and fished before the morning's chores began, taking care to choose the darkest and quietest parts of the Loire. I caught live bait in my cray-pots, keeping them alive and trapped until I could use them to bait my new rod. Then I skimmed them across the water, just lightly enough for their pale bellies to touch the surface, raking the current with the living lure. I caught several pike that way, but they were all youngsters, none of them much longer than a hand or a foot. I pinned them to the Standing Stones all the same, with the stinking strips of water-snake which had hung there all that summer.

Like the pike, I waited.

10

It was early September now, and summer was on the turn. Still hot, there was a new ripeness in the air, something rich and swollen, a sweet scent of honey decay. The bad August rains had spoiled much of the fruit harvest, and what remained was black with wasps, but we picked it anyway; we could not afford waste, and what could not be sold as fresh fruit might still make jam or liqueur for the winter. My mother supervised the operation, giving us all thick gloves to wear and wooden tongs – once used for picking washing out of the boiling vats at the laundry – to pick up the fallen fruit. I remember the wasps were especially mean that year, perhaps scenting the approach of autumn and their coming deaths, for they stung us repeatedly in spite of our gloves as we flung the half-rotten fruit into the big boiling pans for jam. The jam itself was half wasps at first, and Reine, who loathed insects, was almost hysterical at having to scoop their half-dead bodies from the scummy surface of the red liquid with a slatted spoon, flinging them far onto the path in a spray of plum juice, where soon enough their living companions were crawling stickily. Mother had no patience with such behaviour. We were not expected to be afraid of such things as wasps, and when Reine screamed and cried at having to pick up the swarming masses of windfall plums, she spoke to her more sharply than usual.

'Don't be more of a fool than God made you, girl,' she snapped. 'Do you think the plums will pick themselves? Or do you expect the rest of us to do it for you?'

Reine whimpered, hands held out stiffly in front of her, her face twisted with loathing and fear.

My mother's tone grew dangerous. For a moment her voice sounded waspy, buzzing with menace.

'Go to it,' she said, 'or I'll give you something to whine about,' and she pushed Reinette hard towards the pile of plums we had collected, a pile of spongy, half-fermented fruit, volatile with wasps. Reinette found herself in a swarm of insects and screamed, recoiling towards my mother, eyes closed so that she did not see the sudden spasm of rage which crossed Mother's face. For a moment Mother looked almost blank, then she grabbed Reinette, who was still screaming hysterically, by the arm and marched her quickly, wordlessly towards the house. Cassis and I looked at each other but made no move to follow. We knew better than that. When Reinette began to scream more loudly, each scream punctuated by a sound like the crack of a small air-rifle, we simply shrugged and went back to work among the wasps, using the wooden tongs to scoop drifts of spoiled plums into the bins which lined the path.

After what seemed like a long while, the sounds of Reinette being whipped ceased, and she and my mother came out of the house, Mother still holding the piece of washing line she had used, and set to work again in silence, Reinette sniffing occasionally and wiping at her reddened eyes. After a while Mother's tic began again, and she went to her room, leaving us with terse instructions to finish picking up the windfalls and to put the jam on to boil. She never mentioned the incident later, or seemed even to recall its having happened, though I heard Reinette tossing and whimpering in the night and saw the red weals on her legs as she put on her nightdress.

Unusual though it was, it was far from the last unusual thing Mother was to do that summer, and it was very soon forgotten, except by Reinette, of course. We had other things to think about.

11

I had seen little of Paul that summer; with Cassis and Reinette out of school he kept his distance. But by September the new term was close to starting, and Paul began to come round more often. Though I liked Paul well enough, I felt uneasy about him meeting Tomas, so I often avoided him, hiding in the bushes at the side of the river until he'd gone, ignoring his calls or pretending not to notice when he waved at me. After a while he seemed to get the message, because he stopped coming altogether.

It was at this point that Mother began to grow really strange. Since the incident with Reinette we had watched her with the wary caution of primitives at the feet of their god. Indeed, she was a kind of idol to us, a thing of arbitrary favours and punishments, and her smiles and frowns were the vane upon which our emotional weather turned. Now, with September on the turn and school starting for the two eldest in a week's time, she became almost a parody of her former self, enraged at the slightest tiny thing – a dishcloth left beside the sink, a plate on the draining board, a speck of dust on the glass of a framed photograph. Her headaches plagued her almost daily. I almost envied Cassis and Reinette, spending long days in school, but our own primary school had closed, and I was not old enough to join them in Angers until the following year.

I used the orange bag often. Terrified that my mother might discover the trick, I still couldn't stop myself. Only when she took her pills was she quiet, and she only took them when she smelled oranges. I hid my supply of orange peel deep in the anchovy barrel and brought it out when necessary. It was risky, but it often brought me five or six hours of much-needed peace.

Between these brief moments of amnesty the campaign between us continued. I was growing fast; I was already as tall as Cassis, and taller than Reinette. I had my mother's sharp face, her dark, suspicious eyes, her straight, black hair. I resented this similarity more than her strangeness, and as summer festered into autumn I felt my resentment grow until I was almost stifled with it. There was a piece of mirror in our bedroom, and I found myself looking into it in secret. I'd never taken a great deal of interest in my appearance before, but now I became curious, then critical. I counted my shortcomings and was dismayed to find so many. I would have liked to have curly hair, like Reinette, and full, red lips. I sneaked the film post-cards from beneath my sister's mattress and learned each one by heart. Not with sighs and ecstasies, but with gritted-teeth desperation. I twisted my hair with rags to make it curl. Fiercely I pinched the pale brown buds of my breasts to make them grow. Nothing worked. I remained the image of my mother; sullen, inarticulate and clumsy. There were other strange-nesses. I had vivid dreams, from which I awoke gasping and sweating, though the nights were turning cold. My sense of smell was enhanced, so that on some days I could smell a burning hayrick right across Hourias' fields with the wind in the opposite direction, or I knew when Paul had been eating smoked ham or what my mother was making in the kitchen before I even got into the orchard. For the first time I was aware of my own smell, my salty, fishy, warm smell, which persisted even when I rubbed my skin with lemon balm and peppermint, and the sharp oily scent of my hair. I had stomach cramps – I who was never sick – and headaches. I began to wonder if my mother's strangeness was something I had inherited, a terrible, mad secret into which I was being drawn.

Then I awoke one morning to find blood on the bedsheet. Cassis and Reinette were getting ready to cycle to school and paid little attention to me. Instinctively I dragged the cover over the stained sheet and pulled on an old skirt and jumper before running down to the Loire to investigate my affliction. There was blood on my legs, and I washed it in the river. I tried to make a bandage for myself out of old handkerchiefs, but the injury was too deep, too complex for that. I felt as if I were being torn apart, nerve by nerve.

It never occurred to me to tell my mother. I had never heard of menstruation – Mother was obsessively prim regarding bodily functions – and I assumed that I was badly hurt, maybe even dying. A careless fall somewhere in the woods, a poison mushroom, bleeding me from the inside out, perhaps even a poisonous thought. We didn't go to church – my mother disliked what she called *la curaille* and sneered at the crowds on their way to Mass – and yet she had given us a strong awareness of sin. 'Badness will get out somehow,' she would say, and we were full of badness to her, like wineskins bloated with a bitter vintage, always to be watched, tapped, every look and mutter indicative of the deeper, instinctive badness we hid.

I was the worst. I understood this. I saw it in my eyes in the mirror, so like hers with their flat, animal insolence. You can call death with a single bad thought, she used to say, and that summer all my thoughts had been bad. I believed her. Like a poisoned animal I hid; climbed up to the top of the Lookout Post and lay curled on the wooden floor of the treehouse, waiting for death. My belly ached like a rotten tooth. When death didn't come I read one of Cassis' comics for a while, then lay looking up at the bright canopy of leaves until I fell asleep.

12

She explained to me later as she handed me the clean sheet. Expressionless but for that look of appraisal which she always wore in my presence, mouth thinned almost to invisibility and eyes barbed-wire jags in her pallor.

'It's the curse come early,' she said. 'You'd better have these.' And she gave me a wad of muslin squares, almost like a child's nappies. She did not tell me how to use them.

'Curse?' I'd stayed away all day in the treehouse, expecting to die. Her lack of expression infuriated and confused me. I'd always loved drama. I'd imagined myself dead at her feet, flowers at my head, a marble gravestone saying, 'Beloved Daughter'. I'd told myself that I must have seen Old Mother without knowing it. I was cursed.

'Mother's curse,' she said, as if in agreement. 'You'll be like me now.'

She said nothing more. For a day or two I was afraid, but I did not speak to her about it, and I washed the muslin squares in the Loire. After that the curse ended for a time, and I forgot about it.

Except for the resentment. It was focused now, honed somehow by my fear, and my mother's refusal to comfort. Her words haunted me – 'you'll be like me now' – and I began to imagine myself changing imperceptibly, growing more like her in sly insidious ways. I pinched my skinny arms and legs because they were hers. I slapped my cheeks to give them more colour. One day I cut off my hair – so closely that I nicked my scalp in several places – because it refused to curl. I tried to pluck my eyebrows, but I was unskilled at the task and had already taken most of them off when Reinette found me, squinting over mirror and tweezers with a deep crease of rage between my eyes.

Mother barely noticed. My story that I had scorched off my hair and eyebrows trying to light the kitchen boiler seemed to satisfy her. Only once – this must have been on one of her good days – as we were in the kitchen making *terrines de lapin*, she turned to me with an oddly impulsive look on her face.

'Do you want to go to the pictures today, 'Boise?' she asked abruptly. 'We could go together, you and me.'

The suggestion was so untypical of my mother that I was startled. She never left the farm except on business. She never wasted money on entertainment. Suddenly I noticed that she was wearing a new dress – as new as those straitened days allowed, anyway – with a daring red bodice. She must have made it from scraps in her room during the nights she couldn't sleep, because I had never seen it before. Her face was slightly flushed, almost girlish, and there was rabbit blood on her outstretched hands.

I recoiled. It had been a gesture of friendship, I knew that. To reject it was unthinkable, and yet there was too much unspoken stuff between us to make it possible. For a second I imagined going to her, letting her arms come around me, telling her everything . . .

The thought was immediately sobering.

Telling her what? I asked myself sternly. There was too much to say. There was nothing to say. Nothing at all. She looked at me quizzically.

"Boise? What about it?' Her voice was unusually soft, almost caressing. I had a sudden, appalling picture of her in bed with my father, arms outstretched, with that same look of seduction. 'We never do anything but work,' she said quietly. 'We never seem to have any time. And I'm so tired.'

It was the first time I could remember hearing her complain. Again I felt the urge to go to her, to feel warmth from her, but it was impossible. We were not used to such things. We hardly ever touched. The idea seemed almost indecent.

I muttered something graceless about having seen the film already.

For a moment the bloodstained hands remained, beckoning. Then her face closed and I felt a sudden stab of fierce exhilaration. At last, in our long, bitter game I had scored a point.

'Of course,' she said tonelessly. There was no more talk of going to the cinema, and when I went to Angers that Thursday with Cassis and Reine to see the very film I had claimed to have seen already, she made no comment. Perhaps she had already forgotten.

13

That month our arbitrary, unpredictable mother was filled with a new set of caprices. One day cheerful, singing to herself in the orchard as she supervised the last of the picking, the next snapping our heads off if we dared to come near her. There were unexpected gifts: sugar lumps, a precious square of chocolate and a blouse for Reine, made of Madame Petit's famous parachute silk and sewn with tiny pearl buttons. She must have made that in secret, too, like the red-bodice dress, for I had not seen her cutting the cloth or fitting it, but it was beautiful. As usual, no word accompanied the gift, simply an awkward, abrupt silence, in which any mention of thanks or appreciation would have seemed inappropriate.

'She looks so pretty,' she wrote in the album. 'Almost a woman already, with her father's eyes. If he wasn't already dead I might feel jealous. Maybe 'Boise feels it, with her funny little froggy face, like mine. I'll try to find something to please her. It isn't too late.'

If only she'd said something, instead of setting it down in that tiny, encrypted writing. As it was, these small acts of generosity – if that was what they were – enraged me even more, and I found myself looking for ways to reach her again, as I had that time in the kitchen.

I make no apologies. I wanted to hurt her. The old cliché stands true: children are cruel. When they cut, they reach the bone with a truer aim than any adult, and we were feral little things, merciless when we scented weakness. That moment of reaching out in the kitchen was fatal for her, and maybe she knew it, but it was too late. I had seen weakness in her, and from that moment I was unrelenting. My loneliness yawned hungrily inside me, opening deeper, blacker galleries in my heart, and if there were times when I loved her too, loved her with achy, needful desperation, I banished the thought with memories of her absence, her coldness, her anger. My logic was wonderfully mad; I would make her sorry, I told myself. I would make her hate me.

I dreamed often of Jeannette Gaudin, of the white gravestone with the angel, and white lilies in a vase at the head. 'Beloved Daughter'. Sometimes I awoke with tears on my face, my jaw aching, as if I had ground my teeth for hours. Sometimes I awoke confused, certain that I was dying. The water-snake had bitten me after all, I told myself woozily, in spite of all my precautions. It had bitten me, but instead of dying quickly – white flowers, marble, tears – it was turning me into my mother. I moaned in my hot half-sleep, holding my shorn head in my hands.

There were times when I used the orange bag out of sheer spite and secret revenge for the dreams. I heard her pacing in her room, sometimes talking to herself. The morphine jar was almost empty. Once she threw something heavy against the wall and it shattered; later we found the pieces of her mother's clock in the rubbish, the dome smashed to pieces, the clock face cracked down the middle. I felt no pity. I would have done it myself if I'd dared.

Two things kept me sane through that September. First, my hunt for the pike. I caught several using Tomas' suggestion of live bait – the Standing Stones were rank with their corpses and the air was a purple shimmer, crackling with flies – and though Old Mother still remained elusive, I was sure I was getting close. I imagined that for every pike I caught she would be watching, her rage and her recklessness growing. The lust for vengeance would claim her at last, I told myself. She could not ignore this attack on her people for ever. However patient, however impassive she might be, there would come a time when she would not be able to stop herself. She would come out, she would fight, and I would have her. I persisted, and vented my rage on the corpses of the victims with growing ingenuity, sometimes using what was left as bait for my cray-pots.

My second source of comfort was Tomas. We saw him weekly when he could get away, almost always on a Thursday, which was his day off. He came by motor-bike, which he hid, along with his uniform, in the bushes behind the Lookout Post, often with a parcel of black-market stuff to be shared between us. Strangely enough, we had got so used to his visits that his presence alone would have been enough for us, but we hid the fact, each in his or her own way. In his presence we changed: Cassis grew nonchalant, showing off with desperate bravado – 'Watch how I can swim the Loire at the fastest point. Watch how I steal honeycomb from the wild bees' – Reine was kittenish and shy, peeping at him from darkened eyes and pouting her pretty lipsticked mouth. I despised Reine's posturing. Since I knew I could not compete with my sister at her game, I went out of my way to outdare Cassis in everything he did. I swam across deeper and more dangerous stretches of river. I dived for longer periods of time. I swung from the topmost branches of the Lookout Post, and when Cassis dared to match me, I swung upside down, knowing his secret fear of heights, laughing and screaming apelike at the others below. With my cropped hair I was more boyish than any boy, and already Cassis was beginning to show traces of the softness which would overtake him in middle age. I was tougher and harder than he was. I was too young to understand fear as he did,

201

risking my life gaily in order to steal a march on my brother. I was the one who invented the Root Game which was to become one of our favourites, and I spent hours practising, so that I was almost always the winner.

The principle of the game was simple. Along the banks of the Loire, shrunken now since the end of the rains, grew a profusion of tree roots, washed bare by the passage of the river. Some were as thick as a girl's waist, others were mere fingerlings, drooping down into the current, often reattaching themselves to the yellow soil a metre or so underwater, so they formed loops of woody matter in the murkiness. The object of the game was to dive through these loops – some of them very tight – jack-knifing the body abruptly down and through and back again. If you missed the loop first time in the murky dark water, or resurfaced without having gone through, or if you refused a dare, then you were out. The person who could do the most loops, without missing any, won.

It was a dangerous game. The root loops always occurred at the fastest parts of the river, where the banks were steeply eroded. Snakes lived in the hollows under the roots, and if the bank collapsed it was possible to remain trapped beneath the fallen soil. It was virtually invisible, and you had to grope underneath the rootlets for the way out. It was always a possibility that someone might get caught, jammed in place by the savage current until they drowned, but this, of course, was the game's beauty and its appeal.

I was very good at it. Reine seldom played, and was driven frequently to hysterics as we competed to impress, but Cassis could never refuse a challenge. He was still stronger than I was, but I had the advantage of a slighter build and more supple spine. I was an eel, and the more Cassis bragged and postured, the stiffer he grew. I don't remember ever losing.

The only times I saw Tomas alone was when Cassis and Reine had misbehaved at school. Only then were they obliged to stay behind on Thursdays after the rest had left, sitting at their little desks in the detention hall, conjugating verbs or writing lines. It happened rarely as a rule, but this was a difficult time for everyone. The school was still occupied. Teachers were scarce, and classes might run to fifty or sixty pupils at once. Their patience was worn thin; any little thing might do it – a word spoken out of turn, a bad test result, a playground fight, a forgotten lesson. I prayed for it to happen.

The day it did was unique. I remember it as clearly as some dreams, a memory more coloured and defined than the rest, a perfect transparency among the blurry, uncertain events of that summer. For a single day everything turned in perfect synchronicity, and for the first time since I could remember I felt a kind of tranquillity, a peace with myself and my world, a feeling that, if I chose, I could make this perfect day last for ever. It is a feeling I have never quite regained, though I thought I felt something a little like it on each of the days my daughters were born, and perhaps again once or twice with Hervé, or when a dish I was cooking turned out exactly right. But this was the real thing, the elixir, the never-to-be-forgotten.

Mother had been ill the evening before. Not my doing, this time; the orange bag was useless, having been heated up so often in the past month that the peel was blackened and charred, its smell barely perceptible. No, this was just one of her usual bad spells, and after a while she took her pills and went to bed, leaving me to my own devices. I awoke early and took off to the river before Cassis and Reine were awake. It was one of those red-gold early October days, the air crisp and tart and heady as applejack, and even at five the sky was the clear, purplish-blue which only the finest of autumn days brings. There are maybe three such days in a year, and this was one of them. I sang as

203

I lifted my traps, and my voice bounced off the misty banks of the Loire like a challenge. It was the mushroom season, so after I had brought my catch back to the farm and cleaned it out, I took some bread and cheese for breakfast and set out into the woods to hunt for mushrooms. I was always good at that. Still am, to tell the truth, but in those days I had a nose like a truffle pig's. I could *smell* those mushrooms out, the grey *chanterelle*, and the orange, with its apricot scent, the *bolet* and the *petit rose* and the edible puffball and the browncap and the bluecap. Mother always told us to take our mushrooms to the chemist's to ensure we had not gathered anything poisonous, but I never made a mistake. I knew the meaty scent of the *bolet* and the dry, earthy smell of the browncap mushroom. I knew their haunts and their breeding grounds. I was a patient collector.

It was almost noon when I returned to the house, and Cassis and Reinette should have been back from school, but as yet there was no sign of either of them. I cleaned the mushrooms and put them in a jar of olive oil to marinade, with some thyme and rosemary. I could hear Mother's deep, druggy breathing from behind her bedroom door.

Twelve thirty came and went. They should have been back by now. Tomas usually came by two at the latest. I began to feel a tiny spike of excitement pricking at my belly. I went into our bedroom and looked at myself in Reinette's mirror. My hair had begun to grow out, but it was still as short as a boy's at the back. I put on my straw hat, though it was long past high summer, and thought I looked better.

One o'clock. They were over an hour late. I imagined them in the detention hall with the sun slanting through the high windows and the smell of floor polish and old books in their nostrils. Cassis would be sullen; Reinette sniffling furtively. I smiled. I took Reinette's precious lipstick from the hiding place beneath her mattress and smeared some on my mouth.

I looked at myself critically, then I applied the same colour to my eyelids and repeated the procedure. I looked different, I thought approvingly, almost pretty. Not pretty like Reinette or her actress pictures, but today that didn't matter. Today Reinette wasn't there.

At one thirty I made my way to the river and our usual meeting place. I watched for him from the Lookout Post, half expecting him not to turn up – such good fortune seemed to belong to another person, not to me – and smelling the warm sappy scent of the crisp red leaves from the branches all around. Another week and the Lookout Post would be useless for the next six months, the treehouse bare as a house on a hill, but today there was still enough foliage to hide me from view. Delicious tremors went through me, as if someone were playing a delicate bone xylophone just above my pelvis, and my head rang with an indescribably light feeling. Today anything was possible, I told myself giddily. Anything at all.

Twenty minutes later I heard the sound of a motorbike on the road, and I leaped from the tree towards the river as quickly as I could. The sensation of giddiness was stronger now, so that I felt strangely disoriented, walking on ground which was barely there. A feeling of power almost as great as my joy cascaded over me. For today, Tomas was *my* secret, my possession. What we said to each other would be ours alone. What I said to him . . .

He was stopping by the verge, one quick glance behind to see if anyone had seen him, then dragging the bike down into the tamarisks by the long sandbank. I watched, oddly reluctant to show myself now that the moment had come, suddenly shy of our aloneness, our new intimacy. I waited for him to take off his uniform jacket and hide it in the undergrowth. Then he looked around. He was carrying a parcel wrapped with string, and there was a cigarette at the corner of his mouth.

'The others aren't here.' I tried to make my voice adult to match his gaze, suddenly conscious of the lipstick on my mouth and eyes, wondering whether he would comment. If he laughed, I thought fiercely, if he laughed . . . But Tomas simply smiled. 'Fine,' he said casually. 'Just you and me, then.'

14

As I said, it was a perfect day. It's difficult from the distance of sixty-five years to explain the tremulous joy of those few hours. At nine one is so raw that a single word is sometimes enough to draw blood, and I was more sensitive than most, almost *expecting* him to spoil everything. I never asked myself whether I loved him. It was irrelevant to the moment, and impossible to equate what I felt – that aching, desperate joy – with the language of Reinette's favourite movies. And yet that was what it was. My confusion, my loneliness, the strangeness of my mother and the separation from my sister and brother had formed a kind of hunger, a mouth opening instinctively to any scrap of kindness, even from a German, a cheery extortionist who cared for nothing but keeping his information channels open.

I tell myself now that that was all he wanted. Even so, some part of me denies it. That wasn't all it was. There was more to it than that. He took pleasure in meeting me, in talking to me. Why else would he have stayed so long? I remember every word, every gesture, every intonation. He talked about his home in Germany, of *Bierwurst* and *Schnitzel*, of the Black Forest and the streets of Old Hamburg and the Rheinland, of *Feuerzangenbowle*, with a burning orange studded with cloves in a bowl of steaming punch, and *Keks* and *Strudel* and *Backofen* and *Frikadelle* with mustard and the apples which used to grow in his grandfather's garden before the war, and I talked about Mother and her pills and her strangeness and the orange bag and the cray-pots and the broken clock with the cracked face, and how when I got my wish I would wish for this day to go on for ever and ever.

He looked at me then, and an oddly adult look passed between us, like some variant of Cassis' staring-out game. This time I was the first to look away.

'I'm sorry,' I muttered.

'It's OK,' he told me, and somehow it was. We picked some more mushrooms and some wild thyme – so much more strongly scented than the cultivated variety, with its tiny purple flowers – and some late strawberries under a stump. As he climbed over a deadfall of birches I touched his back fleetingly, under the pretence of steadying myself, and felt the warmth of his skin sear into my palm for hours after that, like a brand. And then we sat by the river and watched the red disk of the sun go behind the trees, and for a moment I was sure I saw something, black against the black water, something half visible in the centre of a great V of ripples – a mouth, an eye, the oil-slick curve of a rolling flank, a double row of fangs whiskered with ancient fish-hooks – something of awesome, unbelievable proportions, which vanished the moment I tried to give it a name, leaving nothing but ripples and a churning of troubled water where it might have been.

I leaped to my feet, my heart hammering wildly. 'Tomas! Did you *see* that?'

Tomas looked at me lazily, cigarette stub between his teeth. 'Floating log,' he told me laconically. 'Log in the current. See them all the time.'

'It wasn't!' My voice was high and trembling with excitement. 'I saw it Tomas! It was *her*, it was *her*. Old Mother, Old Moth—' With a sudden, lurching burst of speed, I began to run towards the Lookout Post to fetch my fishing rod. Tomas gave a chuckle.

'You'll never make it,' he said. 'Even if it was the old

pike, and believe me, *Backfisch*, no pike ever grows to be *that* big.'

'It *was* Old Mother,' I insisted stubbornly. 'It was. It was. Twelve feet long, Paul says, and black as pitch. It couldn't have been anything else. It *was* her.'

Tomas smiled.

I met his bright, challenging gaze for a second or two and then dropped it, abashed.

'It was,' I repeated, half under my breath. 'It was. I know it was.'

Well, I often wondered about that. Maybe it was just a floating log, as Tomas said. Certainly, when I finally caught her, Old Mother was nothing like twelve feet in length, though she was definitely the biggest pike any of us had ever seen. Pikes don't ever grow as long as that, I tell myself, and what I saw – or thought I saw – on the river that day was easily as big as one of the crocodiles that Johnny Weissmuller used to wrestle with on Saturday mornings at the Majestic.

But that's an adult reasoning. In those days there were no such barriers to belief as logic or realism. We saw what we saw, and sometimes, if what we saw made adults laugh, who was to say where the truth lay? In my heart I know I saw a monster that day, something as old and cunning as the river itself, something no-one could ever catch. She took Jeannette Gaudin. She took Tomas Leibniz. She almost took me.

PART FOUR

La Mauvaise Réputation

1

'Clean and gut the anchovies and rub inside and out with salt. Fill each one generously with rock salt and branches of *salicorne*. Place in the barrel *with the heads facing upwards* and cover with salt by layers.'

Another affectation. When you opened the barrel they would be there, standing on their tails in the gleaming grey salt, staring in mute fishy appeal. Remove what is needed for the day's cooking and pack the rest into place with more salt and *salicorne*. In the darkness of the cellar they looked desperate, like drowning children in a well.

Snip off that thought quickly, like the head of a flower.

My mother writes in blue ink, the script neat and slanting. Beneath it she has added something in a more careless hand, but it's in bilini-enverlini, an exotic scrawl in red grease pencil, like lipstick: 'Toulini fonini nislipni' – out of pills.

She'd had them since the beginning of the war, using them at first with care, once a month or less, then more recklessly as that strange summer advanced and she smelt oranges all the time.

'Y does his best to help,' she wrote raggedly. 'It gives both of us a little relief. He gets the pills from La Rép, from a man Hourias knows there. Other comforts, too, I guess. I know better than to ask. He isn't made of stone, after all. Not like me. I try not to care. It's pointless. He is discreet. I should be grateful. He looks after me in his way, but it's useless. We are divided. He lives in the light. The thought of my suffering dismays him. I know this, and still I hate him for being what he is.'

Then, later, after my father's death:

'Out of pills. The German says he can get some more, but he doesn't come. It's a kind of madness. I would sell my children for a night's sleep.'

This last entry, unusually, has a date. That's how I know. She was jealous with her pills, hiding the bottle away at the bottom of a drawer in her room. Sometimes she would take the bottle out and turn it over. It was brown glass, the label still showing a few barely legible words in German.

Out of pills.

That was the night of the dance, the night of the last orange.

2

'Hey, *Backfisch*, almost forgot.' Turning, he threw it carelessly, like a boy pitching a ball, to see if I'd catch. He was like that, pretending to forget, teasing me, risking the prize in the murky Loire if I was slow or clumsy. 'Your favourite.'

I caught it easily, left-handed, and grinned.

'Tell the others to come by La Mauvaise Réputation tonight.' Winked, eyes glinting cat-green with mischief. 'Might be some fun.'

Of course, Mother would never have let us go out at night. Though the curfew remained largely unenforceable in the remoter villages such as ours, there were other dangers. Night hid more illicit goings-on than we could guess, and by then a number of off-duty Germans had occasionally taken to stopping by at the café for drinks. Apparently they liked to get out of Angers and away from the suspicious eyes of the SS. In the course of our meetings Tomas had mentioned this, and sometimes I heard the sounds of motorbikes on the distant road and thought of him riding home. I saw him clearly in my mind's eye, hair blown back by the wind, the moonlight shining on his face and the cold white sweep of the Loire. The motorbike rider might have been anyone, of course, but I always thought of Tomas.

Today, however, was different. Emboldened, perhaps, by our secret time together, anything seemed possible. Slinging his uniform jacket over his shoulders, Tomas

215

waved lazily as he drove off, kicking up a cloud of yellow Loire dust beneath his wheels, and suddenly my heart swelled unbearably. Loss flooded through me in a hot-cold wash and I ran after him, tasting his dust, waving my arms for long after his bike vanished down the Angers road, tears beginning to crawl pink channels across my face's mud-mask.

It wasn't enough.

I'd had my day, my one perfect day, and already my heart was boiling with rage and dissatisfaction. I clocked the sun. Four hours. An impossible time, a whole afternoon, and yet it wasn't enough. I wanted more. More. The discovery of this new appetite within me made me bite my lips in desperation; the memory of the brief contact between us still burning on my hand. Several times I lifted my palm to my lips and kissed the burning place his skin had left. I lingered over his words as if they were poetry. I relived every precious moment to myself, with growing disbelief, as on winter mornings I try to recall the summer. But it is an appetite that no amount of feeding can satisfy. I wanted to see him again, that day, that minute. I had wild thoughts of us running away together, of living in the forest away from people, of building him a tree-house and eating mushrooms and wild strawberries and chestnuts until the war was over.

They found me at the Lookout Post, the orange in one hand, lying on my back and staring into the autumn canopy.

'S-s-said she'd b-be here,' said Paul – he always stammered badly when Reine was there. 'S-s-saw her g-oing into the w-woods when I was fishing.' He looked shy and awkward beside Cassis, conscious of his scruffy blue dungarees – cut-down from one of his uncle's overalls – and his bare feet in their wooden clogs. His old dog, Malabar, was with him, tied with a length of green gardening twine. Cassis and Reine wore their school clothes, and Reinette's hair was tied with a yellow silk ribbon. I always wondered why

216

Paul dressed so shabbily when his mother was a seamstress.

'Are you all right?' Cassis' voice was sharp with anxiety. 'When you didn't come home, I thought—' He cast a quick, dark look at Paul, then one of warning to me. '*You know who* hasn't been here, has he?' he whispered, clearly wishing that Paul would leave.

I nodded. Cassis made a gesture of annoyance. 'What did I tell you?' he said in a low, furious voice. 'What did I say? Never be alone with—' Another glance at Paul. 'Anyway, we'd better be going home now,' he said in a louder voice. 'Mother will be starting to get worried, and she's making a *pavé*. You'd better hurry up and—'

But Paul was looking at the orange in my hand.

'You g-got another un,' he said in his slow, curious way.

Cassis gave me a look of disgust – *why couldn't you hide it, stupid? Now we'll have to share it with him*.

I hesitated. Sharing was not in my plan. I needed the orange for tonight. And yet I could see Paul was already curious. Ready to talk.

'I'll give you some if you don't tell,' I said at last.

'Where's it f-from?'

'Swapped it down the market,' I said glibly. 'For some sugar and parachute silk. Mother doesn't know.'

Paul nodded, then looked shyly at Reine. 'We could all sh-share it now,' he said tentatively. 'I've gotta knife.'

'Give it to me,' I said.

'I'll do it,' said Cassis at once.

'No, it's mine,' I said. 'Let me.'

I was thinking rapidly. Of course I might be able to retrieve some of the orange peel, but I didn't want Cassis to suspect.

I turned my back on them to divide the orange, slicing carefully to avoid cutting my hand. Cutting quarters would have been easy – slice down the

217

middle, then slice again – but this time I needed to cut an extra piece, large enough for my purpose but too small to be immediately noticeable as missing from the rest, a piece I could slip into my pocket for later. As I sliced it I saw that Tomas' gift was a Seville blood orange, a *sanguine*, and for an instant I was transfixed by the red juice dripping from my fingers.

'Hurry up, clumsy,' said Cassis impatiently. 'How long does it take to cut an orange into quarters?'

'I'm trying,' I snapped. 'The skin's tough.'

'L-let m-m-m-' Paul made a move towards me, and for a second I was sure he'd seen it, the fifth piece, no more than a sliver really, before I slid it into my sleeve and out of sight.

'It's all right,' I said. 'I've done it now.'

The pieces were uneven. I had done the best I could, but still there was one quarter which was noticeably bigger than the rest, and another which was very small. I took the small piece. I noticed Paul gave the large one to Reine.

Cassis watched in disgust. 'I told you you should have let me do it,' he said. 'Mine isn't a proper quarter. You're so clumsy, 'Boise.'

I sucked my piece of orange in silence. After a while Cassis stopped grumbling and ate his. I saw Paul watching me with an odd expression, but he didn't say anything.

We threw our pieces of peel into the river. I did manage to save one piece of mine in my mouth, but I threw in the rest, uneasily aware of Cassis' eyes on me, and was relieved to see him relax a little. I wondered what he might have suspected. I transferred the bitten-off piece of peel into my pocket with the illicit fifth quarter, feeling pleased. I just hoped it would be enough.

I showed the others how to clean their hands and mouths with mint and fennel and to rub under their fingernails with mud to hide the orange-peel stain, then we went home through the fields to where

Mother, singing tonelessly to herself in the kitchen, was preparing dinner.

Sweat the onion and shallots in olive oil with some fresh rosemary, mushrooms and a small leek. Add a handful of dried tomatoes, basil and thyme. Cut four anchovies lengthways and place in the pan. Leave for five minutes.

''Boise, some anchovies from the barrel. Four big ones.'

I went down to the cellar with a dish and the wooden tongs so that the salt would not crack open the skin of my palms. I brought out the fish, then the orange bag in its protective jar. I added the new piece of orange, squeezing the oil and juice onto the old peel to revive it, then chopped what was left with my penknife and tied it into the bag. The scent was immediate and pungent. I sealed the bag back into the jar, rubbed the glass clean of salt and placed it in my apron pocket so that no more of the precious scent could escape. I touched my palms briefly against the salted fish so that Mother would be deceived.

Add a cupful of white wine and the parboiled, floury potatoes. Add cooking scraps – bacon rind, leftover meat or fish – and a tablespoon of oil. Cook on a very low heat for ten minutes without stirring or lifting the lid.

I could hear her singing to herself in the kitchen. She had a monotonous, rather grating voice, which rose and fell at intervals.

'Add the raw unsoaked millet' – hnn hnnn – 'and turn off the heat. Leave covered for' – hnn hnnn – 'ten minutes without stirring or' – hnnnn – 'until the juices have been absorbed. Press into a shallow dish' – hnn hnn hnnn – 'brush with oil and bake until crisp.'

With a keen eye to what was happening in the kitchen I put the orange bag under the heating pipes for the last time.

I waited.

For a time I was sure it wasn't going to work. Mother stayed in the kitchen, humming to herself in that tuneless, dogged way. As well as the *pavé* there was also a cake black with berries and bowls of green salad and tomatoes. Almost a celebration dinner, though what we had to celebrate I couldn't guess. Mother was like that sometimes; on good days there would be a feast, and on bad we would make do with cold pancakes and a smear of *rillettes*. Today she seemed almost fey, her hair falling from its usually severe scraped-back style into casual tendrils, her face moist and pink with the heat of the fire. There was a feverish quality about her, in the way she spoke to us, the quick, breathless hug she gave Reine as she came in – a rarity almost as unusual as her brief episodes of violence – the tone in her voice, the way her hands moved in the basin, on the chopping board, with quick, nervous flutterings of the fingers.

Out of pills.

A crease between her eyes, creases around her mouth, her strained, effortful smile. She looked at me as I handed her the anchovies and gave a smile of peculiar sweetness, a smile which, a month ago, a day ago, might almost have softened my heart.

''Boise.'

I thought of Tomas sitting by the river bank. I thought of the thing I had seen, the oil-slick, monstrous beauty of its flank against the water. *I wish, I wish* . . . he'd be there tonight, I told myself, at La Mauvaise Réputation, jacket slung casually across a chair back. I imagined myself grown suddenly movie-star beautiful and refined, silk dress billowing out behind me, everyone staring. *I wish, I wish*. If I'd only had my rod . . .

My mother was staring at me with that expression of strange, almost embarrassing vulnerability.

''Boise?' she repeated. 'Are you all right? Do you feel ill?'

220

I shook my head in silence. The wave of self-hatred which struck me was whiplash-quick, a revelation. *I wish, I wish.* I made my face sullen. *Tomas. Only you. For ever.*

'I've got to check my traps,' I told her in my dead voice. 'I won't be long.'

''Boise!' I heard her call after me, but I ignored her. I ran to the river, checked each trap twice, certain that *this* time, *this* time, when I needed that wish . . .

All empty. I threw the small-fry – bleaks; gudgeons; flat, small-snouted eels – back into the river in sudden, searing rage.

'*Where are you?*' I screeched across the silent water. '*Where are you, you sly old bitch?*'

Below my feet the dim Loire flowed unmoved, brown and mocking. *I wish, I wish.* I picked up a stone from the bank and threw it as far as I could, wrenching my shoulder painfully.

'*Where are you? Where are you hiding?*' My voice sounded hoarse and shrill, like my mother's. The air sizzled with my fury. '*Come out and show yourself! Dare you! DARE YOU!*'

Nothing. Nothing but the brown snaky river and the sandbanks lying half drowned in the failing light. My throat felt raw and scraped. Tears stung the corners of my eyes like wasps.

'I know you can hear me,' I said in a low voice. 'I know you're there.' The river seemed to agree with me. I could hear the silky sounds of the water against the bank at my feet.

'I know you're there,' I said again, almost caressingly. Everything seemed to be listening to me now, the trees with their turning leaves, the water, the burnt autumn grass.

'You know what I want, don't you?' Again that voice which sounded like someone else's. That adult, seductive voice. 'You know.'

I thought of Jeannette Gaudin then and the water-snake, of the long brown bodies hanging up against the

Standing Stones and the feeling I'd had earlier that summer a million years ago, the *conviction*. It was an abomination, a monster. No-one could make a pact with a monster.

I wish. I wish.

I wondered whether Jeannette had stood where I was now, barefoot and looking over the water. What did she wish for? A new dress? A doll to play with? Something else?

White cross. 'Beloved Daughter'. Suddenly it didn't seem such a terrible thing to be dead and beloved, a plaster angel at your head and silence.

I wish. I wish.

'I'd throw you back,' I whispered slyly. 'You know I would.'

For a second I thought I saw something, bristle-black in the water, a shining silent something like a mine, all teeth and metal. But it was just my imagination.

'I would,' I repeated softly. 'I'd throw you back.'

But if it had been there at all, it wasn't now. Beside me a frog belched suddenly, absurdly. It was getting cold. I turned and went back across the fields the way I'd come, picking a few ears of corn to excuse my late arrival.

After a while I began to smell the *pavé* cooking, and I quickened my step.

3

'I've lost her. I'm losing them all.'

It's there in my mother's album, opposite a recipe for blackberry cake. Tiny migraine letters in black ink, the lines crossed and recrossed, as if even the code in which she writes is not enough to hide the fear she hides from us and from herself.

She looked at me today as if I wasn't there. I wanted so hard to take her in my arms, but she's grown so much and I'm afraid of her eyes. Only R-C keeps a little softness but B doesn't feel like my child any more. My mistake was thinking children were like trees. Prune them back and they'll grow sweeter. Not true. Not true. When Y died I made them grow up too fast. I didn't want them to be children. Now they're harder than me. Like animals. My fault. I made them that way. Oranges in the house again tonight, but no-one smells them but me. My head aches. If only she could put her hand on my forehead. No more pills. The German says he can get some more, but he doesn't come. 'Boise. Late home tonight. Like me, divided.

It sounds like gibberish, but her voice in my mind is suddenly very clear. It is sharp and plaintive, the voice of a woman hanging on to her sanity with every bit of her strength.

'The German says he can get some more, but he doesn't come.'

Oh, Mother. If only I'd known.

4

Paul and I read through the album little by little during those lengthening nights. I deciphered the code whilst he wrote down and cross-referenced everything by means of small cards, trying to put events in sequence. He never commented, not even when I passed over certain sections without telling him why. We averaged two or three pages a night, not a great deal, but by October we had covered almost half the album. For some reason it seemed a less arduous task than when I'd tried it alone, and we would often sit late into the night remembering the old days of the Lookout Post and the rituals at the Standing Stones, the good days before Tomas. Once or twice I even came close to telling him the truth, but I always stopped just in time.

No, Paul mustn't know.

My mother's album was only one story, one with which he was already partly familiar. But the story *behind* the album . . . I looked at him as we sat together, the bottle of Cointreau between us and the copper pot of coffee simmering on the stove behind. Red light from the fire lit his face and outlined his old yellow moustache in flame. He caught me looking at him – seems he does that more and more nowadays – and smiled.

And it wasn't so much the smile as something *behind* the smile – a look, a kind of searching, wry look – which made my heart beat faster and my face flush with more than the heat of the fire. If I told him, I thought suddenly to myself, that look would go from his face. I couldn't tell him. Not ever.

5

When I came in the others were already at the table. Mother greeted me with her strange, forced cheeriness, but I could tell she was at the end of her tether. The smell of orange stung my sensitized nostrils. I watched her intently. We ate in silence.

The celebration dinner was heavy, like eating clay, and my stomach rebelled against it. I pushed food about on my plate until I was sure she was looking elsewhere, then transferred it into my apron pocket for later disposal. I need not have worried. In the state she was in, I don't think she would have noticed if I'd thrown it against the wall.

'I smell oranges.' Her voice was brittle with desperation. 'Have any of you brought oranges into the house?'

Silence. We looked at her blankly, expectant.

'Well? Have you? Brought oranges?' Voice rising now, a plea, an accusation.

Reine looked at me suddenly, guiltily.

'Of course not.' I made my voice flat and sullen. 'Where would we get oranges?'

'I don't know.' Her eyes were narrow with suspicion. 'The Germans, perhaps. How should I know what you do all day?'

This was so close to the truth that for a moment I was startled, but I didn't let it show. I gave a shrug, very conscious of Reinette watching me. I shot her a warning look – *Give the game away, would you?*

Reinette turned back to her cake. I kept on watching my mother, staring her out. She was better at it than Cassis, her eyes expressionless as sloes. Then she stood up abruptly, almost knocking over her plate and half dragging the tablecloth with her.

'What are you staring at now?' she cried at me, stabbing at the air with her hands. 'What are you staring at, damn you? What is there to see?'

I gave another shrug. 'Nothing.'

'That isn't true.' Voice like a bird's, sharp and precise as a woodpecker's beak. 'You're always staring at me. Staring. What at? Thinking what, you little bitch?'

I could smell her distress and fear, and my heart swelled with victory. Her eyes dropped from mine. I did it, I thought. I did it. I won.

She knew it, too. She looked at me for another few seconds, but the battle was lost. I gave a tiny smile which only she could see. Her hand crept to her temple in the old gesture of helplessness. 'I have a headache,' she said with difficulty. 'I'm going to lie down.'

'Good idea,' I said tonelessly.

'Don't forget to wash the plates,' she said, but it was only noise. She knew she'd lost. 'No putting them away still wet. No leaving—' Then she broke off, silent, staring into space for half a minute. A statue, frozen mid-movement, mouth half-open. The rest of the sentence hung between us for an uneasy half minute.

'Plates on the draining board all night,' she finished at last, and stumbled off down the passageway, pausing once to check the bathroom, where there were no more pills.

We – Cassis, Reinette and I – looked at each other.

'Tomas said to meet him at La Mauvaise Réputation tonight,' I told the others. 'He said there might be some fun.'

Cassis looked at me. 'How did you do that?' he said.

'Do what?' I echoed.

'You know.' His voice was low and urgent, almost fearful. In that moment he seemed to have lost all authority over us. I was the leader now, the one to whom the rest would look for guidance. The strange thing was that, though I realized this at once, I felt scarcely any satisfaction. There were other things on my mind.

I ignored his question. 'We'll wait until she's asleep,' I decided, 'an hour, maybe two at the most, then we'll make our way across the fields. No-one will see us. We can hide out in the alley and watch out for him.'

Reinette's eyes lit up, but Cassis looked sceptical. 'What for?' he asked at last. 'What are we going to do when we get there? We've got nothing to tell him, and he already left the film magazines—'

I glared at him. 'Magazines,' I snapped. 'Is that all you ever think about?'

Cassis looked sullen. 'He said something interesting might happen,' I said. 'Aren't you curious?'

'Not really. It mightn't be safe. You know what Mother—'

'You're just chicken,' I said fiercely.

'I'm not!' He was, though. I could see it in his eyes.

'Chicken.'

'I just don't see the point in—'

'Dare you,' I said.

Silence. Cassis gave a sudden, pleading look at Reine. I began to stare him out. He held my gaze for a second or two, then turned away.

'Baby stuff,' he said with mock indifference.

'*Double* dare you.'

Cassis made a furious gesture of helplessness and defeat. 'Oh, all right, but I tell you, it's going to be a pointless waste of time.'

I laughed in triumph.

6

The Café de la Mauvaise Réputation – La Rép to its
regulars. wooden floor, polished bar with an old piano
standing beside it – of course, nowadays half the keys
are missing and there's a planter of geraniums where
the works used to be – a row of bottles – no optics in
those days – and glasses hanging on hooks under and
around the bar. The sign has been replaced by a blue
neon thing and there are machines and a jukebox, but
in those days there was nothing but the piano and a
few tables, which you could move against the walls if
anyone happened to want to dance.

Raphaël could play when he wanted to, and
occasionally someone – one of the women, Colette
Gaudin or Agnès Petit – might sing. No-one had
a record player in those days, and the radio was
forbidden, but the café was said to be a lively place in
the evenings, and we sometimes heard music from
there even across the fields if the wind was blowing
in the right direction. That was where Julien Lecoz
lost his south pasture at cards – rumour had it that
he'd bet his wife as well, but no-one would take him
up on the offer – and it was the second home of the
local drunks, who would sit on the *terrasse* smoking
or playing *pétanque* by the steps. Paul's father was
there often, much to our mother's disapproval, and
though I never saw him drunk, he never seemed to be
quite sober either, smiling vaguely at passers-by and
showing his big, square yellow dentures. It was a place

where we never went. We were territorial creatures and regarded certain places as peculiarly our own, though others belonged to the village, the adults, places of mystery or indifference – the church, the post office where Michelle Hourias sorted the mail and gossiped over the counter, the little school where we had spent our earliest years but which now stayed boarded-up.

La Mauvaise Réputation.

We stayed away partly because our mother told us to. She had a peculiar hatred of drunkenness, dirt and loose-living, and the place epitomized all of these to her. Though she was not a churchgoer, she retained an almost puritan view of life, believing in hard work, a clean house and polite, well-mannered children. When she had to walk past the place she would do so with her head lowered protectively, a scarf crossed at her thin chest, her mouth pursed against the sounds of music and laughter from within. Strange that such a woman, such a self-controlled, order-loving woman, should have fallen victim to drug addiction.

'Like the clock,' she writes in her album, 'I am divided. When the moon rises I am not myself.' She went to her room so that we would not see her change.

It was a shock to me to realize, after reading those secret passages in the album, that she went regularly to La Mauvaise Réputation. Once a week or more she went there, after dark and in secret, hating every moment and hating herself for her need. She did not drink. No. Why should she when there were dozens of bottles of cider or *prunelle* or even *calva* from her native Brittany in the cellar? Drunkenness, she told us once in a rare moment of confidence, is a sin against the fruit, the tree, the wine itself. It is an outrage, an abuse, just as rape is an abuse of the act of love. She flushed then, turning away gruffly – 'Reine-Claude, the oil and some basil, quickly!' – but the thought stayed with me. Wine, distilled and nurtured from bud into fruit, and then through all the processes that make it what it is, deserves better than to be guzzled by some sot with a headful of nonsense. It deserves reverence, joy, gentleness.

Oh, she understood wine, my mother. She understood the sweetening process, the fermentation, the seething and mellowing of life in the bottle, the darkening, the slow transformations, the birth of a new vintage in a bouquet of aromas, like a magician's bunch of paper flowers. If only she'd had time and patience for us. A child is not a fruit tree. She understood that too late. There is no recipe to take a child into sweet, safe adulthood. She should have known that.

Of course, drugs are still sold in La Mauvaise Réputation. Even I know that; I'm not so old that I can't recognize the sweet jazzy reek of pot over the haze of beer and frying. God knows I smelled it often enough across the road from the snack wagon. I've got a nose, even if that idiot Ramondin hasn't, and the air was yellow with it some nights, when the bikers came. Recreational drugs, they call them nowadays, and give them fancy names. But there wasn't really any such thing in Les Laveuses in those days. The jazz clubs of St Germain-des-Prés were still a decade away, and besides, they never really reached us, not even in the Sixties. No, my mother went to La Mauvaise Réputation out of need, simple need, because that was where most of the trading took place. Black-market trading, cloth and shoes and less innocuous things like knives, guns and ammunition. Everything had its place at La Rép, cigarettes and brandy and picture postcards of naked women, nylon stockings and lace underwear for Colette and Agnès, who wore their hair loose and reddened their cheekbones with old-fashioned rouge so they looked like Dutch dolls, one high crimson spot on each cheek and a round bud on the lips, like Lillian Gish.

Round the back, the secret societies, the communists, the malcontents, the would-bes and the

232

heroes made plans. In the bar, the talkers held court and passed little packages to each other, or whispered in undertones and drank to future undertakings. In the woods, a few wore soot on their faces and cycled to meetings in Angers, braving the curfew. Sometimes – very infrequently – you could hear shots from the other side of the river.

How Mother must have hated it.

But that was where she got the pills. She wrote it all in her album – pills for her migraines, morphine from the hospital, three at a time at first, and then six, ten, twelve, twenty. Her suppliers varied. At first it was Philippe Hourias. Julien Lecoz knew someone, a voluntary worker. Agnès Petit had a cousin, a friend of a friend in Paris. Guilherm Ramondin, the one with the wooden leg, could be persuaded to exchange some of his own medication for wine or money. Small packages – a couple of tablets in a twist of paper, an ampoule and a syringe, a blister of pills – anything with a morphine base. Of course, there was no getting anything from the doctor. In any case, the nearest was in Angers, and all the supplies were needed to treat our soldiers. After her own supplies ran out, she scrounged, sold and swapped. She kept the list in her album.

March 2, 1942. Guilherm Ramondin, 4 tablets morphine against 12 eggs.
March 16, 1942. Françoise Petit, 3 tablets morphine against bottle calvados.

She sold her jewellery – the single row of pearls she is wearing in her wedding photo, her rings, the diamond-chip earrings she had from her mother – in Angers. She was ingenious. Almost as much as Tomas, in her way, though she was always fair in her dealings. With a little ingenuity, she managed.

Then the Germans came.

One or two at a time at first. Some in uniform, some

out. The bar fell silent at their entrance, but they made up for that by their merriment, their laughter, the rounds they drank, standing up unsteady at closing time, with a smile to Colette or Agnès and a careless handful of coins thrown onto the counter. Sometimes they brought women. We never recognized them, the fur-collared girls from town. Girls with nylon stockings and sheer dresses and hair rolled into movie-star confections bristling with hairgrips, and plucked-thin eyebrows and red-black gleaming lips with white teeth, and drooping, long-fingered hands over wine-glasses. They only came at night, on the backs of the Germans' motorcycles, squealing with shrill delight as they sped through the night, hair flying. Four women, four Germans. Every now and again the women changed, but the Germans stayed the same.

She writes about them in her album, her first glimpse of them.

Filthy Boche and their whores. Looked at me in my overall, smiled behind their hands. I'd like to kill them. Looked at them watching me and I felt old. Ugly. Only one has kind eyes. The girl beside him bored him, I could tell. Cheap, stupid girl, stocking seams drawn on in grease pencil. I could almost feel sorry for her. But he smiled at me. Had to bite my tongue to stop myself from smiling back.

Of course, I have no proof that it was Tomas she wrote about. It might have been anyone in those few scrawled lines. There is no description, nothing to suggest it might have been him, and yet somehow I am certain that it was. Only Tomas could have made her feel that way. Only Tomas could have made me feel that way.

It's all in the album. You can read it if you want to, if you know where to look. There is no sequence to events. Other than with the details of her secret transactions there are scarcely any dates. But she was meticulous in her fashion. She described La Rép as it was so clearly that, reading it years later, I felt a thickness in my throat. The noise, music, smoke, beer, voices raised in laughter or drunken ribaldry. No wonder we were not allowed near the place. She was too ashamed of her own involvement, too afraid of what we might learn from one of the regulars.

On the night we crept over there we were to be disappointed. We had imagined a secret den of adult vices. I'd expected naked dancers, women with rubies in their navels and hair down to their waists. Cassis, still feigning indifference, had seen Resistance fighters in his mind's eye, black-clad guerrillas with hard eyes beneath their night camouflage. Reinette imagined herself, rouged and pomaded, with a fur stole around her shoulders, sipping Martinis. But that night, looking through the murky window, there seemed to be nothing of interest. Only a few old men at tables, a backgammon board, a pack of cards, the old piano and Agnès with her parachute-silk blouse open to the third button, leaning against it and singing. It was still early. Tomas had not yet arrived.

May 9, a German soldier (Bavarian), 12 high-dosage morphine tablets against one chicken, a sack of sugar and a side of bacon. May 25, German soldier (fat neck), 16 high-dose morphine tablets against 1 bottle *calva*, a sack of flour, a packet of coffee, 6 jars of preserves.

Then a last entry, the date deliberately vague:

September, T/L, bottle 30 high-dose morphine tablets.

For the first time she fails to write her own contribution to the deal. Perhaps it is merely carelessness; the writing is barely legible, scrawled in a hurry. Perhaps this time she has paid more than she cares to write. What was the price? Thirty tablets must have seemed a prize of almost unimagined riches. No need to return to La Rép for a while. No more bartering with drunken louts like Julien Lecoz. I imagine she must have paid a great deal for the peace of mind those thirty tablets gave her. What exactly did she pay for that peace of mind? Information? Something else?

We waited in what later became the car park. In those days it was no more than a dumping area for rubbish, where the bins were kept and where deliveries – barrels of beer or occasionally merchandise of a more illicit nature – were made. A wall ran halfway along the back of the building, then disappeared in a tangle of elders and blackberry bushes. The back door was open – even in October it was stifling hot – and a bright yellow light fanned across the ground from the taproom. We sat on the wall, ready to drop down onto the other side if anyone came too near, and waited.

7

As I said, it hasn't changed much. A few lights, some machines, more people, but still the same Mauvaise Réputation, the same people with different hairstyles, the same faces. Going in there today you might almost imagine yourself back there, with the old sots and the young men with their girls in tow and the smell of beer and perfume and cigarettes over everything.

I went there myself, you know, when the snack wagon came. Paul and I hid, just as Cassis, Reine and I hid on the night of the dance, in the car park. Of course, there were cars in it then. It was cold, too, and raining. The elders and the blackberry tangle have gone, and now there's only tarmac and a new wall behind which lovers go, or drunks when they want to piss. We were looking out for Dessanges, our Luc with his sharp, handsome face, but waiting there in the dark with the new neon sign going blink-blink against the wet tarmac, I might have been nine again, and Tomas in the back room with a girl on each arm – funny tricks time plays on you. There was a double row of motor-bikes in the car park, gleaming wetly.

It was eleven o'clock. I felt suddenly stupid, leaning against the new concrete wall like a silly girl spying on the adults, the world's oldest nine-year-old, with Paul next to me and his old dog in tow on its inevitable leash of twine. Stupid and beaten, two old people watching a bar from the dark. For what? A burst of music from the jukebox – nothing I could identify.

Even the instruments are alien nowadays, electronic things with no need for mouths or fingers to play them. A girl's laugh, high and unpleasant. For a moment the door fanned open and we saw him clearly, a girl on each arm. He was wearing a leather jacket which must have cost 2,000 francs or more in a Paris shop. The girls were silky and red-mouthed and very young in their thin-strapped dresses. I felt a sudden cold despair.

'Look at us.' I realized that my hair was wet, my fingers stiff as sticks. 'James Bond and Mata Hari. Let's go home.'

Paul looked at me in that reflective way he has. Anyone else might not have seen the intelligence in his eyes, but I did. Silently, he took my hand between his. His hands felt comfortingly warm, and I could feel the rows of callouses on his palms.

'Don't give up,' he said.

I shrugged. 'We're doing no good here,' I said. 'Just making fools of ourselves. Face it, Paul, we're never going to get the better of Dessanges, so we might as well get that into our thick, stubborn heads right now. I mean—'

'No, you don't.' His voice was slow and almost amused. 'You never give up, Framboise. You never did.'

Patience. His patience, kind and stubborn enough to wait out a lifetime.

'That was then,' I told him without meeting his eyes.

'You haven't changed so much, Framboise.'

Maybe that's true. There's something in me still, something hard and not necessarily good. I still feel it occasionally, a hard cold something, like a stone inside a clenched fist. I always had it, even in the old days, something mean and dogged and just clever enough to hang on for as long as it took to win. As if Old Mother had somehow got inside me that day, and, going for the heart, had instead been swallowed by that inner mouth of mine. A fossil fish inside a fist of stone – I saw a picture of one once in one of Ricot's dinosaur books – eating itself in its stubborn spite.

'Perhaps I ought to change,' I said softly. 'Perhaps I should.'

I think that for a while I really meant it, too. I was tired, you understand. Tired beyond anything. Two months on and we'd tried, God knows, we'd tried everything. We watched Luc, we reasoned with him, we built elaborate fantasies: a bomb under his caravan, a hit man from Paris, a stray shot from a sniper's rifle at the Lookout Post. Oh yes, I could have killed him. My anger exhausted me, but my fear kept me awake throughout the night so that my days were broken glass and my head ached all the time. It was more than simply the fear of exposure; after all, I was Mirabelle Dartigen's daughter. I had her spirit. I cared about the restaurant, but even if the Dessanges put me out of business, even if no-one in Les Laveuses spoke to me ever again, I knew I could fight it out. No, my true fear – kept secret from Paul and barely acknowledged even to myself – was something far darker and more complex. It lurked in the depths of my mind, like Old Mother in her slimy bed, and I prayed no lure would ever tempt it out.

I received two more letters, one from Yannick and one addressed to me in Laure's writing. I read the first with growing unease. In it Yannick was plaintive and cajoling. He had been going through a bad time. Laure didn't understand him, he said. She constantly used his financial dependency as a weapon against him. They had been trying for a child for three years without success, and she blamed him for that, too. She had mentioned divorce.

According to Yannick, the loan of my mother's album would change all that. What Laure needed was something to occupy her mind, a new project. Her career needed a boost. Yannick knew I couldn't be so heartless as to refuse.

I burnt the second letter unopened. Perhaps it was

the memory of Noisette's flat, factual notes from Canada, but I found my nephew's confidences pitiful and embarrassing. I did not want to know any more. Undaunted, Paul and I prepared for a final siege.

This was to be our last hope. I'm not sure what we expected; it was only sheer obstinacy that kept us going. Perhaps I still needed to win, just as I had that last summer at Les Laveuses. Perhaps it was my mother's harsh, unreasonable spirit in me, refusing to be beaten. Give up now, I told myself, and her sacrifice would have been for nothing. I fought for both of us, and thought that even my mother might have been proud.

I had never imagined that Paul would prove such an invaluable support. Watching the café had been his idea, just as it was he who discovered the Dessanges address on the back of the snack wagon. I had come to rely heavily on Paul in those months, and to trust his judgement. We often sat guard together, a blanket tucked over our feet as the nights grew colder, a pot of coffee and a couple of glasses of Cointreau between us. In small ways, he made himself indispensable. He peeled vegetables for the evening's cooking, brought in firewood and gutted fish. Even though visitors to Crêpe Framboise were rare – I stopped opening altogether midweek, and even at weekends the presence of the snack wagon discouraged all but the most determined customers – he would keep watch in the restaurant, wash dishes and mop floors. And nearly always in silence, the comfortable silence of long intimacy, the simple silence of friendship.

'Don't change,' he said at last.

I'd turned to go, but he kept my hand in his and I couldn't pull away. I could see raindrops gleaming on his beret and against his moustache.

'I think I might have got something,' said Paul.

'What?' My voice was rough with weariness. All I wanted to do was lie down and sleep. 'For God's sake, what now?'

'It might be nothing.' Careful now, with a slowness that made me want to scream in frustration. 'Wait here. Just want to, you know, check something.'

'What, here?' I almost shrieked. 'Paul, you just wait a—'

But he was already gone, moving with a poacher's speed and silence towards the taproom door. Another second and he was gone.

'*Paul!*' I hissed furiously. 'Paul! Don't think I'm going to wait out here for you! Damn you, Paul!'

But I did. As the rain soaked into the collar of my good autumn coat, creeping slowly into my hair and dribbling cold fingerlings between my breasts, I had plenty of time to realize that no, I hadn't really changed all that much after all.

8

Cassis, Reinette and I had been waiting for over an hour when they arrived. Once we were outside La Rép, Cassis shed all pretence at indifference and watched avidly through the crack in the doorway, pushing us back when we tried to take our turns. My interest was limited. Until Tomas arrived there could be nothing much to see, after all. But Reine was persistent.

'I want to see,' she wailed. 'Cassis, you mean thing, I want to *see*!'

'There's nothing there,' I told her impatiently. 'Nothing but old men at tables and those two tarts with their mouths painted red.' I'd only caught a glimpse at the time, but how I remember. Agnès at the piano and Colette with a tight green wrap-over cardigan, revealing thrusting breasts like cannon shells. I still remember where everyone was, Martin and Jean-Marie Dupré playing cards with Philippe Hourias, fleecing him, as usual, by all appearances; Henri Lemaître sitting by the bar with an everlasting *demi* and an eye on the ladies; François Ramondin and Arthur Lecoz, Julien's cousin, discussing something furtive in a corner with Julien Lanicen and Auguste Truriand, and old Gustave Beauchamp on his own by the window, beret pulled down over his hairy ears and a stub of a pipe jammed between his lips. I remember them all. With a struggle I can see Philippe's cloth cap lying on the bar next to him, I can smell the tobacco smoke – by then the precious tobacco was heavily laced with dandelion leaves and stank like a green-stick fire – and the smell of chicory coffee. The scene has the stillness of a tableau, the golden glow of nostalgia overridden by the dark-red flare of burning. Oh, I remember. I only wish I didn't.

When at last they came, we were stiff and bad-tempered from crouching against the wall and Reinette was almost in tears. Cassis had been watching through the doorway and we had found a place under one of the smeary windows where we could just distinguish shapes moving dimly in the smoky light. It was I who heard them first, the distant sound of motorbikes getting closer on the Angers road, then blatting down the dirt track with a muffled series of small explosions. Four bikes. I suppose we should have expected the women. If we had read Mother's album we would certainly have known, but we were profoundly innocent in spite of everything, and the reality shocked us a little. I suppose it was because, as they entered the bar, we could see that these were real women – tight twinsets, fake pearls, one carrying her pointed high-heeled shoes in one hand, the other fumbling in her handbag for a compact – not especially pretty and not even very young. I'd expected glamour. But these were only ordinary women, like my mother, sharp-faced, hair held back with metal grips, backs arched to an impossible camber by those agonizing shoes. Three ordinary women.

Reinette was gaping.

'Look at her shoes!' Her face, pressed against the smeared glass, was pink with delight and admiration. I realized that she and I were seeing different things, that my sister still saw movie-star glamour in the nylon stockings, fur collars, crocodile handbags, fluffy ostrich feathers, diamond-cluster earrings and elaborate hairstyles. For the next minute she continued to murmur to herself in tones of ecstasy. 'Look at her hat! Ohhh! Her dress! *Ohh!*'

Cassis and I both ignored her. My brother was

243

studying the boxes which had been brought on the back of the fourth motorbike. I was watching Tomas.

He stood slightly aside from the rest, one elbow on the bar. I saw him say something to Raphaël, who began to draw glasses of beer. Heinemann, Schwartz and Hauer settled themselves at a free table near the window with the women, and I noticed old Gustave drew away to the other side of the room with a sudden expression of disgust, taking his glass with him. The other drinkers behaved much as if they were used to such visits, even nodding to the Germans as they crossed the room, Henri giving the eye to the three women even after they sat down. I felt a sudden, absurd stab of triumph that Tomas remained unescorted. He stayed at the bar for a while, talking with Raphaël, and I had a chance to watch his expressions, his careless gestures, his cap pushed back at a jaunty angle and his uniform jacket left hanging open over his shirt. Raphaël said little, his face wooden and polite. Tomas seemed to sense his dislike, but appeared more amused than angry. He lifted his glass in a slightly mocking way and drank to Raphaël's health. Agnès began to play the piano, a waltzy tune with a brittle plink-plink on one of the high notes where one of the keys had been damaged.

Cassis was getting bored.

'Nothing's happening,' he said in a sullen voice. 'Let's go.'

But Reinette and I were fascinated, she by the lights, the jewellery, the glass, the smoke from an elegant lacquer cigarette holder held between painted nails, and I . . . by Tomas, of course. It didn't matter whether anything was happening. I would have derived equal pleasure from watching him alone and sleeping. There was a charm in watching him in secret like this. I could put my hands on the blurry glass and cup his face between them. I could put my lips to the window and imagine his skin against mine. The other three Germans had been drinking more heavily, fat Schwartz with a woman on his knee, one hand riding her skirt higher and higher up her legs, so that occasionally I was able to catch a glimpse of her brown stocking top and the pinkish garter which held it. I noticed, too, that Henri had moved closer to the group, ogling the women, who screeched like peacocks at every pleasantry. The card players had stopped their game to stare, and Jean-Marie, who seemed to have won the most, moved casually across the bar towards Tomas. Jean-Marie pushed money across the scuffed surface, and Raphaël brought more drinks. Tomas looked once, briefly, behind him at the group of drinkers and smiled. It was a short conversation, and it must have passed unnoticed by anyone who was not deliberately observing Tomas. I imagine that only I saw the transaction, a smile, a mutter, a piece of paper pushed across the bar and quickly hidden in the pocket of Tomas' coat. It didn't surprise me. Tomas traded with everyone. He had that gift. We watched and waited for another hour. I think Cassis dozed. Tomas played the piano for a while as Agnès sang, but I was pleased to see that he showed little interest in the women who fawned and caressed him. I felt proud of him for that. Tomas had better taste.

Everyone had drunk rather a lot at this stage. Raphaël produced a bottle of *fine* and they drank it neat in coffee cups but without the coffee. A card game started between Hauer and the Dupré brothers, with Philippe and Colette watching and drinks as stakes. I could hear their laughter through the glass as Hauer lost again, though there was no ill feeling, as the drinks were already paid for. One of the town women fell over onto her ankle and sat on the floor, giggling, hair falling over her face. Only Gustave Beauchamp remained aloof, refusing an offer of *fine* from Philippe and keeping as far from the Germans as possible. He caught Hauer's eye once and said something under his breath, but as Hauer didn't catch it, he just looked at him coolly for a moment before returning to the game. It happened again though, a few minutes later, and this time Hauer, the only one of the group apart from Tomas who could understand French, stood up, one hand going to the belt where he kept his pistol. The old man glowered at him, his pipe jutting out between his yellow teeth like the barrel of an old tank.

For a moment the tension between them was paralysing. I saw Raphaël make a movement towards Tomas, who was watching the scene with unruffled amusement. A silent exchange passed between them. For a second or two I thought he might let it go on, just to see what would happen. The old man and the German faced each other, Hauer fully two heads taller than Gustave, his blue eyes bloodshot and the veins in his forehead like bloodworms against his brown skin. Tomas looked at Raphaël and smiled. *What do you think?* said the smile. *Seems a pity to step in just when things were getting exciting. What do you think?* Then he stepped forward, almost casually, to his friend, while Raphaël manoeuvred the old man out of harm's way. I don't know what he said, but I think Tomas saved old Gustave's life then, one arm around Hauer's shoulder and the other gesturing vaguely in the direction of the boxes they had brought with them on the back of the fourth motorcycle, the black boxes which had so intrigued Cassis and which now stood against the piano waiting to be opened.

Hauer glared at Tomas for a moment. I could see his eyes narrowed to cuts in his thick cheeks, like slices in a piece of bacon rind. Then Tomas said something else and he relaxed, laughing with a troll's roar above the sudden renewal of sound in the taproom, and the moment was over. Gustave shuffled off into a corner to finish his drink, and everyone went over to the piano where the boxes were waiting.

For a while I could see nothing but bodies. Then I heard a sound, a musical note much clearer and sweeter than that of the piano, and when Hauer turned towards the window he was holding a trumpet.

Schwartz had a drum and Heinemann an instrument I did not recognize – later I found out it was a clarinet, though I'd never seen such a thing before. The women moved aside to allow Agnès to reach the piano, then Tomas moved back into my field of vision with his saxophone slung over one shoulder like an exotic weapon. For a second I thought it *was* a weapon. Beside me, Reinette took in a long, wavery breath of awe. Cassis, his boredom forgotten, leaned forwards, almost pushing me out of the way. It was he who identified the instruments for the rest of us. We had no record player at home, but Cassis was old enough to remember the music we used to listen to on the radio, before such things were forbidden, and he'd seen pictures of Glenn Miller's band in the magazines he loved so much.

'That's a clarinet.' He sounded very young suddenly, like his sister in her awe over the town women's shoes. 'And Tomas has got a saxophone. Oh, where did they *get* them? They must have requisitioned them. Trust Tomas to find . . . Oh, I hope they play them; I hope they—'

I don't know how good they were. I had no point of comparison at all, and we were so flushed with the excitement and wonder of it that anything would have charmed us. I know it seems ridiculous now, but in those days we heard music so seldom – the piano at La Mauvaise Réputation, the church organ for those who went to Mass, Denis Gaudin's violin on 14 July or Mardi Gras, when we danced in the streets. Not so much of that after the war started, of course, but we still did for a while, at least until his violin was eventually requisitioned, like everything else. But now the sounds – exotic, unfamiliar sounds as unlike La Mauvaise Réputation's old piano as opera from barking – arose from the taproom, and we drew closer to the window so as not to miss a note. At first the instruments did little but make odd wailing sounds – I imagine they were tuning up, but we didn't know that

– then they began to play a bright, sharp-sounding tune we did not recognize, though I think it might have been some kind of jazz. A light beat from the drum, a throaty burble from the clarinet, but from Tomas' saxophone a string of bright notes, like Christmas lights, sweetly wailing, harshly whispering, rising and falling above the half discordant whole, like a human voice magically enhanced and containing the entire human range of softness, brashness, coaxing and grief.

Of course, memory is such a subjective thing. Perhaps that's why I feel tears in my eyes as I recall that music, music for the end of the world. In all probability it was nothing like my memory of it – a group of drunken Germans hammering out a few bars of jazz blues on stolen instruments – but for me it was magic. It must have had some effect on the others, too, because in a few minutes they were dancing, some alone and others in pairs, the town women in the arms of the card-playing Dupré brothers, and Philippe and Colette with their faces close together. It was a kind of dance we had never seen before, a gyrating, bump-grinding dance, where ankles went over and tables were shunted by rotating backsides and laughter shrilled over the sounds of the instruments and even Raphaël tapped his foot and forgot to look wooden. I don't know how long it lasted; maybe less than an hour; maybe just a few minutes. I know we joined in, gleeful outside the window, jigging and gyrating like small demons. The music was *hot* and the heat burned off us like alcohol in a flambée, with a sharp, sour smell, and we whooped like Indians, knowing that with the volume of the sound indoors we could make as much noise as we pleased and still remain unheard. Fortunately I was watching the window all the time, because I was the one to see old Gustave leave. I gave the alarm at once, and we dived behind the wall just in time to see him stumbling out into the freshening night, a stooped, dark figure with the glowing bowl of his pipe making a red rose on his face. He was drunk, but not debilitated. In fact, I believe he had heard us, for he stopped alongside the wall and peered sharply into the shadows at the back of the building, one hand pressed against the angle of the porch to stop himself from falling.

'Who's there?' His voice was querulous. 'Is there anybody there?'

We kept quiet behind the wall, stifling giggles.

'Anybody?' repeated old Gustave; then, apparently satisfied, he muttered something barely audible to himself and began to move again. He came as far as the wall, knocked out his pipe against the stones. A spark shower floated down onto our side, and I clapped my hand onto Reinette's mouth to stop her from screaming. Then silence for a moment. We waited, barely daring to breathe. Then we heard the sound of him pissing luxuriantly, endlessly against the wall, giving out a little old man's grunt of satisfaction as he did so. I grinned in the dark. No wonder he'd been so eager to know if anyone was there. Cassis nudged me furiously, one hand over his mouth. Reine made a disgusted face. Then we heard sounds of him fastening his belt buckle again, and a few shuffling steps towards the café. Then nothing. We waited for a few minutes.

'Where is he?' whispered Cassis at last. 'He hasn't gone. We'd have heard him.'

I shrugged. In a sliver of moonlight I could see Cassis' face shining with sweat and anxiety. I gestured towards the wall. 'Look and see,' I mouthed. 'Maybe he's passed out or something.'

Cassis shook his head. 'Maybe he's spotted us,' he said grimly. 'Just waiting for one of us to stick our head up, and pow!'

I shrugged again and carefully looked over the top of the wall. Old Gustave hadn't passed out; but he was sitting on his stick with his back to us, watching the café. He was quite still.

'Well?' said Cassis as I ducked back behind the wall.

I told him what I had seen.

'What's he *doing*?' said Cassis, white with frustration.

I shook my head.

'Damn the old idiot! He'll have us waiting here all night!'

I put my finger to my lips. '*Shh*. There's someone coming.'

Old Gustave must have heard them, too, for as we ducked further behind the wall into the blackberry tangles we heard him come over. Not as quietly as we had, and if he'd come over a few metres to the left he would have landed right on top of us. As it was, he fell into a mess of brambles, cursing and flailing with his stick, and we retreated even further into the thicket. We were in a kind of tunnel made up of rolls of blackberry hedge and goose-grass, and for youngsters of our age and agility it looked as if it might be possible to crawl along underneath it until we reached the road. If we could do that, we might be able to avoid climbing back over the wall altogether, and thus be able to escape unseen into the darkness.

I had almost made up my mind to try this out when I heard the sound of voices from the other side of the wall. One was a woman's voice. The other spoke German only, and I recognized it as Schwartz. I could still hear the music playing in the bar, and I guessed that Schwartz and his lady friend had crept out unremarked. From my vantage point in the blackberry tangle I could see their figures dimly above the wall, and I gestured to Reinette and Cassis to stay where they were. I could see Gustave, too, some distance from us and unaware of our presence, huddled against the bricks at his side and watching through one of the cracks in the masonry. I heard the woman's laughter, high and a little nervous, then Schwartz's thick voice saying something in German. He was shorter than she was, troll-like next to her slim figure, and the way he leaned into her neck seemed oddly

250

carnivorous, as did the sounds he uttered while doing so – slurping, mumbling sounds, like a man in a hurry to finish his dinner. As they moved from behind the back porch the moonlight caught them garishly, and I saw Schwartz's big hands fumbling at the woman's blouse – '*Liebchen, Liebling*' – and heard her laughter shriller than ever – '*hihihihi*' – as she thrust her breasts into his hands. Then they were no longer alone. A third figure came from behind the porch, but the German seemed unsurprised by his arrival, because he nodded briefly at the newcomer, though the woman seemed oblivious, and turned back to the business in hand while the other man looked on, silent and avid, his eyes gleaming out of the darkness of the porch like an animal's. It was Jean-Marie Dupré.

It didn't occur to me then that Tomas might have arranged this meeting. The spectacle of the woman as trade in exchange for something else; a favour perhaps, or a tin of black-market coffee. I made no connection between the interchange I had witnessed between them in the bar and this; in fact I wasn't even sure what *this* was, it was so far removed from the little knowledge I had of such things. Cassis would have known, of course, but he was still crouching behind the wall with Reinette. I beckoned to him frantically, thinking that perhaps this was the time, while the three protagonists were still absorbed in themselves, to make good our escape. Nodding, he began to move towards me through the thicket, leaving Reinette in the shadow of the wall, only her white parachute-silk blouse visible from where we waited.

'Damn her. Why doesn't she follow?' hissed Cassis at last. The German and the town woman had moved closer to the wall so that we could hardly see what was going on. Jean-Marie was close by them – close enough to watch, I thought, feeling suddenly guilty and sick at the same time – and I could hear their breathing, the thick, piggy breathing of the German and the harsh, excited breathing of the watcher, with the high, muffled squeal of the woman between them both, and I was suddenly glad I couldn't see what was happening, glad that I was too young to understand, because the act seemed impossibly ugly, impossibly messy, and yet they were enjoying it, eyes rolling in the moonlight and mouths gaping fishily. And now the German was thudding the woman against the wall in short, percussive bursts, and I could hear her head and backside hitting the bricks and her squealing voice – 'Ah! Ah! Ah!' – and his growling – '*Liebchen, ja Liebling, ach ja*' – and I wanted to stand up and run for it there and then, all my cool falling from me in a great prickly wave of panic. I was about to follow my instinct, half standing, turning towards the road, measuring the distance between myself and escape – when abruptly the sounds stopped and a man's voice, very loud in the sudden stillness, snapped, '*Wer ist das?*'

It was then that Reinette, who had been moving softly towards us all the time, panicked. Instead of freezing, as we had done when Gustave challenged the dark, she must have thought he had spotted her, because she stood up and began to run, startling with the moonlight on her white silk blouse, and fell into the blackberry bushes with a cry, twisting her ankle to one side and sitting there wailing, with her ankle held between her hands and her white face turning helplessly towards us and her mouth moving desperately and without words.

Cassis moved quickly. Swearing beneath his breath, he ran through the thicket in the opposite direction, elder branches whipping at his face as he went and brambles snagging barbs of flesh from his ankles. Without a backward look at either of us, he vaulted the wall on the other side and disappeared onto the road.

'*Verdammt!*' It was Schwartz. I saw his pale moony face over the top of the wall and flattened myself invisibly into the bushes. '*Wer war das?*'

Hauer, who had joined him from the back room, shook his head, '*Weiß nicht. Etwas da drüben!*' He pointed. Three faces appeared over the top of the wall. I could only hide myself behind the dark foliage and hope that Reinette would have the sense to make a dash for it as soon as possible. At least I hadn't run away, I thought contemptuously, like Cassis. Dimly I realized that back in La Rép, the music had stopped.

'Wait, there's someone still there,' said Jean-Marie, peering over the wall. The town woman joined him, her face white as flour in the moonlight. Her mouth looked black and vicious against that unnatural pallor.

'Why, the little trollop!' she said shrilly. 'You! Get up this minute! Yes, *you*, hiding behind the wall. *Spying* on us.' Her voice was high and indignant, and maybe a little guilty. Reine stood up slowly, obediently. Such a good girl, my sister. Always so quick to respond to the voice of authority. Much good it did her. I could hear her breathing, the quick, panicky hiss in her throat as she faced them. Her blouse had pulled out of her skirt as she fell, and her hair had come down and blew about her face.

Hauer said something softly to Schwartz in German. Schwartz reached over the wall to haul Reinette over onto their side.

For a few seconds she allowed herself to be hoisted, unprotesting. She was never the quickest thinker, and of the three of us she was by far the most docile. An order from an adult and her first instinct was to obey without question.

Then she seemed to understand. Perhaps it was Schwartz's hands on her, or maybe she understood what Hauer had murmured, but she began to struggle. Too late. Hauer was holding her still while Schwartz stripped off her blouse. I saw it go sailing over the wall like a white banner in the moonlight. Then another voice – Heinemann, I think – shouted something in

German, then my sister was screaming, high, breathless cries – '*Ah! Ah! Ah!*' of disgust and terror. For a second I saw her face above the wall, her hair flying out around her, her arms clawing the night, and Schwartz's beery, grinning face turned towards her. Then she disappeared, though the sounds continued, the gluttonous sounds of the men, and the town woman shrilling in what might have been triumph, 'Serve her right, little whore. Serve her right.'

And through it all the laughter, that piggy *heh-heh-heh* which cuts through my dreams even now some nights, that and the saxophone music, so like a human voice, so like his voice.

I hesitated for maybe thirty seconds. No more, though it seemed like longer to me as I bit my knuckles to aid concentration and crouched in the undergrowth. Cassis had already escaped. I was only nine. What could I do? But even though I only understood very dimly what was going on, still I could not leave her. I stood up and opened my mouth to scream – in my mind's eye Tomas was near by and would stop the whole thing – except that someone was already climbing clumsily over the wall, someone with a stick, which he used to lash at the onlookers with more rage than efficiency. Someone who roared in a furious, cavernous voice, 'Filthy Boche! Filthy Boche!'

It was Gustave Beauchamp.

I ducked back into the undergrowth. I could see very little of what was happening now, but I was aware of Reinette picking up her blouse and running whimpering back along the wall to the road. I might have joined her then, but for curiosity and the sudden elation which washed over me as I heard the familiar voice calling through the pandemonium: 'It's all right! It's all right!'

My heart leapt.

I heard him push his way through the little crowd – others had joined the fight now and I heard the sound of old Gustave's stick connect twice more, making a sound like someone kicking a cabbage. Soothing words – Tomas' voice – in French and German: 'It's all right now, calm down. *Verdammt*. Calm it, can't you Fränzl, you've done enough in one day.' Then Hauer's angry voice, and confused protests from Schwartz.

Hauer, his voice trembling with rage, shouted at Gustave, 'That's twice you've tried it with me tonight, you old *Arschloch*.'

Tomas shouting something unintelligible, then there was a great cry from Gustave, cut off suddenly by a sound like a sack of flour hitting a stone granary floor; a terrible thwack against the stone, then silence as shocking as an icy shower.

It lasted thirty seconds or more. No-one spoke. No-one moved.

Then Tomas' voice, cheerily casual. 'It's all right. Go back into the bar, finish your drinks. The wine must finally have got to him.'

There was an uneasy murmur, a whisper, a flutter of protest. A woman's voice; Colette, I think. 'His eyes . . .'

'Just the drink.' Tomas' voice was brisk and light. 'An old man like that. Doesn't know when to stop.' His laugh was utterly convincing, and yet I knew he was lying. 'Fränzl, you stay and help me get him home. Udi, get the others inside.'

As soon as the others had returned to the bar I heard the piano music begin again and a woman's voice lifting in a nervous warble to the tune of a popular song. Left alone, Tomas and Hauer began to talk in rapid, urgent undertones.

Hauer: *Leibniz, was muß—'*

'*Halt's Maul!*' Tomas broke in sharply. Moving to the place where I guessed the old man's body had fallen, he knelt down. I heard him move Gustave, then speak to him a couple of times softly in French: 'Old man. Wake up, old man.'

Hauer said something rapid and angry in German, which I did not catch. Then Tomas spoke, slowly and clearly, and it was more from the tone of his words than the words themselves that I understood. Slowly, deliberately, the words almost amused in their cool contempt.

'*Sehr gut, Fränzl,*' said Tomas crisply. '*Er ist tot.*'

9

'Out of pills.' She must have been desperate. That terrible night, with the scent of oranges all around her and nothing to which she could cling.

'I would sell my children for a night's sleep.'

Then, under a pasted-in recipe clipped from a newspaper, in writing so small my old eyes needed a magnifying glass to make out the words:

> TL came again. Said there had been a problem at La Rép. Some soldiers got out of hand. Said R-C might have seen something. Brought pills.

Could those pills have been thirty high-dose morphine-based tablets? For her silence. Or were the pills for something else entirely?

10

Paul came back half an hour later. He wore the slightly sheepish expression of a man who expects to be scolded, and he smelled of beer.

'I had to buy a drink,' he said apologetically. 'It would have looked odd if I'd just stayed staring at them.'

By then I was half soaked and irritable. 'Well?' I demanded. 'What's your big discovery?'

Paul shrugged. 'Maybe nothing,' he said reflectively. 'I'd rather . . . ah . . . wait till I've checked a few things before getting your hopes up.'

I looked him in the eye. 'Paul Désiré Hourias,' I declared. 'I've waited for you in the rain for ages. I've stood in the stink of this café watching for Dessanges because you thought we might learn something. I haven't complained *once*' – he gave me a satirical look at this point, which I ignored – 'That makes me practically a *saint*,' I said sternly. 'But if you *dare* to try to keep me in the dark, if you so much as *think* about it—'

Paul made a lazy gesture of defeat. 'How did you know my middle name was Désiré?' he asked.

'I know everything,' I said, without smiling.

11

I don't know what they did after we ran away. A couple of days later old Gustave's body was found in the Loire by a fisherman outside of Courlé. The fish had been at him already. No-one mentioned what had happened at La Mauvaise Réputation, though the Dupré brothers seemed more furtive than ever, and an unusual silence hung over the café. Reinette didn't mention what had happened, and I pretended I'd run off at the same time as Cassis, so she didn't suspect what I'd seen. But she had changed; she seemed cold, almost aggressive. When she thought I wasn't looking she would touch her hair and face compulsively, as if checking for something out-of-place. She avoided school for several days, claiming she had stomach ache.

Surprisingly, Mother indulged her. She sat with her, mixing her hot drinks and talking to her in a low, urgent voice. She moved Reinette's cot into her own room, something she had never done before for either myself or Cassis. Once I saw her give her two tablets, which Reinette took reluctantly, protesting. From my spy place behind the door I caught a snatch of their conversation, in which I thought I caught the word 'curse'. Reinette was quite ill for some days after the pills, but recovered soon enough, and no more was said about the incident.

There was little relating to this in the album. On one page my mother writes, 'R-C fully recovered' under a pressed marigold and a recipe for wormwood tisane. But I've always had my suspicions. Could the pills have been some kind of a purgative, in case of an unwanted pregnancy? Could they have been the pills to which Mother refers in the journal entry? And was TL Tomas Leibniz?

I think Cassis might have guessed something, but he was far too absorbed in his own affairs to take great notice of Reinette. Instead he learned his lessons, read his magazines, played in the woods with Paul and pretended nothing had happened. Perhaps, for him, nothing had.

I tried to talk to him about it once.

'Something happened? What do you mean, something happened?' We were sitting at the top of the Lookout Post, eating mustard sandwiches and reading *The Time Machine*. It had been my favourite story that summer, and I never tired of it. Cassis looked at me, his mouth full, his eyes not quite meeting mine.

'I'm not sure.' I was careful what I said, watching his placid face over the hard cover of the book. 'I mean, I only stayed a minute longer, but—' It was difficult to put it into words. There were no words for that kind of thing in my vocabulary. 'They nearly caught Reinette,' I said lamely. 'Jean-Marie and the others. They . . . they pushed her down against the wall. They tore her blouse,' I said.

There was more, if only I could find the words. I tried to recall the feelings of horror, of guilt which had come over me then; the feeling that I was about to witness some ugly, compelling mystery, but somehow everything had become unclear, grainy, like images in a dream.

'Gustave was there,' I continued desperately.

Cassis was getting irritable. 'So?' he said in a sharp voice. 'So what? He was always there, the old tosspot. So what's new about that?' And still his eyes refused to meet mine, lingering on the page, skittering to and fro like dead leaves in the wind.

'There was a fight. A kind of fight.' I had to say it. I knew he didn't want me to, saw his fixed gaze deliberately avoiding me, concentrating on the page, and wishing I'd shut up.

Silence. In silence our wills fought each other, he with his years and his experience, me with the weight of my knowledge.

'Do you think maybe—'

He turned on me then, ferociously, his eyes bright with rage and terror. 'Think what, for Christ's sake? Think *what*?' he spat. 'Haven't you done enough already, with your *deals* and your plans and your clever *ideas*?' He was panting, his face hectic and very close to mine. 'Don't you think you've done enough?'

'I don't know what—' I was almost in tears.

'Well, *think*, why don't you?' yelled Cassis. 'Let's say you suspect something, shall we? Let's say you know why old Gustave died.' He paused to watch my reaction, his voice lowering to a harsh whisper. 'Let's say you suspect someone. Who're you going to tell? The police? Mother? The fucking Foreign Legion?' I watched him, feeling wretched but not showing it, staring him out in my old insolent way.

'We couldn't tell anyone,' said Cassis in an altered voice. 'Not anyone. They'd want to know how we knew. Who we'd been talking to. And if we said' – his eyes flicked away from mine – 'if ever we said *anything*, to *anyone*—' He broke off suddenly and turned back to his book. Even his fear had gone, replaced instead by a wary indifference.

'It's a good thing we're just kids, isn't it?' he remarked in a new, flat voice. 'Kids are always playing at stuff. Finding things out, detectives, things like that. Everyone knows it isn't real. Everyone knows we just make it up.'

I stared at him. 'But Gustave,' I said.

'Just an old man,' said Cassis, unconsciously echoing Tomas. 'Fell in the river, didn't he. Drank too much wine. Happens all the time.'

I shivered.

'We never saw anything,' said Cassis stolidly. 'Not you, not me, not Reinette. Nothing happened, all right?'

I shook my head. 'I did see. I did.'

But Cassis would not look at me again, retreating behind the pages of his book, where Morlocks and Eloi warred furiously behind the safe barriers of fiction. And every time I tried to talk to him about it subsequently he pretended not to understand, or to think I was playing some kind of game. In time, perhaps he even came to believe it.

Days passed. I removed all traces of the orange bag from under my mother's pillow, as well as the orange peel hidden in the anchovy barrel, and I buried them in the garden. I had the feeling that I wouldn't be using them again.

'Woke at six this morning,' she writes, 'for the first time in months. Strange how everything looks different. When you haven't slept it's as if the world is sliding away bit by bit. The ground isn't quite in line with your feet. The air seems full of shiny, stinging particles. I feel I've left a part of myself behind, but I can't remember what. They look at me with such solemn eyes. I think they're afraid of me. All but 'Boise. She's not afraid of anything. I want to warn her that it doesn't last for ever.'

She was right about that. It doesn't. I knew that as soon as Noisette was born – my Noisette, so sly, so hard, so like myself. She has a child now, a child I've never seen except in a picture. She calls her Pêche. I often wonder how they manage, alone, so far away from home. Noisette used to look at me like that, with those hard black eyes of hers. Remembering now, I realize she looks more like my mother than me.

Only a few days after the dance at La Rép, Raphaël came to call. He made some excuse – buying wine or something – but we knew what he really wanted.

Cassis never admitted it, of course, but I could see it in Reine's eyes. He wanted to find out what we knew. I imagine he was worried; more so than the rest because it was his café, after all, and he felt responsible. Maybe he was simply guessing. Maybe someone had talked. In any case, he was nervous as a cat when my mother opened the door, his eyes darting into the house behind her, then out again. Since the dance, business at La Mauvaise Réputation had been bad. I'd heard someone at the post office – it might have been Lisbeth Genêt – saying that the place had gone to the dogs, that Germans went there with their whores, that no decent person would be seen there, and though no-one had yet made the connection between what had happened that night and the death of Gustave Beauchamp, there was no saying when the talk would begin. It was a village, after all, and in a village no-one can keep a secret for long.

Well, Mother didn't give him what you'd call a warm welcome. Maybe she was too conscious of us watching them, too aware of what he knew about her. Maybe her illness made her sharp, or maybe it was just her naturally surly temperament. Either way, he didn't come back, though a week later he and everyone who had been at La Réputation the night of the dance was dead, so perhaps he just didn't get the chance.

Mother makes only one reference to his visit: 'That fool Raphaël called. Too late as usual. Told me he knew where he could get me some pills. I said no more.'

No more. Just like that. If it had been another woman I wouldn't have believed it, but Mirabelle Dartigen was no ordinary woman. No more, she said. And that was her last word. To my knowledge she never took morphine again, though that too might have been because of what happened rather than from sheer force of will. Of course, by then there were to be no more oranges, ever again. I think even I had lost my taste for them.

PART FIVE

Harvest

1

I told you much of what she wrote was lies. whole paragraphs of them, tangled into the truth like bind-weed into a hedge, further obscured by the mad jargon she used, lines crossed and recrossed, words folded and inverted so that each one is a struggle of my will against hers to extract meaning from the code.

'Walking down by the river today. I saw a woman flying a kite made of plywood and oildrums. Wouldn't have imagined such a thing could fly. Big as a tank but painted so many colours, and ribbons flying from the tail. I thought' – at this point some words are obscured by an olive-oil stain, bleeding the ink a deep violet into the paper – 'but she leaped onto the crossbar and swung into the air. Didn't recognize her at first, though I thought it might have been Minette, but' – a larger stain here obscures most of the rest, though there are a few words still visible. 'Beautiful' is one of them. Scrawled across the top of the paragraph she has written the word 'seesaw' in ordinary script. Below, a scratchy diagram which might represent almost anything, but which seems to show a stick figure standing on a swastika shape.

In any case, it doesn't matter. There was no kite woman. Even the reference to Minette makes no sense; the only Minette we ever knew was an elderly distant cousin of my father, to whom people would kindly allude as 'eccentric', but who referred to her many cats as 'my babies' and who could sometimes be seen suckling kittens at her breast in public places, her face tranquil above her sagging, scandalous flesh.

I'm only saying this so you'll understand. There were all kinds of fanciful tales in Mother's album, stories of meetings with long-dead people, dreams disguised as fact, prosaic impossibilities – rainy days converted to bright ones; an imaginary guard dog; conversations which never happened, some of them quite dull; a kiss from a friend long since vanished. Sometimes she mixed truth with lies so effectively that even I am no longer sure which is which. Besides, there is no apparent purpose. Perhaps it was her illness talking, or the delusions of her addiction. I don't know if the album was meant for any eyes but hers. Nor does it act as a memoir. In places it is almost a diary, but not quite; the irregular sequence robs it of logic and usefulness. Maybe this is why it took me so long to understand what was staring me in the face, to see the reason for her actions and the terrible repercussions of my own. Sometimes the phrases are doubly hidden, crammed between the lines of recipes in tiny, scratching script. Maybe that's how she wanted it to be. Between her and myself, at last. A labour of love.

Green Tomato jam. Cut green tomatoes into pieces, like apples, and weigh them. Place in a bowl with 1 kg of sugar to the same weight of fruit. Awoke at three again this morning and went to find my pills. Forgot again that I'd none left. When the sugar is melted – to stop it burning add 2 glasses of water if required – stir with a wooden spoon. I keep thinking that if I go to Raphaël he might find me another supplier. I daren't go to the Germans again, not after what happened, I'd rather die first. Then add the tomatoes and boil gently, stirring very frequently. Skim off the residue at intervals with a slatted spoon. Sometimes dying seems better than this. At least I wouldn't have to worry about waking up, ha ha. I keep thinking about the children. I'm afraid Belle Yolande has honey fungus. Have to dig away the infected roots or it will spread to them all. Allow to boil gently for about two hours, maybe a little less. When the jam sticks to a small plate it is ready. I feel so angry, with myself, with him, with them. With myself most of all. When that idiot Raphaël told me, I had to bite my lips till they bled so I wouldn't give myself away. I don't think he noticed. I said I knew already, that girls were always getting into mischief, that nothing had come of it. He seemed relieved, and when he'd gone I took the big hatchet and chopped wood until I could hardly stand, wishing all the time it was his face.

You see, her narrative is unclear. Only in retrospect does it begin to make a little sense. And, of course, she gave nothing away of her conversation with Raphaël. I can only imagine what took place – his anxiety; her stony, impassive silence; his guilt. It was his café, after all. But Mother wouldn't have given anything away. Pretending she knew was a defensive measure, throwing up a barrier against his unwanted concern. Reine could look after herself, she must have said. Besides, nothing really happened. Reine would be more careful in future. We could only be happy that nothing worse had happened.

T told me it wasn't his fault, but Raphaël says he stood by and did nothing. The Germans were his friends, after all. Perhaps they paid for Reine the way they did for those town women T brought with him.

What lulled our suspicions was that she never mentioned the incident to us. Maybe she simply didn't know how – her distaste of anything which reminded her of bodily functions was acute – or maybe she thought it was something better left alone. But her album reveals her growing rage, her violence, her dreams of retribution. 'I wanted to chop at him until there was nothing left,' she writes. When I read it

269

for the first time I was certain she was referring to Raphaël, but now I'm not so sure. The intensity of her hatred speaks of something deeper, darker. A betrayal, perhaps. Or a thwarted love.

'His hands were softer than I expected,' she writes below a recipe for apple-sauce cake. 'He looks very young, and his eyes are the exact same colour as the sea on a stormy day. I thought I would hate it, hate him, but there is something about his gentleness. Even in a German. I wonder whether I am insane to believe what he promises. I'm so much older than he is. And yet I'm not so old. Perhaps there's time.'

There is no more at this point, as if she is ashamed at her own boldness, but I find small references throughout the album, now that I know where to look. Single words, phrases broken by recipes and gardening reminders, coded even from herself. And the poem.

> This sweetness
> scooped
> like some bright fruit

For years I assumed that it was fantasy, like so many of the other things she mentions. My mother could never have had a lover. She lacked the capacity for tenderness. Her defences were too good, her sensual impulses sublimated into her recipes, into creating the perfect *lentilles cuisinées*, the most ardent *crême brûlée*. It never occurred to me that there might be any truth in these, the most unlikely of her fantasies. Remembering her face, the sour turn of her mouth, the hard lines of her cheekbones, the hair scraped back into a knot at the back of her head, even the story of the kite woman seemed more likely.

And yet I came to believe it. Maybe it was Paul who started me thinking. Maybe the day when I caught myself looking at my reflection in the mirror, with a red scarf round my head and my birthday earrings – a present from Pistache, never before worn – dangling coquettishly. I'm sixty-five years old, for pity's sake. I ought to know better. And yet there's something in the way he looks at me that sets my old heart lurching like a tractor engine. Not the lost, frantic feeling I had for Tomas. Not even the sense of temporary reprieve that was Hervé's gift to me. No, this is something different again; a feeling of peace. The feeling you get when a recipe turns out perfectly right – a perfectly risen soufflé, a flawless *sauce hollandaise*. It's a feeling that tells me *any* woman can be beautiful in the eyes of a man who loves her.

I have taken to creaming my hands and face before I go to bed at night, and the other day I brought out an old lipstick, cracked and clotted with disuse, and blotted a little of the colour onto my lips before rubbing it off in guilty confusion. What am I doing? And why? At sixty-five, surely I've passed the age at which I should decently think of such things. But the severity of my inner voice fails to convince me. I brush my hair with greater care than usual and pin it back with a tortoiseshell comb. There's no fool like an old fool, I tell myself sternly.

And my mother was nearly thirty years younger.

I can look at her photograph now with a kind of mellowing. The mixed emotions I felt for so many years, the bitterness and the guilt, have diminished so that I can see – really see – her face. Mirabelle Dartigen, the tight, pinched features and the hair yanked so savagely back that it hurts to look at it. What was she afraid of, the lonely woman in the picture? The woman of the album is so different, the wistful woman of the poem, laughing and raging behind her mask, sometimes flirtatious, sometimes coldly murderous in her imaginings. I can see her quite clearly, not yet forty, her hair only touched with grey, her black eyes still bright. A lifetime of work has not yet stooped her, and the muscles of her arms are hard and firm. Her breasts are firm too beneath the severe succession of grey aprons, and sometimes she looks at her naked body in the mirror behind her wardrobe door and imagines her long lonely widowhood, the descent into old age, the scraps of youth falling from her, the sagging lines of her belly dropping into pouchy flaps at her hips, the skinny thighs throwing the bulging knees into sharp relief. There is so little time, the woman tells herself. I can almost hear her voice now from beneath the pages of her album. So little time.

And who would come, even in a hundred years of waiting? Old Lecoz with his rheumy lubricious eye? Or Alphonse Fenouil or Jean-Pierre Truriand? Secretly she dreams of a soft-voiced stranger. In her mind's eye she sees him, a man who could see beyond what she has become to what she might have been.

Of course, there's no way I can know what she felt, but I feel closer to her now than I ever was, almost close enough to hear that voice from the brittle pages of the album, a voice which tries so hard to hide its true nature, the passionate, desperate woman behind the cold façade.

You understand that this is merely speculation. She never mentions his name. I can't even prove she had a lover, let alone that it was Tomas Leibniz. But something in me tells me that where I might fail on the details, the essence is true. It might have been so many men, I tell myself. But my secret heart tells me it could have been only Tomas. Perhaps I am more like her than I would like to think. Perhaps she knew that, and leaving me the album was her way of trying to make me understand.

Perhaps, at last, an attempt at ending our war.

2

We didn't see Tomas until almost a fortnight after the dance at La Mauvaise Réputation. That was partly because of Mother – still half crazy with insomnia and migraines – and partly because we sensed that something had changed. We all sensed it: Cassis, hiding behind his comic books; Reine in her new, blank silence; even myself. Oh, we longed for him. All three of us did. Love is not something you can turn off like a tap, and we were already trying, in our way, to excuse what he had done, what he had abetted.

But the ghost of old Gustave Beauchamp swam beneath us like the menacing shadow of a sea monster. It touched everything. We played with Paul almost in the way we had before Tomas, but our games were half-hearted, pushing us to fake exuberance to hide the fact that the life had gone out of them. We swam in the river, ran in the woods, climbed trees with more energy than ever before, but behind it all we knew we were waiting, aching and itching with impatience, for him to come. I think we all believed he might be able to make it better, even then.

I certainly thought so. He was always so sure, so arrogantly self-confident. I imagined him with his cigarette hanging from his lips and his cap pushed back, the sun in his eyes and that smile lighting his face. That smile which lit the world.

But Thursday came and went, and we saw nothing of Tomas. Cassis looked for him at school, but there was no sign of him in any of his usual places. Hauer, Schwartz and Heinemann were also strangely absent, almost as if they were avoiding contact. Another Thursday came and went. We pretended not to notice, did not even mention his name to each other, though we may have whispered it in our dreams, going through the motions of life without him as if we didn't care whether we saw him again or not. I became almost frenzied now in my hunt for Old Mother. I checked the traps I had laid ten or twenty times a day, and was always setting new ones. I stole food from the cellar in order to make new and tempting baits for her. I swam out to the Treasure Stone and sat there for hours with my rod, watching the gracious arc of the line as it dipped into the water and listening to the sounds of the river at my feet.

Raphaël called to see Mother again. Business at the café was poor. Someone had painted 'COLLAB-ORATOR' on the back wall in red paint, and someone threw stones at his windows one night so that now they had to be boarded up. I listened at the door as he spoke in a low urgent voice to Mother.

'It isn't my fault, Mirabelle,' he said. 'You have to believe that. I wasn't responsible.'

My mother made a noncommittal sound between her teeth.

'You can't argue with the Germans,' said Raphaël. 'You have to treat them as you would any other customer. It isn't as if I was the only one.'

Mother shrugged. 'In this village, perhaps you are,' she said indifferently.

'How can you say that? You were pleased enough yourself at one time.'

Mother lunged forward. Raphaël took a hasty step back, rattling the plates on the dresser. Her voice was low and furious. 'Shut up, you fool,' she hissed. 'That's *over*, do you hear? Over. And if I even suspect you've said a word to *anyone* . . .'

Raphaël's face was sallow with fear, but he tried to

bluster. 'I'm not having anyone calling me a fool,' he began in a shaking voice.

'I'll call you a fool and your mother a whore if I want to.' My mother's voice was hard and shrill. 'You're a fool and a coward, Raphaël Crespin, and we both know it.' She was standing so close to him that I could hardly see his face, though I could still see his hands splayed out on either side of her, as if in entreaty. 'But if you or anyone talks about this, God help you. If my *children* get to hear anything because of you' – I could hear her breathing, harsh as dead leaves in the tiny kitchen – 'then I'll kill you,' whispered my mother, and Raphaël must have believed her, because his face was white as curd when he left the house, his hands shaking so badly he jammed them into his pockets.

'Anyone messes with my children and I'll kill the bastards,' spat my mother in his wake, and I saw him wince, as if her words were poison. 'Kill the bastards,' repeated my mother, even though Raphaël was almost down to the gate by then, half running, head lowered as if against a strong wind.

They were words that would return to haunt us.

She was in vicious humour all day. Even Paul caught the lash of her tongue when he came to ask Cassis to play. Mother, who had been silently brewing trouble since Raphaël's visit, launched such a fierce and un-provoked attack upon him that he was able only to stare at her, his mouth working, his voice locked into an agonizing stutter – 'I'm so-so-so-so. I'm so-so-so—'

'Talk properly, you cretin!' screamed my mother in her glassy voice, and for a second I thought I saw Paul's mild eyes light with something almost savage, then he turned without uttering a word and fled jerkily towards the Loire, his voice returning as he did and ululating behind him in a series of weird, desperate trills as he ran.

'Good riddance!' shouted my mother after him, slamming the door.

'You shouldn't have said that,' I said stonily to her back. 'It isn't Paul's fault he stammers.'

My mother turned to look at me, her eyes like agates. 'You would side with him,' she said in a flat voice. 'If it was a choice between me and a Nazi, you'd side with the Nazi.'

3

It was then that the letters began to arrive. Three of them, scribbled on thin blue-lined notepaper and pushed under the door. I found her in the act of picking one up, and she crammed it into the pocket of her apron, almost screaming at me to get into the kitchen, I wasn't fit to be seen, get that soap and scrub, scrub. There was a note in her voice which reminded me of the orange bag, and I made myself scarce, but I remembered the letter and later, when I found it pasted into the album between a recipe for *boudin noir* and a magazine cutting on how to remove boot-polish stains, I recognized it at once.

'We now what youve bean doing,' it read in small, shaky letters. 'Weve bean watchen you and we now wat to do with colaboraters.' Underneath she has written in bold red letters, 'Learn to spell, ha ha!' but her words look overlarge, over-red, as if she is trying too hard to appear unconcerned. Certainly she never spoke to us of the notes, though in retrospect I realize that her abrupt changes of mood might have been related to their secret arrival. Another suggests that the writer knew something about our meetings with Tomas.

Weve sene your kids with him so dont try to deny it. We now wat your game is. You think youre so good better than the rest of us well youre nothing but a Boch whoar and your kids are seling stuff to the germans. Wat do you think of that.

The writing might belong to anyone. Certainly the script is uneducated, the spelling atrocious, but it might have been written by anyone in the village. My mother began to behave even more erratically than usual, shutting herself in the farmhouse for most of the day and watching any passers-by with a suspicion verging on paranoia.

The third letter is the worst. I suppose there were no more, though she might simply have decided not to keep them, but I think this is the last.

You dont deserve to live, Nazi whoar and your stuckup kids. Bet you didnt now theyre selling us to the germans. Ask them wear all the stuff coms from. They keep it in a place theyve got in the woods. They get it of a man calld Lybnits I think hes calld. You now him. And we now you.

The same night someone painted a scarlet 'C' on our front door and 'NAZI WHOAR' across the side of the chicken hut, though we painted over it before anyone could see what had been written. And October dragged on.

4

Paul and I came back from La Mauvaise Réputation late that night. The rain had stopped, but it was still cold – either nights have got colder or I've begun to feel it more than I ever did in the old days – and I was impatient and bad-tempered. But the more impatient I got, the quieter Paul seemed to be, until we were both glowering at each other in silence, our breath puffing out in great billows of steam as we walked.

'That girl,' said Paul at last. His voice was quiet and reflective, almost as if he were speaking to himself. 'She looked very young, didn't she?'

I was annoyed by the seeming irrelevance. 'What girl, for heaven's sake?' I snapped. 'I thought we were going to find a way to get rid of Dessanges and his grease wagon, not to give you an excuse to ogle girls.'

Paul ignored me. 'She was sitting next to him,' he said slowly. 'You'll have seen her go in. Red dress, high heels. Comes to the wagon pretty often, too.'

As it happened I did remember her. I recalled a vague sulky blur of red mouth under a slice of black hair. One of Luc's regulars from town. 'So?'

'That's Louis Ramondin's daughter. Moved to Angers a couple of years ago, you know, with her mother, Simone, after the divorce. You'll remember them.' He nodded as if I'd given him a civil answer instead of a grunt. 'Simone went back to her maiden name, Truriand. The girl would be fourteen, maybe fifteen nowadays.'

'So?' I still couldn't understand his interest in this. I took out my door key and fitted it into the lock.

Paul continued in his slow, thoughtful way. 'Certainly no older than fifteen, I'd say,' he repeated.

'All right,' I said tartly. 'I'm glad you found something to liven up your evening. Pity you didn't ask for her shoe size, too, then you'd *really* have something to dream about.'

Paul gave me his lazy smile. 'You're actually jealous,' he said.

'Not at all,' I said with dignity. 'I just wish you'd go dribble on someone else's carpet, you dirty old lecher.'

'Well, I was thinking,' said Paul slowly.

'Well done,' I said.

'I was thinking, maybe Louis – being a *gendarme* and all – maybe he'd draw the line at his daughter being involved – at fifteen, maybe even fourteen – with a man – a *married* man – like Luc Dessanges.' He gave me a little look of triumph and amusement. 'I mean, I know times have changed since you and I were young, but fathers and daughters, especially policemen . . .'

I yelped. '*Paul!*'

'Smokin' those sweet cigarettes, too,' he added in the same reflective tone. 'The kind they used to have in the jazz clubs, way back.'

I stared at him in awe. 'Paul, this is almost *intelligent.*'

He shrugged modestly. 'Been doing some asking around,' he said. 'Thought something might come to me sooner or later.' He paused. 'That's why I took a little time in there,' he added. 'Wasn't sure if I'd be able to persuade Louis to come over and see for himself.'

I gaped. 'You *brought* Louis? While I was waiting outside?'

Paul nodded.

'Pretended I'd had my wallet taken in the bar. Made sure he got an eyeful.' Another pause. 'His daughter was kissing Dessanges,' he explained. 'That helped a bit.'

'Paul,' I declared, 'you can dribble over every carpet in the house if you want to. You have my full permission.'

'I'd rather dribble over *you*,' said Paul, with an extravagant leer.

'Dirty old man.'

5

Luc came back to the snack wagon the next day to find Louis waiting for him. The *gendarme* was in full uniform, his usually vague and pleasant face wearing an expression of almost military indifference. There was an object in the grass beside the wagon which looked something like a child's trolley.

'Watch this,' said Paul to me from the window.

I left my place at the stove, where the coffee was beginning to boil.

'Just you watch this,' said Paul.

The window was open a crack, and I could smell the smoky Loire mist as it rolled over the fields. The scent was as nostalgic as burning leaves.

'*Hé, là!*' Luc's voice was quite clear where we stood, and he walked with the carefree assurance of one who knows himself to be irresistible. Louis Ramondin just stared at him impassively.

'What's that he's got with him?' I asked Paul softly, with a gesture towards the machine on the grass. Paul grinned.

'Just watch,' he advised.

'Hey, how's it going?' Luc reached into his pocket for his keys. 'Must be in a hurry for breakfast, *hein*? Been waiting long?'

Louis just watched him without a word.

'Listen to this.' Luc made an expansive gesture. 'Pancakes, farmhouse sausage, egg and *bacon à l'anglaise. Le breakfast Dessanges*. Plus a big pot of my very blackest, very meanest *café noirissime*, because I can tell you've had a rough night.' He laughed. 'What was it, *hein*? Stakeout at the church bazaar? Someone molesting the local sheep? Or was it the other way around?'

Still Louis said nothing. He remained quite still, like a toy policeman, one hand on the handle of the trolley thing in the grass.

Luc shrugged and opened the snack-wagon door.

'I guess you'll be a bit more vocal when you've had my Breakfast Dessanges.'

We watched for a few minutes as Luc brought out his awning and the pennants which advertised his daily menus. Louis stood stolidly beside the snack wagon, seeming not to notice. Every now and again Luc sang out something cheerful at the waiting police-man. After a time I heard the sound of music from the radio.

'What's he waiting for?' I demanded impatiently. 'Why doesn't he say something?'

Paul grinned. 'Give him time,' he advised. 'Never quick on the uptake, the Ramondins, but once you get them going . . .'

Louis waited fully ten minutes. By that time Luc was still cheery but bewildered, and had all but aban-doned any attempt at conversation. He had begun to heat the cooking plates for the pancakes, his paper hat tilted jauntily back from his forehead. Then, at last, Louis moved. Not far; he simply went to the back of the snack wagon with his trolley and vanished from sight.

'What is that thing, anyway?' I asked.

'Hydraulic jack,' replied Paul, still smiling. 'They use them in garages. Watch.'

And as we watched, the snack wagon began to tilt forwards, ever so slowly. Almost imperceptibly at first, then with a sudden lurch which brought Dessanges out of his galley quicker than a ferret. He looked angry, but he looked scared, too, taken off-balance for the first time in this whole sorry game, and I liked that look just fine.

'What the fuck d'you think you're doing!' he yelled at Ramondin, half incredulous. 'What is this?'

Silence. I saw the wagon tilt again, just a little. Paul and I craned our necks to see what was going on.

Luc glanced briefly at the wagon to make sure it wasn't damaged. The awning hung askew and the box had tilted drunkenly, like a shack built on sand. I saw the look of calculation come back into his face, the careful, sharp look of a man who not only has aces up his sleeve, but who believes he owns the whole pack.

'Had me going there for a minute,' he said in that cheery, relentless voice. 'Hey, you really had me going. Knocked me sideways, you might say.'

We heard nothing from Louis, but thought we saw the wagon tilt a little more. Paul found that from the bedroom window we could see the rear of the snack wagon, so we moved for a better view. Their voices were thin but audible in the cool morning air.

'Come on, man,' said Luc, a flicker of nerves in his voice now. 'Joke over, OK. Get the wagon back on its feet again and I'll make you my breakfast special. On the house.'

Louis looked at him. 'Certainly, sir,' he said pleasantly, but the wagon tipped a little further forward anyway. Luc made a rapid gesture towards it, as if to steady it.

'I'd step away if I were you, sir,' suggested Louis mildly. 'It doesn't look very stable to me.' The wagon tipped another fraction.

'What do you think you're playing at?' I could hear the angry note in his voice returning.

Louis only smiled. 'Windy night last night, sir,' he observed gently, with another touch at the hydraulic jack at his feet. 'Whole bunch of trees got blown down over by the river.'

I saw Luc stiffen. His rage made him graceless, his head jerking like that of a rooster getting ready for a fight. He was taller than Louis, I noticed, but much slighter. Louis, short and stocky, with the look of his great-uncle Guilherm, had spent most of his life getting into fights. That's why he got to be a policeman in the first place. Luc took a step forward.

'You just let go of that jack right now,' he said in a low, threatening voice.

Louis smiled. 'Certainly, sir,' he said. 'Whatever you say.'

We saw it in a kind of inevitable slow motion. The snack wagon, perched precariously on its edge, swung back as its support was removed. There was a crash as the contents of the galley – plates, glasses, cutlery, pans – were suddenly and violently displaced and hurled into the far side of the wagon with a splash of broken crockery. The wagon continued to move backwards in a lazy arc, propelled by its own momentum and the weight of its displaced furniture. For a moment it seemed as if it might right itself. Then it toppled, slowly and almost ponderously, onto its side on the grass verge with a crash that shook the house and rattled the cups on the downstairs dresser so loudly we heard it from our lookout in the bedroom.

For seconds the two men just looked at each other, Louis with an expression of concern and sympathy, Luc in disbelief and increasing fury. The snack wagon lay on its side in the long grass, sounds of tinkling and breakage settling gently inside its belly.

'Oops,' said Louis.

Luc made a furious dash at Louis. For a second something blurred between them, arms and fists moving too fast for me to see properly. Then Luc was sitting in the grass with his hands over his face, and Louis was helping him up with that kind expression of sympathy.

'Dear me, sir, how could that have happened? Taken over faint for a moment, were we? It's the shock; it's quite natural. Take it easy.'

Luc was spluttering with rage. 'Have you – any –

fucking – *idea* what you've done, you moron?' His words were unclear because of the way he held his hands in front of his face. Paul said later that he'd seen Louis' elbow jab him neatly across the bridge of the nose, though it all happened a bit too quickly for me to catch. Pity. I'd have enjoyed seeing that.

'*My lawyer's going to take you to the fucking cleaner's*. Be almost worth it to see you. Shit! I'm bleeding to death.' Funny, but I could hear the family resemblance now, more pronounced than it had been before. Something about the way he emphasized syllables; the thwarted squeal of a spoilt city boy who has never had anything denied him. For a moment there I could have sworn he sounded just like his sister.

Paul and I went downstairs then – I don't think we could have stayed indoors for another minute – and out to watch the fun. Luc was standing by, not so pretty now with blood dripping from his nose and his eyes watering. I noticed he had fresh dogshit on one of his expensive Paris boots. I held out my handkerchief. Luc gave me a suspicious glance and took it. He began to dabble at his nose. I could tell he hadn't understood yet; he was pale, but he had a stubborn kind of fighting look on his face, the look of a man who has lawyers and advisers and friends in high places to run to.

'You saw that, didn't you?' he spat. 'You saw what that fucker did to me?' He looked at the bloody handkerchief with a kind of disbelief. His nose was swelling nicely, and so were his eyes. 'You both saw him hit me, didn't you?' insisted Luc. 'In broad daylight. I could *sue* you for every *penny*.'

Paul shrugged. 'Didn't see much myself,' he said in his slow voice. 'We old people, we don't see as well as we used to. Don't hear as well, either.'

'But you were watching,' insisted Luc. 'You *must* have seen.' He caught me grinning and his eyes narrowed. 'Oh, I understand,' he said unpleasantly. 'This is what it's all about, is it? Thought you could get your pet *gendarme* to intimidate me, did you?' He glared at Louis.

'If this is really the best you can do between you' – he pinched his nostrils shut to stop the bleeding.

'I don't think there's any call to go casting aspersions,' said Louis stolidly.

'Oh, you don't?' snapped Luc. 'When my lawyer sees—'

Louis interrupted him. 'It's natural you should be upset. The wind blowing your café over like that. I can understand you didn't know what you were doing.'

Luc stared at him in disbelief.

'Terrible night last night,' said Paul kindly. 'First of the October storms. I'm sure you'll be able to claim on the insurance.'

'Of course, it was bound to happen,' I said. 'A high-sided vehicle like that by the side of a road. I'm only surprised it didn't happen earlier.'

Luc nodded. 'I see,' he said softly. 'Not bad, Framboise. Not bad at all. I see you've been hard at work.' His tone was almost coaxing. 'But even without the wagon, you know there's a lot more I can do. A lot more *we* can do.' He tried a grin, then winced and dabbed at his nose again. 'You might as well give them what they want,' he continued in the same almost-seductive tone. '*Hé*, Mamie. What do you say?'

I'm not sure what I would have answered. Looking at him I felt old. I'd expected him to give in, but he looked less beaten at that moment than he'd ever been, his sharp face expectant. I'd given it my best shot – *our* best shot, Paul and I – and even so, Luc seemed invincible. Like children trying to dam a river, we'd had our moment of triumph – that look on his face; it was almost worth it just for that – but in the end, however brave the effort, the river always wins. Louis had spent his childhood by the side of the Loire, too, I told myself. He must have known. All he had done was get himself into trouble. I imagined an army of lawyers, advisers, city police – our names in the

287

papers, our secret business revealed. I felt tired. So tired.

Then I saw Paul's face. He was smiling that slow sweet smile of his, looking almost half-witted but for the lazy amusement in his eyes. He yanked his beret down over his forehead in a gesture which was somehow final and comic and heroic at the same time, like the world's oldest knight pulling down his visor for a last tilt at the enemy. I felt a sudden crazy urge to laugh.

'I think we can, ah, sort it out,' Paul said. 'Maybe Louis here got carried away a little. All the Ramondins were a little, ah, quick to take offence. It's in the blood.' He smiled apologetically, then turned to address Louis. 'There was that business with Guilherm. Who was he, your grandmother's brother?' Dessanges listened in growing irritation and contempt.

'Grandfather's,' corrected Louis.

Paul nodded. 'Aye, hot blood, the Ramondins. All of 'em.' He was lapsing into dialect again – one of the things Mother always held most against him, that and his stutter – and his accent was thicker now than I ever remember it back in the old days. 'I remember how they led the rabble that night against the farmhouse, with old Guilherm at the front with his wooden leg, and all for that business at La Mauvaise Réputation. Seems it's kept that bad reputation all this time.'

Luc shrugged his shoulders. 'Look, I'd love to hear today's selection of Quaint Country Tales from Long Ago. But what I'd *really* like—'

'T'was a young man started it all,' continued Paul inexorably. 'Not unlike yourself, I'd say he was. A man from the city, *hein*, from the foreign, who thought he could wrap the poor stupid Loire people round his finger.'

He gave me a quick look, as if checking an emotional barometer somewhere in my face. 'Came to a bad end, though. Didn't he?'

'The worst,' I said thickly. 'The very worst.'

Luc was watching us both, his eyes wary. 'Oh?' he said.

I nodded. '*He* liked young girls, too,' I said in a voice which sounded dim and distant to my own ears. 'Played them along. Used them to find out things. They'd call that corruption nowadays.'

''Course, in those days most of the girls didn't have fathers,' said Paul blandly. ''Cause of the war.'

I saw Luc's eyes kindle with understanding. He gave a small nod, as if marking a point. 'This is something to do with last night, is it?' he said.

I ignored the question. 'You *are* married, aren't you?' I asked.

He nodded again.

'Pity if your wife had to be involved in all this,' I went on. 'Corruption of minors – nasty business. I don't see how she could avoid getting involved.'

'You'll never get that one to stick,' said Luc quickly. 'The girl wouldn't—'

'The girl is my daughter,' said Louis simply. 'She would do – say – whatever she felt was right.'

Again, the nod. He was cool enough, I'll give him that.

'Fine,' he said at last. He even managed a little smile. 'Fine. I get the message.' He was relaxed in spite of everything; his pallor came from anger rather than fear. He looked at me directly, an ironic twist at his mouth.

'I hope the victory was worth it, Mamie,' he said with emphasis. 'Because come tomorrow you're going to need every bit of comfort you can get. Come tomorrow your sad little secret is going to be splashed across every magazine and newspaper in the country. Just time for a couple of phone calls before I move on. After all, it really has been *such* a dull party, and if our friend here thinks his little bitch of a daughter even *began* to make it worthwhile—' He broke off to grin viciously at Louis, and gaped as the policeman's handcuffs snapped sharply over first one wrist, then the other.

'*What?*' He sounded incredulous and close to laughter. 'What the fuck do you think you're doing now? Adding abduction to the list? Where do you think this is? The Wild West?'

Louis gave him his stolid look.

'It's my duty to warn you, sir,' he said, 'that violent and abusive behaviour cannot be tolerated, and that it is my duty—'

'*What?*' Luc's voice rose almost to a scream. '*What* behaviour? *You're* the one who hit *me*! You can't—'

Louis looked at him with polite reproach. 'I have reason to believe, sir, that, given your erratic behaviour, you may be under the influence of alcohol, or some other intoxicating substance, and that for your own safety I feel it my duty to keep you under supervision.'

'You're arresting me?' demanded Luc, disbelieving. 'You're *charging* me?'

'Not unless I'm obliged to, sir,' said Louis reproachfully. 'But I'm sure these two witnesses here will testify to abusive, threatening behaviour, violent language and disorderly conduct' – he gave a nod in my direction – 'I'll have to ask you to accompany me to the station, sir.'

'*There is no fucking station!*' screamed Luc.

'Louis uses the basement of his house for drunk and disorderlies,' said Paul quietly. ''Course, we haven't had one for a while, not since Guguste Tinon went on that bender five years ago.'

'But I have a root cellar which is entirely at your disposal, Louis, if you think there's a danger he might pass out on his way into the village,' I suggested blandly. 'There's a good strong lock on it, and no way he could do himself any harm.'

Louis appeared to consider this. 'Thank you, *veuve* Simon,' he said at last. 'I think perhaps that would be for the best. At least until I can work out where to go from here.' He looked critically at Dessanges, who was pale now with something more than rage.

'You're crazy, all three of you,' said Dessanges softly.

''Course, I'll have to search you first,' said Louis calmly. 'Can't have you burning the place down or anything. Could you empty your pockets for me, please?'

Luc shook his head. 'I just don't believe this,' he said.

'I'm sorry sir,' persisted Louis. 'But I'll have to ask you to empty your pockets.'

'Ask away,' retorted Luc sourly. 'I don't know what you're expecting to get from all this, but when my lawyer hears about it—'

'I'll do it,' suggested Paul. 'I don't suppose he can reach his pockets with his hands cuffed, anyway.'

He moved quickly, in spite of his seeming clumsiness, his poacher's hands patting Luc's clothing and extracting its contents – a lighter, some roll-up papers, car keys, a wallet, a packet of cigarettes. Luc struggled uselessly, swearing. He looked about him, as if expecting to see someone to whom he might call for help, but the street was deserted.

'One wallet.' Louis checked the contents. 'One cigarette lighter, silver; one mobile phone.' He began to open the packet of cigarettes and shake out the contents into his palm. Then, on Louis' hand, I saw something I didn't recognize. A small irregular block of some blackish-brown stuff, like old treacle toffee.

'I wonder what this is?' said Louis blandly.

'Fuck you!' said Luc sharply. 'That isn't mine. You planted it on me, you old bastard!' This to Paul, who looked at him in slow-witted surprise. 'You'll never get it to stand—'

'Maybe not,' said Louis indifferently. 'But we can try, can't we?'

6

Louis left Dessanges in the root cellar as promised. He could keep him for twenty-four hours, he told us, before he had to charge him. With a curious glance at both of us and a careful lack of expression in his voice, he informed us that we had that time in which to conclude our business. A good lad, Louis Ramondin, in spite of his slowness. Too like his great-uncle Guilherm for comfort, though, and that I suppose blinded me at first to his essential goodness. I only hoped he would not have cause to regret it soon enough.

At first Dessanges raved and yelled in the root cellar. Demanded his lawyer, his phone, his sister Laure, his cigarettes. Claimed his nose hurt, that it was broken, that for all he knew there were bone shards working their way into his brain that minute. He hammered against the door, pleaded, threatened, swore. We ignored him, and eventually the sounds ceased. At twelve thirty I brought him some coffee and a plate of bread and *charcuterie*, and he was sulky but calm, that look of calculation back in his eyes.

'You're just delaying the moment, Mamie,' he told me as I cut the bread into slices. 'Twenty-four hours is all you've got, because as you know, as soon as I make that phone call—'

'Do you actually *want* this food?' I snapped at him sharply. ''Cause it won't hurt you to go hungry for a while, and that way I wouldn't have to listen to your nasty talk any more. Right?'

He gave me a dirty look, but said nothing else on the subject.

'Right,' I said.

7

Paul and I pretended to work for the rest of the afternoon. it was a Sunday and the restaurant was shut, but there was still work to be done in the orchard and the vegetable garden. I hoed and pruned and weeded until my kidneys felt like hot glass and sweat ringed my armpits. Paul watched me from the house, not knowing I was also watching him.

Those twenty-four hours; they itched and fretted at me like a bad case of nettle-rash. I knew I should be doing *something*, but what I could do in twenty-four hours was beyond my ability to decide. We had foiled one Dessanges – temporarily, at least – but the others were still as free and full of malice as ever. And time was short. Several times I made it to the phone box in front of the post office, manufacturing errands just so I could be near it, and once I even went as far as dialling the number, but cut it off before anyone answered as I realized I had absolutely no idea of what I ought to say. It seemed that wherever I looked I saw the same terrible truth staring out at me, the same awful set of alternatives. Old Mother, with her mouth open and bristling with fish-hooks, her eyes glassy with rage, myself pulling against that dreadful pressure, biting against it like a minnow on a line, as if the pike were some part of myself I was struggling to tear free, some black part of my own heart writhing and thrashing on the line, some terrible, secret catch . . .

It came down to one of two options. My mind might

play with other possibilities – that Laure Dessanges might promise to leave me alone in exchange for her little brother's release – but the deep-down practical part of my mind knew they wouldn't work. We'd only gained one thing by our actions so far – time – and I could feel the prize slipping from me second by second, even as I racked my brains to find out how I could use it. If not, by the following day Luc's prediction – 'Come tomorrow your sad little secret is going to be splashed across every magazine and newspaper' – would stand before us in hard print, and I'd lose everything: the farm, the restaurant, my place in Les Laveuses . . . The only alternative, I knew, was to use the truth as a weapon. But although that might win me back my home and my business, who could say what the effect might be on Pistache, on Noisette, on Paul?

I gritted my teeth in frustration. No-one should have to make that choice, I wailed inwardly. No-one.

I hoed at a line of shallots so hard and blindly that I forgot myself and began to gouge at the ripening plants, sending the shiny little onions flying with the weeds. I wiped the sweat from my eyes and found I was crying.

No-one should have to choose between a life and a lie. And yet *she* had, Mirabelle Dartigen, the woman in the picture with her fake pearls and shy smile, the woman with the sharp cheekbones and scragged-back hair. She'd given it up, all of it – the farm, the orchard, the little niche she'd carved for herself, her grief, the truth – buried it without a backward glance and moved on. Only one fact is missing from her album, so carefully collated and cross-referenced, one thing she couldn't possibly have written because she couldn't possibly have known. One fact remains to complete our story. One fact.

If it wasn't for my daughters and for Paul, I told myself, I'd tell all of it. If only to spite Laure, if only to rob her of her triumph. But there Paul was, so quiet and unassuming, so humble in his silence that he managed to get past my defences before I even realized it. Paul, always something of a joke with his stammer and his ratty old blue dungarees; Paul, with his poacher's hands and his easy smile. Who would have thought it would be Paul, after all these years? Who would have thought that after so many years I would find my way back home?

I almost phoned several times. I found the number in one of my old magazines. Mirabelle Dartigen was long dead, after all. I had no need to haul her about the weird water of my heart like Old Mother on her line. A second lie would not change her now, I told myself. Nor would revealing the truth at this point allow me to atone. But Mirabelle Dartigen is a stubborn woman, even in death. Even now I can feel her, *hear* her, like the wail of wires on a windy day – that shrill, confused treble which is all that remains of my memory of her. No matter that I never knew how much I really loved her. Her love, that flawed and stony secret, drags me with it into the murk.

And yet. It wouldn't be *right*. Paul's voice inside me, relentless as the river. It wouldn't be right to live a lie. I wished I didn't have to choose.

8

It was almost sunset when he came to find me. I'd been working in the garden for so long that the ache in my bones had become a screeching, jarring imperative. My throat was dry and full of fish-hooks. My head swam. Still I turned away from him as he stood silently at my back, not speaking, not needing to speak, just waiting, biding his time.

'What do you want?' I snapped at last. 'Stop *staring* at me, for heaven's sake, and get on with something useful.'

Paul said nothing. I could feel the back of my neck burning. At last I turned round, flinging the hoe across the vegetable patch and screaming at him in my mother's voice.

'You cretin! Can't you keep away from me? You miserable old fool!' I wanted to hurt him, I think. It would have been easier if I'd been able to hurt him, make him turn from me in rage or pain or disgust, but he faced me out – funny, I'd always thought I was better at that game than anyone – with his inexorable patience, not moving, not speaking, just waiting for me to reach the end of my line so that he could speak his piece. I turned away furiously, afraid of his words and his terrible patience.

'I made our guest some dinner,' he said at last. 'P'raps you'd like some, too.'

I shook my head. 'I don't want anything except to be left alone,' I told him.

Behind me I heard Paul sigh. 'She was just the same,' he said. 'Mirabelle Dartigen. Never would take help from anyone. No, not even from herself.' His voice was quiet and reflective. 'You're a lot like her, you know. Too much like her for your own good, or anybody's.'

I bit back a sharp reply and would not look at him.

'Set herself aback everyone with her stubbornness,' continued Paul. 'Never knowing they'd have helped her if she'd said. But she never said, did she? She never told a soul.'

'I don't suppose she could,' I said numbly. 'Some things you can't. You . . . just can't.'

'Look at me,' said Paul.

His face looked rosy in the last flare of the sunset, rosy and young in spite of the lines and the nicotine moustache. Behind him the sky was a raw red barbed with clouds.

'Comes a time *someone* has to tell,' he said reasonably. 'I've not been reading your ma's scrapbook for all this time for nothing, and whatever you might think, I'm not quite such a fool as all that.'

'I'm sorry,' I said. 'I didn't mean to say that.'

Paul shook his head dismissively. 'I know. I'm not smart, like Cassis or you, but seems to me sometimes that it's the smart ones get lost the soonest.' He smiled and tapped his temple with one extended knuckle. 'Too much goin' on in here,' he said kindly. 'Far too much.'

I looked at him.

'See, it isn't the *truth* that hurts,' he continued. 'If she'd seen that, none of this might ever have happened. If she'd just asked them for help, 'stead of goin' her own way, like she always did—'

'No.' My voice was flat and final. 'You don't understand. She never knew the truth. Or if she did, she hid it, even from herself. For *our* sake. For *mine*.' I was choking now, a familiar taste rising up from my sour belly, cramping me with its sourness. 'It wasn't up

to her to tell the truth. It was up to *us*. To *me*.' I
swallowed painfully. 'It could only have been me,'
I said with an effort. 'Only I knew the whole story.
Only I could have had the *guts*—'

I stopped to look at him again – his sweet and rueful
smile; his stooped shoulders, like those of a mule who
has carried long and heavy loads in patience and peace
of mind. How I envied him. How I wanted him.

'You do have the guts,' said Paul at last. 'You always
did.'

We looked at each other. Silence between us.

'All right,' I told him at last. 'Let him go.'

'Are you sure? The drugs Louis found in his
pocket—'

I gave a laugh which sounded strangely carefree in
my dry mouth. 'You and I both know there were no
drugs. A harmless fake, that's all, which you planted
on him when you went through his pockets.' I laughed
again at his startled look. 'Poacher's fingers, Paul,
poacher's hands. Did you think you were the only one
with a suspicious mind?'

Paul nodded. 'What will you do then?' he asked. 'As
soon as he tells Yannick and Laure . . .'

I shook my head.

'Let him tell them,' I said. I felt light inside, lighter
than I had ever felt before; thistledown on the water. I
felt laughter rising up inside me, the mad laughter of a
person who is about to throw everything she possesses
to the wind. I put my hand into my apron pocket and
drew out the scrap of paper with the telephone number
written on it.

Then, thinking better of it, I fetched my little address
book. After a moment's searching, I found the right
page.

'I think I know what to do now,' I said.

9

Apple and dried-apricot clafoutis. Beat the eggs and flour together with the sugar and melted butter until the consistency is thick and creamy. Add the milk, little by little, beating all the time. The final consistency should be a thin batter. Rub a dish generously with butter, and add the sliced fruit to the batter. Add cinnamon and allspice and put it into the oven at a medium temperature. When the cake has begun to rise, add brown sugar to the top and dot with butter. Bake until the top is crisp and firm to the touch.

It had been a meagre harvest. The drought, followed by the disastrous rains, had seen to that. And yet the end-of-October harvest festival was something we all looked forward to with anticipation, even Reine, even Mother, who made her special cakes and left bowls of fruit and vegetables on the window ledge, and baked loaves of extravagant and intricate loveliness – a wheat sheaf, a fish, a basket of apples – to sell at the Angers market. The village school had closed the previous year when the teacher moved to Paris, but the Sunday school was still going.

That day all the Sunday-schoolers filed around the fountain – paganly decorated with flowers, fruit and wreaths of corn, pumpkins and coloured squash, hollowed and cut into lantern shapes – dressed in their best clothes, holding candles and singing. The service continued in the church, where the altar was draped in green and gold, and the hymns, resounding across the square where we listened, fascinated by the lure of things forbidden, dealt with the reaping of the chosen and the burning of the chaff. We waited until the service was over, and joined in the festivities with the rest while the *curé* remained to take confession in church and the harvest bonfires burned smoky-sweet at the corners of the bare fields.

It was then that the fair began. The harvest fair, with wrestling and racing and all kinds of competitions – dancing, ducking for apples, pancake-eating, goose-racing – and hot gingerbread and cider given out to the winners and losers, and baskets of home-made produce sold at the fountain while the Harvest Queen sat smiling on her yellow throne and showered passers-by with flowers.

This year we had hardly seen it coming. Most other years we would have awaited the celebration with an impatience greater than Christmas, for presents were scarce in those days and December is a poor time for celebration. October, fleeting and sappy-sweet with its reddish-gold light and early white frosts and the leaves turning brilliantly, is a different matter, a magical time, a last gleeful defiance in the face of the approaching cold. Other years we would have had the pile of wood and dead leaves waiting in a sheltered spot weeks in advance, the necklaces of crab apples and bags of nuts waiting, our best clothes ironed and ready and our shoes polished for dancing. There might have been a special celebration at the Lookout Post, wreaths hung on the Treasure Stone and scarlet flower heads dropped into the slow brown Loire, pears and apples sliced and dried in the oven, garlands of yellow corn plaited and worked into braids and dollies for good luck around the house, tricks planned against the unsuspecting and bellies rumbling in hungry anticipation.

But this year there was little of that. The sourness after the night at La Mauvaise Réputation had begun our descent, and with it the letters, the rumours, graffiti on the walls, whispering behind our backs and polite silences to our faces. It was assumed that there could be no smoke without fire. The accusations – 'NAZI WHOAR' painted in red on the side of the hen house, painted and repainted in spite of our attempts to wash them clean – coupled with Mother's refusal to acknowledge or deny the gossip, along with reports of her visits to La Rép, exaggerated and passed hungrily from mouth to mouth, were enough to whet suspicions even more keenly. Harvest time was a sour affair for the Dartigen family that year.

The others built their bonfires and sheaved their wheat. Children picked over the rows to make sure none of the grain was lost. We gathered the last of the apples – what wasn't rotten through with wasps, that is – and stored them away in the cellar on trays, each one separate so that rot couldn't spread. We stored our vegetables in the root cellar in bins and under loose coverings of dry earth. Mother even baked some of her special bread, though there was little market for her baking in Les Laveuses, and sold it impassively in Angers. I remember how we took a cartload of loaves and cakes to market one day, how the sun shone on the burnished crusts – acorns, hedgehogs, little grimacing masks – like on polished oak. A few of the village children refused to speak to us. On the way to school one day someone threw clods of earth at Reinette and Cassis from a stand of tamarisks by the riverside. As the day approached, girls began to appraise each other, brushing their hair with special care and washing their faces with oatmeal, for on festival day one of them would be chosen to be the Harvest Queen and would wear the barley crown and carry the pitcher of wine. I was totally uninterested in this. With my short straight hair and froggy face I was never going to be Harvest Queen. Besides, without Tomas nothing mattered very much. I wondered if I would ever see him again. I sat by the Loire with my traps and my fishing rod and watched. I couldn't stop myself from believing that somehow, if I caught the pike, Tomas would return.

10

Harvest day morning was cold and bright, with the dying-ember glow peculiar to October. Mother had stayed up the night before, out of a kind of stubbornness rather than a love of tradition, making gingerbread and black buckwheat pancakes and blackberry jam, which she placed in baskets and gave to us to take to the fair. I wasn't planning on going. Instead, I milked the goat and finished my few Sunday chores, then began to make my way towards the river. I had just placed a particularly ingenious trap there, a series of crates and drums tied together with chicken wire and baited with fish scraps right at the edge of the river bank, and I was eager to test it out. I could smell cut grass on the wind with the first of the autumn bonfires, and the scent was poignant, centuries old, a reminder of happier times. I felt old, too, trudging through the maize fields to the Loire. I felt as if I'd already lived a long, long time.

Paul was waiting for me at the Standing Stones. He looked unsurprised to see me, glancing briefly at me from his fishing before returning to the cork floater on the water.

'Aren't you going to the f-fair?' he asked.

I shook my head. I realized I hadn't seen him once since Mother chased him from the house, and I felt a sudden pang of guilt at having so completely forgotten my old friend. Maybe that's why I sat down next to him. Certainly it was not for the sake of companionship; my need for solitude was stifling me.

'Me n-neither.' He looked morose, almost sour-faced that morning, his eyes drawn together in a frown of concentration which was unsettlingly adult. 'All those idiots getting d-drunk and d-dancing about. Who needs it?'

'Not me.' At my feet, the brown eddies of the river were hypnotic. 'I'm going to check all my traps, then I thought I'd try the big sandbank. Cassis says there are pike there sometimes.'

Paul gave me a cynical look. 'Never g-get her,' he told me tersely.

'Why not?'

He shrugged. 'You j-just won't, that's all.'

We fished side by side for a time, as the sun warmed our backs slowly and the leaves fell yellow-red-black, one by one into the silky water. We heard the church bells ringing sweet and distant across the fields, signalling the end of Mass. The fair would begin within ten minutes.

'Are the others going?' Paul shifted a bloodworm from its warming place in his left cheek and speared it expertly onto the hook.

I shrugged. 'Don't care,' I said.

In the silence which followed I heard Paul's stomach rumble loudly.

'Hungry?'

'Nah.'

It was then that I heard it, clear as memory on the Angers road. Almost imperceptible at first, but growing louder, like the drone of a sleepy wasp. Louder like the buzz of blood in the temples after a breathless run across the fields. The sound of a single motorbike.

A sudden burst of panic. Paul must not see him. If it was Tomas I *must* be alone, and my heart's sick lurch of joy told me, told me with a clear rapturous certainty, that it was Tomas.

Tomas.

'Perhaps we could just have a look in,' I said with fake indifference.

Paul made a noncommittal sound.

'There'll be gingerbread,' I told him slyly. 'And baked potatoes and roasted sweetcorn and pies and sausage in the coals of the bonfire.'

I heard his stomach rumble a little louder.

'We could sneak in and help ourselves,' I suggested.

Silence.

'Cassis and Reine will be there.'

At least I hoped they would. I was counting on their presence to enable me to make a quick getaway and back to Tomas. The thought of his closeness, the unbearable, hot joy which filled me at the thought of seeing him, was like baking stones under my feet.

'W-will *she* be there?' His voice was low with a hate which might in other circumstances have surprised me. I never imagined Paul to be the kind to bear a grudge. 'I mean your m-m-m-' He grimaced with the effort. 'Your m-m-m-Your m-m-m-'

I shook my head.

'Shouldn't think so,' I interrupted more sharply than I intended. 'God, Paul, it drives me crazy when you do that.'

Paul shrugged indifferently. I could hear the sound of the motorbike clearly now, maybe a mile or two up the road. I clenched my fists so hard that my fingernails scarred my palms.

'I mean,' I said in a gentler tone. 'I mean it doesn't matter really. She just doesn't understand, that's all.'

'Will she b-be there?' insisted Paul.

I shook my head. 'No,' I lied. 'She said she'd be clearing out the goat shed this morning.'

Paul nodded. 'All right,' he said mildly.

11

Tomas might wait at the Lookout Post for an hour or so. The weather was warm; he would hide his motorbike in the bushes and smoke a cigarette. If there was nobody around he might risk a dip in the river. If after that time no-one had appeared, he would scribble a message for us and leave it, perhaps with a parcel of magazines or sweets carefully packed in newspaper, at the top of the Lookout Post, in the fork under the platform. I knew; he'd done it before. In that time I could easily get into the village with Paul, then double back as soon as no-one was watching. I would not tell Reinette or Cassis that he was here. I felt a burst of greedy joy at the thought, imagining his face lit up by a smile of welcome, a smile which would be mine alone. With that thought I almost rushed Paul towards the village, my hot hand tight round his cool one, my sweaty hair hanging in my eyes.

The square around the fountain was already half filled with people. More people were filing out of the church – children holding candles, young girls with crowns of autumn leaves, a handful of young men fresh from confession, Guilherm Ramondin amongst them, ogling the girls prior to reaping a new crop of sinful thoughts. More, if they could get it; harvest was the time for it, after all, and there was precious little else to look forward to. I saw Cassis and Reinette standing a little way away from the main body of the crowd. Reine was wearing a red flannel dress and a

307

necklace of berries, and Cassis was eating a sugared pastry. No-one seemed to be talking to them, and I could sense the little circle of isolation about them. Reinette was laughing, a high, brittle sound, like the scream of a seabird. A little distance away from them my mother stood watching, a basket of pastries and fruit in one hand. She looked very drab amongst the festival crowd, her black dress and headscarf jarring against the flowers and bunting. At my side I felt Paul stiffen.

A group of people by the side of the fountain began a cheery song. Raphaël was there, I think, and Colette Gaudin, and Paul's uncle Philippe Hourias, a yellow scarf tied incongruously about his neck, and Agnès Petit in her Sunday frock and patent shoes, a crown of berries on her hair. I remember her voice rising above the others for a moment – it was untrained, but very sweet and clear – and I felt a shiver raise the hairs on the nape of my neck, as if the ghost she was to become had walked prematurely over my grave. I still remember the words she sang:

> *A la claire fontaine j'allais me promener*
> *J'ai trouvé l'eau si belle que je m'y suis baignée*
> *Il y a longtemps que je t'aime*
> *Jamais je ne t'oublierai.*

Tomas, if it had been Tomas, would be at the Lookout Post by now. But Paul at my side showed no sign of mingling with the crowd. Instead he looked at my mother's figure across from the fountain and bit his lips nervously.

'I thought you said she wouldn't b-be here,' he said.

'I didn't know,' I said.

We stood watching for a while as people came out of the church and moved to refresh themselves. There were jugs of cider and wine resting on the ledge around the fountain, and many of the women had, like my mother, brought loaves and brioche and fruit to distribute at the church door. I noticed that my mother kept her distance, though, and few came near enough to claim the food she had so carefully prepared. Her face remained impassive, however, almost indifferent. Only her hands gave her away; her white, nervous hands clenched so tightly against the basket's handle. Her lips were bitten white against her pale face.

I fretted. Paul gave no sign of leaving my side. A woman – Francine Crespin, I think, Raphaël's sister – held out a basket of apples to Paul, then, seeing me, let her smile stiffen. Few people had missed the writing on the hen-house wall.

The priest came out of the church. Père Froment, his weak, mild eyes bright today with the knowledge that his people were united, his gilt crucifix mounted on a wooden pole and held in the air like a trophy. Behind him, two altar boys carried the Virgin on her yellow-and-gold dais, decorated with berries and autumn leaves. The Sunday-schoolers turned to the little procession with their candles held in the air and began to sing a harvest hymn. Girls primped and practised their smiles. I saw Reinette turn, too. Then came the Harvest Queen's yellow throne, carried by two young men from inside the church. It was only straw, with head and armrests made of corn sheaves and a cushion of autumn leaves, but for a moment, with the sun shining on it, it might just as easily have been gold.

There were maybe a dozen girls of the right age waiting by the fountain. I remember them all: Jeannette Crespin in her too-tight Communion dress, redheaded Francine Hourias with her mass of freckles that no amount of washing with bran could fade, Michèle Petit with her tight braids and eyeglasses. None of them could hold a candle to Reinette. They knew it, too. I could see it in the way they watched her, set slightly apart from the others in her red dress, with her long hair unbound and berries woven into her curls, with envy and suspicion. With a little satisfaction, too: no-one would vote for Reine Dartigen as Harvest Queen this year. Not this year, not with the rumours flying about us, like dead leaves in the wind.

The priest was speaking. I listened with mounting impatience. Tomas would be waiting. I had to leave soon if I was not to miss him. At my side, Paul was staring at the fountain with that look of half-stupid intensity in his face.

'It has been a year of many trials.' The *curé*'s voice was a soothing drone, like the distant bleating of sheep. 'But your faith and your energy have brought us through once again.' I sensed an impatience akin to mine from the people in the crowd. They had already listened to a long sermon. Now was the time for the crowning of the queen, for the dancing and celebration. I saw a small child reach for a piece of cake from her mother's basket and eat it quickly, unnoticed, behind her hand, with furtive, greedy bites.

'Now is a time for celebration.' That was more like it. I heard a low shushing from the crowd, a murmur of approbation and impatience. Père Froment felt it, too.

'I only ask that you show moderation in all things,' he bleated, 'remembering what it is that you are celebrating, without Whom there could be no harvest and no rejoicing.'

'Get on with it, *Père*!' cried a rough, cheery voice from the side of the church. Père Froment looked affronted and resigned at the same moment.

'All in good time, *mon fils*,' he admonished. 'As I was saying, now is the time to begin our Lord's festival by naming the Harvest Queen – a girl between the ages of thirteen and seventeen – to rule over our celebrations and wear the barley crown.'

A dozen voices interrupted, crying out names, some of them quite ineligible. Raphaël yelled out, 'Agnès Petit!' and Agnès, who wasn't a day under thirty-five, blushed in delighted embarrassment, looking, for a moment, almost pretty.

'Murielle Dupré!'

'Colette Gaudin!' Wives kissed their husbands and shrieked mock-indignation at the compliment.

'Michèle Petit!' That was Michèle's mother, doggedly loyal.

'Georgette Lemaître!' This was Henri volunteering his grandmother, aged ninety or more and cackling wildly at the joke.

Several young men called out for Jeannette Crespin, and she blushed furiously behind her hands. Then Paul, who had been standing in silence at my side, suddenly stepped forwards.

'Reine-Claude Dartigen!' he called loudly, without stammering, and his voice was strong and almost adult, a man's voice, quite unlike his own, slow, hesitant drawl. 'Reine-Claude Dartigen!' he called again, and people turned to look at him curiously, murmuring. 'Reine-Claude Dartigen!' he called once again, and walked across the square towards the astounded Reinette with a necklace of crab apples in his hand.

'Here, this is for you,' he said in a softer voice, but still with no trace of a stutter, and flung the necklace over Reinette's head. The little red-and-yellow fruit glowed in the reddish October light.

'Reine-Claude Dartigen,' said Paul once more and, taking Reine's hand, led her the few steps to the straw throne. Père Froment said nothing, an uneasy smile on his lips, but allowed Paul to place the barley crown on Reinette's head.

'Very good,' said the priest softly. 'Very good.' Then, in a louder voice, 'I hereby name Reine-Claude Dartigen this year's Harvest Queen!'

It might have been impatience at the thought of so much wine and cider waiting to be drunk. It might have been the surprise of hearing poor little Paul Hourias speak without stammering for the first time in his life. It might have been the sight of Reinette sitting on the throne with her lips like cherries and the sun shining through her hair like a halo. Most of them clapped. A few even cheered and called out her name – all of them men, I noticed, even Raphaël and Julien Lanicen, who were at La Mauvaise Réputation that night. But some of the women did not applaud. Only a few abstained, only a handful, but enough. Michèle's mother, for one, and spiteful gossips like Marthe Gaudin and Isabelle Ramondin. But they were still few, and although some looked uneasy, they joined their voices to the rest. Some even clapped as Reine threw flower heads and fruit from her basket at the Sunday-school children. I caught a glimpse of my mother's face then as I began to creep away, and was struck by the sudden look on her face, the sudden soft, warm look – cheeks flushed and eyes almost as bright as in the forgotten wedding photograph – the headscarf pulling from her hair as she almost ran to Reinette's side. I think I was the only one to see it. Everyone else was looking at my sister. Even Paul was looking at her from his place at the side of the fountain, the stupid look back on his face as if it had never left. Something inside me twisted. Moisture stung my eyes so sharply that for a second I was sure that some insect – a wasp, perhaps – had lit onto my eyelid.

I dropped the pastry I had been eating and turned, unnoticed, to go. Tomas was waiting for me. Suddenly it was very important to believe that Tomas was waiting. Tomas, who loved me. Tomas, only Tomas, for ever. For a moment I turned back, fixing the scene into my mind. My sister the Harvest Queen, the most beautiful Harvest Queen ever crowned, the sheaf in one hand and in the other a round bright fruit – an apple, maybe, or a pomegranate – pressed into her palm by Père Froment, their eyes meeting, he smiling in his sweet, sheepy way, my mother, the smile freezing on her bright face in a sudden gesture of recoil, her voice coming to me thinly over the sound of the merry crowd – 'What's that? For God's sake, what's that? Who gave you that?'

I ran then, while attention was diverted from me.

Almost laughing, with the invisible wasp still stinging at my eyelids, I ran as fast as I could back to the river, my thoughts a blur. Every now and again I had to stop to quiet the spasms that cramped my stomach, spasms eerily like laughter, but which sent tears spurting from my eyes. That orange! Stored with care and love for just this occasion, kept hidden in tissue paper for the Harvest Queen, globed in her hand as Mother . . . as Mother . . . The laughter was like acid inside me, but the pain was exquisite, rolling me to the ground, tugging at me like fish-hooks. The look on my mother's face convulsed me whenever I thought of it, the look of pride turning to fear – no, *terror* – at the sight of a single, tiny orange. Between spasms I ran as fast as I could, calculating that it might take ten minutes to arrive at the Lookout Post, adding to that the time we had spent at the fountain – twenty at least – gasping with fear that Tomas might already have left.

This time I'd ask him, I promised myself. I'd ask him to take me with him this time, wherever he was going, back to Germany or into the woods, on the run for ever. Whatever he wanted as long as he and I . . . he and I. I prayed to Old Mother as I ran, brambles snagging at my bare legs unheeded. Please, Tomas. Please. Only you. For ever. I met no-one on my mad run across the fields. Everyone else was at the festival. By the time I reached the Standing Stones I was calling his name out loud, my voice shrill as a peewit's in the silky silence of the river.

Could he already have gone?

'Tomas! Tomas!' I was hoarse from laughing, hoarse with fear. '*Tomas! Tomas!*'

I almost didn't see him, he was so quick. Sliding out of a stand of bushes, one hand clamping around my wrist, the other over my mouth. For a second I hardly even recognized him – his face dark – and I struggled wildly, trying to bite his hand, making small birdlike sounds against his palm.

'Shh, *Backfisch*, what the hell are you trying to do?' I recognized his voice and stopped struggling.

'Tomas. Tomas.' I couldn't stop saying his name, the familiar scent of tobacco and sweat from his clothes filling my nostrils. I clutched his coat close to my face in a way I would never have dared two months ago. In the secret darkness of it, I kissed the lining with desperate passion. 'I knew you'd come back. I knew you would.'

He looked at me, saying nothing. 'Are you alone?' His eyes looked narrower than usual, wary. I nodded.

'Good. I want you to listen.' He spoke very slowly, emphatically, enunciating every word. There was no cigarette at the corner of his mouth, no gleam in his eyes. He seemed to have got thinner in the past few weeks, his face sharper, his mouth less generous.

'I want you to listen carefully.'

I nodded my obedience. Whatever you want, Tomas. My eyes felt bright and hot. Only you, Tomas. Only you. I wanted to tell him about my mother and Reine and the orange, but sensed that this was the wrong time. I listened.

'There may be men coming to the village,' he said. 'Black uniforms. You know what that means, don't you?'

I nodded. 'German police,' I said. 'SS.'

'That's right.' He spoke in a clipped, precise tone very unlike his usual careless drawl. 'They may ask questions.'

I looked at him without comprehension.

'Questions about me,' said Tomas.

'Why?'

'Never mind why.' His hand was still tight, almost painfully so, around my wrist. 'There are things they might ask you. Things about what we've been doing.'

'You mean the magazines and stuff?'

'That's right. And about the old man at the café. Gustave. The one who drowned.' His face looked grim and drawn. He turned my face to look at his, coming

314

very close. I could smell cigarette smoke on his collar and on his breath. 'Listen, *Backfisch*. This is important. You mustn't tell them anything. You've never seen me. You weren't at La Rép the night of the dance. You don't even know my name. All right?'

I nodded.

'Don't forget,' insisted Tomas. 'You don't know anything. You've never spoken to me. Tell the others.'

I nodded again, and he seemed to relax a little.

'Something else, too.' His voice had lost its harshness, becoming almost caressing. It made me feel soft inside, like warm caramel. I looked at him expectantly.

'I can't come here again,' he said gently. 'Not for a while, anyway. It's getting too dangerous. I only just managed to get away with it last time.'

I was silent for a moment. 'We could meet at the cinema instead,' I suggested shyly. 'Like we used to do. Or in the woods.'

Tomas shook his head impatiently. 'Aren't you listening?' he snapped. 'We can't meet at all. Not anywhere.'

Cold prickled over my skin like snowflakes. My mind was a surging black cloud.

'For how long?' I whispered at last.

'A long time.' I could feel his impatience. 'Maybe for ever.'

I flinched and began to shake. The prickling had turned to a hot stinging sensation, like rolling in nettles. He took my face in his hands.

'Look, Framboise,' he said slowly. 'I'm sorry. I know you—' he broke off then, suddenly. 'I know it's hard.' He grinned, a fierce but somehow rueful grin, like a wild animal trying to mimic friendliness.

'I brought you some things,' he said at last. 'Magazines, coffee.' Again that tight, cheery grin. 'Chewing gum, chocolate, books.'

I looked at him in silence. My heart felt like a lump of cold clay.

'Just hide them, won't you?' His eyes were bright, the

315

eyes of a child sharing a delightful secret. 'And don't tell anyone about us. Not anyone at all.'

He turned to the bush from which he had sprung and pulled out a parcel tied up with string.

'Open it,' he urged.

I stared at him dully.

'Go on.' His voice was tight with enforced cheer. 'It's yours.'

'I don't want it.'

'Ah, *Backfisch*, come *on*.' He reached out to put his arm around me, but I pushed him away.

'*I said I don't want it!*' It was my mother's voice again, screamy and sharp, and suddenly I hated him for bringing it out of me. '*I don't want it, don't want it!*'

He grinned at me helplessly. 'Ah, come on,' he repeated. 'Don't be like that. I only—'

'We could run away,' I said abruptly. 'I know lots of places in the woods. We could run away and no-one would ever know where to find us. We could eat rabbits and things, mushrooms, berries.' My face was burning. My throat felt sore and parched. 'We'd be safe,' I insisted. 'No-one would know.' But I could see from his face that it was useless.

'I can't,' he said with finality.

I could feel tears welling up in my eyes.

'Can't you even s-stay for a while?' I sounded like Paul now, humble and stupid, but I couldn't help it. Part of me would have liked to let him go in icy, prideful silence, without a word, but the words stumbled out of my mouth unbidden.

'Please? You could have a cigarette, or a swim, or we c-could go f-ishing.'

Tomas shook his head.

I felt something inside me begin to collapse with slow inevitability. In the distance I heard a sudden clanking of metal against metal.

'Just a few minutes? *Please*?' How I hated the sound of my voice then, that stupid, hurt pleading. 'I'll show you my new traps. I'll show you my pike pot.'

316

His silence was damning, patient as the grave. I could feel our time slipping from me, inexorably. Again I heard the distant clanking of metal against metal, the sound of a dog with a tin can tied to his tail, and suddenly I recognized that sound. A wave of desperate joy submerged me.

'Please! It's important!' High and childish now, and with the hope of salvation, closer to tears than ever, heat spilling from my eyelids and clogging my throat. 'I'll tell if you don't stay. I'll tell, I'll tell, I'll—'

He nodded once, impatiently.

'Five minutes. Not a minute more. All right?'

My tears stopped. 'All right.'

12

Five minutes. I knew what I had to do. It was our last chance – my last chance – but my heart, beating like a hammer, filled my desperate mind with a wild music. He'd given me five minutes. Elation filled me as I dragged him by the hand towards the big sandbank where I'd laid my last trap. The prayer which filled my mind as I ran from the village was a yammering, deafening imperative now – *only you only you oh Tomas please oh please please please* – my heart beating so hard that it threatened to burst my eardrums.

'Where are we going?' His voice was calm, amused, almost disinterested.

'I want to show you something,' I gasped, pulling harder at his hand. 'Something important. Come on!'

I could hear the tin cans I had tied to the oil drum rattling. There was something in there, I told myself with a sudden shiver of excitement. Something big. The tins bobbed furiously on the water, rattling the drum. Below, the two crates secured together with chicken wire rocked and churned under the surface.

It had to be. It just *had* to be.

From its hiding place beneath the banking I pulled out the wooden pole which I used to manoeuvre my heavy traps to the surface. My hands were shaking so badly that at the first try I almost dropped the pole into the water. With the hook secured to the end of the pole, I detached the crates from the floater and pushed the big drum away. The crates bucked and pranced.

318

'It's too *heavy*!' I screamed.

Tomas was watching me in some bewilderment.

'What the hell is that?' he asked.

'Oh please. *Please*.' I was heaving at the crates, trying to drag them up the steep banking. Water ran out of the slatted sides of the boxes. Something large and violent slid and thrashed about inside.

At my side I heard Tomas' low laugh.

'Oh you *Backfisch*,' he gasped. 'I think you've got it at last. That old pike. *Lieber Gott*, but it must be huge!'

I was hardly listening. My breath rasped my throat like sandpaper. I could feel my bare heels in the mud, sliding helplessly towards the water. The thing in my hands was dragging me in, inch by inch.

'I'm not going to lose her!' I gasped harshly. 'I'm not! I'm not!' I took one step up the bank, pulling the sodden crates after me, then another. I could feel the slippery yellow mud beneath my feet threatening to bring my legs from under me. The pole dug cruelly into my shoulders as I fought for leverage. And at the back of my mind was the rapturous knowledge that *he* was watching, that if only I could drag Old Mother from her hiding place, then my wish . . . my wish . . .

One step, then another. I dug my toes into the clay and dragged myself higher. One more step, my burden getting lighter as water poured from the crates. I could feel the creature inside hurling itself in fury against the sides of the box. One step more.

Then nothing.

I pulled, but the crates did not move. Crying out in frustration, I threw myself as far as I could up the banking, but the crate was stuck fast. A root, perhaps, dangling from the bare bank like the stub of a rotten tooth, or a floating log wedged in the chicken wire. 'It's *stuck*!' I cried desperately. 'The damn trap's stuck on something!'

Tomas gave me a comical look.

319

'It's only an old pike,' he said with a hint of impatience.

'Please, Tomas,' I gasped. 'If I drop it she'll get away. Reach down and pull it loose. Please.'

Tomas shrugged and took off his jacket and shirt, leaving them neatly on a bush.

'I'm not getting mud on my uniform,' he observed mildly.

My arms trembling with the effort, I held the pole whilst Tomas investigated the obstruction.

'It's a clump of roots,' he called to me. 'Looks as if one of the slats has come free, and got caught in the roots. It's stuck tight.'

'Can you reach it?' I called.

He shrugged. 'I'll try.' Pulling off his trousers to hang them beside the rest of his uniform and leaving his boots beside the banking, I saw him shiver as he entered the water – it was deep there – and heard him swear comically.

'I must be crazy,' said Tomas. 'It's freezing in here.' He was standing almost to his shoulders in the sleek brown water. I remember how the Loire parted at that point, the current just hard enough to make little pale frills of foam around his body.

'Can you reach it?' I yelled to him. My arms were filled with burning wires, my head pounding furiously. I could still feel the pike, half in water, as it flung itself mightily against the sides of the crate.

'It's down here,' I heard him say. 'Just below the surface. I think' – a plashing sound as he ducked momentarily and resurfaced sleek as an otter – 'a little further down' – I leaned against the pull with all of my weight. My temples burned and I felt like screaming in pain and frustration. Five seconds, ten seconds – almost passing out now, red-black flowers blooming against my eyelids and the prayer: *please oh please I'll let you go I swear I swear just please please Tomas only you Tomas only you for ever only*.

Then, without warning, the crate released. I skidded

up the banking, almost losing my grip on the pole as I did, the freed trap bouncing after me. With blurred vision and the taste of metal in my throat I dragged it to safety on the bank, driving splinters of the broken crate under my fingernails and into my already blistered palms. I tore at the chicken wire, stripping the skin from my hands, certain that the pike had got away. Something slapped at the side of the box – slap-slap-slap. The fierce wet sound of a face-flannel against an enamel basin – 'Look at that face, 'Boise, it's a disgrace! Come here and let me see to that' – I was suddenly reminded of Mother and how she used to scrub us when we wouldn't get washed, sometimes until we bled.

Slap-slap-slap. The sound was weaker now, less persistent, though I knew a fish could live for minutes, even twitching for as long as half-an-hour after it was caught. Through the slats, in the darkness of the crate, I could see a huge shape the colour of dark oil, and now and again the gleam of its eye, like a single ballbearing, rolling at me in a stripe of sunlight. I felt a stab of joy so fierce it felt like dying.

'Old Mother,' I whispered hoarsely. 'Old Mother. I wish. I wish. Make him stay. Make Tomas stay.' I whispered it quickly so that Tomas wouldn't hear what I was saying, and then, when he didn't come up the banking immediately, I said it again, in case the old pike hadn't heard the first time: 'Make Tomas stay. Make him stay for ever.'

Inside the crate, the pike slapped and floundered. I could make out the shape of its mouth now, a sour, downturned crescent, whiskered with steel from previous attempts at capture, and I was filled with terror at its size, pride at my victory, crazed, engulfing relief. It was over. The nightmare which had begun with Jeannette and the water-snake, the oranges and Mother's descent into madness, it all ended here on the river bank. This girl in her muddied skirt and bare feet, her short hair scruffed with mud and her face shining, this box, this fish, this man looking almost a boy, without his uniform and with his hair dripping. I looked around impatiently.

'Tomas! Come and look!'

Silence. Only the small sounds of the river plapping against the muddy hollow of the banking. I stood up to look over the edge.

'Tomas!'

But there was no sign of Tomas. Where he had dived down there was an unbroken creamy smoothness the colour of *café au lait*, with only a few bubbles on the surface.

'Tomas!'

Maybe I should have felt panic. If I'd responded there and then maybe I would have caught him in time, avoided the inevitable somehow. I tell myself this now. But then, still dizzy with my victory, my legs trembling with exertion and fatigue, I could only remember the hundreds of times he and Cassis had played this game, diving deep under the surface of the water and pretending they were drowned, hiding in hollows under the sandbank to resurface, red-eyed and laughing, as Reinette screamed and screamed. In the box Old Mother slap-slapped imperiously. I took another couple of steps towards the edge.

'Tomas?'

Silence. I stood there for a moment, which seemed like for ever. I whispered, 'Tomas?'

The Loire hissed silkily beneath my feet. Old Mother's slapping had grown feeble in the crate. Along the rotten banking the long yellow roots reached into the water like witches' fingers. And I knew.

I had my wish.

When Cassis and Reine found me two hours later I was lying dry-eyed by the river bank with one hand on Tomas' boots and the other on a broken packing crate containing the remains of a big fish, which was already beginning to stink.

322

13

We were still only children. We didn't know what to do. We were afraid. Cassis perhaps more than the rest of us, because he was older and he understood rather better than we did what would happen if we were linked with Tomas' death. It was Cassis who dragged Tomas from under the banking, freeing his ankle from behind the root that had snagged him. Cassis, too, who removed the remainder of his clothes and bundled them together, tying them with his belt. He was crying, but there was something hard in him that day, something we had never seen before. Perhaps he used up his lifetime's reserve of bravery that day, I thought afterwards. Perhaps that was why he fled later into the soft forgetfulness of drink. Reine was useless. She sat on the bank throughout, crying, her face mottled and almost ugly. It was only when Cassis shook her and said she had to promise – *promise!* – that she showed any reaction, nodding dimly through her tears and sobbing, *'Tomas. Oh Tomas!'* Perhaps that was why, in spite of everything, I never really managed to hate Cassis. He stood by me that day, after all, and that was more than anyone else did. Until now, that is.

'You have to understand this.' His boy's voice, unsteadied by fear, still sounded oddly like an echo of Tomas'. 'If they find out about us, they'll think *we* killed him. They'll shoot us.' Reine watched him with huge, terrified eyes. I looked over the river, feeling strangely indifferent and unaffected. No-one would shoot *me*. I'd caught Old Mother. Cassis slapped me sharply on the arm. He looked sick, but dogged.

"Boise, are you listening?"

I nodded.

'We have to make it look as if someone else did it,' said Cassis. 'The Resistance or someone. If they think he drowned –' He paused to glance superstitiously at the river. 'If they find out he went *swimming* with us, they might talk to the others, Hauer and the rest, and –' Cassis gave a convulsive swallow. There was no need to say more. We looked at each other.

'We have to make it look like' – he looked at me, almost pleading – 'you know, an execution.'

I nodded. 'I'll do it,' I said.

It took us a while to understand how to fire the gun. There was a safety catch. We took it off. The gun was heavy and greasy-smelling. Then came the question of where to shoot. I said the heart, Cassis the head. A single shot should do it, he said, just there at the temple, to make it look like a Resistance job. We tied his hands with string to make it look more authentic. We muffled the sound of the shot with his jacket, but even so the noise, flat and yet with a peculiar resonance which went on and on, seemed to fill the whole world.

My grief had gone deep, too deep for me to feel anything but an enduring numbness. My mind was like the river, smooth and shiny on the surface, filled with cold beneath it. We dragged Tomas to the edge and tipped him into the water. Without his clothes or identity tags, we knew he would be virtually unidentifiable. By tomorrow, we told ourselves, the current might have rolled him all the way to Angers.

'But what about his clothes?' There was a bluish tinge around Cassis' mouth, though his voice was still strong. 'We can't risk just tipping them into the river. Someone might find them, and know.'

'We could burn them,' I suggested.

Cassis shook his head. 'Too much smoke,' he said

324

shortly. 'Besides, you can't burn the gun, or the belt, or the tags.' I shrugged disinterestedly. In my mind I saw Tomas roll softly into the water, like a tired child into bed, again and again. Then I had the idea.

'The Morlock hole,' I said.

Cassis nodded.

'All right,' he said.

14

The well looks much as it did then, though someone has placed a concrete plug over it nowadays so that children don't fall in. Of course, we have running water now. In my mother's day the well was the only drinking water we had apart from the overspill from the rain gutter, which we only used for watering. It was a giant brick cylindrical affair, rising some five feet off the ground, with a handpump to draw off the water. At the top of the cylinder a padlocked wooden lid prevented accidents and contamination. Sometimes, when the weather was very dry, the well water was yellow and brackish, but for most of the year it was sweet. After reading *The Time Machine*, Cassis and I had gone through a phase of playing Morlocks and Eloi around the well, which reminded me, in its grim solidity, of the dark holes into which the creatures had vanished.

We waited until night was almost falling before returning home. We carried the bundle of Tomas' clothes with us, hiding it in a thick patch of lavender bushes at the end of the garden until nightfall. We brought the unopened parcel of magazines, too – not even Cassis was interested in opening it after what had happened. One of us would have to make an excuse to go out, said Cassis – by that, of course, he meant *I* would have to do it – quickly retrieve the bundle and throw it into the well. The key to the padlock hung on the back of the door with the rest of our house keys – it was even labelled 'well', Mother's passion for neatness being what it was – and could easily be removed and replaced without Mother noticing. After that, said Cassis with that unaccustomed harshness in his voice, the rest was up to us. We had never known, never heard of a Tomas Leibniz. We had never spoken to any German soldiers. Hauer and the others would keep their mouths shut if they knew what was good for them. All we had to do was look stupid and say nothing at all.

15

It was easier than we expected. Mother was having another of her bad spells and was too preoccupied with her own suffering to notice our pale faces and muddy eyes. She whisked Reine away to the bathroom immediately, claiming she could still smell oranges on her skin, and rubbed her hands with camphor and pumice until Reinette screamed and pleaded. They emerged twenty minutes later, Reine with her hair bound up in a towel and smelling strongly of camphor, my mother, dull and hard-mouthed with suppressed rage. There was no supper for us.

'Make it yourselves if you want any,' Mother advised us. 'Running about the woods like gypsies. *Flaunting* yourselves in the square like that—' she almost moaned, one hand touching her temple in the old warning gesture. There was a silence, during which she stared at us as if we were strangers, then she retired to her rocking chair by the fireside and twisted her knitting savagely in her hands, rocking and glaring into the flames.

'Oranges,' she said in her low voice. 'Why would you want to bring oranges into the house? Do you hate me so much?' But who she was talking to was unclear, and none of us dared answer her. I'm not sure what we would have said anyway.

At ten o'clock she went to her room. It was already late for us, but Mother, who often seemed to lose track of time during her bad spells, said nothing. We stayed in the kitchen for a while, listening to the sounds of her preparing for bed. Cassis went to the cellar for something to eat, returning with a piece of *rillettes* wrapped in paper and half a loaf of bread. We ate, though none of us was very hungry. I think perhaps we were trying to avoid talking to each other.

The act, the terrible act we had abetted, still hung in front of us like a dreadful fruit. His body, his pale Northern skin almost bluish in the dapple of the leaves, his averted face, his sleepy, boneless roll into the water. Kicking leaves over the shattered mess at the back of his head – strange that the bullet hole should be so small and neat at the point of entry – then the slow, regal splash into the water. Black rage blotted out my grief. You cheated me, I thought to myself. You cheated. You cheated me.

It was Cassis who broke the silence first. 'You ought to, you know, do it now.'

I gave him a look of hate.

'You ought to,' he insisted. 'Before it gets too late.'

Reine looked at us both with those appealing heifer's eyes.

'All right,' I said tonelessly. 'I'll do it.'

Afterwards I went back to the river once again. I don't know what I expected to see there – the ghost of Tomas Leibniz, perhaps, leaning against the Lookout Post and smoking – but the place was oddly normal, without even the eerie quietness I might have expected in the wake of such a dreadful thing. Frogs croaked and water plashed softly against the hollow of the bank. In the cool grey moonlight the dead pike stared at me with its ball-bearing eyes and its jagged, drooling mouth. I could not rid myself of the idea that it was not dead, that it could hear every word, that it was listening.

'I hate you,' I told Old Mother.

It stared at me in glassy contempt. There were discarded fish-hooks all around its mean toothy mouth, some almost healed over with time. They looked like strange fangs.

'I'd have let you go,' I told it. 'You knew I would.' I lay in the grass beside it, our faces almost touching. The stench of rotting fish mingled with the dank smell of the ground. 'You cheated me,' I said.

In the pale light the old pike's eyes looked almost knowing. Almost triumphant.

I'm not sure how long I stayed out that night. I think I dozed a little, for when I awoke the moon was further downriver, glancing its crescent off the smooth milky water. It was very cold. Rubbing the numbness from my hands and feet I sat up, then carefully picked up the dead pike. It was heavy, slimed with mud from the river, and there were jagged remnants of fish-hook crusted into its gleaming flanks, like pieces of carapace. In silence I took it to the Standing Stones, where I had nailed the corpses of water-snakes all through that summer. I hooked it through the lower jaw onto one of the nails. The flesh was tough and elastic; for a moment I wasn't sure the skin would break, but with an effort I managed. Old Mother hung open-mouthed above the river in a snakeskin skirt that trembled in the breeze.

'At least I got you,' I said softly.

At least I got you.

330

16

I almost missed the first call.

The woman who answered was working late – it was ten past five already – and had forgotten to switch on the answering machine. She sounded very young and bored, and I felt my heart sink at the sound of her voice. I blurted my message through lips which felt oddly numb. I'd have liked an older woman, one who would remember the war, one who might remember my mother's name, and for a moment I was sure she'd hang up and tell me all that ancient history was finished now, no-one wanted to know any more.

In my mind I even heard her say it. I stretched out my hand to cut the connection.

'Madame? Madame?' Her voice was urgent. 'Are you still there?'

With an effort, 'Yes.'

'Did you say *Mirabelle Dartigen*?'

'Yes. I'm her daughter. Framboise.'

'Wait. Please wait.' The voice was almost breathless behind the professional politeness, all trace of boredom gone. 'Please, *don't* go away.'

17

I had expected an article, a feature at most, maybe with a picture or two. Instead they talked to me about film rights, foreign rights to my story and a book. But I couldn't write a book, I told them, appalled. I can *read*, all right, but as for *writing* . . . At my age, too? It doesn't matter, they tell me soothingly. It can be ghost-written.

Ghostwritten. The word makes me shiver.

At first I thought I was doing it as revenge on Laure and Yannick. To rob them of their little glory. But the time for that is over. As Tomas once said, there's more than one way of fighting back. Besides, they seem pitiful to me now. Yannick has written to me several times, with increasing urgency. He is in Paris at the moment. Laure is suing for a divorce. She has not tried to contact me, and in spite of myself I feel a little sorry for them both. After all, they have no children. They have no idea of the difference that makes between us.

My second call was to Pistache. My daughter answered almost at once, as if she were expecting me. Her voice sounded calm and remote. In the background I could hear a dog barking and Prune and Ricot playing a noisy game.

'Of course I'll come,' she said mildly. 'Jean-Marc can look after the children for a few days.' My sweet Pistache, so patient and undemanding. How can she know what it feels like to have that hard place inside? She never had it. She may love me, perhaps even forgive me, but she can never really understand. Perhaps it's better for her this way.

The last call was long-distance. I left a message, struggling with the unfamiliar accent, the impossible words. My voice sounded old and wavery, and I had to repeat the message several times to make myself heard against the sounds of crockery, talk and the distant jukebox. I only hoped it would be enough.

18

What happened next is common knowledge. They found Tomas almost at once, not twenty-four hours after what happened at Les Laveuses and nowhere close to Angers. Instead of rolling with the current far away, he'd been washed up on a sandbank half a mile from the village, only to be found by the same group of Germans who had found his motorbike, hidden in a stand of bushes under the road from the Standing Stones. We heard from Paul what was rumoured in the village: that a Resistance group had shot a German guard who had caught them out after the curfew; that a communist sniper had shot him for his papers; that it was an execution by his own people following the discovery that he was trading German army-issue goods on the black market. The Germans were suddenly all over the village, black uniforms and grey, conducting house-to-house searches.

Their attention to our house was perfunctory. There was no man there, after all, simply a pack of brats with their sick mother. I answered the door when they came knocking and led them around the house, but they seemed more interested in what we knew about Raphaël Crespin than anything else. Paul told us later that Raphaël had disappeared earlier that day, or maybe some time during the night. Disappeared without a trace and taking his money and papers with him, while in the basement of La Mauvaise Réputation the Germans had found a cache of weapons and explosives big enough to blow up all of Les Laveuses twice over.

The Germans came to our house twice and searched it from root cellar to attic, then seemed to lose interest altogether. I noticed in passing, with little surprise, that the SS officer who accompanied the search party was the same jovial red-faced man who had commented on our strawberries early that summer. He was still red-faced and jovial in spite of the nature of his investigation, scruffing my head carelessly as he went by and making sure the soldiers left everything neat after their passage. A message in French and German went up on the church door, inviting anyone with knowledge of the affair to volunteer information. Mother remained in her room with one of her migraines, sleeping during the day and talking to herself at night.

We slept badly, visited by nightmares.

When it finally happened, it was with a sense of anti-climax. It was over before we even knew about it, six o'clock that morning against the west wall of Saint Benedict's church, close to the fountain where, only two days before, Reinette had sat with the barley crown on her head, throwing flowers.

Paul came to tell us. His face was pale and blotchy, one prominent vein standing out on his forehead as he told us in a voice which was one long stammer. We listened in appalled silence, benumbed, wondering, perhaps, how it could have come to this, how such a small seed as ours could have blossomed into this bloody flower. Their names fell against my ears like stones falling into deep water. Ten names, never to be forgotten, never in my life: Martin Dupré, Jean-Marie Dupré, Colette Gaudin, Philippe Hourias, Henri Lemaître, Julien Lanicen, Arthur Lecoz, Agnès Petit, François Ramondin, Auguste Truriand. Playing through my memory like the refrain of a song which you know will never leave you alone, surprising me out of sleep, pounding through my dreams, counter-pointing the movements and rhythms of my life with

335

relentless precision. Ten names. One for each of the ten who had been at La Mauvaise Réputation that night.

We gathered later that it was Raphaël's disappearance that decided it. The cache of weapons in the basement suggested that the café owner had connections with resistance groups. No-one really knew. Perhaps the entire outfit was a blind for carefully organized resistance activity, or maybe Tomas' death had been a simple case of retaliation for what had happened to old Gustave a few weeks earlier, but whatever it was, Les Laveuses paid a heavy price for its little rebellion. Like late-summer wasps, the Germans sensed the end coming and retaliated with instinctive savagery.

Martin Dupré, Jean-Marie Dupré, Colette Gaudin, Philippe Hourias, Henri Lemaître, Julien Lanicen, Arthur Lecoz, Agnès Petit, François Ramondin, Auguste Truriand. I wondered if they fell silently, like figures in a dream, or whether they wept, pleaded and clawed at each other in their efforts to escape. I wondered whether men checked over the bodies afterwards, one still twitching and staring, but silenced at last with the butt of a pistol, one soldier lifting a bloody skirt to expose a sleek stretch of thigh. Paul told me it was over in a second. No-one was allowed to watch, and soldiers stood with guns at the shuttered windows. I imagine them still, behind their shutters, eyes pressed avidly to cracks and knotholes, mouths half open in stupid shock. Then the whispering, their voices lowered, stifled, spilling words as if they might help them understand.

'They're coming! There's the Dupré boys. And Colette, Colette Gaudin. Philippe Hourias. Henri Lemaître – why, he wouldn't hurt a fly; he's hardly sober ten minutes in the day – old Julien Lanicen. Arthur Lecoz. And Agnès, Agnès Petit. And François Ramondin. And Auguste Truriand.'

From the church where the early service was already

beginning comes a sound of voices raised. A harvest hymn. Outside the closed doors, two soldiers stand guard with bored, sour faces. Père Froment bleats out the words while the congregation mutter along. Only a few dozen people today, their faces harsh and accusing, for rumour has it the priest has made a deal with the Germans to ensure cooperation. The organ blats out the tune at top volume, but even so the shots are audible outside against the west wall, the muted percussion of the bullets as they strike the old stone, something which will stick in the flesh of every member of that congregation like an old fish-hook, half healed over and never to be pulled out. At the back of the church someone begins to sing 'La Marseillaise' but the words sound beery and over-loud in the sudden lull and the singer falls silent, embarrassed.

I see it all in my dreams, clearer than memory. I see their faces. I hear their voices. I see the sudden, shocking transition from living to dead. But my grief has gone down too far for me to reach it, and when I awake with tears on my face it is with a strange feeling of surprise, almost of indifference. Tomas has gone. Nothing else has any meaning.

I suppose we were in shock. We didn't speak to each other about it, but went our separate ways, Reinette to her room, where she would lie on her bed for hours, looking at her movie pictures; Cassis to his books, looking increasingly middle-aged to me now, as if something in him had collapsed; me to the woods and the river. We paid little attention to Mother during that time, though her bad spell continued as before, lasting longer than the worst of them that summer. But by then we had forgotten to fear her. Even Reinette forgot to flinch before her rages. We had killed, after all. Beyond that, what was there to fear?

My hate had no focus as yet, like my rage – Old Mother was nailed to the stone and could not therefore be blamed for Tomas' death – but I could feel it moving, watching, like the eye of a pinhole camera, clicking away in the darkness, noting everything. Emerging from her room after another sleepless night, Mother looking white and worn and desperate. I felt my hate tighten at the sight of her, shrinking to an exquisite black diamond point of understanding.

You it was you it was you.

She looked at me as if she'd heard. ''Boise?' Her voice was shaking, vulnerable.

I turned away, feeling the hate in my heart like a nugget of ice.

Behind me, I heard her stricken intake of breath.

19

Next it was the water. That week, the well water, which was usually sweet and clean, began to run brownish, like peat, and it had an odd taste to it, something bitter and burnt-tasting, as if dead leaves had been raked into the cylinder. We ignored it for a day or two, but it only seemed to get worse. Even Mother, whose bad spell was finally coming to an end, noticed it.

'Perhaps something's got into the water,' she suggested.

We stared at her with our customary blankness.

'I'll have to go and look,' she decided.

We waited for discovery with an outward display of stoicism.

'She can't prove anything,' said Cassis desperately. 'She can't *know*.'

Reine whimpered. 'She will, she will,' she whined. 'She'll find everything and she'll know.'

Cassis bit his fist savagely, as if to stop himself from screaming. 'Why didn't you tell us there was coffee in the parcel?' he moaned. 'Didn't you *think*?'

I shrugged. Alone of all of us, I remained serene.

Discovery never came. Mother came back from the well with a bucketful of dead leaves and proclaimed the water clear.

'It's probably sediment from the river swells,' she

said, almost cheerily. 'When the level drops it will run clear again. You'll see.'

She locked the well's wooden lid again, and took to carrying the key at her belt. We had no opportunity to check it again.

'The parcel must have sunk to the bottom,' decided Cassis at last. 'It was heavy, wasn't it? She won't even be able to see it unless the well runs dry.' We all knew there was little chance of that. And by summer the parcel's contents would have been reduced to mush at the bottom of the well.

'We're safe,' said Cassis.

20

Recipe for *crème de framboise liqueur*.

> I recognized them at once. For a while I thought it was just a bundle of leaves and pulled it out with a pole to clear the water. Clean the raspberries and wipe off the bristles. Soak in warm water for half an hour. Then I saw it was a parcel of clothes tied together with a belt. I didn't have to go through the pockets to know at once. Drain the water from the fruit and place in a large jar so as to cover the bottom. Thickly layer over with sugar. Repeat layers until jar is half full. At first I couldn't think. I told the children I'd cleared the well and went to my room to lie down. I locked the well. I couldn't think straight. Cover the fruit and sugar with cognac, making sure not to disturb the layers, then fill with cognac to top of jar. Leave for at least eighteen months.

The writing is neat and close-written in the strange hieroglyphics she uses when she wants her words to remain secret. I can almost hear her voice as she speaks, the slightly nasal intonation, the matter-of-factness of the terrible conclusion.

> I must have done it. I've dreamed of violence so often, and this time I must have really done it right. His clothes in the well, his name tags in his pocket. He must have come round again, and I did it: shot him, stripped him and threw him into the river. I can almost remember it now,

341

but not quite, like a dream. So many things seem like dreams to me now. Can't say I'm sorry. After what he did to me, what he did, what he let them do to Reine, to me, to the children, to me.

The words are illegible at this point, as if terror has taken over the pen and sent it skating across the page in a desperate scrawl, but she takes control again almost immediately.

I have to think of the children. Can't think it's safe any more for them. He was using them all the time. All that time I thought it was me he wanted, but it was the children he was using. Keeping me sweet so he could use them some more. Those letters. Spiteful words, but that's what it took to open my eyes. What were they doing at La Rép? What else did he have planned for them after? Maybe it's a good thing, what happened to Reine. It spoiled things for him, at least. Things finally got out of control. Someone died. That wasn't in his plan. Those other Germans were never really a part of it. He was using them, too. To take the blame, if that's what it took. And now my children.

More of the mad scrawl:

I wish I could remember. What did he offer me this time for my silence? More pills? Did he really think I could sleep knowing what I'd paid for them? Or did he smile and touch my face in that special way, as if nothing had changed between us? Was that what made me do it?

The words are legible but shaking, forced into control by a mighty effort of will.

There's always a price. Not my children, though. Take someone else. Anyone. Take the whole village if you like. It's what I think to myself when I see their faces in my

dreams, that I did it for my children. I should send them
to Juliette's for a while. Finish up here and collect them
when the war's over. Safe there. Safe from me. Send
them away, my sweet Reine Cassis 'Boise. Most of all my
little 'Boise. What else can I do? And when will it ever
end?

She breaks off here; a neat recipe in red ink for
rabbit casserole separates this from the final paragraph, which is written in a different colour and a
different style, as if she has thought about this at
length.

It's all arranged. I'll send them to Juliette's. They'll be safe
there. I'll make up some tale to keep the gossip-mongers
happy. I can't leave the farm like this; the trees need care
over the winter. Belle Yolande still has signs of fungus; I'll
have to sort that out. Besides, they'll be safer without me.
I know that now.

I can't begin to imagine what she must have felt.
Fear, remorse, despair, and the terror that at last she
was going insane, that the bad spells had opened a
nightmare door from her dreams into the real world,
threatening everything she loved. But her tenacity
cut through it all. This stubbornness I inherited from
her, the instinct to hold onto what was hers if it killed
her.

No, I never realized what she was going through. I
had my own nightmares. But even so I had begun to
hear the rumours in the village, rumours which grew
ever louder and more menacing and which Mother,
as always, failed to deny or even to notice. The graffiti
on the hen house had begun a trickle of ill-will
and suspicion which now, after the executions at the
church, began to flow more freely. People grieve in
different ways, some silently, some in anger, some in
spite. Rarely does grief bring out the best in people,
despite what local historians like to tell you, and Les

Laveuses was no exception. Chrétien and Murielle Dupré, shocked into brief silence at the death of their two boys, turned upon each other, she shrewish and vicious, he boorish, glaring at one another over the pews in church – she with a new bruise over one eye – with something close to hate. Old Gaudin turned in upon himself like a turtle getting ready for hibernation. Isabelle Ramondin, always a spiteful tongue at the best of times, became milky and false, looking at folk from her huge blue-black eyes, her soft chin trembling tearily. I suspect maybe she started it. Or maybe it was Claude Petit, who had never had a good word to say for his sister while she was alive, but who now seemed the picture of fraternal grief, or Martin Truriand who would inherit all his father's business now that his brother was dead – seems like death always brings out the rats from the woodwork in any place, and in Les Laveuses the rats were envy and hypocrisy, false piety and greed. Within three days it seemed that everyone was looking askance at everyone else. People gathered in twos and threes to talk in whispers, and fell silent as you approached. They broke into unexplained tears one minute and knocked out their friends' teeth the next, and little by little, even I realized that the hushed conversations, the sideways glances, the muttered imprecations all happened most often when we were around, when we went to the post office to collect the mail or to the Hourias farm to fetch milk or to the hardware shop for a box of masonry nails. Every time, the same looks, the same whispers. Once it was a stone flung at my mother from behind a milking shed, another time clods of earth thrown at our door after curfew. Women turned away without greeting us. More graffiti, this time on our walls.

'NAZI WHORE', one read. Another on the side of the goat shack read, 'OUR BROTHERS AND SISTERS DIED FOR YOU'.

But Mother treated it all with indifferent contempt. She bought her milk from Crécy when the Hourias

344

farm ran dry, and posted her letters in Angers. No-one spoke directly to her, but when Francine Crespin spat at her feet one Sunday morning on the way back from church, Mother spat back, right in Francine's face, with remarkable speed and accuracy.

As for us, we were ignored. Paul still spoke to us occasionally, though not when anyone else was there to see. Adults seemed not to notice us, but from time to time someone like crazy Denise Lelac might give us an apple or a piece of cake to stuff in our pockets, murmuring in her cracked old voice, 'Take it. Take it, for God's sake. It's a pity you children should be caught up in such a business,' before hurrying on her way, her black skirts dragging in the sour yellow dust and her shopping basket clutched tightly in her bony fingers.

By Monday everyone was saying that Mirabelle Dartigen had been the Germans' whore, and that was why her family had been spared retribution. By Tuesday some people had recalled that our father had once expressed sympathy for the Germans. On Wednesday night a group of drunks – La Mauvaise Réputation had long since closed, and people grow bitter and violent drinking alone – came to yell abuse at our closed shutters and to throw stones. We stayed in our bedroom with the light off, trembling and listening to the half-familiar voices, until Mother went out to break it up. That night they went quietly. The following night they left noisily. Then came Friday.

It was just after supper when we heard them coming. It had been grey and dank all day, as if an old blanket had been thrown across the sky, and people were hot and prickly. Night brought little comfort, rolling a whitish mist across the fields so that our farmhouse seemed an island, mist seeping damply under doors and around window frames. We had eaten in silence as had become usual, and with little appetite, though I remember Mother had made an effort to make what we liked best. Bread freshly baked and scattered with poppy seeds, butter from Crécy, *rillettes*, slices of *andouillette* from last year's pig, hot sizzling pieces of *boudin* in its grease, and black buckwheat pancakes toasted in the pan, as crispy and fragrant as autumn leaves on the plate. Mother, trying hard to be cheerful, served us sweet cider from earthen *bolées*, but took none for herself. I remember she smiled constantly and painfully throughout the meal, sometimes giving a sharp bark of false laughter, though none of us said anything funny.

'I've been thinking.' Her voice was bright and metallic. 'Thinking we may need a change of air.' We looked indifferently at her. The smell of grease and cider was overpowering.

'I was thinking of going to visit Tante Juliette in Pierre-Buffière,' she continued. 'You'd like it there. It's in the mountains, on the Limousin. There are goats and marmots and—'

'There are goats here,' I said in a flat voice.

Mother gave another of those brittle, unhappy laughs. 'I should have known you'd have some objection,' she said.

I met her eyes with mine. 'You want us to run away,' I said.

For a minute she pretended not to understand.

'I know it sounds like a long way to go,' she said with that forced cheeriness. 'But it's really not that far, and Tante Juliette will be so pleased to see us all.'

'You want us to run away because of what people are saying,' I said. 'That you're a Nazi whore.'

Mother flushed. 'You shouldn't listen to gossip,' she said in a sharp voice. 'Nothing good ever comes of it.'

'Oh, so it isn't true, then?' I asked simply to embarrass her. I knew it wasn't, and couldn't *imagine* it to be true. I'd seen whores before. Whores were pink and plump, soft and pretty, with wide, vapid eyes and

346

painted mouths like Reinette's cinema actresses. Whores laughed and squealed and wore high shoes and carried leather handbags. Mother was old, ugly, sour. Even when she laughed it was ugly.

'Of course not.' Her eyes did not meet mine.

Insistently: 'So why are we running away?'

Silence. And in the sudden silence we heard it, the first harsh murmur of voices outside, and in it the clanking of metal and kicking of feet, even before the first stone hit the shutters. The sound of Les Laveuses in all its petty spite and vengeful anger, people no longer people now – no Gaudins or Lecozes or Truriands or Duprés or Ramondins – but members of an army. Peering out of the window, we saw them gathered outside our gate, twenty, thirty or more of them, mostly men, but some women, too. Some with lamps or torches, like a late harvest procession, some with pocketfuls of stones. As we watched, and light from our kitchen spilled out across into the yard, someone turned to the window and threw another stone, which cracked the old wooden frame and sprayed glass into the room. It was Guilherm Ramondin, the man with the wooden leg. I could hardly see his face in the flickering reddish light of the torches, but I could feel the weight of his hate, even through the glass.

'*Bitch!*' His voice was hardly recognizable, thickened by something more than drink. 'Come out, bitch, before we decide to come in there and get you!' A kind of roar accompanied his words, punctuated by stamping, cheering and a volley of fistfuls of gravel and clods which spattered against our half-closed shutters.

Mother half-opened the broken window and shouted out. 'Go home, Guilherm, you fool, before you pass out and someone has to carry you!' Laughter and jeering from the crowd. Guilherm shook the crutch on which he had been leaning.

'Brave talk for a German bitch!' he yelled. His voice

sounded rough and beery, though his words were barely slurred. 'Who told them about Raphaël, eh? Who told them about La Rép? Was it you, Mirabelle? Did you tell the SS that they killed your lover?'

Mother spat out of the window at them. 'Brave talk?' Her voice was shrill and high. 'You're the one to be talking bravery, Guilherm Ramondin! Brave enough to be standing drunk outside an honest woman's house, frightening her kids! Brave enough to get sent home in the first week of battle while my husband got killed!'

At this Guilherm gave a roar of fury. Behind him the crowd joined in hoarsely. Another volley of stones and earth hit the window, sending pieces of earth spattering across the kitchen floor.

'You bitch!' They were through the gate now, pushing it up and off its rotten hinges with ease. Our old dog barked once, twice, then fell quiet with a sudden yelp. 'Don't think we don't know! Don't think Raphaël didn't tell anyone!' His triumphant hateful voice rang out even above the rest. In the red darkness below the window I could see his eyes as they reflected the firelight like a crazywork of broken glass. 'We know you were trading with them, Mirabelle! We know Leibniz was your lover!' From the window, Mother hurled a jug of water onto the nearest members of the crowd. 'Cool you off!' she screamed furiously. 'You think that's all people can think about? You think we're all at your level?'

But Guilherm was already through the gate and pounding on the door, undeterred. 'Get out here, bitch! We know what you've been doing!' I could see the door trembling on its latch beneath the pressure of his blows. Mother turned to us, her face blazing with rage.

'Get your things. Get the cash box from under the sink. Get our papers.'

'Why? But—'

'Get them, I tell you!'

We fled.

At first I thought the crash – a terrible sound that shook the rotten floorboards – was the sound of the door coming down. But when we returned to the kitchen we saw that Mother had pulled the dresser across the door, breaking many of her precious plates in the process, and was using it to barricade the entrance. The table, too, had been dragged towards the door, so that if the dresser gave way no-one could enter. She was holding my father's shotgun in one hand.

'Cassis, check the back door. I don't think they've thought of that yet, but you never know. Reine, stay with me. 'Boise . . .' She looked at me strangely for a moment, her eyes black and bright and unreadable, but was unable to finish her sentence, for at that moment a terrible weight crashed against the door, splintering the top half right out of the frame and exposing a slice of night sky. Faces reddened by fire and fury appeared in the frame, boosted up onto the shoulders of their comrades. One of the faces belonged to Guilherm Ramondin. His smile was ferocious.

'Can't hide in your little house,' he gasped. 'Coming to get you, bitch. Coming to pay you back for what . . . you did . . . to'

Even then, with the house coming down about her, my mother managed a sour laugh.

'Your father?' she said in a high, scornful voice. 'Your father, the martyr? François? The hero? Don't make me laugh!' She raised the shotgun so that he could see it. 'Your father was a pathetic old drunkard who'd piss on his shoes more often than not when he wasn't sober. Your father—'

'My father was Resistance!' Guilherm's voice was shrieky with rage. 'Why else would he go to Raphaël's? Why else would the Germans take him?'

Mother laughed again. 'Oh, *Resistance*, was he?' she said. 'And old Lecoz? I suppose he was Resistance, too, was he? And poor Agnès? And Colette?' For the first time that night Guilherm faltered. Mother took a step towards the broken door, shotgun levelled.

'I'll tell you this for nothing, Ramondin,' she said. 'Your father was no more Resistance than I'm Joan of Arc. He was a sad old sot, that was all, who liked to talk too much and who couldn't have got it up if he'd stuck a wire through it first. He just happened to be in the wrong place at the wrong time, just like the rest of you idiots out there. Now get yourselves home, all of you.' She fired a single shot into the air. '*All of you!*' she yelled.

But Guilherm was stubborn. He winced when the shards of pulverized wood grazed his cheek, but did not drop down.

'*Someone* killed that Boche,' he said in a more sober voice. 'Someone executed him. Who else but Resistance? And then someone tipped them off to the SS. Someone from the village. Who else but you, Mirabelle? Who else?'

My mother began to laugh. In the firelight I could see her face, flushed and almost beautiful in her rage. Around her lay the ruins of her kitchen. Her laughter was terrible.

'You want to know, Guilherm?' There was a new note in her voice, a note almost of joy. 'You really won't go home until you *know*?' She fired the gun again into the ceiling, making plaster fall like bloody feathers in the firelight. '*You really want to fucking know?*'

I saw him flinch at the word more than the blast from the shotgun. It was all right for men to swear in those days, but for a woman to do so – a decent woman, at least – was almost unthinkable. I understood that in her own words she had condemned herself, but my mother didn't seem to have finished.

'I'll tell you the truth, shall I, Ramondin?' she said. Her voice was breaking with laughter, hysteria, I suppose, but in that moment I was sure she was enjoying herself. 'I'll just tell you how it *really* happened, shall I?' She nodded gaily. 'I didn't have to report *anyone* to the Germans, Ramondin. And do you know why? Because *I* killed Tomas Leibniz! I killed him! Don't you believe me? *I killed him!*' I could hear her dry-firing the shotgun, though both barrels were empty. Her capering shadow on the kitchen floor was red and black and giant. Her voice rose to a scream. 'Does that make you feel better, Ramondin? I killed him! I was his whore all right, and I'm not sorry. I killed him, and I'd kill him again if I had to. I'd kill him a thousand times. What d'you think of that? What do you fucking think of that?'

She was still screaming as the first torch hit the kitchen floor. That went out, though Reinette began to cry as soon as she saw the flames, but the second caught the curtains, and the third the cracked ruin of the dresser. Guilherm's face at the top of the door had vanished now, but I could hear him shouting orders outside. Another torch, a sheaf of straw much like those from which the Harvest Queen's throne was made, came flying over the top of the dresser and landed smouldering in the centre of the kitchen. Mother was still screaming, out-of-control, 'I killed him, you cowards! I killed him, and I'm glad I did, and I'll kill you, every one of you, any one of you tries to mess with me and my children!' Cassis tried to take her arm and she flung him back against the wall.

'The back door,' I called to him. 'We'll have to go out through the back.'

'What if they're waiting?' whimpered Reine.

'*What if!*' I yelled impatiently. From outside came rumours and catcalls, like a fairground turned suddenly savage. I caught my mother by the arm, Cassis took the other. Together we dragged her, still raving and laughing, to the back of the house. Of course they were waiting. Their faces were red with firelight. Guilherm barred our way, flanked by Lecoz, the butcher, and Jean-Marc Hourias, looking slightly embarrassed but grinning like a sickle. Too drunk, maybe, or perhaps still too wary, building themselves up to the act of murder like children playing double-dare. They had already set fire to the hen house and the goat-shack, and the stench of burning feathers married with the dank chill of the fog.

'You're not going anywhere,' said Guilherm sourly. Behind us the house whispered and snickered as the flames took.

Mother reversed the butt of the old rifle and, with a gesture almost too quick to see, punched Guilherm in the chest with it. He went down. For a second there was a gap where he had been, and I leaped through it, pushing under elbows and wriggling between an undergrowth of legs, sticks and pitchforks. Someone grabbed me by the hair, but I was slick as an oiled eel, scrabbling away into the hot crowd. I felt myself pinned, suffocated between a sudden surge of bodies. I clawed my way to air and space, barely feeling the blows which fell upon me. I sprinted across the field into the darkness, taking cover behind a stand of raspberry canes. Somewhere far behind me I thought I could hear my mother's voice, beyond fear now, enraged and screaming. She sounded like an animal defending her young.

The stink of smoke was getting stronger. In the front of the house something collapsed with a splintering crash, and I felt a soft buffet of heat reach me across the field. Someone, I think it was Reine, screamed thinly.

The crowd was a shapeless thing, all hate. Its shadow reached as far as the raspberry canes and beyond. Beyond it I was just in time to see the far gable of the house collapse in a spray of fireworks. A chimney of superheated air rose redly into the night, sending spume and firecrackers squawking into the grey sky like a geyser of flame.

A figure broke from the shapelessness of the crowd and ran across the field. I recognized Cassis. He made a dash for the maize, and I guessed he would make for the Lookout Post. A couple of people started to follow him, but the burning farm held many of them hypnotized. Besides, it was Mother they wanted. I could make out her words now over the twin throats of the crowd and the fire. She was calling our names.

'Cassis! Reine-Claude! 'Boise!'

I stood up behind the raspberry canes, ready to run if anyone came towards me. Standing on the tips of my toes I glimpsed her briefly. She looked like something in a fisherman's tale, caught on all sides but thrashing furiously, her face red and black with fire and blood and smoke, a monster of the deep. I could see some other faces, too: Francine Crespin, her sheep-eyed saintly face distorted into a scream of hatred; old Guilherm Ramondin like something from the dead. There was fear in their hatred now, the kind of super-stitious fear that can only be cured by destruction and murder. It had taken them a long time to get to it, but their killing time had come. I saw Reinette slink out from one side of the crowd into the maize. No-one tried to stop her. By then most of them, blinded by bloodlust, would have been hard put to recognize who she was, anyway.

Mother went down. I may have imagined a single hand rising above the grimacing faces. It was like something from one of Cassis' books, *Plague of Zombies* or *Valley of the Cannibals*. All that was missing were the jungle drums. But the worst part of the horror was that I knew those faces, glimpsed mercifully briefly in the gleeful dark. That was Paul's father. That was Jeannette Crespin, who'd almost been Harvest Queen, barely sixteen and with blood across her face. Even sheepy Père Froment was there, though whether he was trying to keep order or was himself contributing to the chaos it was impossible to tell. Sticks and fists hammered onto my mother's head and back, she holding herself tight like a curled fist, like a woman with a baby in her arms, still screaming defiance, though muffled now by the hot weight of flesh and hate.

Then came the shot.

We all heard it, even above the noise; the yark of a large-gauge weapon, a double-barrelled shotgun perhaps, or one of the antique barkers still hoarded in farm attics or under floorboards in villages all over France. It was a wild shot, though Guilherm Ramondin felt it scorch his cheek and promptly voided his bladder in terror, and heads whipped round curiously to see from where it had come. No-one knew. Beneath their suddenly frozen hands my mother began to crawl, bleeding now from a dozen places, her hair dragged out so the scalp showed slick in patches, a sharp stick actually pushed *through* the back of her hand so the fingers splayed out helplessly.

The sound of the fire – Biblical, apocalyptic – was now the only sound. People waited, remembering perhaps the sound of the execution squad in front of Saint-Jérôme's, trembling before their own bloody intentions. A voice came – from the maize field, perhaps, or from the burning house, or even the sky itself – a booming, authoritative man's voice, impossible to ignore or disobey.

'Leave them!'

My mother continued to crawl. Uneasily, the crowd parted to let her through, like wheat before the wind.

'Leave them! Go home!'

The voice sounded a little familiar, people said later. There was an inflection they recognized but couldn't quite identify. Someone cried hysterically, 'It's Philippe Hourias!' But Philippe was dead. A shiver went through the people. My mother reached the open field, staggering defiantly to her feet. Someone reached out to stop her, then thought better of it. Père Froment bleated something weak and well-meaning. A couple of angry cries faltered and died in the superstitious silence. Warily, insolently, without turning my face away from their collective gaze, I began to make my way towards my mother. I could feel my face burning with the heat, my eyes full of reflected firelight. I took her good hand.

The wide, dark expanse of Hourias' maize field lay before us. We plunged into it without a word. No-one followed us.

21

I went to Tante Juliette's with Reinette and Cassis. Mother stayed a week, then moved away, perhaps out of guilt or fear, but ostensibly for the sake of her health. We only saw her a few times after that. We understood that she'd changed her name, reverting to her maiden name again, and had moved back to Brittany. Details after that were sketchy. I heard she was making a reasonable living in a bakery, baking her old specialities. Cooking always was her first love. We stayed with Tante Juliette, moving away ourselves as soon as we decently could; Reine to try for the movies for which she had so long yearned, Cassis escaping to Paris, I into a dull but comfortable marriage. We heard that the farmhouse in Les Laveuses had been only partially gutted by the fire, that the outhouses were mostly undamaged and that of the main building, only the front section was completely destroyed. We could have gone back, but word of the massacre at Les Laveuses had already spread. Mother's admission of guilt in front of three dozen witnesses; her words – 'I was his whore, I killed him and I'm not sorry' – as much as the sentiments she had expressed against her fellow villagers, sufficed to condemn her. A monument was erected to the ten martyrs of the Great Massacre, and later, when such things became curiosities to be contemplated at leisure, when the ache of loss and terror had diminished a little, it became clear that the hostility against Mirabelle Dartigen and her children was unlikely to dwindle. I had to face the truth; I would never return to Les Laveuses. Never again. And for a long time I didn't even realize how badly I wanted to.

22

The coffee's still boiling on the stove. Its smell is
bitterly nostalgic, a black burnt-leaf smell, with a hint
of smoke in the steam. I drink it very sweet, like a
shock victim. I think I can begin to understand how
my mother must have felt, the wildness, the freedom
of throwing everything away.

Everyone has gone. The girl with her little tape-
recorders and her mountain of tapes, the photographer.
Even Pistache has gone home, at my own insistence,
though I can still almost feel her arms around me, and
the last touch of her lips against my cheek. My good
daughter, neglected for so long in favour of my bad
one. But people change. At last I feel I can talk to you
now, my wild Noisette, my sweet Pistache. Now I can
hold you in my arms without that feeling of drowning
in silt. Old Mother is dead at last; her curse ended. No
disaster will strike if I dare to love you.

Noisette answered my call late last night. Her voice
was tight and cautious, like mine; I pictured her leaning as I do, her narrow face suspicious, against the
tiled surface of the bar. There is little warmth in her
words, coming as they do across cold miles and wasted
years, but occasionally, when she speaks of her child, I
think I can hear something in her voice. Something
like the beginning of softness. It makes me glad.

I will tell her in my own time, I think; little by little,
drawing her in. I can afford to be patient; after all, I
know the technique. In a way she needs this story

more than anyone – certainly more than the public, gawping at old scandals – even more than Pistache. Pistache doesn't bear grudges. She takes people as they are, honestly and with kindness. But Noisette needs this story, and her daughter, Pêche, needs it, too, if the spectre of Old Mother is not to raise its head again one day. Noisette has her own demons. I only hope I am no longer one of them.

The house feels oddly hollow and uninhabited now that everyone has left. A draught skitters a few dead leaves across the tiles. And yet I do not feel quite alone. Absurd to imagine ghosts remaining in this old house. I've lived here so long and never felt a single shiver of a presence, and yet today I feel . . . someone just behind the shadows, a quiet presence, discreet and almost humble, waiting . . .

My voice was sharper than I intended. 'Who's there? *I said who's there?*' It rang with a metallic sound against the bare walls, the tiled floor. He stepped out into the light and I was suddenly close to laughter, closer to tears at his presence.

'Smells like good coffee,' he said in his mild way.

'God, Paul. How do you manage to walk so *quietly*?'

He grinned.

'I thought you . . . I thought—'

'You think too much,' said Paul simply, moving towards the stove. His face looked yellow-gold in the dim lamplight, his droopy moustache giving him a doleful expression, belied by the quick light in his eyes. I tried to think how much he'd overheard of my story. Sitting in the shadows like that, I'd quite forgotten he was there.

'Talk a lot, too,' he said, not unkindly, pouring himself a cup of coffee. 'Thought you'd be talking all week, the way you went at it.' He gave me a quick, sly grin.

'I needed them to understand,' I began stiffly. 'And Pistache—'

359

'People understand more'n you give 'em credit for.' He took a step towards me and put his hand against my face. He smelled of coffee and old tobacco. 'Why did you hide yourself for so long? What good was it goin' to do?'

'There were . . . things I just couldn't bear to tell,' I faltered. 'Not to you, not to anyone. Things I thought would bring the whole world crashing down around me. You don't know, you've never done anything like—'

He laughed, a sweet, uncomplicated sound. 'Oh, Framboise. Is that what you think? That I don't know what it's like to keep a secret?' He took my dirty hand in both of his. 'That I'm too stupid even to *have* a secret?'

'That's not what I thought—' I began. But it was. God help me, it was.

'You think you can carry the whole world on your back,' said Paul. 'Well, listen to this.' He was lapsing into dialect again, and in certain words I could hear a tremor of his childhood stutter. The combination made him sound very young. 'Those anonymous letters. Remember the letters, 'Boise? The ones with the bad spellings? And the writing on the barn door?'

I nodded.

'Remember how she h-hid those letters when you came into the hall? Remember how you could tell she'd got one because of the look on her face, and the way she'd stamp about, looking scared, and angry, and h-hateful *because* she was scared and angry, and about how you hated her specially on those days, hated her so much you could have killed her yourself?'

I nodded.

'That was me,' said Paul simply. 'I wrote 'em, every one myself. Bet you didn't even know I *could* write, did you. And a pretty poor job I made of it for all the work I put into writing 'em. To get my own back. Because she called me a cretin that day afront of you, and Cassis, and Reine-C-C-C.' He screwed up his face in sudden frustration, flushing furiously. 'Afront of Reine-Claude,' he finished quietly.

'I see.'

Of course. Like all riddles, it was clear as starlight when you knew the answer. I remembered the look on his face whenever Reinette was around, the way he would flush and stammer and fall silent, even though when he was with me his voice was almost normal. I remembered the look of sharp, untinctured hatred in his eyes that day – 'Talk properly, you cretin!' – and the eerie wail of grief and fury which trailed across the fields in his wake. I remembered the way he would sometimes look at Cassis' comic books with a look of fierce concentration – Paul, who we all knew couldn't read a word. I remembered a look of appraisal in his face as I gave out the pieces of orange, an odd feeling at the river of sometimes being watched – even that last time, that last day with Tomas – even then, God, even then.

'I never meant for it to go so far. I wanted her to be sorry, but I never meant for that other stuff to happen. It got out of hand, though. Like those things do. Like a fish too big to reel in, that takes your line away with it. I tried to make amends, though, at the end. I did try.'

I stared at him.

'Good God, Paul.' Too amazed even to be angry, even assuming there was still a place left in me for anger. 'It was you, wasn't it? You with the shotgun, that night at the farm? *You* hiding in the field?'

Paul nodded. I couldn't stop staring at him, seeing him, perhaps, for the first time.

'You *knew*? All this time, and you knew everything?'

He shrugged. 'You all thought I was soft,' he said without bitterness. 'Thought all that could be going on right under my nose and that I still wouldn't notice.' He gave his slow, sad smile. 'Suppose that's it now, though. With you and me. Suppose it's over.'

I tried to think clearly, but the facts refused to lock into place. For so many years I'd thought that

Guilherm Ramondin had started it, Guilherm who led the night of the fire. Or perhaps Raphaël, or one of the Families. And now to hear that all the time it was Paul, my own sweet, slow Paul, barely twelve years old and open as the summer sky. Begun it and ended it, too, with the hard, inevitable symmetry of seasons turning. When I finally spoke it was to say something entirely different, something that surprised us both.

'Did you love her so much, then?' My sister Reinette, with her high cheekbones and her glossy curls. My sister the Harvest Queen, lipsticked and crowned with berries, a sheaf of wheat in one hand and basket of apples under her arm. That's how I'll always remember her, you know. That clear, perfect picture in my mind. I felt an unexpected prick of jealousy close to my heart.

'The same way you loved him, perhaps,' said Paul calmly. 'The way you loved Leibniz.'

The fools we were when we were children. The hurting, hopeful fools. I spent my life dreaming of Tomas, through my married days in Brittany, through my widowhood, dreaming of a man like Tomas, with his careless laughter and his sharp, river-coloured eyes, the Tomas of my wish – you, Tomas. Only you for ever – Old Mother's curse made terrible flesh.

'It took a little time, you know,' said Paul, 'but I got over it. I let go. It's like swimming against the current. It exhausts you. After a while, whoever you are, you just have to let go, and the river brings you home.'

'Home.' My voice sounded strange in my ears. His hands over mine felt rough and warm as an old dog's pelt. I had the strangest picture of us both, standing there in the failing light like Hansel and Gretel, grown old and grey in the witch's house, finally closing the gingerbread door behind them.

Just let go, and the river brings you home. It sounded so easy.

'We've waited a long time, 'Boise.'

I turned my face away. 'Too long, perhaps.'

'I don't think so.'

362

I took a deep breath. This was the moment. To explain that it was all over, that the lie between us was too old to erase, too big to climb over, that *we* were too old, for pity's sake, that it was ridiculous, that it was impossible, that besides, besides . . .

He kissed me then, on the lips, not a shy old-man's kiss, but something else altogether, something that left me feeling shaken, indignant and strangely hopeful. His eyes shone as slowly he drew something out of his pocket, something which glowed red-yellow in the lamplight . . . A string of crab apples.

I stared at him as he drew the necklace gently over my head. It lay against my breasts, the fruit glossy, round and shining.

'Harvest Queen,' whispered Paul. 'Framboise Dartigen. Only you.'

I could smell the good, tart scent of the little fruit against my warming skin.

'I'm too old,' I said shakily. 'It's too late.'

He kissed me again, on the temple, then at the corner of the mouth. Then, from his pocket again, he drew a plait of yellow straw, which he placed around my forehead like a crown.

'It's never too late to come home,' he said, and pulled me gently, insistently towards him. 'All you have to do is stop moving away.'

Resistance is like swimming against the current, exhausting and pointless. I turned my face towards the curve of his shoulder, as if into a pillow. Around my neck the crab apples gave off a pungent, sappy scent, like the Octobers of our childhood.

We toasted our homecoming with sweet black coffee and croissants and green tomato jam made to my mother's recipe.

THE END

COASTLINERS

Joanne Harris

'IF JOANNE HARRIS DIDN'T EXIST, SOMEONE WOULD HAVE TO
INVENT HER'
The Express

Joanne Harris' eagerly awaited new novel, Coastliners, is once again
set in France, this time on a wind-blasted island off the Atlantic
coast. It is the story of Mado, a young woman who returns to the
island and tries to stop the decline of her father's fishing village by
pulling the community together to fight the encroaching tides and
rival commercial interests. Also a powerful love story and peopled
with a rich galaxy of characters, Coastliners was inspired by the
island the author used to visit every summer as a child.

0 385 60172 7

AVAILABLE FROM
DOUBLEDAY

BLACKBERRY WINE

Joanne Harris

'TOUCHING, FUNNY AND CLEVER'
Daily Telegraph

Jay Mackintosh is trapped by memory in the old familiar landscape
of his childhood, more enticing than the present, and to which he
longs to return. A bottle of home-brewed wine left to him by a
long-vanished friend seems to provide both the key to an old mystery
and a doorway into another world. As the unusual properties of the
strange brew takes effect, Jay escapes to a derelict farmhouse in the
French village of Lansquenet, where a ghost from the past waits to
confront him, and the reclusive Marise – haunted, lovely and
dangerous – hides a terrible secret behind her closed shutters.
Between them, a mysterious chemistry. Or could it be magic?

'A LIVELY AND ORIGINAL TALENT'
Sunday Times

'JOANNE HARRIS HAS THE GIFT OF CONVEYING HER DELIGHT
IN THE SENSUOUS PLEASURES OF FOOD, WINE, SCENT AND
PLANTS . . . [*BLACKBERRY WINE*] HAS ALL THE APPEAL OF A
VELVETY SCENTED GLASS OF VINTAGE WINE'
Daily Mail

0 552 99800 1

BLACK SWAN

CHOCOLAT

Joanne Harris

"SENSUOUS AND THOUGHT-PROVOKING . . . SUBTLE AND
BRILLIANT'
Daily Telegraph

When an exotic stranger, Vianne Rocher, arrives in the French
village of Lansquenet and opens a chocolate boutique directly
opposite the church, Father Reynaud identifies her as a serious
danger to his flock – especially as it is the beginning of Lent, the
traditional season of self-denial. War is declared as the priest
denounces the newcomer's wares as the ultimate sin.

Suddenly Vianne's shop-cum-café means that there is somewhere for
secrets to be whispered, grievances to be aired, dreams to be tested.
But Vianne's plans for an Easter Chocolate Festival divide the whole
community in a conflict that escalates into a 'Church not Chocolate'
battle. As mouths water in anticipation, can the solemnity of the
Church compare with the pagan passion of a chocolate éclair?

For the first time here is a novel in which chocolate enjoys its true
importance. Rich, clever and mischievous, *Chocolat* is a literary feast
for all the senses.

'MODDY AND ATMOSPHERIC . . . A RICHLY TEXTURED TALE'
Independent

'MOUTHWATERING . . . A FEELGOOD BOOK OF THE FIRST
ORDER. AS YOU ARE LURED BY THE PLOT AND THE
WONDERFUL DESCRIPTIONS, YOUR SENSES ARE LEFT REELING.
READ IT'
Observer

'IS THIS THE BEST BOOK EVER WRITTEN? TRULY EXCELLENT
. . . HARRIS' ACHIEVEMENT IS NOT ONLY IN HER STORY, IN HER
INSIGHT AND HUMOUR AND THE WONDERFUL PICTURE OF
SMALL-TOWN LIFE IN RURAL FRANCE, BUT ALSO IN HER
WRITING'
Literary Review

0 552 99848 6

BLACK SWAN

LA CUCINA

Lily Prior

'WONDERFUL. A FESTIVAL OF LIFE AND ALL ITS PLEASURES'
Joanne Harris

A delicious début novel set in Sicily about a shy librarian with a broken heart whose passion for cooking leads to an expected love affair.

La Cucina combines the sensuous pleasures of love and food, simmering in the heat of a Sicilian kitchen. Rosa Fiore is a solitary middle-aged woman who has resigned herself to a loveless life, and expresses her passionate nature through her delicious cooking. Then, one day, she meets an enigmatic chef, known only as l'Inglese, whose research on the heritage of Sicilian cuisine leads him into Rosa's library and into her heart. They share one sublime summer of discovery, during which l'Inglese awakens the power of Rosa's sexuality, and together they reach new heights of culinary passion. When he vanishes unexpectedly, Rosa returns to her family's estate to grieve for her lost love only to find a new fulfilment, as well as many surprises, in the magic of her beloved Cucina.

A love song to Italy, *La Cucina* is a celebration of all things sensual. It spills over with intense images, colours, fragrances, and exuberant characters, all reflecting the splendour of the Sicilian countryside in which it is set.

'A HEADY CONCOCTION, BY TURNS FUNNY, FRIGHTENING, SAD AND JOYFUL'
Valerie Martin

0 552 99909 1

BLACK SWAN

A SELECTED LIST OF FINE NOVELS
AVAILABLE FROM BLACK SWAN

99588	6	**THE HOUSE OF THE SPIRITS**	*Isabel Allende*	£7.99
99820	6	**FLANDERS**	*Patricia Anthony*	£6.99
99734	X	**EMOTIONALLY WEIRD**	*Kate Atkinson*	£6.99
99860	5	**IDIOGLOSSIA**	*Eleanor Bailey*	£6.99
99922	9	**A GOOD HOUSE**	*Bonnie Burnard*	£6.99
99854	0	**LESSONS FOR A SUNDAY FATHER**	*Claire Calman*	£5.99
99767	6	**SISTER OF MY HEART**	*Chitra Banerjee Divakaruni*	£6.99
99836	2	**A HEART OF STONE**	*Renate Dorrestein*	£6.99
99587	8	**LIKE WATER FOR CHOCOLATE**	*Laura Esquivel*	£6.99
99910	5	**TELLING LIDDY**	*Anne Fine*	£6.99
99851	6	**REMEMBERING BLUE**	*Connie May Fowler*	£6.99
99759	5	**DOG DAYS, GLENN MILLER NIGHTS**	*Laurie Graham*	£6.99
99890	7	**DISOBEDIENCE**	*Jane Hamilton*	£6.99
99893	1	**CHOCOLAT**	*Joanne Harris*	£6.99
99800	1	**BLACKBERRY WINE**	*Joanne Harris*	£6.99
99867	2	**LIKE WATER IN WILD PLACES**	*Pamela Jooste*	£6.99
99737	4	**GOLDEN LADS AND GIRLS**	*Angela Lambert*	£6.99
99959	8	**BACK ROADS**	*Tawni O'Dell*	£6.99
99909	1	**LA CUCINA**	*Lily Prior*	£6.99
99777	3	**THE SPARROW**	*Mary Doria Russell*	£7.99
99865	6	**THE FIG EATER**	*Jody Shields*	£6.99
99952	0	**LIFE ISN'T ALL HA HA HEE HEE**	*Meera Syal*	£6.99
99819	2	**WHISTLING FOR THE ELEPHANTS**	*Sandi Toksvig*	£6.99
99872	9	**MARRYING THE MISTRESS**	*Joanne Trollope*	£6.99
99864	8	**A DESERT IN BOHEMIA**	*Jill Paton Walsh*	£6.99
99673	4	**DINA'S BOOK**	*Herbjørg Wassmo*	£7.99
99723	4	**PART OF THE FURNITURE**	*Mary Wesley*	£6.99